Robert E. Howard's
SAILOR STEVE COSTIGAN

ROBERT E. HOWARD'S
SAILOR STEVE
COSTIGAN

THE COMPLETE COLLECTION OF PUBLISHED STORIES

By **ROBERT E. HOWARD**
Edited and annotated by **FINN J.D. JOHN**

Pulp-Lit
PRODUCTIONS
Corvallis, Oregon

First edition: Softcover

ISBN: 978-1-63591-352-1

Cover art:

Cover art adapted from the September 1934 issue of *Adventure* magazine, featuring an illustration by John Newton Howitt.

Pulp-Lit Productions
P.O. Box 77
Corvallis, Oregon

http://pulp-lit.com

TABLE *of* CONTENTS

1934: Magic Carpet and Dempsey's Fight magazine.

INTRODUCTION.

ROBERT E. HOWARD'S BRAND OF COMEDY.

I t's a strange quirk of history that Robert E. Howard is not much remembered today as a writer of comedy.

This is especially strange, because in the early 1930s that was what he was most known for.

Robert E. Howard was, not to beat around the bush too much, a comedic genius. And he came by it honestly: he grew up in the land of Pecos Bill and Davey Crockett, a land of tall tales spun with wry humor by master storytellers.

It's Davy Crocket — the secular patron saint of Texas — who's likely most responsible for Howard's sense of humor. The tall tales of Davy Crockett's alleged adventures are not much remembered today; but in

their time they were known and followed by virtually everyone, and formed something like a national mythology for the nascent United States. They were delivered, by several different publishers, in the form of Davy Crockett almanacs.

By the 1910s, when Howard was developing his craft, the golden years of Crockett almanacs were 60 years in the past — but they were far from forgotten. They were published from the 1830s through the 1850s, stopping just before the Civil War broke out.

The Crockett almanacs were regular almanacs of the type familiar to rural families today, with tables of sunrise and sunset times, phases of the moon, expected temperatures, recommended dates on which to plant various crops, and so forth; but between every set of tables was one or two tall tales of the exploits of Davy Crockett, accompanied by woodcut pictures. The tales were written in a sort of frontier patois as first-person accounts.

A good example of the style is one published in 1837, titled "Crockett Riding his Pet Bear Up a Tree":

"If ever a set o' blood-thirsty human critters were suddenaciously socked an astonished to stupification, it war a party o' Mexican scouts that got arter me an my pet bar Death Hug, determined to take us both alive an exhibit us as the ninth wonder o' Creation. You see, I had jist mounted Death Hug, an were travellin at about twenty miles an hour, with some important news to General Houston, when a party o' snake eyed Mexican scouts seed me comin and commenced surroundin me for instanter captivation; they couldn't bear the idea o' killin two sich tempten curiosities o' nater, so they closed up with pinted gun prongs, thinkin to make us surrender in course; but I gin him a tickle under the fore paw, an he jumped clar over thar heads, an put off like a whirlwind. Dreckly a hull squad o' twenty more headed us with thar gun prongs held up so tarnal high that Death Hug couldn't come it, but seein a hickory tree right between us, I jist wheeled Death Hug around instanterly, pinted up the tree, an

take me for a two-legged Rhinocerous, if the critter didn't walk up that are trunk with me on his back about as slick as a pinter (panther) goin up to roost, ran out the limb onto another tree, an another, an down agin, an then made off clar, jist as they war shootin into No. 1."

Other stories in the same almanac bear headlines like "Crockett Drinking Up the Gulf Between the United States and Texas," "Crockett and Ben Hardin Making Their Escape from a Tornado by Mounting a Streak of Lightning," and "Crockett's Wonderful Escape by Driving his Pet Alligator Up Niagara Falls."

Now, it has to be said that the real David Crockett — the actual historical figure, a former frontiersman and onetime member of Congress who died at the Alamo — would likely not have approved of some of the stories attributed to him after his death. The real David Crockett had no use for Andrew Jackson, bitterly opposing him for his Indian policies. The legend, though, introduced himself in the pages of his almanac as "that same David Crockett, fresh from the backwoods, half horse, half alligator, a little tetched with the snappin turtle — can wade the Mississippi, leap the Ohio, ride upon a streak a lightning, an slip without a scratch down a honey locust tree — can whip my weight in wildcats — and whip any man opposed to Jackson."

A cursory glance at the text of any one of the Sailor Steve Costigan stories will show the similarities with the Davy Crocket almanac yarns. Of course, the Costigan tales are far more professional and subtly crafted — the original Crockett tales were pounded out by anonymous contract writers to fill space, and their quality varies pretty widely. And Steve Costigan himself is a more believable character than Davy Crockett — although, as you will no doubt have noticed, that's not saying much. Costigan is far larger than life, especially in his ability to absorb punishment from the fists of his opponents in the ring.

And this is richly ironic, because the stories Howard wrote starring this oversized, underbrained, generally unbelievable character feel more authentic than the stories Howard is best known for. They are, in a very real sense, more than just pulp literature; they are anthropological artifacts of pre-oil-boom frontier Texas.

The Costigan stories are, of course, quite different from the ones

Robert E. Howard as he appeared in 1934.

that Howard used to break into the business. Howard got his start as a professional storyteller in 1925, at the age of 17, when he broke into *Weird Tales* magazine with "In the Forest of Villefère," a sympathetic story of a reluctant werewolf.

But by then he'd already made a reputation for himself around his home town as a teller of humorous tall tales in the style of Davy Crockett.

He also had a reputation as an amateur boxer of no mean skill.

So it surely wasn't much of a surprise to anyone when, a few years later, looking to expand his markets beyond the Solomon Kane and King Kull sword-and-sorcery pieces he was regularly placing in *Weird Tales*, he came up with the idea of combining Davy Crockett-style tall tales with boxing stories, and pitching them to one of the then-popular pulp magazines devoted to action in the ring.

It took Howard some experimentation to get the formula just right. The result, when he did, was Sailor Steve Costigan, the adorably wooden-headed but spectacularly iron-fisted merchant mariner who blows around through exotic ports of call, getting swindled by dishy fast-talking dames, punching his way into and out of various kinds of legal trouble, and winning prizefights in which the amount of damage given and taken is enough to kill twenty or thirty real guys.

The combination turned out to be a huge winner for Fight Stories, the new pulp that he was targeting with them.

With Costigan, there was always a prizefight in the story, and it was full of descriptive action of the type boxing fans could envision and relate to.

There was enough other action that one did not have to even care about boxing to enjoy the stories. But for people who knew their boxing, a Steve Costigan tale was a really satisfying read. Howard would probably have been surprised if he'd know how many members of the sports world's royalty — journalists, promoters, even big-name prize-fighters — were regular readers and counted themselves among Steve Costigan's fans.

A word of warning, before we get started: The Steve Costigan stories are all, by modern standards, full of racism.

Mostly this takes the form of slurs and disparaging references to people of Asian descent, since most of the stories take place in Asiatic ports — although there are also several racial slurs relating to people of Hispanic/Latino and African ancestry as well. This was not considered a big deal in the early 1930s.

Ironically, what was considered a big deal in those days was swearing. On occasions when Sailor Costigan is called upon to "swear like a sailor," readers have to use their imagination. So, "F-bombs" were strictly verboten, but "N-bombs" were just fine.

Reading these stories today can be an awkward experience for any modern reader of any ethnicity, although obviously more so for those of non-European ancestry. It's important to keep in mind that they are, essentially, cultural artifacts of a very different time.

The PIT *of the* SERPENT.

ALTERNATE TITLE: MANILA MANSLAUGHTER

This short story was first published in the July 1929 issue of Fight Stories *magazine.*

THE MINUTE I stepped ashore from the *Sea Girl,* merchantman, I had a hunch that there would be trouble. This hunch was caused by seeing some of the crew of the *Dauntless.* The men on the *Dauntless* have disliked the *Sea Girl's* crew ever since our skipper took their captain to a cleaning on the wharfs of Zanzibar—them being narrow-minded that way. They claimed that the old man had a knuckle-duster on his right, which is ridiculous and a dirty lie. He had it on his left.

Seeing these roughnecks in Manila, I had no illusions about them, but I was not looking for no trouble. I am heavyweight champion of the *Sea Girl,* and before you make any wisecracks about the non-importance of that title, I want you to come down to the forecastle and look over Mushy Hansen and One-Round Grannigan and Flat-Face O'Toole and Swede Hjonning and the rest of the man-killers that make up the *Sea Girl's* crew. But for all that, no one can never accuse me of being quarrelsome, and so instead of following my natural instinct and knocking seven or eight of these bezarks for a row, just to be ornery, I avoided them and went to the nearest American bar.

1

After a while I found myself in a dance hall, and while it is kind of hazy just how I got there, I assure you I had not no great amount of liquor under my belt—some beer, a few whiskeys, a little brandy, and maybe a slug of wine for a chaser like. No, I was the perfect chevalier in all my actions, as was proven when I found myself dancing with the prettiest girl I have yet to see in Manila or elsewhere. She had red lips and black hair, and oh, what a face!

"Say, miss," said I, the soul of politeness, "where have you been all my life?"

"Oooh, la!" said she, with a silvery ripple of laughter. "You Americans say such theengs. Oooh, so huge and strong you are, senyor!"

I let her feel of my biceps, and she give squeals of surprise and pleasure, clapping her little white hands just like a child what has found a new pretty.

"Oooh! You could just snatch little me oop and walk away weeth me, couldn't you, senyor?"

"You needn't not be afraid," said I, kindly. "I am the soul of politeness around frails, and never pull no rough stuff. I have never soaked a woman in my life, not even that dame in Suez that throwed a knife at me. Baby, has anybody ever give you a hint about what knockouts your eyes is?"

"Ah, go 'long," said she, coyly— "Ouch!"

"Did somebody step on your foot?" I ask, looking about for somebody to crown.

"Yes—let's sit theese one out, senyor. Where did you learn to dance?"

"It comes natural, I reckon," I admitted modestly. "I never knew I could till now. This is the first time I ever tried."

From the foregoing you will see that I am carrying on a quiet conversation, not starting nothing with nobody. It is not my fault, what happened.

Me and this girl, whose name is Raquel La Costa, her being Spanish that way, are sitting peacefully at a table and I am just beginning to get started good telling her how her eyes are like dark pools of night (pretty hot, that one; I got it offa Mushy Hansen, who is all poetical like), when I notice her looking over my shoulder at somebody. This irritates me slightly, but I ignore it, and having forgotten what I was saying, my mind being slightly hazy for some reason, I continue:

"Listen, cutey—hey, who are you winkin' at? Oh, somethin' in your eye, you say? All right, as I was sayin', we got a feller named Hansen on board the *Sea Girl* what writes po'try. Listen to this:

"Oh, the road to glory lay
Over old Manila Bay.
Where the Irish whipped the Spanish
On a sultry summer day."

At this moment some bezark came barging up to our table and, ignoring me, leaned over and leered engagingly at my girl.

"Let's shake a hoof, baby," said this skate, whom I recognized instantly as Bat Slade, champion box fighter of the *Dauntless*.

Miss La Costa said nothing, and I arose and shoved Slade back from the table.

"The lady is engaged at present, stupid," says I, poking my jaw out. "If you got any business, you better 'tend to it."

"Don't get gay with me, Costigan," says he, nastily. "Since when is dames choosin' gorillas instead of humans?"

By this time quite a crowd had formed, and I restrained my natural indignation and said, "Listen, bird, take that map outa my line uh vision before I bust it."

Bat is a handsome galoot who has a way with the dames, and I knew if he danced one dance with my girl he would figure out some way to do me dirt. I did not see any more of the *Dauntless* men; on the other hand, I was the only one of the *Sea Girl's* crew in the joint.

"Suppose we let the lady choose between us," said Bat. Can you beat that for nerve? Him butting in that way and then giving himself equal rights with me. That was too much. With a bellow, I started my left from the hip, but somehow he wasn't there—the shifty crook! I miss by a yard, and he slams me with a left to the nose that knocks me over a chair.

My brain instantly cleared, and I realized that I had been slightly lit.

I arose with an irritated roar, but before hostilities could be renewed, Miss La Costa stepped between us.

"Zut," said she, tapping us with her fan. "Zut! What is theese? Am I a common girl to be so insult' by two great tramps who make fight over me in public? Bah! Eef you wanta fight, go out in ze woods or some place where no one make scandal, and wham each other all you want. May ze best man win! I will not be fight over in public, no sir!"

AND WITH THAT she turned back and walked away. At the same time, up came an oily-looking fellow, rubbing his hands together. I mistrust a bird what goes around rubbing his hands together like he was in a state of perpetual self-satisfaction.

"Now, now, boys," said this bezark, "le's do this right! You boys wanta fight. Tut! Tut! Too bad, too bad! But if you gotta fight, le's do it right, that's what I say! Let fellers live together in peace and enmity if they can, but if they gotta fight, let it be did right!"

"Gi' me leeway—and I'll do this blankety-blank right," says I, fairly shaking with rage. It always irritates me to be hit on the nose without a return and in front of ladies.

"Oh, will you?" said Bat, putting up his mitts. "Let's see you get goin', you—"

"Now, now, boys," said the oily bird, "le's do this right! Costigan, will you and Slade fight for me in my club?"

"Anywheres!" I roar. "Bare-knuckles, gloves, or marlin-spikes!"

"Fine," says the oily bird, rubbing his hands worse than ever. "Ah, fine! Ah—um—ah, Costigan, will you fight Slade in the pit of the serpent?"

Now, I should have noticed that he didn't ask Slade if he'd fight, and I saw Slade grin quietly, but I was too crazy with rage to think straight.

"I'll fight him in the pit of Hades with the devil for a referee!" I roared. "Bring on your fight club—ring, deck, or whatever! Let's get goin'."

"That's the way to talk!" says the oily bird. "Come on."

He turned around and started for the exit, and me and Slade and a few more followed him. Had I of thought, I would have seen right off that this was all working too smooth to have happened impromptu, as it were. But I was still seething with rage and in no shape to think properly.

Howthesomever, I did give a few thoughts as to the chances I had against Slade. As for size, I had the advantage. I'm six feet, and Slade is two inches shorter; I am also a few pounds heavier but not enough to make much difference, us being heavyweights that way. But Slade, I knew, was the shiftiest, trickiest leather-slinger in the whole merchant marine. I had never met him for the simple reason that no match-maker in any port would stage a bout between a *Sea Girl* man

and a *Dauntless* tramp, since that night in Singapore when the bout between Slade and One-Round Grannigan started a free-for-all that plumb wrecked the Wharfside A. C. Slade knocked Grannigan out that night, and Grannigan was then champion slugger aboard the *Sea Girl*. Later, I beat Grannigan.

As for dope, you couldn't tell much, as usual. I'd won a decision over Boatswain Hagney, the champion of the British Asiatic naval fleet, who'd knocked Slade out in Hong Kong, but on the other hand, Slade had knocked out Mike Leary of the *Blue Whale*, who'd given me a terrible beating at Bombay.

These cogitations was interrupted at that minute by the oily bird. We had come out of the joint and was standing on the curb. Several autos was parked there, and the crowd piled into them. The oily bird motioned me to get in one, and I done so.

Next, we was speeding through the streets, where the lights was beginning to glow, and I asked no questions, even when we left the business section behind and then went right on through the suburbs and out on a road which didn't appear to be used very much. I said nothing, however.

AT LAST WE stopped at a large building some distance outside the city, which looked more like an ex-palace than anything else. All the crowd alighted, and I done likewise, though I was completely mystified. There was no other houses near, trees grew dense on all sides, the house itself was dark and gloomy-looking. All together I did not like the looks of things but would not let on, with Bat Slade gazing at me in his supercilious way. Anyway, I thought, they are not intending to assassinate me because Slade ain't that crooked, though he would stop at nothing else.

We went up the walk, lined on each side by tropical trees, and into the house. There the oily bird struck a light and we went down in the basement. This was a large, roomy affair, with a concrete floor, and in the center was a pit about seven feet deep, and about ten by eight in dimensions. I did not pay no great attention to it at that time, but I did later, I want to tell you.

"Say," I says, "I'm in no mood for foolishness. What you bring me away out here for? Where's your arena?"

"This here's it," said the oily bird.

"Huh! Where's the ring? Where do we fight?"

"Down in there," says the oily bird, pointing at the pit.

"What!" I yell. "What are you tryin' to hand me?"

"Aw, pipe down," interrupted Bat Slade. "Didn't you agree to fight me in the serpent pit? Stop grouchin' and get your duds off."

"All right," I says, plumb burned

up by this deal. "I don't know what you're tryin' to put over, but lemme get that handsome map in front of my right and that's all I want!"

"Grahhh!" snarled Slade, and started toward the other end of the pit. He had a couple of yeggs with him as handlers. Shows his caliber, how he always knows some thug; no matter how crooked the crowd may be, he's never without acquaintances. I looked around and recognized a pickpocket I used to know in Cuba, and asked him to handle me. He said he would, though, he added, they wasn't much a handler could do under the circumstances.

"What kind of a deal have I got into?" I asked him as I stripped. "What kind of a joint is this?"

"This house used to be owned by a crazy Spaniard with more mazuma than brains," said the dip, helping me undress. "He yearned for bull fightin' and the like, and he thought up a brand new one. He rigged up this pit and had his servants go out and bring in all kinds of snakes. He'd put two snakes in the pit and let 'em fight till they killed each other."

"What! I got to fight in a snake den?"

"Aw, don't worry. They ain't been no snakes in there for years. The Spaniard got killed, and the old place went to ruin. They held cock fights here and a few years ago the fellow that's stagin' this bout got the idea of buyin' the house and stagin' grudge fights."

"How's he make any money? I didn't see nobody buyin' tickets, and they ain't more'n thirty or forty here."

"Aw, he didn't have no time to work it up. He'll make his money bettin'. He never picks a loser! And he always referees himself. He knows your ship sails tomorrow, and he didn't have no time for ballyhooin'. This fight club is just for a select few who is too sated or too vicious to enjoy a ordinary legitimate prize fight. They ain't but a few in the know—all this is illegal, of course—just a few sports which don't mind payin' for their pleasure. The night Slade fought Sailor Handler they was forty-five men here, each payin' a hundred and twenty-five dollars for admission. Figure it out for yourself."

"Has Slade fought here before?" I ask, beginning to see a light.

"Sure. He's the champion of the pit. Only last month he knocked out Sailor Handler in nine rounds."

Gerusha! And only a few months ago me and the Sailor—who stood six-four and weighed two-twenty—had done everything but knife each other in a twenty-round draw.

"Ho! So that's the way it is," said I. "Slade deliberately come and started trouble with me, knowin' I wouldn't get a square deal here, him bein' the favorite and—"

"No," said the dip, "I don't think so. He just fell for that Spanish frail. Had they been any malice afore-thought, word would have circulated among the wealthy sports of the town. As it is, the fellow that owns the joint is throwin' the party free of charge. He didn't have time to work it up. Figure it out—he ain't losing nothin'. Here's two tough sailors wanting to fight a grudge fight—willin' to fight for nothin'. It costs him nothin' to stage the riot. It's a great boost for his club, and he'll win plenty on bets."

The confidence with which the dip said that last gave me cold shivers.

"And who will he bet on?" I asked.

"Slade, of course. Ain't he the pit champion?"

While I was considering this cheering piece of information, Bat Slade yelled at me from the other end of the pit:

"Hey, you blankey dash-dot-blank, ain't you ready yet?"

He was in his socks, shoes and underpants, and no gloves on his hands.

"Where's the gloves?" I asked. "Ain't we goin' to tape our hands?"

"They ain't no gloves," said Slade, with a satisfied grin. "This little riot is goin' to be a bare-knuckle affair. Don't you know the rules of the pit?"

"You see, Costigan," says the oily bird, kinda nervous, "in the fights we put on here, the fighters don't wear no gloves—regular he-man grudge stuff, see?"

"Aw, get goin'!" the crowd began to bellow, having paid nothing to get in and wanting their money's worth. "Lessee some action! What do you think this is? Start somethin'!"

"Shut up!" I ordered, cowing them with one menacing look. "What kind of a deal am I getting here, anyhow?"

"Didn't you agree to fight Slade in the serpent pit?"

"Yes but—"

"Tryin' to back out," said Slade nastily, as usual. "That's like you *Sea Girl* tramps, you—"

"Blank, exclamation point, and asterisk!" I roared, tearing off my undershirt and bounding into the pit. "Get down in here you blank-blank semicolon, and I'll make you look like the last rose of summer, you—"

Slade hopped down into the pit at the other end, and the crowd began to fight for places at the edge. It was a cinch that some of them was not going to get to see all of it. The sides of the pit were hard and rough, and the floor was the same way, like you'd expect a pit in a concrete floor to be. Of course they was no stools or anything.

"Now then," says the oily bird, "this is a finish fight between Steve Costigan of the *Sea Girl*, weight one-eighty-eight, and Battling Slade, one-seventy-nine, of the *Dauntless*, bare-knuckle champion of the Philippine Islands, in as far as he's proved it in this here pit. They will fight three-minute rounds, one minute rest, no limit to the number of rounds. There will be no decision. They will fight till one of 'em goes out. Referee, me.

"The rules is, nothing barred except hittin' below the belt—in the way of punches, I mean. Break when I say so, and hit on the breakaway if you wanta. Seconds will kindly refrain from hittin' the other man with the water bucket. Ready?"

"A hundred I lay you like a rug", says Slade.

"I see you and raise you a hundred," I snarl.

The crowd began to yell and curse, the timekeeper hit a piece of iron with a six-shooter stock, and the riot was on.

NOW, UNDERSTAND, THIS was a very different fight from any I ever engaged in. It combined the viciousness of a rough-and-tumble with that of a legitimate ring bout. No room for any footwork, concrete to land on if you went down, the uncertain flare of the lights which was hung on the ceiling over us, and the feeling of being crowded for space, to say nothing of thinking about all the snakes which had fought there. Ugh! And me hating snakes that way.

I had figured that I'd have the advantage, being heavier and stronger. Slade couldn't use his shifty footwork to keep out of my way. I'd pin him in a corner and smash him like a cat does a rat. But the bout hadn't been on two seconds before I saw I was all wrong. Slade was just an overgrown Young Griffo. His footwork was second to his ducking and slipping. He had fought in the

7

pit before, and had found that kind of fighting just suited to his peculiar style. He shifted on his feet just enough to keep weaving, while he let my punches go under his arms, around his neck, over his head or across his shoulder.

At the sound of the gong I'd stepped forward, crouching, with both hands going in the only way I knew.

Slade took my left on his shoulder, my right on his elbow, and, blip-blip! his left landed twice to my face. Now I want to tell you that a blow from a bare fist is much different than a blow from a glove, and while less stunning, is more of a punisher in its way. Still, I was used to being hit with bare knuckles, and I kept boring in. I swung a left to the ribs that made Slade grunt, and missed a right in the same direction.

This was the beginning of a cruel, bruising fight with no favor. I felt like a wild animal, when I had time to feel anything but Slade's left, battling down there in the pit, with a ring of yelling, distorted faces leering down at us. The oily bird, referee, leaned over the edge at the risk of falling on top of us, and when we clinched he would yell, "Break, you blank-blanks!" and prod us with a cane. He would dance around the edge of the pit trying to keep in prodding distance, and cussing when the crowd got in his way, which was all the time. There was no room in the pit for him; wasn't scarcely room enough for us.

Following that left I landed, Slade tied me up in a clinch, stamped on my instep, thumbed me in the eye, and swished a right to my chin on the breakaway. Slightly infuriated at this treatment, I curled my lip back and sank a left to the wrist in his midriff. He showed no signs at all of liking this, and retaliated with a left to the body and a right to the side of the head. Then he settled down to work.

He ducked a right and came in close, pounding my waist line with short jolts. When, in desperation, I clinched, he shot a right uppercut between my arms that set me back on my heels. And while I was off balance he threw all his weight against me and scraped me against the wall, which procedure removed a large area of hide from my shoulder. With a roar, I tore loose and threw him the full length of the pit, but, charging after him, he side-stepped somehow and I crashed against the pit wall, head-first. Wham! I was on the floor, with seventeen million stars flashing before me, and the oily bird was counting as fast as he could, "Onetwothreefourfive—"

I bounded up again, not hurt but slightly dizzy. Wham, wham, wham! Bat came slugging in to finish me. I swished loose a right that was labeled T.N.T., but he ducked.

"Look out, Bat! That bird's dangerous!" yelled the oily bird in fright.

"So am I!" snarled Bat, cutting my lip with a straight left and weaving away from my right counter. He whipped a right to the wind that made me grunt, flashed two lefts to my already battered face, and somehow missed with a venomous right. All the time, get me, I was swinging fast and heavy, but it was like hitting at a ghost. Bat had maneuvered me into a corner, where I couldn't get set or defend myself. When I drew back for a punch, my elbow hit the wall. Finally I wrapped both arms around my jaw and plunged forward, breaking through Slade's barrage by sheer weight. As we came together, I threw my arms about him and together we crashed to the floor.

Slade, being the quicker that way, was the first up, and hit me with a roundhouse left to the side of the head while I was still on one knee.

"Foul!" yells some of the crowd.

"Shut up!" bellowed the oily bird. "I'm refereein' this bout!"

As I found my feet, Slade was right on me and we traded rights. Just then the gong sounded. I went back to my end of the pit and sat down on the floor, leaning my back against the wall. The dip peered over the edge.

"Anything I can do?" said he.

"Yeah," said I, "knock the daylights out of the blank-blank that's pretendin' to referee this bout."

Meanwhile the aforesaid blank-blank shoved his snoot over the other end of the pit, and shouted anxiously, "Slade, you reckon you can take him in a couple more rounds?"

"Sure," said Bat. "Double your bets; triple 'em. I'll lay him in the next round."

"You'd better!" admonished this fair-minded referee.

"How can he get anybody to bet with him?" I asked.

"Oh," says the dip, handing me down a sponge to wipe off the blood, "some fellers will bet on anything. For instance, I just laid ten smackers on you, myself."

"That I'll win?"

"Naw; that you'll last five rounds."

AT THIS MOMENT the gong sounded and I rushed for the other end of the pit, with the worthy intention of effacing Slade from the face of the earth. But, as usual, I underestimated the force of my rush and the length of the pit. There didn't seem to be room enough for Slade to get out of my way, but he solved this problem by dropping on his knees, and allowing me to fall over him, which I did.

"Foul!" yelled the dip. "He went down without bein' hit!"

"Foul my eye!" squawked the oily bird. "A blind man could tell he slipped, accidental."

We arose at the same time, me none the better for my fiasco. Slade took my left over his shoulder and hooked a left to the body. He followed this with a straight right to the mouth and a left hook to the side of the head. I clinched and clubbed him with my right to the ribs until the referee prodded us apart.

Again Slade managed to get me into a corner. You see, he was used to the dimensions whereas I, accustomed to a regular ring, kept forgetting about the size of the blasted pit. It seemed like with every movement I bumped my hip or shoulder or scraped my arms against the rough cement of the walls. To date, Slade hadn't a mark to show he'd been in a fight, except for the bruise on his ribs. What with his thumbing and his straight lefts, both my eyes were in a fair way to close, my lips were cut, and I was bunged up generally, but was not otherwise badly hurt.

I fought my way out of the corner, and the gong found us slugging toe to toe in the center of the pit, where I had the pleasure of staggering Bat with a left to the temple. Not an awful lot of action in that round; mostly clinching.

The third started like a whirlwind. At the tap of the gong Slade bounded from his end and was in mine before I could get up. He slammed me with a left and right that shook me clean to my toes, and ducked my left. He also ducked a couple of rights, and then rammed a left to my wind which bent me double. No doubt—this baby could hit!

I came up with a left swing to the head, and in a wild mix-up took four right and left hooks to land my right to the ribs. Slade grunted and tried to back-heel me, failing which he lowered his head and butted me in the belly, kicked me on the shin, and would have did more, likely, only I halted the proceedings temporarily by swinging an overhand right to the back of his neck which took the steam out of him for a minute.

We clinched, and I never saw a critter short of a octopus which could appear to have so many arms when clinching. He always managed to not only tie me up and render me helpless for the time being, but to stamp on my insteps, thumb me in the eye and pound the back of my neck with the edge of his hand. Add to this the fact that he frequently shoved me against the wall, and you can get a idea what kind of a bezark I was fighting. My superior weight and bulk did not have no advantage. What was needed was skill and speed, and the fact that Bat was somewhat smaller than me was an advantage to him.

Still, I was managing to hand out some punishment. Near the end of that round Bat had a beautiful black eye and some more bruises on his ribs. Then it happened. I had plunged after him, swinging; he sidestepped out of the corner, and the next instant was left-jabbing me to death while I floundered along the wall trying to get set for a smash.

I swished a right to his body, and while I didn't think it landed solid, he staggered and dropped his hands slightly. I straightened out of my defensive crouch and cocked my right, and, simultaneous, I realized I had been took. Slade had tricked me. The minute I raised my chin in this careless manner, he beat me to the punch with a right that smashed my head back against the wall, laying open the scalp. Dazed and only partly conscious of what was going on I rebounded right into Slade, ramming my jaw flush into his left. Zam! At the same instant I hooked a trip-hammer right under his heart, and we hit the floor together.

Zowie! I could hear the yelling and cursing as if from a great distance, and the lights on the ceiling high above seemed dancing in a thick fog. All I knew was that I had to get back on my feet as quick as I could.

"One—two—three—four," the oily bird was counting over the both of us, "five—Bat, you blank-blank, get up!—Six—seven—Bat, blast it, get your feet under you!—eight— Juan, hit that gong! What kind of a timekeeper are you?"

"The round ain't over yet!" yelled the dip, seeing I had begun to get my legs under me.

"Who's refereein' this?" roared the oily bird, jerking out a .45. "Juan, hit that gong!—Nine!"

Juan hit the gong and Bat's seconds hopped down into the pit and dragged him to his end, where they started working over him. I crawled back to mine. Splash! The dip emptied a bucket of water over me. That freshened me up a lot.

"How you comin'?" he asked.

"Great!" said I, still dizzy. "I'll lay this bird like a rug in the next round! For honor and the love of a dame! 'Oh, the road to glory lay—'"

"I've seen 'em knocked even more cuckoo," said the dip, tearing off a cud of tobacco.

THE FOURTH! SLADE came up weakened, but with fire in his eye. I was all right, but my legs wouldn't work like they should. Slade was in far better condition. Seeing this, or probably feeling that he was weak-ening, he threw caution to the winds and rushed in to slug with me.

The crowd went crazy. Left-right-left-right! I was taking four to one, but mine carried the most steam. It couldn't last long at this rate.

The oily bird was yelling advice and dashing about the pit's edge like a lunatic. We went into a clinch, and he leaned over to prod us apart as usual. He leaned far over, and I don't know if he slipped or somebody shoved him. Anyway, he crashed down on top of us just as we broke and started slugging. He fell between us, stopped somebody's right with his chin, and flopped, face down— through for the night!

By mutual consent, Bat and me suspended hostilities, grabbed the fallen referee by his neck and the slack of his pants, and hove him up into the crowd. Then, without a word, we began again. The end was in sight.

Bat suddenly broke and backed away. I followed, swinging with both hands. Now I saw the wall was at his back. Ha! He couldn't duck now! I shot my right straight for his face. He dropped to his knees. Wham! My fist just cleared the top of his skull and crashed against the concrete wall.

I heard the bones shatter and a dark tide of agony surged up my arm, which dropped helpless at my side. Slade was up and springing for me, but the torture I was in made me forget all about him. I was nauseated, done up—out on my feet, if you get what I mean. He swung his left with everything he had—my foot slipped in some blood on the floor—his left landed high on the side of my skull instead of my jaw. I went down, but I heard him squawk and looked up to see him dancing and wringing his left hand.

The knockdown had cleared my brain somewhat. My hand was numb and not hurting so much, and I realized that Bat had broke his left hand on my skull like many a man has did. Fair enough! I came surging up, and Bat, with the light of desperation in his eyes, rushed in wide open, staking everything on one right swing.

I stepped inside it, sank my left to the wrist in his midriff, and brought the same hand up to his jaw. He staggered, his arms fell, and I swung my left flush to the button with everything I had behind it. Bat hit the floor.

About eight men shoved their snoots over the edge and started counting, the oily bird being still out. They wasn't all counting together, so somehow I managed to prop myself up against the wall, not wanting to make no mistake, until the last man had said "ten!" Then everything began to whirl, and I flopped down on top of Slade and went out like a candle.

LET'S PASS OVER the immediate events. I don't remember much about them anyhow. I slept until the middle of the next afternoon, and I know the only thing that dragged me out of the bed where the dip had dumped me was the knowledge that the *Sea Girl* sailed that night and that Raquel La Costa probably would be waiting for the victor—me.

Outside the joint where I first met her, who should I come upon but Bat Slade!

"Huh!" says I, giving him the once over. "Are you able to be out?"

"You ain't no beauty yourself," he retorted.

I admit it. My right was in a sling, both eyes was black, and I was generally cut and bruised. Still, Slade had no right to give himself airs. His left was all bandaged, he too had a black eye, and moreover his features was about as battered as mine. I hope it hurt him as much to move as it did me. But he had the edge on me in one way—he hadn't rubbed as much hide off against the walls.

"Where's that two hundred we bet?" I snarled.

"Heh, heh!" sneered he. "Try and get it! They told me I wasn't counted out officially. The referee didn't count me out. You didn't whip me."

"Let the money go, you dirty, yellow crook," I snarled, "but I whipped you, and I can prove it by thirty men. What you doin' here, anyway?"

"I come to see my girl."

"Your girl? What was we fightin' about last night?"

"Just because you had the sap's luck to knock me stiff don't mean Raquel chooses you," he answered savagely. "This time, she names the man she likes, see? And when she does, I want you to get out!"

"All right," I snarled. "I whipped you fair and can prove it. Come in here; she'll get a chance to choose between us, and if she don't pick the best man, why, I can whip you all over again. Come on, you—"

Saying no more, we kicked the door open and went on in. We swept the interior with a eagle glance, and then sighted Raquel sitting at a table, leaning on her elbows and gazing soulfully into the eyes of a handsome bird in the uniform of a Spanish naval officer.

We barged across the room and come to a halt at her table. She glanced up in some surprise, but she could not have been blamed had she failed to recognize us.

"Raquel," said I, "we went forth and fought for your fair hand just like you said. As might be expected, I won. Still, this incomprehensible bezark thinks that you might still have some lurkin' fondness for him, and he requires to hear from your own rosy lips that you love another—meanin' me, of course. Say the word and I toss him out. My ship sails tonight, and I got a lot to say to you."

"Santa Maria!" said Raquel. "What ees theese? What kind of a bizness is theese, you two tramps coming looking like theese and talking gibberish? Am I to blame eef two great tramps go pound each other's maps, ha? What ees that to me?"

"But you said—" I began, completely at sea, "you said, go fight and the best man—"

"I say, may the best man win! Bah! Did I geeve any promise? What do I care about Yankee tramps what make the fist-fight? Bah! Go home and beefsteak the eye. You insult me, talking to me in public with the punch' nose and bung' up face."

"Then you don't love either of us?" said Bat.

"Me love two gorillas? Bah! Here is my man—Don Jose y Balsa Santa Maria Gonzales."

She then gave a screech, for at that moment Bat and me hit Don Jose y Balsa Santa Maria Gonzales simultaneous, him with the right and me with the left. And then, turning our backs on the dumfounded Raquel, we linked arms and, stepping over the fallen lover, strode haughtily to the door and vanished from her life.

"AND THAT," SAID I, as we leaned upon the bar to which we had made our mutual and unspoke agreement, "ends our romance, and the glory road leads only to disappointment and hokum."

"Women," said Bat gloomily, "are the bunk."

"Listen," said I, remembering something, "how about that two hundred you owe me?"

"What for?"

"For knockin' you cold."

"Steve," said Bat, laying his hand on my shoulder in brotherly fashion, "you know I been intendin' to pay you that all along. After all, Steve, we are seamen together, and we have just been did dirt by a woman of another race. We are both American sailors, even if you are a harp, and we got to stand by each other. Let bygones be bygones, says I. The fortunes of war, you know. We fought a fair, clean fight, and you was lucky enough to win. Let's have one more drink and then part in peace an' amity."

"You ain't holdin' no grudge account of me layin' you out?" I asked, suspiciously.

"Steve," said Bat, waxing oratorical, "all men is brothers, and the fact that you was lucky enough to crown me don't alter my admiration and affection. Tomorrow we will be sailin' the high seas, many miles apart. Let our thoughts of each other be gentle and fraternal. Let us forgit old feuds and old differences. Let this be the dawn of a new age of brotherly affection and square dealin'."

"And how about my two hundred?"

"Steve, you know I am always broke at the end of my shore leave. I give you my word I'll pay you them two hundred smackers. Ain't the word of a comrade enough? Now le's drink to our future friendship and the amicable relations of the crews of our respective ships. Steve, here's my hand! Let this here shake be a symbol of our friendship. May no women ever come between us again! Good-bye, Steve! Good luck! Good luck!"

And so saying, we shook and turned away. That is, I turned and then whirled back as quick as I could—just in time to duck the right swing he'd started the minute my back was turned, and to knock him cold with a bottle I snatched off the bar.

The BULL DOG BREED.

ALTERNATE TITLE: YOU GOT TO KILL A BULLDOG

This short story was first published in the February 1930 issue of Fight Stories *magazine.*

"AND SO," CON-CLUDED the Old Man, "this big bully ducked the seltzer bottle and the next thing I knowed I knowed nothin'. I come to with the general idee that the *Sea Girl* was sinkin' with all hands and I was drownin'—but it was only some chump pourin' water all over me to bring me to. Oh, yeah, the big French cluck I had the row with was nobody much, I learned—just only merely nobody but Tiger Valois, the heavyweight champion of the French navy—"

Me and the crew winked at each other. Until the captain decided to unburden to Penrhyn, the first mate, in our hearing, we'd wondered about the black eye he'd sported following his night ashore in Manila. He'd been in an unusual bad temper ever since, which means he'd been acting like a sore-tailed hyena. The Old Man was a Welshman, and he hated a Frenchman like he hated a snake. He now turned on me.

"If you was any part of a man, you big mick ham," he said bitterly, "you wouldn't stand around and let a blankety-blank French so-on and so-forth layout your captain. Oh, yeah, I know you wasn't there, then, but if you'll fight him—"

"Aragh!" I said with sarcasm, "leavin' out the fact that I'd stand a great chance of gettin' matched with Valois—why not pick me somethin' easy, like Dempsey? Do you realize you're askin' me, a ordinary ham-an'-egger, to climb the original and only Tiger Valois that's whipped everything in European and the Asian waters and looks like a sure bet for the world's title?"

"Gerahh!" snarled the Old Man. "Me that's boasted in every port of the Seven Seas that I shipped the toughest crew since the days of Harry Morgan—" He turned his back in disgust and immediately fell over my white bulldog, Mike, who was taking a snooze by the hatch. The Old Man give a howl as he come up and booted the innocent pup most severe. Mike instantly attached hisself to the Old Man's leg, from which I at last succeeded in prying him with a loss of some meat and the pants leg.

The captain danced hither and yon about the deck on one foot while he expressed his feelings at some length and the crew stopped work to listen and admire.

"And get me right, Steve Costigan," he wound up, "the *Sea Girl* is too small for me and that double-dash dog. He goes ashore at the next port. Do you hear me?"

"Then I go ashore with him," I answered with dignity. "It was not Mike what caused you to get a black eye, and if you had not been so taken up in abusin' me you would not have fell over him.

"Mike is a Dublin gentleman, and no Welsh water rat can boot him and get away with it. If you want to banish your best A.B. mariner, it's up to you. Till we make port you keep your boots off of Mike, or I will personally kick you loose from your spine. If that's mutiny, make the most of it—and, Mister First Mate, I see you easin' toward that belayin' pin on the rail, and I call to your mind what I done to the last man that hit me with a belayin' pin."

There was a coolness between me and the Old Man thereafter. The old nut was pretty rough and rugged, but good at heart, and likely he was ashamed of himself, but he was too stubborn to admit it, besides still being sore at me and Mike. Well, he paid me off without a word at Hong Kong, and I went down the gangplank with Mike at my heels, feeling kind of queer and empty, though I wouldn't show it for nothing, and acted like I was glad to get off the old tub. But since I growed up, the *Sea Girl's* been the only home I knowed, and though I've left her from time to time to prowl around loose or to make a fight tour, I've always come back to her.

Now I knowed I couldn't come back, and it hit me hard. The *Sea Girl* is the only thing I'm champion of, and as I went ashore I heard the sound of Mushy Hansen and Bill O'Brien trying to decide which should succeed to my place of honor.

WELL, MAYBE SOME will say I should of sent Mike ashore and stayed on, but to my mind, a man that won't stand by his dog is lower down than one which won't stand by his fellow man.

Some years ago I'd picked Mike up wandering around the wharfs of Dublin and fighting everything he met on four legs and not averse to tackling two-legged critters. I named him Mike after a brother of mine, Iron Mike Costigan, rather well known in them higher fight circles where I've never gotten to.

Well, I wandered around the dives and presently fell in with Tom Roche, a lean, fighting engineer that I once knocked out in Liverpool. We meandered around, drinking here and there, though not very much, and presently found ourselves in a dump a little different from the general run. A French joint, kinda more highbrow, if you get me. A lot of swell-looking fellows was in there drinking, and the bartenders and waiters, all French, scowled at Mike, but said nothing. I was unburdening my woes to Tom, when I noticed a tall, elegant young man with a dress

suit, cane and gloves stroll by our table. He seemed well known in the dump, because birds all around was jumping up from their tables and waving their glasses and yelling at him in French. He smiled back in a superior manner and flourished his cane in a way which irritated me. This galoot rubbed me the wrong way right from the start, see?

Well, Mike was snoozing close to my chair as usual, and, like any other fighter, Mike was never very particular where he chose to snooze. This big bimbo could have stepped over him or around him, but he stopped and prodded Mike with his cane. Mike opened one eye, looked up and lifted his lip in a polite manner, just like he was sayin': "We don't want no trouble; go 'long and leave me alone."

Then this French dipthong drawed back his patent leather shoe and kicked Mike hard in the ribs. I was out of my chair in a second, seeing red, but Mike was quicker. He shot up off the floor, not for the Frenchman's leg, but for his throat. But the Frenchman, quick as a flash, crashed his heavy cane down across Mike's head, and the bulldog hit the floor and laid still. The next minute the Frenchman hit the floor, and believe me he laid still! My right-hander to the jaw put him down, and the crack his head got against the corner of the bar kept him there.

I bent over Mike, but he was already coming around, in spite of the fact that a loaded cane had been broken over his head. It took a blow like that to put Mike out, even for a few seconds. The instant he got his bearings, his eyes went red and he started out to find what hit him and tear it up. I grabbed him, and for a minute it was all I could do to hold him. Then the red faded out of his eyes and he wagged his stump of a tail and licked my nose. But I knowed the first good chance he had at the Frenchman he'd rip out his throat or die trying. The only way you can lick a bulldog is to kill him.

Being taken up with Mike I hadn't had much time to notice what was going on. But a gang of French sailors had tried to rush me and had stopped at the sight of a gun in Tom Roche's hand. A real fighting man was Tom, and a bad egg to fool with.

By this time the Frenchman had woke up; he was standing with a handkerchief at his mouth, which latter was trickling blood, and honest to Jupiter I never saw such a pair of eyes on a human! His face was dead white, and those black, burning eyes blazed out at me—say, fellows!—they carried more than hate and a desire to muss me up! They was mutilation and sudden death! Once I seen a famous duelist in Heidelberg who'd killed ten men in sword fights—he had just such eyes as this fellow.

A gang of Frenchies was around him all whooping and yelling and jabbering at once, and I couldn't understand a word none of them said. Now one come prancing up to

Tom Roche and shook his fist in Tom's face and pointed at me and yelled, and pretty soon Tom turned around to me and said: "Steve, this yam is challengin' you to a duel— what about?"

I thought of the German duelist and said to myself: "I bet this bird was born with a fencin' sword in one hand and a duelin' pistol in the other." I opened my mouth to say "Nothin' doin'—" when Tom pipes: "You're the challenged party—the choice of weapons is up to you."

At that I hove a sigh of relief and a broad smile flitted across my homely but honest countenance. "Tell him I'll fight him," I said, "with five-ounce boxin' gloves."

Of course I figured this bird never saw a boxing glove. Now, maybe you think I was doing him dirty, pulling a fast one like that— but what about him? All I was figuring on was mussing him up a little, counting on him not knowing a left hook from a neutral corner— takin' a mean advantage, maybe, but he was counting on killing me, and I'd never had a sword in my hand, and couldn't hit the side of a barn with a gun.

Well, Tom told them what I said and the cackling and gibbering bust out all over again, and to my astonishment I saw a cold, deadly smile waft itself across the sinister, handsome face of my tete-a-tete.

"They ask who you are," said Tom. "I told 'em Steve Costigan, of America. This bird says his name is

Francois, which he opines is enough for you. He says that he'll fight you right away at the exclusive Napoleon Club, which it seems has a ring on account of it occasionally sponsoring prize fights."

AS WE WENDED our way toward the aforesaid club, I thought deeply. It seemed very possible that this Francois, whoever he was, knew something of the manly art. Likely, I thought, a rich clubman who took up boxing for a hobby. Well, I reckoned he hadn't heard of me, because no amateur, however rich, would think he had a chance against Steve Costigan, known in all ports as the toughest sailor in the Asian waters—if I do say so myself—and champion of—what I mean—ex-champion of the *Sea Girl*, the toughest of all the trading vessels.

A kind of pang went through me just then at the thought that my days with the old tub was ended, and I wondered what sort of a dub would take my place at mess and sleep in my bunk, and how the forecastle gang would haze him, and how all the crew would miss me—I wondered if Bill O'Brien had licked Mushy Hansen or if the Dane had won, and who called hisself champion of the craft now—

Well, I felt low in spirits, and Mike knowed it, because he snuggled up closer to me in the rickshaw that was carrying us to the Napoleon Club, and licked my hand. I pulled

his ears and felt better. Anyway, Mike wouldn't never desert me.

Pretty ritzy affair this club. Footmen or butlers or something in uniform at the doors, and they didn't want to let Mike in. But they did— oh, yeah, they did.

In the dressing room they give me, which was the swellest of its sort I ever see, and looked more like a girl's boodwar than a fighter's dressing room, I said to Tom: "This big ham must have lots of dough— notice what a hand they all give him? Reckon I'll get a square deal? Who's goin' to referee? If it's a Frenchman, how'm I gonna follow the count?"

"Well, gee whiz!" Tom said, "you ain't expectin' him to count over you, are you?"

"No," I said. "But I'd like to keep count of what he tolls off over the other fellow."

"Well," said Tom, helping me into the green trunks they'd give me, "don't worry none. I understand Francois can speak English, so I'll specify that the referee shall converse entirely in that language."

"Then why didn't this Francois ham talk English to me?" I wanted to know.

"He didn't talk to you in anything," Tom reminded me. "He's a swell and thinks you're beneath his notice—except only to knock your head off."

"H'mm," said I thoughtfully, gently touching the slight cut which Francois' cane had made on Mike's incredibly hard head. A slight red mist, I will admit, waved in front of my eyes.

When I climbed into the ring I noticed several things: mainly the room was small and elegantly furnished; second, there was only a small crowd there, mostly French, with a scattering of English and one Chink in English clothes. There was high hats, frock-tailed coats and gold-knobbed canes everywhere, and I noted with some surprise that they was also a sprinkling of French sailors.

I sat in my corner, and Mike took his stand just outside, like he always does when I fight, standing on his hind legs with his head and forepaws resting on the edge of the canvas, and looking under the ropes. On the street, if a man soaks me he's likely to have Mike at his throat, but the old dog knows how to act in the ring. He won't interfere, though sometimes when I'm on the canvas or bleeding bad his eyes get red and he rumbles away down deep in his throat.

TOM WAS MASSAGING my muscles light-like and I was scratching Mike's ears when into the ring comes Francois the Mysterious. Oui! Oui! I noted now how much of a man he was, and Tom whispers to me to pull in my chin a couple of feet and stop looking so goofy. When Francois threw off his silk embroidered bathrobe I saw I was in for a rough session, even if this bird was only an amateur. He was one of these fellows that look like a fighting man, even if they've never seen a glove before.

A good six one and a half he stood, or an inch and a half taller than me. A powerful neck sloped into broad, flexible shoulders, a limber steel body tapered to a girlishly slender waist. His legs was slim, strong and shapely, with narrow feet that looked speedy and sure; his arms was long, thick, but perfectly molded. Oh, I tell you, this Francois looked more like a champion than any man I'd seen since I saw Dempsey last.

And the face—his sleek black hair was combed straight back and lay smooth on his head, adding to his sinister good looks. From under narrow black brows them eyes burned at me, and now they wasn't a duelist's eyes—they was tiger eyes. And when he gripped the ropes and dipped a couple of times, flexing his muscles, them muscles rippled under his satiny skin most beautiful, and he looked just like a big cat sharpening his claws on a tree.

"Looks fast, Steve," Tom Roche said, looking serious. "May know somethin'; you better crowd him from the gong and keep rushin'—"

"How else did I ever fight?" I asked.

A sleek-looking Frenchman with a sheik mustache got in the ring and, waving his hands to the crowd, which was still jabbering for Francois, he bust into a gush of French.

"What's he mean?" I asked Tom,

and Tom said, "Aw, he's just sayin' what everybody knows—that this ain't a regular prize fight, but an affair of honor between you and— uh—that Francois fellow there."

Tom called him and talked to him in French, and he turned around and called an Englishman out of the crowd. Tom asked me was it all right with me for the Englishman to referee, and I tells him yes, and they asked Francois and he nodded in a supercilious manner. So the referee asked me what I weighed and I told him, and he hollered: "This bout is to be at catch weights, Marquis of Queensberry rules. Three-minute rounds, one minute rest; to a finish, if it takes all night. In this corner, Monsieur Francois, weight 205 pounds; in this corner, Steve Costigan of America, weight 190 pounds. Are you ready, gentlemen?"

'Stead of standing outside the ring, English style, the referee stayed in with us, American fashion. The gong sounded and I was out of my corner. All I seen was that cold, sneering, handsome face, and all I wanted to do was to spoil it. And I very nearly done it the first charge. I came in like a house afire and I walloped Francois with an overhand right hook to the chin—more by sheer luck than anything, and it landed high. But it shook him to his toes, and the sneering smile faded.

TOO QUICK FOR the eye to follow, his straight left beat my left hook, and it packed the jarring kick that marks a puncher. The next minute, when I missed with both hands and got that left in my pan again, I knowed I was up against a master boxer, too.

I saw in a second I couldn't match him for speed and skill. He was like a cat; each move he made was a blur of speed, and when he hit he hit quick and hard. He was a brainy fighter—he thought out each move while traveling at high speed, and he was never at a loss what to do next.

Well, my only chance was to keep on top of him, and I kept crowding him, hitting fast and heavy. He wouldn't stand up to me, but back-pedaled all around the ring. Still, I got the idea that he wasn't afraid of me, but was retreating with a purpose of his own. But I never stop to figure out why the other bird does something.

He kept reaching me with that straight left, until finally I dived under it and sank my right deep into his midriff. It shook him—it should of brought him down. But he clinched and tied me up so I couldn't hit or do nothing. As the referee broke us Francois scraped his glove laces across my eyes. With an appropriate remark, I threw my right at his head with everything I had, but he drifted out of the way, and I fell into the ropes from the force of my own swing. The crowd howled with laughter, and then the gong sounded.

"This baby's tough," said Tom, back in my corner, as he rubbed my belly muscles, "but keep crowdin' him, get inside that left, if you can. And watch the right."

I reached back to scratch Mike's nose and said, "You watch this round."

Well, I reckon it was worth watching. Francois changed his tactics, and as I come in he met me with a left to the nose that started the claret and filled my eyes full of water and stars. While I was thinking about that he opened a cut under my left eye with a venomous right-hander and then stuck the same hand into my midriff. I woke up and bent him double with a savage left hook to the liver, crashing him with an overhand right behind the ear before he could straighten. He shook his head, snarled a French cuss word and drifted back behind that straight left where I couldn't reach him.

I went into him like a whirlwind, lamming head on full into that left jab again and again, trying to get to him, but always my swings were short. Them jabs wasn't hurting me yet, because it takes a lot of them to weaken a man. But it was like running into a floating brick wall, if you get what I mean. Then he started crossing his right—and oh, baby, what a right he had! Blip! Blim! Blam!

His rally was so unexpected and he hit so quick that he took me clean off my guard and caught me wide open. That right was lightning! In a second I was groggy, and Francois beat me back across the ring with

both hands going too fast for me to block more than about a fourth of the blows. He was wild for the kill now and hitting wide open.

Then the ropes was at my back and I caught a flashing glimpse of him, crouching like a big tiger in front of me, wide open and starting his right. In that flash of a second I shot my right from the hip, beat his punch and landed solid to the button. Francois went down like he'd been hit with a pile driver—the referee leaped forward—the gong sounded!

As I went to my corner the crowd was clean ory-eyed and not responsible; and I saw Francois stagger up, glassy-eyed, and walk to his stool with one arm thrown over the shoulder of his handler.

But he come out fresh as ever for the third round. He'd found out that I could hit as hard as he could and that I was dangerous when groggy, like most sluggers. He was wild with rage, his smile was gone, his face dead white again, his eyes was like black fires—but he was cautious. He side-stepped my rush, hooking me viciously on the ear as I shot past him, and ducking when I slewed around and hooked my right. He backed away, shooting that left to my face. It went that way the whole round; him keeping the right reserved and marking me up with left jabs while I worked for his body and usually missed or was blocked. Just before the gong he rallied, stag-gered me with a flashing right hook to the head and took a crushing left hook to the ribs in return.

THE FOURTH ROUND come and he was more aggressive. He began to trade punches with me again. He'd shoot a straight left to my face, then hook the same hand to my body. Or he'd feint the left for my face and drop it to my ribs. Them hooks to the body didn't hurt much, because I was hard as a rock there, but a continual rain of them wouldn't do me no good, and them jabs to the face was beginning to irritate me. I was already pretty well marked up.

He shot his blows so quick I usually couldn't block or duck, so every time he'd make a motion with the left I'd throw my right for his head haphazard. After rocking his head back several times this way he quit feinting so much and began to devote most of his time to body blows.

Now I found out this about him: he had more claws than sand, as the saying goes. I mean he had everything, including a lot of stuff I didn't, but he didn't like to take it. In a mix-up he always landed three blows to my one, and he hit about as hard as I did, but he was always the one to back away.

Well, come the seventh round. I'd taken plenty. My left eye was closing fast and I had a nasty gash over the other one. My ribs was beginning to feel the body punishment he was handing out when in close, and my right ear was rapidly assuming the shape of a cabbage. Outside of some ugly welts on his torso, my dancing partner had only one mark on him—the small cut on his chin where I'd landed with my bare fist earlier in the evening.

But I was not beginning to weaken for I'm used to punishment; in fact I eat it up, if I do say so. I crowded Francois into a corner before I let go. I wrapped my arms around my neck, worked in close and then unwound with a looping left to the head.

Francois countered with a sickening right under the heart and I was wild with another left. Francois stepped inside my right swing, dug his heel into my instep, gouged me in the eye with his thumb and, holding with his left, battered away at my ribs with his right. The referee showed no inclination to interfere with this pastime, so, with a hearty oath, I wrenched my right loose and nearly tore off Francois' head with a torrid uppercut.

His sneer changed to a snarl and he began pistoning me in the face again with his left. Maddened, I crashed into him headlong and smashed my right under his heart—I felt his ribs bend, he went white and sick and clinched before I could follow up my advantage. I felt the drag of his body as his knees buckled, but he held on while I raged and swore, the referee would not break us, and when I tore loose, my charming playmate was almost as good as ever.

He proved this by shooting a left to my sore eye, dropping the same hand to my aching ribs and bringing up a right to the jaw that stretched me flat on my back for the first time that night. Just like that! Biff—bim—bam! Like a cat hitting—and I was on the canvas.

Tom Roche yelled for me to take a count, but I never stay on the canvas longer than I have to. I bounced up at "Four!" my ears still ringing and a trifle dizzy, but otherwise O.K.

Francois thought otherwise, rushed rashly in and stopped a left hook which hung him gracefully over the ropes. The gong!

The beginning of the eighth I come at Francois like we'd just started, took his right between my eyes to hook my left to his body—he broke away, spearing me with his left—I followed swinging—missed a right—crack!

He musta let go his right with all he had for the first time that night, and he had a clear shot to my jaw. The next thing I knowed, I was writhing around on the canvas feeling like my jaw was tore clean off and the referee was saying: "—seven—"

Somehow I got to my knees. It looked like the referee was ten miles away in a mist, but in the mist I could see Francois' face, smiling again, and I reeled up at "nine" and went for that face. Crack! Crack! I don't know

what punch put me down again but there I was. I beat the count by a hair's breadth and swayed forward, following my only instinct and that was to walk into him!

FRANCOIS MIGHT HAVE finished me there, but he wasn't taking any chances for he knowed I was dangerous to the last drop. He speared me a couple of times with the left, and when he shot his right, I ducked it and took it high on my forehead and clinched, shaking my head to clear it. The referee broke us away and Francois lashed into me, cautious but deadly, hammering me back across the ring with me crouching and covering up the best I could.

On the ropes I unwound with a venomous looping right, but he was watching for that and ducked and countered with a terrible left to my jaw, following it with a blasting right to the side of the head. Another left hook threw me back into the ropes and there I caught the top rope with both hands to keep from falling. I was swaying and ducking but his gloves were falling on my ears and temples with a steady thunder which was growing dimmer and dimmer— then the gong sounded.

I let go of the ropes to go to my corner and when I let go I pitched to my knees. Everything was a red mist and the crowd was yelling about a million miles away. I heard Francois' scornful laugh, then Tom Roche was dragging me to my corner.

"By golly," he said, working on my cut up eyes, "you're sure a glutton for punishment; Joe Grim had nothin' on you.

"But you better lemme throw in the towel, Steve. This Frenchman's goin' to kill you—"

"He'll have to, to beat me," I snarled. "I'll take it standin'."

"But, Steve," Tom protested, mopping blood and squeezing lemon juice into my mouth, "this Frenchman is—"

But I wasn't listening. Mike knowed I was getting the worst of it and he'd shoved his nose into my right glove, growling low down in his throat. And I was thinking about something.

One time I was laid up with a broken leg in a little fishing village away up on the Alaskan coast, and looking through a window, not able to help him, I saw Mike fight a big gray devil of a sled dog—more wolf than dog. A big gray killer. They looked funny together—Mike short and thick, bow-legged and squat, and the wolf dog tall and lean, rangy and cruel.

Well, while I lay there and raved and tried to get off my bunk with four men holding me down, that blasted wolf-dog cut poor old Mike to ribbons. He was like lightning—like Francois. He fought with the slash and get away—like Francois. He was all steel and whale-bone—like Francois.

Poor old Mike had kept walking

into him, plunging and missing as the wolf-dog leaped aside—and every time he leaped he slashed Mike with his long sharp teeth till Mike was bloody and looking terrible. How long they fought I don't know. But Mike never give up; he never whimpered; he never took a single back step; he kept walking in on the dog.

At last he landed—crashed through the wolf-dog's defense and clamped his jaws like a steel vise and tore out the wolf-dog's throat. Then Mike slumped down and they brought him into my bunk more dead than alive. But we fixed him up and finally he got well, though he'll carry the scars as long as he lives.

And I thought, as Tom Roche rubbed my belly and mopped the blood off my smashed face, and Mike rubbed his cold, wet nose in my glove, that me and Mike was both of the same breed, and the only fighting quality we had was a ever-lasting persistence. You got to kill a bulldog to lick him. Persistence! How'd I ever won a fight? How'd Mike ever won a fight? By walking in on our men and never giving up, no matter how bad we was hurt! Always outclassed in everything except guts and grip! Somehow the fool Irish tears burned my eyes and it wasn't the pain of the collodion Tom was rubbing into my cuts and it wasn't self-pity—it was—I don't know what it was! My grandfather used to say the Irish cried at Benburb when they were licking the socks off the English.

THEN THE GONG sounded and I was out in the ring again playing the old bulldog game with Francois— walking into him and walking into him and taking everything he handed me without flinching.

I don't remember much about that round. Francois' left was a red-hot lance in my face and his right was a hammer that battered in my ribs and crashed against my dizzy head. Toward the last my legs felt dead and my arms were like lead. I don't know how many times I went down and got up and beat the count, but I remember once in a clinch, half-sobbing through my pulped lips: "You gotta kill me to stop me, you big hash!" And I saw a strange haggard look flash into his eyes as we broke. I lashed out wild and by luck connected under his heart. Then the red fog stole back over everything and then I was back on my stool and Tom was holding me to keep me from falling off.

"What round's this comin' up?" I mumbled.

"The tenth," he said. "For th' luvva Pete, Steve, quit!"

I felt around blind for Mike and felt his cold nose on my wrist.

"Not while I can see, stand or feel," I said, deliriously. "It's bulldog and wolf—and Mike tore his throat out in the end—and I'll rip this wolf apart sooner or later."

Back in the center of the ring with my chest all crimson with my own blood, and Francois' gloves soggy and splashing blood and water at every blow, I suddenly realized that his punches were losing some of their kick. I'd been knocked down I don't know how many times, but I now knew he was hitting me his best and I still kept my feet. My legs wouldn't work right, but my shoulders were still strong. Francois played for my eyes and closed them both tight shut, but while he was doing it I landed three times under the heart, and each time he wilted a little.

"What round's comin' up?" I groped for Mike because I couldn't see.

"The eleventh—this is murder," said Tom. "I know you're one of these birds which fights twenty rounds after they've been knocked cold, but I want to tell you this Frenchman is—"

"Lance my eyelid with your pocket-knife," I broke in, for I had found Mike. "I gotta see."

Tom grumbled, but I felt a sharp pain and the pressure eased up in my right eye and I could see dim-like.

Then the gong sounded, but I couldn't get up; my legs was dead and stiff.

"Help me up, Tom Roche, you big bog-trotter," I snarled. "If you throw in that towel I'll brain you with the water bottle!"

With a shake of his head he helped me up and shoved me in the ring. I got my bearings and went forward with a funny, stiff, mechanical step, toward Francois—who got up slow, with a look on his face like he'd rather be somewhere else. Well, he'd cut me to pieces, knocked me down time and again, and here I was coming back for more. The bulldog instinct is hard to fight—it ain't just exactly courage, and it ain't exactly blood lust—it's—well, it's the bulldog breed.

NOW I WAS facing Francois and I noticed he had a black eye and a deep gash under his cheek bone, though I didn't remember putting them there. He also had welts a-plenty on his body. I'd been handing out punishment as well as taking it, I saw.

Now his eyes blazed with a desperate light and he rushed in, hitting as hard as ever for a few seconds. The blows rained so fast I couldn't think and yet I knowed I must be clean batty—punch drunk—because it seemed like I could hear familiar voices yelling my name—the voices of the crew of the *Sea Girl*, who'd never yell for me again.

I was on the canvas and this time I felt that it was to stay; dim and far away I saw Francois and somehow I could tell his legs was trembling and he shaking like he had a chill. But I couldn't reach him now. I tried to get my legs under me, but they wouldn't work. I slumped back on the canvas, crying with rage and weakness.

Then through the noise I heard one deep, mellow sound like an old Irish bell, almost. Mike's bark! He wasn't a barking dog; only on special occasions did he give tongue. This time he only barked once. I looked at him and he seemed to be swimming in a fog. If a dog ever had his soul in his eyes, he had; plain as speech them eyes said: "Steve, old kid, get up and hit one more blow for the glory of the breed!"

I tell you, the average man has got to be fighting for somebody else besides hisself. It's fighting for a flag, a nation, a woman, a kid or a dog that makes a man win. And I got up—I dunno how! But the look in Mike's eyes dragged me off the canvas just as the referee opened his mouth to say "Ten!" But before he could say it—

In the mist I saw Francois' face, white and desperate. The pace had told. Them blows I'd landed from time to time under the heart had sapped his strength—he'd punched hisself out on me—but more'n anything else, the knowledge that he was up against the old bulldog breed licked him.

I drove my right smash into his face and his head went back like it was on hinges and the blood spattered. He swung his right to my head and it was so weak I laughed, blowing out a haze of blood. I rammed my left to his ribs and as he bent forward I crashed my right to his jaw. He dropped, and crouching there on the canvas, half supporting himself on his hands, he was counted out. I reeled across the ring and collapsed with my arms around Mike, who was whining deep in his throat and trying to lick my face off.

THE FIRST THING I felt on coming to, was a cold, wet nose burrowing into my right hand, which seemed numb. Then somebody grabbed that hand and nearly shook it off and I heard a voice say: "Hey, you old shellback, you want to break a unconscious man's arm?"

I knowed I was dreaming then, because it was Bill O'Brien's voice, who was bound to be miles away at sea by this time. Then Tom Roche said: "I think he's comin' to. Hey, Steve, can you open your eyes?"

I took my fingers and pried the swollen lids apart and the first thing I saw, or wanted to see, was Mike. His stump tail was going like anything and he opened his mouth and let his tongue loll out, grinning as natural as could be. I pulled his ears and looked around and there was Tom Roche—and Bill O'Brien and Mushy Hansen, Olaf Larsen, Penrhyn, the first mate, Red O'Donnell, the second—and the Old Man!

"Steve!" yelled this last, jumping up and down and shaking my hand like he wanted to take it off, "you're a wonder! A blightin' marvel!"

"Well," said I, dazed, "why all the love fest—"

"The fact is," bust in Bill O'Brien, "just as we're about to weigh anchor, up blows a lad with the news that you're fightin' in the Napoleon Club with—"

"—and as soon as I heard who you was fightin' with I stopped everything and we all blowed down there," said the Old Man. "But the fool kid Roche had sent for us loafed on the way—"

"—and we hadda lay some Frenchies before we could get in," said Hansen.

"So we saw only the last three rounds," continued the Old Man. "But, boy, they was worth the money—he had you outclassed every way except guts—you was licked to a frazzle, but he couldn't make you realize it—and I laid a bet or two—"

And blow me, if the Old Man didn't stuff a wad of bills in my sore hand.

"Halfa what I won," he beamed. "And furthermore, the *Sea Girl* ain't sailin' till you're plumb able and fit."

"But what about Mike?" My head was swimming by this time.

"A bloomin' bow-legged angel," said the Old Man, pinching Mike's ear lovingly. "The both of you kin have my upper teeth! I owe you a lot, Steve. You've done a lot for me, but I never felt so in debt to you as I do now. When I see that big French ham, the one man in the world I would of give my right arm to see licked—"

"Hey!" I suddenly seen the light, and I went weak and limp. "You mean that was—"

"You whipped Tiger Valois, heavyweight champion of the French fleet, Steve," said Tom. "You ought to have known how he wears dude clothes and struts amongst the swells when on shore leave. He wouldn't tell you who he was for fear you wouldn't fight him; and I was afraid I'd discourage you if I told you at first and later you wouldn't give me a chance."

"I might as well tell you," I said to the Old Man, "that I didn't know this bird was the fellow that beat you up in Manila. I fought him because he kicked Mike."

"Blow the reason!" said the Old Man, raring back and beaming like a jubilant crocodile. "You licked him—that's enough. Now we'll have a bottle opened and drink to Yankee ships and Yankee sailors—especially Steve Costigan."

"Before you do," I said, "drink to the boy who stands for everything them aforesaid ships and sailors stands for—Mike of Dublin, an honest gentleman and born mascot of all fightin' men!"

SAILOR'S GRUDGE.

ALTERNATE TITLE: COSTIGAN VS. KID CAMERA

This short story was first published in the March 1930 issue of Fight Stories *magazine.*

I COME ASHORE AT Los Angeles for peace and quiet. Being heavyweight champion of the *Sea Girl*, whose captain boasts that he ships the toughest crews on the seven seas, ain't no joke. When we docked, I went ashore with the avowed intention of spending a couple of days in ease. I even went to the extent of leaving my white bulldog, Mike, on board. Not that I was intending to do Mike out of his shore leave, but we was to be docked a week at least, and I wanted a couple of days by myself to kinda soothe my nerves. Mike is always trying to remove somebody's leg, and then I have to either pay for the pants or lick the owner of the leg.

So I went ashore alone and drifted into the resident section along the beach. You know, where all them little summer cottages is that is occupied by nice people of modest means and habits.

I wandered up and down the beach watching the kids play in the sand and the girls sunning themselves, which many of them was knockouts, and I soon found I had got into a kind of secluded district where my kind seldom comes. I was dressed in good unassuming clothes, howthesomever, and could not understand the peculiar looks handed my way by the cottage owners.

It was with a start I heard someone say: "Oooh, sailor, yoo-hoo!"

I turned with some irritation. I am not ashamed of my profession, far from it, but I am unable to see why I am always spotted as a seaman even when I am not in my work clothes. But my irritation was removed instantly. A most beautiful little blonde flapper was coyly beckoning me and I lost no time starting in her direction. She was standing by a boat, holding a foolish little parasol over her curly head.

"Mr. Sailor, won't you row for me, please?" she cooed, letting her big baby blue eyes drift over my manly form. "I just adore sailors!"

"Miss," I said politely, rather dizzy from the look she gave me, "I will row you to Panama and back if you say the word!"

And with that I helped her in the boat and got in. That's me, always the perfect cavalier—I have lived a rough life but I always found time to notice the higher and softer things, such as courtesy and etiquette.

Well, we rowed all over the bay—leastways, I rowed, while she laid back under her little pink parasol and eyed me admiringly from under her long silky eyelashes.

We talked about such things as how hot the weather was this time of the year, and how nasty cold weather was when it was cold, and she asked me what ship I was on, and I told her and also told her my name was Steve Costigan, which was the truth; and she said her name was Marjory Harper, and she got me to tell her about my voyages and the like, like girls will. So I told her a lot of stories, most of which I got out of Mushy Hansen's dime novel library.

Being gifted with consideration, I did not tell her that I was a fighting man, well known in all ports as a tough man with the gloves, and the terror of all first mates and buckos afloat, because I could see she was a nice kid of genteel folks, and did not know nothing much about the world at large, though she was a good deal of a little flirt.

When we parted that afternoon I'll admit I had fell for her strong. She promised to meet me at the same place next day and I wended my way back to my hotel, whistling merrily.

THE NEXT MORNING found me back on the beach though I knowed I wouldn't see Marjory till afternoon. I was strolling by a shaded nook, where couples often go in to spoon, when I heard voices raised in dispute. I'm no eavesdropper, but I couldn't help but hear what was said—by the man, at least, because he had a strong voice and was using it. Some kid getting called down by her steady, I thought.

"—I told you to keep away from sailors, you little flirt!" he was saying angrily. "They're not your kind. Never mind how I know you were with some seagoing dub yesterday! That's all! Don't you talk back to me either. If I catch you with him, I'll spank you good. You're going home and stay there."

This was rather strong, I ruminated, and took a dislike right away to this fellow because I despise to hear a man talking rough to a woman. But the next minute I was almost struck dead with surprise and rage. A girl and a man came out of the nook on the other side. Their backs were toward me, but I got a good look at the man's face when he turned his head for a minute, and I saw he was a big handsome young fellow, with a shock of curly golden hair—and the girl was Marjory Harper!

For an instant I stood rooted to the ground, as it were. The big ham! Forbidding a girl to go with me! Abusing sailors! Calling me a dub when he didn't even know me! I was also amazed and enraged at Marjory's actions; she comes along with him as meek as a child and didn't even talk back. Before I could get my scattered wits together, they got into a car and drove off.

Talk about seeing red! And I knowed from this young upstart's build and walk that he was a sailor, too. The hypocrite!

Well, promptly at the appointed time, I was at the place I'd met Marjory the day before, and I didn't much expect her to show up. But she did, looking rather downcast. Even her little parasol drooped.

"I just came to tell you," she said rather nervously, "that I couldn't go rowing today. I must go back home at once."

"I thought you told me you wasn't married," I said bitterly.

She looked rather startled. "I'm not!" she exclaims.

"Well," I said, "I might's well tell you: I heard you get bawled out this mornin' for bein' with me. And I don't understand how come you took it."

"You don't know Bert," she sighed. "He's a perfect tyrant and treats me like a child." She clenched her little fists angrily and tears come into her eyes. "He's a big bully! If I was a man, I'd knock his block off!"

"Where is this Bert now?" I asked with the old sinister calm.

"Over in Hollywood, somewhere," she answered. "I think he's got a small part in a movie. But I can't stay. I musn't let Bert know I've been out to see you."

"Well, ain't I ever goin' to see you again?" I asked plaintively.

"Oh, goodness, no!" she shivered, dabbing her eyes. "I wouldn't dare! It makes Bert furious for me to even look at a sailor."

I ground my teeth gently. "Ain't

this boob a sailor hisself?" I asked mildly.

"Who? Bert? Yes, but he says as a rule they're no good for a nice girl to go with."

I restrained an impulse to howl and bite holes in the beach, and said with an effort at calmness: "Well, I'm goin' now. But remember, I'm comin' back to you."

"Oh, please don't!" she begged. "I'm terribly sorry, but if Bert catches us together, we'll both suffer."

Being unable to stand any more, I bowed politely and left for Hollywood at full speed. For a girl who seemed to have so much spunk, Bert sure had Marjory buffaloed. What kinda hold did he have over her, so he could talk to her like that? Why didn't she give him the gate? She couldn't love a ham like that, not with men like me around, and, anyway, if she'd loved him so much, she wouldn't have flirted with me.

I decided it must be something like I seen once in a movie called "The Curse of Rum," where the villain had so much on the heroine's old man that the heroine had to put up with his orneryness till the hero comes along and bumped him. I decided that Bert must have something on Marjory's old man, and was on the point of going back to ask her what it was, when I decided I'd make Bert tell me hisself.

WELL, I ARROVE in Hollywood and like a chump, started wandering around vaguely in the bare hopes I would run onto this Bert fellow. All to once I thought luck was with me. In a cafe three or four men was sitting talking earnestly and there was Bert! He was slicked up considerably, better dressed and even more handsome than ever. But I recognized that curly gold hair of his.

The next minute I was at the table and had hauled him out of the seat.

"Order my girl around, will ya?" I bellowed, aiming a terrible right at his jaw. He ducked and avoided complete annihilation by a inch, then to my utmost amazement he dived under the table, yelling for help. The next minute all the waiters in the world was on top of me but I flung 'em aside like chaff and yelled: "Come out from under that table, Bert, you big yellow-headed stiff! I'll show you—!"

"Bert—nothin'," howled a little short fat fellow hanging onto my right, "that's Reginald Van Veer, the famous movie star!"

At this startling bit of information I halted in amazement, and the aforesaid star sticking his frightened face out from under the table, I seen I had made a mistake. The resemblance between him and Bert was remarkable, but they wasn't the same man.

"My mistake," I growled. "Sorry to intrude on yuh." And so saying, I threw one waiter under the table and another into the corner and stalked out in silent majesty. Outside I ducked into a alley and beat it down a side street because I didn't know but what they'd have the cops on my neck.

Well, the street lights was burning when I decided to give it up. About this time who should I bump into but Tommy Marks, a kid I used to know in 'Frisco, and we had a reunion over a plate of corned beef and a stein of near beer. Tommy was sporting a small mustache and puttees and he told me that he was a assistant director, yes man, or something in the Tremendous Arts Movie Corporation, Inc.

"And boy," he splurged, "we are filming a peach, a pip and a wow! Is it a knockout? Oh, baby! A prize-fight picture entitled 'The Honor of the Champion,' starring Reginald Van Veer, with Honey Precious for the herowine. Boy, will it pack the theayters!"

"Baloney!" I sniffed. "You mean to tell me that wax-haired Van Veer will stand up and be pasted for art's sake?"

"Well, to tell you the truth." admitted Tommy, "he wouldn't; anyway, the company couldn't take a chance on a right hook ruinin' his profile. By sheer luck and wonderful chance, we found a fellow which looks enough like Reggie to be his twin brother. He's a tough sailor and a real fightin' man and we use him in the fights. For close-ups we use Reggie, made up to look sweaty and bloody, in a clinch with the other

dub, y'see. We'll work the close-ups in between the long shots and nobody'll be able to tell the difference."

"Who's this double?" I asked, smit by a sudden thought.

"I dunno. I picked him up over in Los Angeles. His first name is—"

"Bert!" I yelped.

Tommy looked kinda surprised. "Yeah, it is, come to think of it."

"Ayargh!" I gnashed my teeth. "I'll be around on the lot tomorrer. I got a few words to say to this here Bert."

"Hey!" hollered Tommy, knowing something of my disposition. "You lay off him till this picture is finished! For cat's sake! Tomorrow we shoot the big fight scene. The climax of the picture, see? We got a real fighter for Reggie's opponent—Terry O'Rourke from Seattle and we're payin' him plenty. If you spoil Reggie's double, we'll be out of luck!"

"Well," I snarled, "I'll be on the lot the first thing in the mornin', see? I don't reckon they'll let me in, but I'll be waitin' for Bert when he comes out."

THE NEXT MORNING found me at the Tremendous Arts studio before it was open. Yet, early as it was, I found a group of tough looking gents collected outside the casting office. They was four of them and one I recognized as Spike Monahan, A.B. mariner on the *Hornswoggle*, merchant ship, and as tough a nut as ever walked a deck.

"How come the thug convention, Spike?" I asked.

"Ain'tcha heard?" he responded. "Last night Terry O'Rourke broke his wrist swingin' at a bouncer in a night club and we're here to cop his job. Not that I care for the money so much," he ruminated, "but I want the job uh mussin' up Reggie Van Veer's beautiful countenance."

"Well, you're outa luck," I said, "because they're usin' a double."

"No matter," said all the tough birds, "we craves to bust into the movies."

"Boys," said I, taking off my coat, "consider the matter as closed. I've decided to take the job."

"Steve," said Spike, spitting in his hands, "I have nothin' agin' you. But it is my duty to the nation to put my map on the silver screen and rest the eyes of them fans which is tired of lookin' at varnished mugs like Reggie Van Veer's, and craves to gaze upon real he-men. Don't take this personal-like, Steve."

So saying, he shot over a right hook at my chin. I ducked and dropped him with an uppercut, blocked a swing from another thug and dropped him across Spike with a left hook to the stummick.

I then turned on the other two who was making war-like gestures, stopped a fist with my eye and crashed the owner of the fist with a left hook to the button.

The fourth man now raised a large lump on my head with a glancing blow of a blackjack, and slightly irritated, I flattened his nose with a straight left, jarred loose a couple of ribs with a right, and bringing the same hand up to his jaw, laid him stiff as a wedge.

Spike was now arising and noting the annoyance in his eye and the brass knuckles on his left hand, I did not wait for him to regain his feet but dropped my right behind his ear while he was still in a stooping position. Spike curled up with a cherubic smile on his frightful countenance.

I then threw my coat over my arm and went up to the door of the casting office and about this time it was opened by a small man in spectacles.

"Who are you?" he asked with some surprise, his gaze fixed on my fast blackening eye.

"I'm your new boxer," I answered gently, "takin' the place of Terry O'Rourke."

He looked puzzled.

"I know we sent the word out rather late last night," said he, "but I rather expected several men to be here, from which we could choose."

"They was four other fellers," I answered, "but they decided they wouldn't wait."

He looked past me to where the four galoots was weaving uncertainly off the lot, and he looked back at me and shuddered slightly.

"Come around next month," said he. "We're shooting a jungle picture then."

I didn't get him, but I said: "Well, you ain't tryin' to tell me I don't get this job, are you?"

"Oh, no," he said hastily. "Oh heavens, no! Come right in!"

I FOLLOWED HIM and after winding in and out among a lot of rooms and things I didn't know the use or meaning of, we come into a place which was fixed up like a big stadium, seats, ring and everything. It was still very early, but already swarms of extras was coming in and being arranged in the seats.

The head director come bustling up and looked me over. He acted like he was about half cuckoo and I don't wonder, what with all the noise and the confusion and fellows running up every second to ask him about lights, or sets or costumes or something.

"What's your name?" he snapped. "You look like a fighter. Where're you from?"

"Steve Costi—" I began.

"All right—listen to me. You're Battling O'Hanlon, champion of the British Isles, see? Reggie Van Veer is the champion of America and you're fighting for the title of the world, see? Of course we have a double for Reggie. After we shoot the fight, we'll take some close-ups of you and Reggie in the clinches and run them in at the proper places. Tommy, take this man to the dressing room and fix him up."

Tommy Marks come up on the run and when he seen me, he stopped short and turned pale. He motioned me to follow him, but when I started to speak to him he hissed: "Shut up! I don't know you! I can see where you crumb the deal some way and if it looks like we're friends, I'll lose my job! They'll think I put you up to it!"

Seeing his point, I said nothing and he led me into a dressing room, where I allowed him to smear some kind of goo on my face and touch up my eye brows. I couldn't see that it improved my looks any, but Tommy said it didn't do them any damage because nothing could. I put on the swellest pair of trunks I ever wore and Tommy knotted a British flag about my waist which struck me funny because while I'd often fought men wearing that flag, naturally I'd never thought I'd ever wear it myself. I tried to make him put the flag of the Irish Free State on me instead, but he said they didn't have one. He then give me a fine silk bath robe to put on and so accoutered I sallied forth.

I heard a wild roar as I opened the dressing room door and peeking carefully forth, I saw Reggie Van Veer striding majestically down the aisle, dressed even sweller than I was. Two cameras was grinding away and the director was howling his lungs out, and the crowd of extras in the seats was jumping and whooping just like a fight crowd does when the favorite comes down the aisle.

He clumb into the ring with a

swarm of seconds and handlers, and then Tommy told me to go into the ring. I come swaggering down the other aisle with a bigger gang than his behind me, carrying enough towels and buckets to fit out a army. I was astonished at the pains the movie people had took to make things realistic. I don't know how many extras was being used, but I saw right off that I'd never fought before a bigger crowd even in the real game itself.

I climbed through the ropes, following the instructions which the director yelled at me. I was kind of surprised. I'd always thought they was a lot of rehearsing to do. The referee called us to the center of the ring and they took a close-up of Reggie shaking hands with me, then the cameras quit grinding and Reggie skipped out of the ring, and in come—Bert! He was dressed just like Reggie had been and I was again struck by their strange resemblance.

"Now, then," bellowed the director, "this is going to be one picture that's going to look real! That's why I haven't rehearsed you boys. Go in and fight like you want to, so long as it's a fight! We got the ring well covered and can take you at any angle, so don't worry about getting out of range. This is going to be something new in pictures!

"Now, forget you're actors for the time being. Get into your solid skulls that you're fighters, like you've always been! Make this real! Put

everything you got into it for four rounds. Then, Bert, when I yell at you in the fifth round, you step back and shoot your left to the body. Steve, you drop your guard and then Bert, you crash the right to the jaw! And don't you pull the punch! I want this to be real. Steve, you drop when the right lands—"

I was thinking I'd be very likely to, anyway!

"I ain't going to have no knockout blows landing on the shoulder. The fight fans that see the shows have got so they spot 'em. This is going to appeal to those fans! If you boys get any teeth knocked out or noses broken, you get extra money. All right, get to your corners, and when the gong sounds, come out like they was a grudge between you!"

I COULD ASSURE him of that. I'd been watching Bert from under my lids while the director was talking. He stripped well and from his manner I knowed he was at home in a ring. He was broad-shouldered and lean-hipped and his muscles rolled beautifully. He was about six feet, one inch, and would weigh, I guess, a hundred and ninety-eight pounds, which was a inch taller and eight pounds heavier than me. Altogether he looked a lot like these Greek gods people rave about, but his firm square jaw and steely gray eyes told me I had my work cut out for me.

Well, the gong sounded and we went for each other. I wanted to give him fair warning, so I ducked his left and clinched.

"Never mind what that director cluck said," I snarled in his ear. "One of us is goin' out of here on a stretcher! I got your number, you big ham!"

"I don't even know you," he growled, jerking loose.

"You will!" I grinned savagely, throwing my right at his head with everything I had. He come back with a slashing left hook to the body and then we didn't have no more time for polite conversation.

This boy was fast, and cleverer than me, but he liked to mix it, too. He followed that left hook with a crashing right. I blocked it and landed hard under the eye, then went into a clinch and clubbed him with my right until the referee broke us.

We traded rights to the head and lefts to the body and he brought up a sizzling uppercut which might of tore my head off, hadst it landed. I buckled his knees with a right hook under the heart and he opened a cut under my left eye with a venomous straight right.

He then backed away, sparring and working for my wounded eye with a sharp-shooting left. Much annoyed, I followed him about the ring and suddenly dropped him to his knees with a smashing right cross to the side of the head. He bounced up without a count and flashed a straight left to my sore eye, following it instantly with a right uppercut to the body. I missed a looping right,

landed with my left, took two straight rights in the face to sink my left hook into his belly, and he went into a clinch. We worked out of it and was fighting along the ropes at the gong.

By this time the extras was whooping in earnest and the director was dancing with joy and yelling for us to keep it up. I growled and flashed a meaningful look across at my dancing partner and from the way he bared his strong white teeth at me, I knowed that the director was going to have his wish.

He come out at the gong like a wildcat and had rammed a straight left to my wind and two straight rights to my face before I could get collected. I came back with a wicked right hook under the heart, and missed with the same hand for the jaw. He had evidently decided his straight right was his best ace, for he kept shooting it over my guard and inside my looping left hook. Enraged, I suddenly slipped it, let it go over my left shoulder, and crossed my left hard to his jaw.

He grunted, and I sank my right deep into his ribs before he could recover his balance. He fell into a desperate clinch and hung on, shaking his head to clear it. The referee broke us, and Bert, evidently infuriated, crashed a haymaking right swing to the side of my head which knocked me into the ropes on the opposite side of the ring. As I come out of them, still dizzy, he was on me like a enraged wildcat and lifted me clear off the floor with a slung-shot right uppercut. Now it was me that clinched and it took all the referee's strength to tear us apart.

Bert feinted a straight right again, then shot his left to my heart. I missed a right, got in a good left and then the gong sounded.

AS I SET on my stool and my handlers and seconds went through a lot of motions which wasn't needed, I glanced out over the crowd. My heart give a leap right up into my mouth! On the first row, ringside, sat Marjory!

She was staring at the ring, rather pale. I give her a grin to show she needn't worry about me, but she just looked back kind of frightened. Poor kid, I reckoned she wasn't used to such tough work and was afraid Bert would hurt me. I chuckled gayly at the thought and felt a deep feeling of satisfaction, that she should see me give the big ham the lamming he deserved.

The gong!

Bert come out kind of cautious. He feinted a left, swung his right at my head, missed and backed away. I followed him rather carelessly, ducking another right swing. I thought, the next time he does that I will block it with my left and step in with a right to the jaw. Well, he swung his left, then his right and mechanically I threw up my left to block it. Too late I noticed that he had changed his position in a curious manner and was a lot closer to me than he ought to be. *Bam!* I was on the canvas feeling like my midriff was caved in.

As I got my legs under me, I realized he'd played the old Fitzsimmons shift on me. As he swung his right for a feint, he'd stepped forward with the right leg which brought him inside my guard and in position to drive in a terrific left-hander to the solar plexus. Well, he done so, and it's a good thing for me he didn't land just where he wanted to, and that he didn't have old Fitz's trick of shooting in bone-crushers from a few inches. If he had, I'd still been out.

Well, I got up at nine, Bert rushing in eager-like to finish me. I snapped my right to his jaw and stopped him in his tracks, and followed with a left hook to the body which he partially blocked. Any man which had ever fought me could of told him that I, like most sluggers, was most dangerous when groggy. He seemed rather discouraged and played safe for the rest of the round, which was rather slow, as I wasn't in no mood to push things, myself.

On my stool I cast a jovial grin at Marjory but she didn't seem to be enjoying the game much. Poor kid, I thought, the sight of me on the canvas was too much for her tender little heart. I bet, thought I, that girl is as good as mine, right now.

So it was with visions of wedding rings and vine covered cottages dancing in my head that I went out for the fourth round. Almost instantly these beautiful visions was shook out of my head by a severe right hook and I settled down to the business at hand. Bert was inclined to end matters quick and we traded wallops toe to toe till the ring was swimming before my eyes and I could see from the glazed look in Bert's eyes that he wasn't in no better shape. We then went into a clinch and leaned on each other, shaking our heads till they was partly clear again.

Then Bert started working his old reliable straight right until I give a roar of rage, dived under it and sank my left hook into his midriff, bringing up a right from my knees that would of ended the fight had it landed. In a wild mix-up we both slipped to the canvas, but was up in a second, Bert closing my eye tight as a drum while I battered him with terrific body blows.

Baring his teeth at me, he shot a right to my bobbing head and suddenly bounded back from my return. We had got close to the ropes and he bounded right against them. The next thing he bounced off of them right into me. I'd never seen a heavyweight try that trick before and he caught me off my guard. His right crashed against my chest and I hit the canvas so hard my feet flew straight up and I thought I'd go on through the boards.

But it was the force and weight of the blow that knocked me down; I didn't fall because I was stunned or badly hurt. I was up at the count of nine and opened a cut over Bert's eye with a wild right. I didn't think he'd try that bouncing trick so quick again and he nearly fooled me there. This time he drew my left, jumped back, hit the ropes and came for me so quick I didn't have time to think. By instinct I side-stepped and met him in mid-air with a right hook to the jaw. *Crash!* He hit the canvas and rolled over and over. I ran back to the fartherest corner, but it didn't look like anybody could get up after a wallop like that. But this Bert was a tough baby. The crowd wasn't yelling now.

At seven he had his legs under him and at nine he come up, wobbly, rubber-legged and glass-eyed, still full of fight. I hesitated; I hated to hit him again, but then the thought come of what he'd said about me, and how he'd bullied poor little Marjory and the way he'd abused sailors. I heard the director yell as I shot across the ring, but I paid no heed.

Bert tried to clinch as I came in, but I dropped him face down with a right hook to the jaw. The crowd began to howl and bellow as I went back to the corner, and through the noise I heard the director, who was jumping up and down and tearing his hair. He was yelling: "Bert, get up! Hey, hey! Get up, for cat's sake! If you get knocked out, you'll rooin the picture."

Bert give no sign of obeying and the director howled: "Sound the gong and drag him to his corner! The round's half a minute to go, but the movie fans won't know the difference!"

This was done, much to my disgust and the director began to yell caustic remarks at me.

"Aw, shut up!" I growled. "You said make it real, didn't you?" So he shut up. Well, I was kind of bothered about hitting Bert and him so near helpless, but it's all in the game; he'd of done the same thing to me, and I remembered that he was blackmailing old man Harper and holding Marjory in the grip of his hand—or why else did she take so much off him? So I decided that I ought not to worry over a black hearted villain like Bert, but go out and knock his head off.

THEY GIVE AN extra long time between rounds, to give Bert time to recover and his handlers was working like mad over him. At last I saw him shake his head, then raise it and glare across the ring at me like a hungry tiger. The director was yelling instructions.

"All right now, remember! When I yell: 'Now!' Bert, you shoot the left to the body and you, Steve, drop your guard."

The gong! We rushed together and Bert clinched and gripped me like a gorilla.

"I want to know if you're going to flop this round according to schedule?" he hissed in my ear.

"Be yourself!" I snarled. "Forget that director cluck! This here's between me and you! I'm goin' to lay you like a rug!"

"But what you got it in for me for!" he snarled bewilderedly. "I never saw you before?"

"Aragh!" I roared, jerking loose and whizzing a terrible right past his jaw. He came back with a hard left to the body and another to the jaw while I planted a wicked right under the heart. He threw a right which went over my shoulder, and falling into me, clinched and tied me up.

"You see that little blonde in the first row?" I hissed. "I heard you abusin' and bullyin' her, and if you want to know, that's why I'm goin' to knock you into her lap!"

He shot a quick glance in the direction I jerked my head, and a bewildered look came over his face.

"Why, that girl—" he began, but just then the referee pulled us apart.

"Now, Bert!" howled the director, "shoot the left! Steve, be ready to flop!"

"Baloney!" I snarled over my shoulder, and stuck my own left into Bert's eye. He retaliated with a terrific right to the ribs and the director, sensing that something was going on which wasn't according to schedule, began to leap up and down and tear his hair and doin' other foolish things like cussing and weeping and screaming. But the cameras kept on grinding and we kept on slugging.

Following the right to the body, Bert swished a left which glanced from my head and I crashed a right under his heart. My continual body punching had begun to take the steam out of him, but he made one more rally, landing two blows to my one, but mine had much more kick behind them. Suddenly I threw everything I had into one ferocious burst of slugging. I snapped Bert's head back with a left uppercut I brought from my knees, and crashed my right under his heart. He staggered and I shot my right twice to his head—hooked a left under his heart and crashed another right flush to the jaw. They'd been coming so fast and hard that Bert, in his weakened condition, couldn't stop them. The last right lifted him off his feet and dropped him under the ropes, right in front of Marjory, who had leaped to her feet, with both her little hands pressed to her cheeks, and her pretty mouth wide open.

The referee mechanically started counting, but it was unnecessary. I strode over to my corner, took my bathrobe from the limp hands of a dumfounded handler and was about to climb out of the ring, when the director, who had thrown hisself on the ground and was biting the grass, come to life.

"Grab that idiot!" he howled. "Tie him up! Soak him! Get a cop! He's crazy! The picture's rooint! We're out heavy money! Grab him! If I got a friend in court, I'll send him up for life!"

"Aw, stand away!" I growled at the menials who approached me uncertainly, "this was a private matter between me and Bert."

"But it's going to cost us more than we can afford to pay!" wailed the director, plucking forth strands of his scanty locks and tossing them recklessly on the breeze. "Oh, why didn't you perform according to instructions? The first four rounds were pippins! But that finish—oh, that I should live to see this day!"

WELL, I FELT sorry for him and kind of wished that I'd waited and licked Bert outside, but I didn't see what I could do. Then up rushed Tommy Marks. He began yanking at the director's sleeve.

"Say, boss," he yelped, "I got a great idea! We'll cut that last round at the place where Bert got knocked down the last time! Then we'll start a scene with Reggie Van Veer, see? Splice the shots together—they can fix it in the cutting room, easy!"

"Yeah?" sniffed the director, wiping his eyes. "I should throw Reggie in with that man-eater. He's crazy; I think he's the maniac that tried to kill Reggie down-town yesterday."

"I thought he was Bert," I said.

"And listen," cried Tommy, "the shot will show Reggie getting up off the canvas slowly, with Steve waiting in his corner. Then Steve rushes out, Reggie meets him with a right to the jaw and Steve flops! A sensational k.o. at the end of the greatest fight ever filmed! See? Reggie won't even get hit at all. And nobody can tell the difference."

"Well, how'll I know this cave man won't take a notion to flatten Reggie when he gets him in the ring?"

"Aw, he's got nothin' against Reggie, have you, Steve? That was a private feud between him and Bert, wasn't it, Steve? You'll do it, won't you, Steve?"

"All right," muttered the director. "We'll try it, but don't rush at Reggie too ferociously or he'll jump clean out of the ring."

I had listened to this talk with much impatience. I wanted to square myself with the movie people and was willing to do what I could, but just now I had other business. I signified my willingness to do what they wanted me to do, then I hurried over to the seat where Marjory sat. She was not in it, and I seen her following close behind the handlers which was taking the still groggy blonde battler to his dressing room.

I hastened to her and laid a gentle hand on her little shoulder.

"Marjory," I said, "fear that big fellow no more! I have avenged us both! He will not be apt to bother you again! Tell your old man not to be afraid, no matter what this big flop has on him! Bert will not come between true lovers again, I bet you!"

To my utter amazement and horror, she turned on me with flashing eyes.

"What kind of gibberish are you talking?" she cried furiously. "You big brute! If you ever speak to me again, I'll call a policeman! How dare you speak to me after what you've done to poor Bert? You beast! You villain!"

And with that she swung her little hand and slapped me smack in the face, then with a stamp of her little foot and a burst of tears, she run forward and gently slipped one of Bert's arms about her slim shoulders, cooing to him gently.

I stood gaping after them like a fool, when Tommy pulled my sleeve.

"Hey, let's get on that shot, Steve."

"Say, Tommy," I said, a bit dazed as I followed him, "you see that little dame that belted me in the map just now? Well, what's that bozo, to her?"

"Him?" said Tommy, biting off a chew of tobacco. "Oh, nobody much—just only merely nobody but her big brother!"

At that I let out a howl that could of been heard in Labrador, and right after that I have to act as nurse to Tommy, he havin' swallowed his tobacco when he hears me yap.

Anyhow, I learned you never can tell when women is holdin' something out on you.

FIST *and* FANG.

ALTERNATE TITLE: CANNIBAL FISTS.

This short story was first published in the May 1930 issue of Fight Stories *magazine.*

I'VE FOUGHT ALL my life; sometimes for money, sometimes for fun—once in a while for my life. But the deadliest, most vicious fight I ever fought wasn't for none of them things; no, sir, I was fighting wild and desperate for the privilege of getting a bullet through my brain!

Stand by and I'll tell you why I was fighting so me and my best friend would get shot.

I'm the heavyweight champion of the *Sea Girl*, merchant ship, my name being Steve Costigan. The Old Man is partial to warm waters and island trade, see? Well, we was cruising through the Solomons on our way to Brisbane, taking our time because the Old Man practically growed up in the South Sea trade and knows all the old traders and native chiefs and the like, and is always on the lookout for bargains in pearls and such like.

Well, we hove to at a small island by the name of Roa-Toa which had a small trading post on it. This post was run by the only white man on the islands, a fellow named MacGregor, and him being an old friend of the captain's, we run in for a visit.

The minute the Old Man had stepped onto the ramshackle wharf, Bill O'Brien, my side kick, said to me, he said: "Steve, see that motor launch down there by the wharf? Let's grab it and chase over to Tamaru and see old Togo."

Tamaru was another little island so close to Roa-Toa you could see the top of the old dead volcano. Togo was the chief; that wasn't his name, but it was as near as we could come to pronouncing it. He was a wrinkled old scoundrel and was a terrible sot, but very friendly to the white men.

"The Old Man will likely stop at Tamaru," I said.

"He won't, either," said Bill. "Him and MacGregor will drink up all the whiskey we got on board before he ever weighs anchor from Roa-Toa. He won't stop by Tamaru because he won't have no liquor to give to or trade with old Togo. Come on," said Bill. "We can easy make it in that launch. If we hang around the mate will find somethin' for us to do. Let's get to that launch and scoot before the Old Man or MacGregor sees us. Mac wouldn't let us have it, like as not, if we asked him."

So in a very short time we was heading out to sea, me and Bill, and my white bulldog, Mike. I heard a kind of whooping above the sputter of the motor, and looked back to see the Old Man and MacGregor run out of the trading stores and they jumped up and down and shook their fists and hollered, but we waggled our fingers at them and kept on our course, full speed, dead ahead.

WELL, IN DUE time Tamaru grew up out of the ocean in front of us, all still and dark green, with its dead volcano, and the trees growing up the sides of the mountains.

Togo's village was right on the beach when we was there the year before, but now much to our surprise we found nothing but a heap of ruins. The huts was leveled, trees cut short close to the water's edge, and not a sign of human life.

While we was talking, four or five natives come slithering out of the jungle and approached us very friendly, with broad smiles. Mike bristled and growled, but I put it down to the fact that no white dog likes colored people. According to that, no black dog ought to like white people, but it don't work.

Anyway, these kanakas made us understand in their pidgin English that the village had been moved back in the jungle a way, and they signified for us to come with them.

"Ask 'em how come they moved the village," I told Bill, who could speak their language pretty well, and he said: "Aw, they say the salt water made the babies sick. Don't worry about that; they likely don't know theirselves why they moved. They don't often have no reason for what they do. Let's go see Togo."

"Ask 'em how Togo is," I said, and Bill did, and said: "They says he's as free from pain and sickness as a man can be."

The kanakas grinned and nodded. Well, we plodded after them, and Mike he come along and growled deep down in his throat till I asked him very irritably to please shut up. But he paid no attention.

After awhile we come on to a large open space and there was the village. Just now they wasn't a sign of life, except a few native dogs sleeping in the sun. A chill wiggled up and down my spine.

"Say," I said to Bill, "this is kind of queer; ask 'em where Togo is."

"Where at is Togo?" said Bill, and one of the natives grinned and pointed to a pole set in front of the biggest hut. At first I couldn't make out what he meant. Then I did, and I suddenly got sick at my stomach—and cold at the heart with fear. On top of that pole was a human head! It was all that was left of poor old Togo.

The next second two big kanakas had grabbed each of us from behind, and a couple hundred more came swarming out of the huts.

Bill, he give a yell and ducked, throwing one of his natives clean

over his head, and he twisted half way round and knocked the other cold with a terrible biff on the jaw. Then the one on the ground grabbed Bill by the legs, and another hit him over the head with a club, laying his scalp open and knocking him to his knees.

MEANWHILE I WAS having my troubles. The minute them two grabbed me, Mike went for them, jerked one of them off me, got him down and nearly tore him apart. At the same instant I jammed my elbow backward, and by sheer luck connected with the other one's solar plexus. He grunted and loosened his hold, and I wheeled round to smash him, but as I did, I felt a sharp prick between my shoulders and knowed one of them was holding a spear at my back. I stopped short and stood still. The next minute me and Bill was tied hand and foot. I looked at Bill; he was bleeding plenty from the cut in his head, but he grinned.

Well, all that took something less than a minute. Three or four natives had went for Mike and pulled him off of his victim, which was howling and bleeding like a stuck hog. The said victim staggered away to the nearest hut, looking like a wreck on a lee shore, and the others danced and jumped around Mike trying to stab him with spears and hit him with clubs, without losing a leg at the same time; while Mike tried to eat his way through them to me.

Then while I watched with my heart in my mouth, crack! went a pistol and Mike went down, rolling over and over till he lay still with the blood oozing from his head. I give a terrible cry and began to rave and tear at my ropes; I struggled so wild and desperate that I jerked loose from the kanakas which was holding me, and fell on the ground, being tied up like I was.

Then they pulled me and Bill roughly around to face a big dark fellow who came swaggering up, a smoking pistol in his hand. At first glance it struck me I'd seen him before, but all I wanted to do now was get loose and tear his throat out with my bare hands for killing Mike.

This bezark stopped in front of us, twirling his gun on his forefinger and I looked close at him. If looks and wishes would kill, he would of dropped dead three times in succession. A big, tall, beautifully built native he was, but he didn't look like the rest. He had a kind of yellow tint to his skin, whereas they was golden brown. And his face wasn't open and good natured like theirs was in repose; it was cruel and slant-eyed and thin-lipped. Malay blood there, I quickly seen. A half breed, with the worst blood of both races. He was dressed in just a loin cloth, like the rest, but somewhere, I knowed, I'd seen him in different clothes and different surroundings. Well, if I hadn't been so grieved and mad on

account of Mike, I guess I'd have knowed him right off.

"Well, Meestah Costigan," said the big ham, in a kind of throaty voice, "you visit my island, eh? You like my welcome, maybeso? Maybeso you stay a long time, eh? Glad you come, me; I rather see you than any other man in the world!"

He was still grinning, but when he said the last his heavy jaws come together like the snap of a alligator. And then Bill, who was glaring at him like he couldn't believe his eyes, yelled: "Santos!"

IT ALL COME back to me in a flash! And I would of fell over from sheer surprise, hadst I not been tied and held up. Sure, I remembered! And you ought to, too, if you keep up with even part of the fighters that comes and goes.

A couple of years ago I'd met Santos in a Frisco ring. Yeah! Battling Santos, the Borneo Tiger, that Abie Hussenstein had discovered slaughtering second-raters in Asiatic ports. Abie brought him to America after Santos had cleaned up everything in sight over there.

They is no doubt that the big boy was good. In America he went through his first rank of set-ups like a sickle through wheat. He was fast, fairly clever for a big man, and strong as a bull.

Well, his first first-rater was Tom York, you remember, and Tom outboxed him easy in the first round, but in the second Santos landed a crusher that broke Tom's nose and knocked out four teeth. From then on it was a butchery, and the referee stopped it in the fifth to keep York from being killed. After that the scribes raved over Santos more than ever, called him a second Firpo and said he couldn't miss being champion.

Abie was sparring for matches in the Garden and he sent Santos back to Frisco to pad his k.o. record and keep in trim by toppling some ham-and-eggers. Then, enter a dark man, the villain of the play—otherwise Steve Costigan.

Santos was matched to meet Joe Handler ten rounds in San Francisco. The very day of the fight, Handler sprained his ankle, and they substituted me the last minute. I needn't tell you I went into the ring on the short end of about a hundred to one, with no takers—except the *Sea Girl's* crew, who seem to think I can lick anybody, simply because I've licked all of them.

Well, I reckon the praise and hurrah and all had went to Santos' head. He come out clowning and playing up to the crowd. He feinted at me with his big long brown arms and made faces and wise-cracks, as I come out of my corner. He dropped his gloves, stuck out his jaw and motioned me to hit him. This got a big laugh out of the crowd, and while he was doing that, with his mouth wide open, laughing, I hit him!

I reckon I was closer to him than he thought, for it was a wide open shot. I crashed my right from my knee, and I plunged in behind it with everything I had. I smashed solid on his sagging jaw so hard it numbed my whole arm. I don't see how I come not to tear his jaw clean off. Anyway, he hit the canvas like he figured on staying there indefinite, and they had to carry him to his dressing room to bring him to.

When everybody got their breath back, they yelled "fluke! fluke!" And it was, because Santos would of licked me, if he'd watched hisself. But it finished him; he'd lost his heart, or something.

His next start he dropped a decision to Kid Allison, and he lost two more fights in a row that way. Hussenstein give him the bounce and he dropped out of view. Santos had gone back to stoking, people supposed; the public had forgot all about him, and I had too, nearly. But here he was!

ALL THIS FLASHED through my brain as I stood and gawped at the big cheese. Say, if Santos had looked tigerish in the ring, in civilized settings, he looked deadly now.

He stuck the pistol back into his girdle and said, easy and lazy: "Well, Meestah Costigan, you remember me, eh?"

"Yeah, I do, you dirty half-breed!" I roared. "What you mean shootin' my dog? Lem'me loose, and I'll rip your heart out!"

He bared his white teeth in a kind of venomous smile and gestured lazily toward the pole where old Togo's head was.

"You come to see your old friend, eh? Well, there he is! What left of him. Now Santos is chief! The old man was fool; the young men, they follow Santos. Now we make palaver; you my guests!"

And with that he laughed in a cold deadly way and said something to the kanakas which was holding us. He turned his back and walked toward his hut, them dragging us along anyway. I looked back, though, and my heart give a jump. Old Mike got to his feet kind of groggy and glassy-eyed, and shook his head and looked around for me. He seen me and started toward me; then he seen Santos, and sneaked away among the trees. I give a sigh of relief. Must be the bullet just grazed him enough to knock him out; nobody had seen him get up and hide but me, and he was safe for the time being, at least—which was something me and Bill O'Brien wasn't—and I guess Bill felt the same way for he looked kind of white.

Santos sat down in a chair, which was one the Old Man had give poor old Togo, and we was propped up in front of him.

"Once we meet before, Costigan," he said, "in your country. Now we meet in mine. This my country. I born here. Big fool, me. I leave with white men on ship when very young. I scrub decks; then

shovel coal. I fight with other stokers. I meet Hus'stein and fight for him. He take me to Australia—America; I lick everybody. Everybody yell when I come in ring."

The grin had faded off his map and a wild light was growing in his eyes; they was getting red.

"Then I meet you!" his voice had dropped to a kind of hiss. "They tell me you one big ham. Nothing in the head! I think make people laugh! I hold out my face, say: 'Hit me!' Then I think maybeso the roof fall on me."

He was snarling like a wild beast now; his chest was heaving with rage and his big hands was working like my throat was between them.

"After that, I not so good. People say dirty things now at me. They say: 'Yellow! Glass chin! Throw him out!' Hus'stein say: 'Get out! You no drawing card now!' I go to stoking again. I work my way back to my people; my island."

He give a short grim laugh. He hit his breast with his fist.

"Me king, now! Togo old fool; friend to white man! Bah! I say to young men: make me king! We kill white men, and take rum and cloth and guns like our people did long ago. So I kill Togo, and old men that follow him! And you—" His eyes burned into me.

"You make fool of me," he said slowly. "Aaahhh! I pay you back!" He looked like a madman, gnashing his teeth and rolling his eyes as he roared at us.

I LOOKED AT Bill, uncertain like, and Bill says, nervy enough, but in a kind of unsteady voice: "You don't dast harm a white man. You may be king of this one-horse hunk of mud, but you know blame well if you knock us off, you'll have a British gunboat on your neck."

Santos grinned like a ogre and sank back in his chair. If he'd ever been half way civilized, which I doubt, he had sure reverted back to type again.

"The British have come," said he. "They knocked our village to pieces and killed a few pigs. But we ran away into the jungle and they could no find us. They shoot some shells around and then steam away, the white swine! That was because we fire on a trading boat and kill a sailor."

"Well," said Bill, "the *Sea Girl's* anchored off Roa-Toa and if you harm us, the crew won't leave nobody alive on this island. They won't shoot at you from long range. They'll land and mop up."

"Soon I go to Roa-Toa," said Santos, very placid. "I think I like to be king of Roa-Toa too; I kill MacGregor, and take his guns and all. If your ship come here, I take her, too. You think I no dare kill white man? Eh? Big fool, you."

"Well," I roared, the suspense being too much for me, "what you goin' to do with us, you yellow-bellied half-breed!"

"I kill you both!" he hissed,

smiling and playing with his gun.

"Then do it, and get it over with," I snarled, being afraid I'd blow up if he dragged it out too long. "But, lem'me tell you somethin'—"

"Oh, no," he smiled, "not with the pistol. That is too easy, eh? I want you to suffer like I suffered."

"I don't get yuh," I growled. "It's all in the game. I don't see why you got it in for me. If you'd a-licked me, I wouldn't of kicked. Anyway, you got no cause to bump off Bill, too."

"I kill you all!" he shouted, leaping up again. "And you two—you will howl for death before I get through. Arrgh! You will scream to die—but you will no die till I am ready."

He came close to me and his wild beast eyes burned into mine.

"Slow you will die," he whispered. "Slow—slow! For that blow you strike me, you suffer—and for all I suffer at the hands of your people, you shall suffer ten times ten!"

He stopped and glared at me.

"The Death of a Thousand Cuts shall be yours," he purred. "You know that, eh? Ah, you been to China! I know you know it, because your face go white now!" I reckon mine did, all right. I knew what he meant, and so did Bill. "Me, I show them where to cut," went on Santos, "for I have seen the Chinese torture like those."

I felt froze solid and my clothes were damp with sweat; also I was mad, like a caged rat.

"All right, you black swine!" I

yelled at him, kind of off my bat, I reckon. "Go ahead—do your worst! But remember one thing—remember that I licked you! I knocked you cold! Killin' me won't alter the fact that I'm the best man!"

He screamed like a maddened jungle cat and I thought he'd go clean nuts. I'd sure touched him to the quick there!

"You did no beat me!" he howled. "I was big fool! I let you hit me! White pig, I break you with my hands! I tear your heart out and give it to the dogs!"

"Well, why didn't you?" I asked bitterly. "You had your chance, and you sure muffed it! I licked you then, and I can lick you now. You wouldn't dare look at me crost-wise if my hands wasn't tied. I'll die knowin' that I licked you."

His eyes was red as a blood-mad tiger's now, and they glittered at me from under his thick black brows. He grinned, but they was no mirth in it.

"I fight you again," he whispered. "We fight before I kill you. I give you something to fight for, too: if I whip you, and no kill you—you die under the knives; and your friend, too. If I whip you, and kill you with my hands—your friend die under the cuts. But if you whip me, then I no torture you, but kill you both quick." He tapped his pistol.

Anything sounded better than the thousand cuts business, and, anyway, I'd have a chance to go out fighting.

"And suppose I kill you?" I asked.

He laughed contemptuously. "No chance. But if you do, my people shoot you quick."

"Take him up, Steve," said Bill. "It's the best of a bad bargain, any way you look at it."

"I'll fight you on your own terms," I said to Santos.

He grunted, yelled some orders in his own tongue, and the stage was set for the strangest battle I ever had.

In the open space between the huts, the natives made a big ring, standing shoulder to shoulder, about three deep, the men behind looking over the shoulders of those in front. The kids and women come out of the huts and tried to watch the fight between the men's legs.

A sort of oval-shaped space was left clear. At each end of this space stood a thick post, set deep in the ground. They tied Bill to one of these posts.

"I can't be in your corner this fight, old sea horse," said Bill, kind of drawn-faced, but still grinning.

"Well, in a way you are," I said. "You can't sponge my cuts and wave a towel, but you can yell advice when the goin's rough. Anyway," I said, "you got a good view of the fight."

"Sure," he grinned, "I got a ring-side seat."

About that time the kanakas unfastened my ropes, and I worked my hands and fingers to get the circulation started again. Bill's hands was tied, so we couldn't shake hands, but I clapped him on the shoulder, and we looked at each other a second. Seafaring men ain't much on showing their emotions, and they ain't very demonstrative, but each of us knew how the other felt. We'd kicked around a good many years together—

Well, I turned around and walked to the middle of the oval, and waited. I didn't have to wait long. Santos came from the other end, his head lowered, his red eyes blazing, a terrible smile on his lips. All he wore was a loin cloth; all I had on was an old pair of pants. We was both bare-footed; and, of course, bare-handed.

I'D NEVER SEEN anything like this in my life before. They was no bright lights except the merciless tropic sun; they was no cheering crowds—nothing but a band of savages that wanted our blood; they was no seconds, no referee—only a hard-faced kanaka with gaudy feathers in his hair, holding Santos' pistol. They was no purse but death. A quick death if I won; a long, slow, terrible death if I lost.

Santos was rangy, big, tapering from wide shoulders to lean legs. Speed and power there was in them smooth, heavy muscles. He was six feet one and a half inch tall; heavier than when I first fought him, but the extra weight was hard muscle. I don't believe he had a ounce of fat on him. He must have weighed two hundred, which gave him about ten pounds on me.

For a second we moved in a half circle, wary and deadly, and then he roared and come lashing in like a tidal wave. He shot left and right to my head so fast that for a second I was too busy ducking and blocking to think. He was crazy to knock my head off; he was shipping everything he had in that direction. Well, it's hard to knock a tough man cold with bare-knuckled head punches. The raw 'uns cut and bruise, but they ain't got the numbing shock the padded glove has. You'll notice most of the knock-outs in the old bare-knuckle days was from blows to the body and throat.

The moment I had a breathing space, I hooked a wicked left to the belly. His ridged muscles felt like flexible steel bands under my knuckles, and he merely snarled and lashed back with a right-hander which bruised my forearm when I blocked it. He was fast and his left was chain lightning—he shot it straight, he uppercut, and he hooked, just like that—zip! blip! blam!

The hook flattened my right ear, and almost simultaneously he threw his right with everything he had. I ducked and he missed by a hair's lash. Jerusha! I heard that right sing past my head like a slung shot, and Santos spun off balance and went to his knees from the force of it. He was up like a cat, spitting and snarling, and I heard Bill yell: "For the love of Mike, Steve, watch that right, or he'll knock your head clean off!"

Well, I guess in a ring with ordinary stakes, Santos would have finished me; but this was different. I'm tough any time; now I was fighting for the privilege of me and my pard going out clean. The thought of them sharp little knives put steel in me.

Santos grinned like a devil as he came in again. This time he didn't rush, he edged craftily, left hand out, watching for a chance to shoot his deadly right over. That's once I wished I was clever! But I ain't, and I knew if I tried to box him, I wouldn't have a chance. So I come in sudden and wide open; his right swished through the air and looped around my neck as I ducked and I braced my feet and ripped both hands to his midriff—bam—bam! The next second his left chopped down on the back of my head. I went into a clinch, and his teeth snapped like a wolf's at my throat as I tied him up. He was snarling at me in his language as we worked out of the clinch, and he nailed me on the breakaway with a straight left to the mouth, which instantly began to bleed.

The sight of the blood maddened the kanakas, and they began to yell like jungle beasts. Santos laughed wild and fierce, and began swinging at my head again with both hands. To date he hadn't tried a single body blow. Three times he landed to the side of my head with a swinging left, and I dug my right into his midriff. His right came over, and I blocked it with my elbow, then shot my own right to his belly again. He'd give a kind of sway with his whole body as he let go the right to give it extra force, and his arm would snap through the air like a big steel spring released.

Crash! His left landed on the side of my head, and I seen ten thousand stars. Bam! His right followed, and I blocked it. But this time it landed flush on the upper arm instead of the elbow, and for a second I thought the bone was broke. The whole arm was numb, and, desperate, I crashed into close quarters and ripped short-arm rights to his belly, while he slashed at my head with short hooks. He wasn't so good in close; he didn't like it, and he broke away and backed off, spearing me with his long left as I followed.

BUT MY BLOOD was up now and I kept right on top of him. I slashed a left hook to his face, sank a straight right under his heart—wham! He brought up a left uppercut that nearly ripped my head off. He flailed in with a torrid right, and I hunched my left shoulder just in time to save my jaw. At the same time I shot my right for his jaw and landed solid, but a little high. He swayed like a tall tree, his eyes rolled, but he come back with a screech like a tree cat and flashed a vicious left to my already bleeding mouth. The right came in behind it like a thunderbolt and I done the only thing I could—ducked, and took it high on the front part of my head. Jerusha! It felt like my skull was unjointed! I heard Bill scream as I hit the ground so hard it nearly knocked the breath clean outa me.

It was just like being hit with a hammer. A stream of blood trickled down into my eyes from where the scalp had been laid open.

I dunno why Santos stepped back and let me get up. Force of habit, I guess. Anyway, as I scrambled up, shaking the blood outa my eyes, he give me a ferocious grin and said: "Now I kill you, white man!" And come slithering in to do it. He feinted his left, drew it back, and as he feinted again, I threw my right, wild and overhand, desperate like, and caught him under the cheek bone. Blood spurted and he went back on his heels. I ripped a left to his belly and he grabbed me and held on like a big python, clubbing me with his left till I tore loose.

He nailed me with the right as I went away from him, but it lacked the old jar. I got a hard skull. No man could of landed like he did without hurting his hand some, anyway. But his left was so fast it looked and felt like twins. He shot it at one of my eyes in straight jabs till I felt that eye closing, and then, as I stepped in with a slashing right to the ribs, he came back with a terrible left hook that split my other eyebrow wide open and the lid sagged down like a curtain halfway over the eye.

"Work in close, Steve!" I heard Bill yell, above the howling of the kanakas. "If he keeps you at long range, he'll kill you!"

I'd already decided that! I wrapped both arms around my head and plunged in till my forehead bumped his chin, and then I started ripping both hands to the belly and heart. His left was beating my right cauliflower to a pulp, but I kept blasting away with both hands till the whole world was blind and red; but he was softening. My fists were sinking deeper into his belly at every blow, and I heard him gasp. Then he wrapped his long, snaky arms around me and pinned me tight. As we tussled back and forth, with his breath hot in my ear, he sunk his teeth into my shoulder and worried it like a dog shaking a rat, growling deep in his throat till I tore away by main strength, and brought a stream of blood from his lips with a smashing right hook.

Then Santos went clean crazy. He howled like a wolf and began throwing punches wild and terrible, without aim or timing. He wasn't thinking about that sore right no more. It was like the air was full of flying sledge-hammers. Some he missed from sheer wildness; I blocked till my arms and shoulders ached. Plenty landed. I slashed a left to his face—and crack!—his right bashed into mine, smashing my nose flat. I heard the bones crackle and snap and a red mist waved in front of my eyes so I couldn't see. I felt faintly the impact of another blow, and then I felt the ground under my shoulders.

I lay there, counting to myself; my head was clearing fast. Nobody ever accused me of not being tough! Having my nose broke was a old story. I said to myself: "Nine!" and got to my feet, wrapping both arms around my head and crouching. Santos yelled and battered at my arms while I glared at him over them, and suddenly I unwound and sank my right to the wrist in his belly. Yes, he was getting soft from my continued batterings! His body muscles was getting too sore to contract hard and my fists sank in deep. Santos bent double, but came up with a punishing left uppercut to the jaw that dazed me and before I could recover, he ripped over that sledge-hammer right. It tore my left ear loose from my head and I felt it flap against my cheek.

I was out on my feet; just fighting from the old battle instinct, now. Some kind of a smash sent me back on my heels, and I felt myself falling backward and couldn't stop. Then I fell against something and heard a fierce voice in my ear: "Steve! He's weakening! Just one more smash, old sea horse, and he's yours!"

We had fought back to the end of the oval space and I was leaning against the post where Bill was tied. I made a desperate effort to right myself. Santos was watching me with his hands down and a nasty sneer on his face. He put his hands out

and gripped my shoulders. He was marked pretty well hisself.

"You licked now," he said. "The little knives, now they feast! The Death of a Thousand Cuts, it is yours!"

AT THAT I went kind of crazy, too. I lunged away from the post, and missed with a wild right, and the slaughter recommenced. Santos was mad and bewildered. Well, he wasn't the first fighter who couldn't understand why I kept getting up. My eyes was full of blood and sweat; one was nearly closed, and the sagging lid nearly hid the other. My nose was busted flat, one ear was hanging loose and the other swole out of all proportions. My left shoulder and arm was so numbed from blocking Santos' terrible right, I couldn't lift it but a few inches above my waist line. My wind was giving out; I didn't know how long the fight had been going on; it seemed to me like we'd been fighting for centuries. I dunno what kept me on my feet; I dunno what kept me going. I'd almost got to where I didn't know nor care what they did to me. Sometimes I'd forget what we was fighting for. Sometimes I'd think it was because Santos had killed Mike, then again it would be Bill I'd think he'd killed. Once I thought we was back in the ring in Frisco.

Then I was down on my back, and Santos was kneeling on my chest, strangling me. I tore his hold loose and threw him off, and then we was standing toe to toe, trading slow, hard smashes. Then suddenly Santos shifted his attack for the first time and catapulted a blasting right to my body. Something snapped like a dead stick and I went to my knees with a red-hot knife cutting into my left side.

Santos standing over me, kicked at me with his big bare feet till I caught his legs, and as I clung on and he rained blows down at my head, I heard Bill's voice above the uproar: "You got his goat, Steve! Get up! Get up once and he's licked!"

I got up. I climbed that Malay devil's legs, paying no attention to the punches he showered on me, and as I leaned on his chest and our eyes glared into each other's, I saw a wild, terrible light had come into his—the light that's in a trapped tiger's—scared and bewildered, and dangerous as death. I'd fought him to a standstill—I had his number! And at them thoughts, strength flowed back into my arms. He flailed at me, but the kick was going from his blows; he was nearly punched out.

I stepped back and then drove in again. He was snarling between his teeth, and then he took a deep breath. The instant I saw his midriff go in, I sank my left in to the wrist, and as he bent forward I slugged him behind the ear, and he dropped to his knees. But he come up, gasping and wild. He'd forgot all the boxing he ever knowed, now. I stepped inside his wild swings and crashed my right under his heart, and though it was the most fearful agony to do it, brought up my left to his jaw. He went down on his haunches and I heard, in the deathly silence which had fell, Bill yelling for me to give him the boots. But I don't fight that way—even if I'd of had any boots on.

But Santos wasn't through. He was all savage now, and too primitive to be stopped by ordinary means. I'd fought him to a standstill; he was licked at this game. And he went clean back to the Stone Age. He leaped off the ground, howling and slavering at the mouth, and sprang at me with his fingers spread like talons; not to hit, but to strangle, tear, claw and gnash. And as he came in wide open, I met him with the same kind of punch I'd flattened him with once; a blasting right I brought up from my knee. Crack! I felt his jaw-bone and my hand give way as I landed, and he turned a complete somersault, heels over head, and crashed down on his back a dozen feet away. You'd think that would hold a man, wouldn't you? Well, it would—a man.

It's possible to break a man's jaw with your bare fist, and still not knock him unconscious. Any ordinary man wouldn't be able to do nothing more after that. But Santos wasn't a man, no more; he was a jungle varmint, and he'd gone mad.

BEFORE I COULD tell what he was going to do, he whirled and tore a long-handled battle-axe from the hand of a warrior in the front rank. He must have been on the point of collapse; he'd taken fearful punishment. Where he found strength for his last effort, I dunno. But it all happened in a flash. He had the axe and was looming over me like a black cloud of death before I could move. As he bounded in and swung up the thing above his head, I threw up my right arm. That saved my life; and the axe head missed the arm, but the heavy handle broke my forearm like a match, and knocked me flat on my shoulders.

Santos howled, swung up the axe and leaped again—and a white thunderbolt shot across me and met him in mid-air! Square on the Malay's chest Mike landed, and the impact knocked Santos flat on his back. One terrible scream he gave, and then Mike's iron jaws closed on his throat.

In a second it was the craziest confusion you ever seen. Kanakas whooping and yelling and running and falling over each other doing nothing, and Bill swearing something terrible and tearing at his bonds—and Mike making a bloody mess out of Santos in the middle of all of it. I tried to get up, but I was done. I got to my knees and slumped over again.

THE REST IS all like a dream. I saw the kanaka with the pistol shoot at Mike, and miss—and then, like an echo, come another shot—and the kanaka whooped, clapped his hand to the seat of his loin cloth, and scooted. I heard yelling in white men's voices, shots and a hurrah generally and then into my line of vision—considerably blurred—hove the Old Man, MacGregor, and Penrhyn, the mate, all cursing and whooping, with the whole crew behind them.

"Great Jupiter!" squawked the Old Man, red faced and puffing, as he leaned over me.

"They've kilt Steve! They've beat him to death with axes!"

"He ain't dead!" snarled Bill, twisting at his ropes. "He has just fit the toughest fight I ever seen—will some of you salt pork and biscuit eaters untie me from this post?"

"Rig a stretcher," said the Old Man. "If Steve ain't dead, he's the next thing to it. Hey, what the—!"

At this moment Mike came sauntering over and sat down beside me, licking my hand.

"Wh-who—who is—was—that?" asked the Old Man, kind of white-faced, pointing to what Mike had left.

"That there is what's left of Battlin' Santos, the Borneo Tiger," said Bill, stretching his arms with relish. "History repeats itself, and Steve has just handed him a most artistic trimmin'—are you goopin' swabs goin' to let Steve die here? Get him on board ship, will you?"

"Look about Mike first," I mumbled. "Santos shot him with a pistol."

"Just a graze," pronounced MacGregor, examining Mike's unusually hard head. "Shot him with a pistol, eh? Guess if he'd used a rifle the dawg would of slaughtered the whole tribe. Wait, don't put Costigan on the stretcher till I mop off some of his blood."

I felt his hands feeling around over me, and I cussed when he'd gouge me.

"He'll be all right," he pronounced, "soon's we've set his arm and this rib here, and stitched his ear back on, and took up a few more gashes. And that nose'll need some attention, though I ain't set many noses."

I kind of dimly remember being carried back to the ship, with Mike trotting alongside, and I heard Bill and the Old Man yappin' at each other back and forth.

"—and no sooner had Mac here got through tellin' me that Santos had killed old Togo and set hisself up as king, than we heard the motor launch sputter, and see you two prize jackasses scootin' away into the jaws uh death. We yelled and whooped but you was too smart to listen—"

"How in the name of seven dizzy mermaids did you expect us to hear you with the motor goin'?"

"—and I says, 'Mac,' I says, 'it ain't worth it to save their useless hides, but we got to do it.' And it bein' a well-known fact that a fast motor launch can make more speed than a sailin' vessel, includin' even the *Sea Girl*, which is all we had to rescue you in, we have just now arrove at the village. Hadst it not been for me—"

"Hadst it not been for Steve, you would of found only a few hunks of raw beef. Santos was goin' to carve us, and believe you me when I tell yuh Steve fought him to a standstill! Steve was licked to a frazzle, and didn't know it! Santos had everything, and he made Steve into the hash which now lies on that stretcher, but the old sea horse just naturally outgamed him. Accordin' to rights, Steve shoulda been knocked cold five times."

"Arrumph, arrumph!" growled the Old Man, but I could tell he was that proud he couldn't hardly keep his feet on the ground. "I'd of give the price of a cargo to see that fight. Well, we didn't do like the British gunboat did—anchor off-shore and shell a few huts. We went through that jungle like Neptune goes through the water, and all of the bucks was too interested to know we was comin' till we swarmed out on 'em.

"I'm tellin' you, we'd of scuppered a flock of them, if my crew wasn't the worst aggregation of poor shots on the Seven Seas—"

"Well, hey," said the crew, "we didn't notice you bringin' down nobody on the fly."

"Shut up!" roared the Old Man. "I'm boss here and I'll be respected."

"For cats' sake," I snarled through my pulped lips, "will you cock-eyed sea horses dry up and let a sufferin' man suffer in his own way?"

"Don't think you rate so high, just because you're a little bunged up," growled Bill; but they was a catch in his voice. From the way he gripped my hand, I knowed exactly how he felt.

WINNER TAKE ALL.

ALTERNATE TITLE: SUCKER!

This short story was first published in the July 1930 issue of Fight Stories *magazine.*

M E AND BILL O'Brien was flat broke when we come out of Jerry Rourke's American Bar. Yes, sir— half a hour ashore, and cleaned along by of a land shark with a pair of educated dice. Not having the coin to pay his fine in case my white bulldog Mike followed his usual custom of tearing off some cop's pants leg, I left him with Jerry till I could raise some dough.

Well, me and Bill sallied forth into the night looking for anything that might mean money, experience having told us that you can find mighty near anything in the wharf-side streets of Singapore. Well, what we did find was the last thing we'd of expected.

We was passing a dark alley in the native quarters when we heard a woman screaming: "Help! Help! Help!"

We dashed into the alley imme-diately, and in the faint light we seen a girl struggling with a big Chinee. I seen the flash of a knife and I yelled and dived for him, but he dropped the frail and scooted down the alley like a scared rabbit, ducking the cobble-stone Bill heaved after him.

"Are you hurt, Miss?" I asked with my usual courtesy, lifting her to her feet.

"No, but I'm scared stiff," she answered. "That was a close call—let's get out of here before the big Chinee comes back with a mob."

So we legged it out into the street. Under the light of the street lamps we saw she was a white girl—American by her accent, and not hard to look at either, with her big grey eyes and wavy black hair.

"Where at shall we take you to, Miss?" asked Bill.

"I dance at the Bristol Cabaret," said she. "But let's go into the saloon—the bar-keep's a friend of mine and I want to buy you men a drink. It's the least I can do, for saving my life."

"Don't mention it, Miss," said I with a courtly bow. "We was glad to be of service. Howthesomever, if it will give you any pleasure to buy us a drink, we would not think of refusin'."

"More especially as we have just lost all our jack in a crap game, and are slowly but surely perishin' of thirst," said Bill, who ain't got my natural tact.

So we went in and got a back room to ourselves, and while we was downing our liquor—me and Bill,

that is, because the girl said she never even tasted the stuff—she cupped her chin in her hands and rested her elbows on the table and gazing deep in my eyes, she sighed deeply.

"If I had a big strong man like you to protect me," she said in open admiration, "I wouldn't have to work in joints like the Bristol, and be abused by such swipes as tried to slit my gullet tonight."

I involuntarily expanded my enormous chest and said: "Well, lady, as long as Steve Costigan, A.B. mariner, can stand on his feet and hit with either maulie, you got no call to be afraid of anybody. The best thing, next to fightin', that me and Bill O'Brien here do is aid ladies in distress."

She shook her head wistfully. "You've been very kind to me, but you sailors are all alike—a girl in every port. But—I haven't even introduced myself—my name is Joan Wells, and I'm from Philadelphia."

"We're mighty glad to meet somebody from the States," said Bill. "But why was that slant-eye tryin' to knife you?"

"I—I really shouldn't tell," said she, looking kind of frightened.

"We ain't tryin' to intrude in your private affairs none," I hastened to add.

"I couldn't keep a secret from a man like you," said she with a languishing glance that made my heart skip a beat, "so I'll tell you. Take a look out the door to see that nobody's listening at the key-hole."

Nobody wasn't, so she went on.

"Did you ever hear of the No Sen Tong?" We shook our heads. We knowed in a general way about the big tongs, or merchant houses, which just about controls the Orient, but we hadn't had no experience with them.

"Well," said she, "it's the richest, most secret tong in the world. When I first came here I worked as private secretary for old To Ying, who's one of its highest secret officials. He fired me because I wouldn't let him get fresh with me—the old slant-eyed snake—and I went to work at the Bristol. But once you've been on the inside of an organization like that, you have ways of knowing things that other people don't."

Her eyes sparkled and her fists clenched as she got all excited. "I'm in on the biggest coup of the century!" she exclaimed. "If I live, I'll be a rich woman! Did you ever hear of the Korean Copper Company? No? Well, it's about to go bankrupt. They've never paid a single dividend. Stock's selling at a dollar a share, with no buyers. But, listen! They've hit the biggest copper mine that the world has ever seen! The No Sens are quietly buying up all the stock they can get—at a dollar a share! As soon as I found this out I ran down to the broker's and bought a hundred shares. It took every cent I had. But one of the No Sen spies saw me, and that's why old To Ying tried to have me bumped off. He's afraid I'll squeal.

"Think what a riot there'll be on the stock market tomorrow when the word gets in! Tonight Korean Copper's selling for a dollar! Tomorrow it'll be worth a thousand dollars a share!"

"Hold everything!" I said, kind of dizzy. "You mean you shoot a buck and get a thousand on the spin of the wheel?"

"I sure do—say, why don't you men buy some stock? It's the chance of a lifetime! Most of it has been bought up by the No Sens, but I know where I can get you a few hundred shares."

Bill laughed bitterly. "Sister, it might as well be sellin' for a thousand per right now as far as we're concerned. We ain't got a dime! And my watch is in a pawn-shop in Hong Kong."

"I'd gladly lend you some money," said she, "but I spent all mine on stock—"

"Wait a minute," said I, getting on my feet, "I got a idee. Miss Wells—Joan, is it safe for you to be left alone for a few hours?"

"Sure; the bar-keep goes off duty in a few minutes, and he can see me home."

"All right. I think we can raise some dough. Where can we see you, in say about three hours?"

"Come to the Alley of the Seven Mandarins," said she, "and knock on the door with the green dragon carved on it. I'm going to hide there till the No Sens quit looking for me. I'll be waiting for you," said she, giving my rugged hand a timid, shy little squeeze that made my big, honest heart flutter like a boy's.

THEN ME AND Bill was out in the foggy dim lighted streets and making tracks. I led the way through narrow streets and garbage-strewn back alleys till we was in the toughest section of Singapore's waterfront. It's dangerous in the daytime; it's pure Hades at night.

Right on the wharfs we come to a big ramshackle building, which a struggling sign announced as Heinie Steinman's Grand International Fight Arena. This dump was all lighted up, and was shaking with the ferocious roars which went up inside.

"Hello, Steve; hello, Bill," said the fellow at the door, a dip who knowed us well. "How 'bout a couple good ringside seats?"

"Gangway," said I. "We ain't got no money—but I'm fightin' here tonight."

"G'wan," said he, "you ain't even matched with nobody—"

"One side!" I roared, drawing back my famous right. "I'm fightin' somebody here tonight, get me?"

"Well, go in and fight somebody that's paid to git mutilated!" he squawked, turning slightly pale and climbing up on the ticket counter, so me and Bill stalked haughtily within.

If you want to study humanity in its crudest and most uncivilized form, take in one of Heinie Steinman's fight shows. The usual crowd was there—sailors, long-shoremen, beach-combers, thugs and crooks; men of every breed and color and description, from the toughest ships and the worst ports in the world. Undoubtedly, the men which fights at the International performs to the toughest crowds in the world. The fighters is mostly sailors trying to pick up a few dollars by massa-cring each other.

Well, as me and Bill entered, the fans was voicing their disapproval in a tone that would of curled the hair of a head-hunter. The main event had just driven the patrons into a frenzy by going to the limit, and they was howling like a pack of wolves because they'd been no knockout. The crowd that comes to Heinie's Arena don't make no talk about being wishful to see a exhibition of boxing. What they want is gore and busted noses, and if somebody don't get just about killed they think they have been gypped, and wreck the joint.

Just as me and Bill come in, the principals scurried out of the ring followed by a offering of chair bottoms, bricks and dead cats, and Heinie, who'd been acting as referee, tried to calm the mob—which only irritated them more and somebody hit Heinie square between the eyes with a rotten tomato. The maddened crowd was fast reaching a point where they was liable to do anything, when me and Bill climbed into the ring. They knowed us, and they kind of quieted down a minute and then started yelling fiercer than ever.

"For my sake, Steve," said Heinie, kind of pale, wiping the vegetable out of his eyes, "say somethin' to 'em before they start a riot. Them two hams that just faded away only cake-walked through the bout and these wolves is ready to lynch everybody concerned, particularly includin' me."

"Have you got somebody I can fight?" I asked.

"No, I ain't," he said, "But I'll announce—"

"I don't see no announcer," I growled, and turning to the crowd I silenced them by the simple process of roaring: "Shut up!" in a voice which drowned them all out.

"Listen here, you tin-horn sports!" I bellered. "You've already paid your dough, but do you think you've got your money's worth?"

"No!" they thundered in a voice that started Heinie's knees to knocking. "We been robbed! We been rooked! We been gypped! Give us our money back! Wreck the dump! Hang that Dutchman!"

"Shut up, you Port Mahon baboons!" I roared. "If you're sports enough to jar loose and make up a purse of twenty-five dollars, I'll fight any man in the house to a finish, winner take all!"

At that they lifted the roof. "'At's the stuff!" they whooped. "Shower down gents. We know Steve! He always gives us a run for our money!"

Coins and a few bills began to shower on the canvas, and two men jumped up from among the crowd and started for the ring. One was a red-headed Englishman and the other was a lithe black-haired fellow. They met just outside the ropes.

"One side, bloke," growled the red-head. "H'I'm fightin' this bloody Yank!"

Black-head's right shot out like a battering ram and red-head kissed the floor, and laid still. The mob went into hysterics of joy and the winner hopped over the ropes, followed by three or four of the most villainous looking mugs I ever hope to see.

"I weel fight Costigan!" said he, and Heinie give a deep sigh of relief. But Bill swore under his breath.

"That's Panther Cortez," said he. "And you know you ain't been trainin' close lately."

"Never mind," I growled. "Count the money. Heinie, you keep your hands off that dough till Bill counts it."

"Thirty-six dollars and fifty cents," announced Bill, and I turned to the slit-eyed devil which called hisself Panther Cortez, and growled: "You willin' to fight for that much—winner take all, loser gets nothin' but a headache?"

He grinned with a flash of white fangs. "Sure!—I fight you just for the fun of knocking you cold!"

I turned my back on him with a snarl and, giving Heinie the money to hold, though it was a terrible risk to take, I strode to one of the make-shift dressing rooms, where I was

65

given a pair of dingy trunks, which Heinie pulled off a preliminary boy which had gone on earlier in the evening and was still out.

I gave little thought to my opponent, though Bill kept grouching about the fact that I was going to get so little for knocking out such a man as Cortez.

"You oughta be gettin' at least a hundred and fifty," Bill grumbled. "This Cortez is a mean puncher, and shifty and dirty. He ain't never been knocked out."

"Well," said I, "it ain't never too late to begin. All I want you to do is watch and see that none of his handlers don't sneak around and hit me with a water bottle. Thirty-six shares means thirty-six thousand dollars for us. Tomorrer we'll kick the Old Man in the slats for a token of farewell, and start livin'! No more standin' watch and gettin' sunburnt and froze for somebody else—"

"Hey!" yelled Heinie, looking in at the door, "hurry up, will ya? This crowd's goin' clean nuts waitin'. The Panther's already in the ring."

A S I CLIMBED through the ropes I was greeted by a roar such as must of resembled them given by the Roman mobs when a favorite gladiator was throwed to the lions. Cortez was seated in his corner, smiling like a big lazy jungle cat, the lids drooping down over his glittering eyes in a way that always irritated me.

He was a mixed breed—Spanish, French, Malay and heck knows what else, but all devil. He was the choice fighting man aboard the Water Snake, a British vessel with a shady reputation, and though I'd never fought him, I knowed he was a dangerous man. But, gosh, all he represented to me just then was thirty-six dollars and fifty cents, which in turn represented thirty-six thousand dollars.

Heinie waved his arms and said: "Gents, you all know these boys! Both of them has fought here plenty of times before, and—"

The crowd rose up and drowned him out: "Yeah, we know 'em. Cut the introductions and le's see gore spilt!"

"Weights," yelled Heinie to make hisself heard. "Sailor Costigan of the *Sea Girl*, one hundred ninety pounds! Panther Cortez of the Water Snake, one hundred eighty-five pounds!"

"That's a lie!" roared Bill. "He weighs one-ninety if he weighs a ounce!"

"Aw, stow yer gab, ye bleedin' mick!" snarled one of the Panther seconds, shoving out his lantern jaw. Bill bent his right on that jaw and the limey went over the ropes on his head. The mob applauded madly; things was going just to their taste! All they needed to make it a perfect evening was for me or Cortez to get our neck broke—preferably both of us.

Well, Heinie chased Cortez'

handlers out of the ring, and Bill climbed out, and the slaughter was on. Heinie was referee, but he didn't give us no instructions. We'd fought enough there to know what we was supposed to do, and that was to sock and keep on socking till somebody kissed the canvas and stayed there. The gloves we wore was at least a ounce and a half lighter than the regular style, and nothing was a foul at the International as long as both fellows could stand on their feet.

The Panther was lithe, rangy, quick; taller than me, but not so heavy. We come together in the middle of the ring, and he hit with cat-like speed. Left to the face, right to the body and left to the jaw. Simultaneous I shot my right to his chin, and he hit the canvas on the seat of his trunks. The crowd howled, but he wasn't hurt much, mainly surprised and mad. His eyes blazed. He took the count of nine, though he could of got up sooner, and bounced up, stopping me in my tracks with a hard left to the mouth. I missed with a looping left, took a right to the ribs and landed hard under the heart. He spat in my face and began working his arms like pistons—left, right, left, right, to the face and body while the crowd went nuts. But that was my game; I grinned savagely and braced my feet, boring in and slugging hard with both hands.

A minute of this, and he backed away in a hurry, blood trickling from a cut on his cheek. I was after him

and sank a left deep in his midriff that made him clinch and hold on. On the break he nailed me with a straight right to the head, and followed it up with a hard left to the eye, but failed to land his right, and got a wicked right hook to the ribs. I battered away at his body, but he was all elbows, and, irritated, I switched to his head and nearly tore it off with a blazing right hook just at the gong.

"That round was yours by a mile," said Bill, between exchanging insults with Cortez' handlers. "But watch out; he's dangerous and dirty—"

"I'm goin' to ask Joan to marry me," I said. "I can tell she's fell for me, right off. I dunno why it is, but it seems like they's a fatal fascination about me for women. They can't keep from floppin' for me at first sight—"

The gong sounded and I dashed out to collect that $36.50.

Well, the Panther had found out that he couldn't trade wallops with me, so he come out boxing. I don't mean he tin-canned and rode his bicycle, like some prominent fighters I could mention. He was one baby that could fight and box at the same time, if you get me. When I say he boxed, I mean he feinted me out of position, kept me off balance, speared me with cutting left jabs, ducked my ferocious returns, tied me up in the clinches, nearly ripped my head off with right uppercuts in close, stayed inside my wings, and generally made a sap outa me.

Inside of a minute he had me bleeding at the mouth and nose, and I hadn't landed solid once. The crowd was howling like wolves and Bill was cussing something terrible, but I wasn't worried. I had all night to lick him in, and I knowed I'd connect sooner or later, and I did quicker than I'd thought. It was a smashing right hook under the heart, and it bent Senyor Cortez double. While in this position I clouted him heartily behind the ear and drove him to his knees. He was up without a count, slipped the terrible swing I threw at him, and having clinched and tied me up, scraped his glove laces across my eyes and ground his heel into my instep. He hung on like a regular octopus regardless of my cruel and unusual oaths. Heinie wouldn't pull him loose, and finally we both went to the canvas still clinched in a vise-like embrace.

This mishap threw the crowd into a perfect delirium of delight, which was increased by Cortez earnestly chewing my ear while we writhed on the mat. Driven to frenzy I tore loose, arose and closed the Panther's left eye with a terrible right swing the minute he was on his feet. He came back with a slashing left hook to the body, ripped the same hand to my already battered face, and stopped a straight left with his own map. At that moment the gong rang.

"I'M GOIN' TO kick Heinie Steinman loose from his britches after the fight!" snarled Bill, shaking with rage as he mopped the blood off my mangled ear. "If that wasn't the dirtiest foul I ever seen—"

"I wonder if we couldn't buy a half share with that fifty cents," I meditated. "That'd be five hundred dollars—"

I rushed out for the third frame inclined to settle matters quick, but Cortez had other plans. He opened a cut over my eye with a left hook, ripped a right hook to my sore ear and went under my return. He come up with a venomous right under the heart, ducked my left swing and jabbed me three times on the nose without a return. Maddened, I hurtled into him headlong, grabbed him with my left and clubbed him with my right till he tied me up.

At close quarters we traded short arm rights and lefts to the body and he was the first to back away, not forgetting to flick me in the eye with his long left as he did so. I was right on top of him and suddenly he lowered his head and butted me square in the mouth, bringing a flow of claret that dyed my chin. He instantly ripped in a right uppercut that loosened a bunch of my teeth and backed me into the ropes with a perfect whirlwind of left and right hooks to the head.

With the ropes cutting into my back I rallied, steadied myself and smashed a right under his heart that stopped him in his tracks. A left to the jaw set him back on his heels and rattled his teeth like a castinet, and before I could hit again the gong sounded.

"This is lastin' considerably longer than I thought," I said to Bill, who was mopping blood and talking to Heinie with some heat.

"My gosh, Bill," said Heinie. "Be reasonable! If I stopped this fight and awarded it to Steve or anybody else on a foul, these thugs wouldst tear this buildin' down and hang me to the rafters. They craves a knockout—"

"They're goin' to get one!" I snarled. "Never mind the fouls. Say, Bill, did you ever see such clear, honest eyes as Joan's got? I know women, I wanta tell you, and I never seen a straighter, squarer jane in my life—"

At the gong we went into a clinch and pounded each other's midsections till Heinie broke us. Cortez wasn't taking much chances, fighting wary and cautious. He slashed away with his left, but he kept his right high and never let it go unless he was sure of landing. He was using his elbows plenty in the clinches, and butting every chance he got, but Heinie pretended not to see. The crowd didn't care; as long as a man fought, they didn't care how he fought. Bill was making remarks that would of curled the toes of a Hottentot, but nobody seemed to mind.

About the middle of the lap,

Cortez began making remarks about my ancestors that made me good and mad. My Irish got up, and I went for him like a wild bull, head down and arms hammering. He shot his left and side-stepped, but the left ain't made that can stop me when my temper's up, and I was right on top of him too fast for him to get away. I battered him across the ring, but just as I thought I had him pinned on the ropes he side-stepped and I fell into them myself.

This highly amused the crowd, and Cortez hooked three lefts to my head while I was untangling myself, and when I slewed around and swung, he ducked and crashed my jaw with a right hook he brought up from the floor and which had me groggy for the first time that night. Sensing victory, he shot the same hand three times to my head, knocking me back into the ropes where he sank his left to the wrist in my midriff.

I was dizzy and slightly sick, but I saw Cortez' snarling face in a sort of red haze and I smashed my right square into the middle of that face. He was off his guard—not expecting a return like that and his head went back like it was hinged. The blood splattered, and the crowd howled with relish. I plunged after him, but he crouched and as I came in he went under my swing and hooked his right hard to my groin. Oh Jerusha! I dropped like my legs had been cut from under me, and writhed and twisted on the canvas like a snake with a broken back.

I had to clench my teeth to keep from vomiting and I was sick—nauseated if you get what I mean. I looked up and Heinie, with his face white, was fixing to count over me.

"One!" he said. "Two! Three!"

"You hog-fat nit-wit!" screamed Bill. "If you count him out I'll blow your brains through the back of your skull!"

Heinie shivered like he had a chill; he took a quick look at Bill, then he shot a scared glance at the ravening crowd, and he ducked his head like a tortoise, shut his eyes and kept on counting.

"Four! Five! Six!"

"Thirty-six thousand dollars!" I groaned, reaching for the ropes. The cold sweat was standing out on my brow as I pulled myself up.

"Seven! Eight! Nine!"

I was up, feet braced wide, holding the top rope to keep from falling. Cortez came lunging in to finish me, and I knowed if I let go I'd fall again. I hunched my shoulder and blocked his right, but he ripped his left to my chin and crashed his right high on my temple—and then the gong sounded. He socked me again after the gong, before he went to his corner—but a little thing like that don't cause no comment in the International Fight Arena.

BILL HELPED ME to my corner, cursing between clenched teeth, but, with my usual recuperative powers, I was already recovering from the effects of that foul blow. Bill emptied a bucket-full of cold water over me, and much to Cortez' disgust I come out for the fifth frame as good as new. He didn't think so at first, but a wicked right-hander under the heart shook him to the toes and made him back pedal in a hurry.

I went for him like a whirlwind and, seeming somewhat discouraged, he began his old tactics of hit and run. A sudden thought hit me that maybe all the shares was bought up. This fight looked like it was going on forever; here I was chasing Panther Cortez around the ring and doing no damage, while the No Sens was buying up all the Korean Copper in sight. Every minute a fortune was slipping that much farther away from me, and this rat refused to stand up and be knocked out like a man. I nearly went crazy with fury.

"Come on and fight, you yellow skunk!" I raged, while the crowd yelled blood-thirstily, beginning to be irritated at Cortez' tactics, which was beginning to be more run than hit. "Stand up to it, you white-livered, yellow-bellied, Porchugeeze half-caste!"

They's always something that'll get under a fellow's hide. This got under Cortez'. Maybe he did have some breed blood in him. Anyway, he went clean crazy. He give a howl like a blood-mad jungle-cat, and in spite of the wild yells from his corner, he tore in with his eyes glaring and froth on his lips. Biff! Bim! Bam! I was caught in a perfect whirlwind of punches; it was like being clawed by a real panther. But, with a savage grin, I slugged it out with him. That's my game! He hit three blows to my one, but mine were the ones that counted.

There was the salty tang of blood in my mouth, and blood in my eyes; it reddened Heinie's shirt, and stained the canvas under our feet. It spattered in the faces of the yelling ring-siders at every blow. But my gloves were sinking deep at every sock, and I was satisfied. Toe to toe we slashed and smashed, till the ring swum red and the thunder of our blows could be heard all over the house. But it couldn't last; flesh and blood couldn't stand it. Somebody had to go—and it was Cortez.

Flat on his back he hit, and bounced back up without a count. But I was on him like a blood-mad tiger. I took his left and right in the face without hardly feeling them, and smashed my right under his heart and my left to his jaw. He staggered, glassy eyed; a crashing right to the jaw dropped him under the ropes on his face. Maybe he's there yet. Anyhow, up to the count of ten he didn't bat an eyelash.

"Gimme that dough!" I snarled, jerking it out of Heinie's reluctant hand.

"Hey!" he protested. "What about my cut? Didn't I promote this show? Didn't I stand all the expense? You think you can fight in my ring for nothin'—"

"If I had your nerve I'd be King of Siam," I growled, shaking the blood outa my eyes, and at that moment Bill's right met Heinie's jaw like a caulking mallet meeting a ship's hull, and Heinie went to sleep. The crowd filed out, gabbling incoherently. That last touch was all that was needed to make the night a perfect success for them.

"Here, give this to Cortez when he wakes up!" I snarled, shoving a five-dollar bill—American money—into the hand of one of the Panther's seconds. "He's dirty, but he's game. And he don't know it, but it's the same as me givin' him five thousand dollars. Come on, Bill."

I CHANGED MY clothes in the dressing-room, noting in a cracked mirror that my face looked like I'd fallen afoul a wildcat, and likewise that I had a beautiful black eye or two. We skinned out a side door, but I reckon some thugs in the crowd had seen us get the money—and they's plenty of men in the Singapore waterfront who'd cut your throat for a dime. The second I stepped out into the dark alley-way something crashed against my head, and I went to my knees seeing about a million stars. I come up again and felt a knife-edge lick along my arm. I hit out blind and landed by sheer luck. My right lifted my unseen attacker clean off his feet and dropped him like a sack on the ground. Meanwhile Bill had grappled with

71

two more and I heard the crack as he knocked their heads together.

"You hurt, Steve?" he asked, feeling for me, because it was that dark you couldn't see your hand before you.

"Scratched a little," I said, my head still ringing from the blackjack sock. "Let's get outa here. Looks like we got to lick everybody in Singapore before we get that stock."

We got out of the alley and beat it down the street, people looking kind of funny at us. Well, I guess I was a sight, what with my black eye and cut and battered face, the bump on my head, and my arm bleeding from the knife wound. But nobody said nothing. People in places like that have got a way of minding their own business that politer folks could well copy.

"We better stop by the Waterfront Mission before we go for that stock, Steve," said Bill. "The gospel-shark will bandage your arm and not charge a cent—and keep his mouth shut afterward."

"No, no, no!" said I, becoming irascible because of my hurts and the delay. "We're goin' to get that stock before we do anything else."

We was passing a gambling hall and Bill's eyes lighted as he heard the click and whir of the roulette wheel.

"I feel lucky tonight," he muttered. "I betcha I could run that thirty bucks up to a hundred in no time."

"And I'd give my arm for a shot of licker," I snapped. "But I tell you, we ain't takin' no chances. We can guzzle and play fan-tan and roulette all we want to after we get rich."

After what seemed a century we arrived at the dismal, dark and vile smelling alley that the Chinese call the Alley of the Seven Mandarins—why, I never could figure. We found the door with the green dragon and knocked, and my heart stood still for fear Joan wouldn't be there. But she was. The door opened and she give a gasp as she saw me.

"Quick, don't keep us in suspense," Bill gasped. "Is the stock all took up?"

"Why, no," she said. "I can get you—"

"Then do it, quick," I said, pressing the money into her hand. "There's thirty-one dollars and fifty-cents—"

"Is that all?" she said, like she was considerably disappointed.

"If you'd a seen how I won it, you'd think it was a lot," I said.

"Well," she said. "Wait a minute. The man who owns that stock lives down the alley."

She vanished down the dark alley-way, and we waited with our hearts knocking holes in our ribs for what seemed like hours. Then she came out of the darkness, looking kind of white and ghostly in the shadows, and slipped a long envelope into my hot and sweaty hand. I hove a vast sigh of relief and started to say something, but she put her finger to her lips.

"Shhh! I musn't be seen with you. I must go, now." And before I could say a word, she'd vanished in the dark.

"Open the envelope, Steve," urged Bill. "Let's see what a fortune looks like!"

I opened it and pulled out a slip of paper. I moved over to the lamplight in the street to read what was wrote on it. Then I give a roar that brought faces to every window on the street. Bill jerked the paper from me and glared at it and then he give a maddened howl and joined me in a frenzied burst of horrible talk that brought a dozen cops on the run. We wasn't in no condition to make any coherent reply, and the ensuing riot didn't end till the reserves was called out.

On the paper which was in the envelope Joan Wells gave me in return for my hard-earned money was wrote:

> *This is to certify that you are entitled to thirty-one and a half shares of stock in the Korean Copper Company which was dissolved in the year 1875. Don't worry about the No Sen Tong; it was extinct before the Boxer Rebellion. Of all the suckers that have fallen for this graft, you saps were the easiest. But cheer up; you're out only $31.50, and I took one bonehead for $300. A girl has got to live.*

WATERFRONT FISTS.

ALTERNATE TITLE: STAND UP AND SLUG.

This short story was first published in the September 1930 issue of Fight Stories *magazine.*

THE *Sea Girl* hadn't been docked in Honolulu more'n three hours before Bill O'Brien come legging it down to the pool hall where I was showing Mushy Hansen the fine points of the game, to tell me that he'd got me matched to fight some has-been at the American Arena that night.

"The *Ruffian* is in," said Bill, "and they got a fellow which they swear can take any man aboard the *Sea Girl* to a royal cleanin'. I ain't seen him, but they say he growed up in the back country of Australia and run wild with the kangaroos till he was shanghaied aboard a ship at an early age. They say he's licked everybody aboard the *Ruffian* from the cap'n down to the mess boy—"

"Stow the gab and lead me to some *Ruffian* idjits which is cravin' to risk their jack on this tramp," I interrupted. "I got a hundred and fifty bucks that's burnin' my pockets up."

Well, it was easy to find some lunatics from the *Ruffian*, and after putting up our money at even odds, with a bartender for stakeholder, and knowing I had a tough battle ahead of me and needed some training, I got me a haircut and then went down to the Hibernian Bar for a few shots of hard licker. While me and Bill and Mushy was lapping up our drinks, in come Sven Larsen. This huge and useless Swede has long been laboring under the hallucination that he oughta be champion of the *Sea Girl*, and no amount of battering has been able to quite wipe the idee outa what he supposes to be his brain.

Well, this big mistake come up to me, and scowling down at me, he said: "You Irisher, put oop your hands!"

I set my licker down with a short sigh of annoyance. "With a thousand sailors in port itchin' for a scrap," I said, "you got to pick on me. G'wan—I don't want to fight no shipmate now. Anyway, I got to fight the Ruffian's man in a few hours."

"Aye shood be fightin' him," persisted the deluded maniac. "Aye ought to be champ of dey *Sea Girl*. Come on, you big stiffer!" And so saying he squared off in what he fondly believed was a fighting pose. At this moment my white bulldog, Mike, sensing trouble, bristled and looked up from the bowl of beer he was lapping up on the floor, but seeing it was nobody but Sven, he curled up and went to sleep.

"Don't risk your hands on the big chump, Steve," said Bill disgustedly. "I'll fix him—"

"You stay oot of dis, Bill O'Brien," said the Swede waving his huge fists around menacingly. "Aye will see to you after Aye lick Steve."

"Aw, you're drunk," I said. "A fine shipmate you are."

"Aye am not droonk!" he roared. "My girl told me—"

"I didn't know you had a girl here," said Bill.

"Well, Aye have. And she said a big man like me shood be champion of his ship and she wouldn't have nothings to do with me till Aye was. So put oop your hands—"

"Aw, you're crazy," I snapped, turning back to the bar, but watching him close from the corner of my eye. Which was a good thing because he started a wild right swing that had destruction wrote all over it. I sidestepped and he crashed into the bar. Rebounding with a bloodthirsty beller he lunged at me, and seeing they was no arguing with the misguided heathen, I stepped inside his swing and brought up a right uppercut to the jaw that lifted his whole two hundred and forty-five pounds clean off the floor and stood him on the back of his neck, out cold. Mike, awakened by the crash, opened one eye, raised one ear, and then went back to sleep with a sort of gentle canine smile.

"Y'oughta be careful," growled

Bill, while Mushy sloshed a pitcher of dirty water over the Swede. "You mighta busted yore hand. Whyn't you hit him in the stummick?"

"I didn't wanta upset his stummick," I said. "I've skinned my knuckles a little, but they ain't even bruised much. I've had 'em in too many buckets uh brine."

AT LAST SVEN was able to sit up and cuss me, and he mumbled something I didn't catch.

"He says he's got a date with his girl tonight," Mushy said, "but he's ashamed to go back to her with that welt on his jaw and tell her he got licked."

"Ya," said Sven, rubbing his jaw, "you got to go tell her I can't come, Steve."

"Aw, well," I said, "all right. I'll tell her you fell off the docks and sprained your ankle. Where's she live?"

"She dances at the Striped Cat Cabaret," said Sven.

After downing a finger of Old Jersey Cream, I tightened my belt and me and Mike sauntered forth.

Bill followed me out into the street and said: "Dawg-gone it, Steve, you ought not to go cruisin' off this way, with the fight just a few hours in the offin'. That *Ruffian* crew is crooked as a buncha snakes—and you know what a soft head you are where women is concerned."

"Your remarks is highly insultin', Bill," I returned with my well-known quiet dignity. "I don't reckon no woman ever made a fool outa me. I know 'em like a book. Anyhow, you don't think I'd fall for a dame as encouraged a sap like Sven, do you? Heck, she's probably some big fat wench with a face like a bull terrier. What'd he say her name was—oh, yes, Gloria Flynn. Don't you worry about me. I'll be at the American in plenty uh time."

It was after dark when me and Mike got to the Striped Cat Cabaret which is located in a tough waterfront section of the city. I asked the manager for Gloria Flynn, and he said she'd just finished a dance and was in her dressing room, changing to street clothes. He told me to wait for her at the back exit, which I done. I was standing there when the door opened and some girls come out. I said, taking off my cap, politely, "Which one of you frails is Gloria Flynn, if any?"

You could of knocked me over with a pile-driver when the snappiest, prettiest one of the bunch up and said, "I'm her—and what of it?"

"Well," I said, eyeing her with great admiration, "all I can say is, what does a girl like you want to waste her time with such tripe as Sven Larsen when they is men like me in port?"

"Don't get fresh!" she snapped.

"Oh, I ain't fresh," I assured her. "I just come to tell you that Sven fell off a dock and broke his neck—I mean sprained his ankle, and he can't make the date tonight."

"Oh," she murmured. Then looking close at me, she said, "Who are you?"

"I'm Steve Costigan, the fellow that licked him," I replied thoughtlessly.

"Oh!" she said, kind of breathlessly. "So you're Steve Costigan!"

"Yeah, I am," I said, having spilled the beans anyway. "Steve Costigan, A. B. mariner, and heavyweight champion aboard the trader *Sea Girl*. I knowed you didn't know me, or you wouldn't of persuaded your boy friend to risk his life by takin' a swing at me."

She looked kind of bewildered. "I don't know what you're talking about."

"Oh, it's all right," I hastened to assure her. "Sven told me about you urgin' him to climb me, but it's natural for a frail to want her fellow to be a champ of somethin'. What I can't understand is, what you see in a galoot like Sven."

She gave a kind of hysterical laugh. "Oh, I see. Why, Mr. Costigan—"

"Call me Steve," I beamed.

"Well—Steve," she said with a little embarrassed laugh, "I didn't urge him anything of the sort. I just said he was such a big fellow I bet he could whip anybody aboard his ship—and he said one of the other sailors, Steve Costigan, was champion, and I said I was surprised that anybody could lick him—Sven, I mean. Why, I had no idea he'd get it into his head I wanted him to fight anybody. I do hope you didn't hurt the poor boy."

"Oh, not much," I said, unconsciously swelling out my huge chest, "I always handle my shipmates easy as possible. Though uh course, I'm so powerful some times I hit harder'n I intend to. But say, sister, I know a swell little girl like you wasn't takin' that big squarehead serious. You was just sorry for him because he's so kind of big and awkward and dumb, wasn't you?"

"Well," she admitted, "that was the way of it; he looked lonesome—"

"Well, that's mighty fine of you," I said. "But forget about him now; after the beltin' I give him, he won't want to come back to you, and anyway, he'll find a native girl or a Chinese or somethin'. He ain't like me; a woman's a woman to him and he'll fall for anything in skirts that comes along. Me, I'm a one-woman man. Anyway, kid, it ain't right for you to trail around with a galoot like him. You owe it to yourself to keep company with only the best—me, for instance."

"Maybe you're right," she said, with downcast eyes.

"Sure, I'm always right," I answered modestly. "Now what say we go in and lap up something. All this talkin' I been doin's got my throat dry."

"Oh, I never drink intoxicants," she said with a bright smile. "If you don't mind let's go over here to this ice-cream parlor."

"O.K. with me," I said, "but first lemme introduce you to Mike who can lick his weight both in wildcats and dog biscuits."

Well, Mike, he shook hands with her but he wasn't particular enthusiastic. He ain't no ladies' dog; he treats 'em politely but coldly. Then we went over to the joint where they sold ice cream, and while we was dawdling over the stuff, I let my eyes wander over my charming companion. She was a beauty, no doubt about it; curly yellow hair and big trusting violet eyes.

"WHAT'S A NICE girl like you doin' workin' in a dump like the Striped Cat?" I asked her, and she kind of sighed and hung her head.

"A girl has to do lots of things she don't like to," she said. "I was in a high class stock company which went broke here on account of the manager getting delirium tremens and having to be sent back to his home in England. I had to eat, and this was the only job open for me. Some day I'm going home; my folks live on a dairy farm in New Jersey, and I was a fool ever to leave there. Right now I can see the old white farm house, and the green meadows with the babbling brooks running through them, and the cows grazing."

I thought she was going to cry for a minute, then she kind of sighed and smiled: "It's all in a lifetime, isn't it?"

"You're a brave kid," I said, touched to my shoe soles, "and I wanta see more of you. I'm fightin' some guy at the American Arena in a little while. How about holdin' down a nice ringside seat there, and then havin' supper and a little dancin' afterwards? I can't dance much, but I'm a bear at the supper table."

"Oh," said she, "you're the man that's going to fight Red Roach?"

"Is that his name?" I asked. "Yeah, if he's the man from the *Ruffian*."

"I'd like to go," she said, "but I have to go on in another dance number in half an hour."

"Well," I said, "the fight can't last more'n three or four rounds, not with me in there. How 'bout me droppin' around the Striped Cat afterwards? If you ain't through then, I'll wait for you."

"That's fine," she said, and noting my slightly unsatisfied expression, she said: "If I'd known you were going to fight so soon, I wouldn't have let you eat that ice cream."

"Oh, that won't interfere with my punchin' ability any," I said. "But I would like a shot of hard licker to kind of settle it on my stummick."

That's the truth; sailors is supposed to be hawgs about ice cream and I have seen navy boys eat it in digusting quantities, but it's poor stuff for my belly. Mike had ate the bowl full I give him, but he'd a sight rather had a pan of slush.

"Let's don't go in any of these

saloons," said Gloria. "These water-front bars sell you the same stuff rattlesnakes have in their teeth. I tell you, I've got a bottle of rare old wine not very far from here. I never touch it myself, but I keep it for my special friends and they say it's great. You've time for a nip, haven't you?"

"Lead on, sister," I said, "I've always got time to take a drink, or oblige a beautiful girl!"

"Ah, you flatterer," she said, giving me a little push. "I bet you tell that to every girl you meet."

WELL, TO MY surprise we halted before a kind of ramshackle gymnasium, and Gloria took out a key and unlocked the door.

"I didn't tell you I had a kid brother with me," she said in answer to my surprised glance. "He's a weakly sort of kid, and I have to support him as well as myself. Poor kid, he would come with me when I left home. Well, Mr. Salana, who owns the gym, lets him use the equipment to build himself up; it's healthy for him. This is the boy's key. I keep the wine hidden in one of the lockers."

"Ain't this where Tony Andrada trains?" I asked suspiciously. "'Cause if it is, it ain't no place for a nice girl. They is fighters and fighters, my child, and Tony is no credit to no business."

"He's always been a perfect gentleman towards me," she answered. "Of course I come here only occasionally when my brother is working out—" She opened the door and we went in and then she shut it. To my slight surprise I heard the click as she locked it. She switched on a light and I seen her bending over something. Then she swung around and—wow!—I got the most unexpected, dumfounding surprise of my life to date! When she turned she had a heavy Indian club in both hands, and she heaved it up and crashed it down on my head with everything she had behind it!

Well, I was so utterly dumfounded I just stood and gaped at her, and Mike, he nearly had a fit. I'd always taught him never to bite a woman, and he just didn't know what to do. Gloria was staring at me with eyes that looked like they was going to jump right out of her head. She glanced down at the broken fragments of the Indian club in a kind of stunned way, and then the color all ebbed out of her face, leaving her white as a ghost.

"That's a nice way to do a friend!" I said reproachfully. "I don't mind a joke, but you've made me bite my tongue."

She cringed back against the wall and held out both hands pitifully: "Don't hit me!" she cried, "please don't hit me! I had to do it!"

Well, if I ever seen a scared girl, it was then. She was shaking in every limb.

"You don't need to insult me on top of busting a club on my skull,"

I said with my quiet dignity. "I never hit no woman in my life and I ain't figurin' on it."

All to once she began to cry. "Oh," said she, "I'm ashamed of myself. But please listen—I've lied to you. My brother is a fighter too, and he just about had this fight with Red Roach, when the promoter at the American changed his mind and signed you up instead. This fight would have given us enough to get back to New Jersey where those cows are grazing by the babbling meadows. I—I—thought, when you told me you were the one that's going to fight Roach, I'd fix it so you wouldn't show up, and they'd have to use Billy—that's my brother—after all. I was going to knock you unconscious and tie you up till after the fight. Oh, I know you'll hate me, but I'm desperate. I'll die if I have to live this life much longer," she said passionately. And then she starts to bawl.

Well, I can't see as it was my fault, but I felt like a horse thief anyhow.

"Don't cry," I said. "I'd help you all I can, but I got all my jack sunk on the imbroglio to win by a k.o."

She lifted her tear stained face. "Oh, Steve, you can help me! Just stay here with me! Don't show up at the Arena! Then Billy will get the fight and we can go home! Please, Steve, please, please, please!"

She had her arms around my neck and was fairly shaking me in her eagerness. Well, I admit I got a soft spot in my heart for the weaker sex, but gee whiz!

"Great cats, Gloria," I said, "I'd dive off the Statue uh Liberty for you, but I can't do this. My shipmates has got every cent they got bet on me. I can't throw 'em down that way."

"You don't love me!" she mourned.

"Aw, I do too," I protested. "But dawg-gone it, Gloria, I just can't do it, and please don't coax me, 'cause it's like jerkin' a heart-string loose to say 'No' to you. Wait a minute! I got a idee! You and your brother got some money saved up, ain't cha?"

"Yes, some," she sniffed, dabbing at her eyes with a foolish little lace handkerchief.

"Well, listen," I said, "you can double it—sink every cent you got on me to win by a kayo! It'll be a cinch placin' the dough. Everybody on the waterfront's bettin' one way or the other."

"But what if you lose?" said she.

"Me lose?" I snorted. "Don't make me laugh! You do that—and I can't stay another minute, kid—I'm due at the Arena right now. And say, I'll have some dough myself after the battle, and I'm goin' to help you and your brother get back to them green cows and babblin' farm houses. Now I got to go!"

And before she had time to say another word, I kicked the lock off the door, being in too big a hurry to have her unlock it, and the next second me and Mike was sprinting for the Arena.

I FOUND BILL tearing his hair and walking the dressing room floor.

"Here you are at last, are you, you blankety-blank mick dipthong!" he yelled blood-thirstily. "Where you been? You want to make a nervous wreck outa me? You realize you been committin' the one unpardonable sin, by keepin' the crowd waitin' for fifteen minutes? They're yellin' bloody murder and the crew which is all out front in ringside seats, has been throwin' chairs at the *Ruffian's* men which has been howlin' you'd run out on us. The promoter says if you ain't in that ring in five minutes, he'll run in a substitute."

"And I'll run him into the bay," said I, sitting down and shucking my shoes. "I gotta get my wind back a little. Boy, we had Sven's girl down all wrong! She's a peach, as well as bein' a square-shootin'—"

"Shut up, and get into them trunks!" howled Bill, doing a war-dance on the cap I'd just took off. "You'll never learn nothin'. Listen to that crowd! We'll be lucky if they don't lynch all of us!"

Well, the maddened fans was making a noise like a flock of hungry lions, but that didn't worry me none. I'd just got into my fighting togs when the door opened and the manager of the Arena stuck a pale face in.

"I got a man in place of Costigan—" he began, when he saw me and stopped.

"Gangway!" I snarled, and as I pushed by him, I saw a fellow in trunks coming out of another dressing room. To my amazement it was Tony Andrada, which even had his hands taped. His jaw fell when he seen me, and his manager, Abe Gold, give a howl. They was two other thugs with them—Salana and Joe Cromwell—I'd been in Honolulu enough to know them yeggs.

"What do you think you're doin' here?" I snarled, facing Tony.

"They want me to fight Roach, when you run out—" he begun.

Bill grabbed my arm as I was making ready to slug him. "For cats' sake!" he snarled, "you can lick him after you flatten Roach if you want to! Come on!"

"It's mighty funny he should turn up, right at this time," I growled. "I thought Billy Flynn was to fight Roach if I didn't show up."

"Who's Billy Flynn?" asked Bill as he rushed me up the aisle between howling rows of infuriated fans.

"My new girl's kid brother," I answered as I clumb through the ropes. "If they've did anything to him, I'll—"

My meditations was drowned by the thunders of the mob, who give me cheers because I'd got there, and razzes because I hadn't got there sooner.

On one side of the ring the *Sea Girls* crew lifted the roof with their wild whoops and on the other side the *Ruffian's* roughnecks greeted me with coarse, rude squawks and impolite remarks.

Well, I glanced over to the opposite corner and saw Red Roach for the first, and I hope the last, time. He was tall and raw-boned, and the ugliest human I ever seen. He had freckles as big as mess pans all over him; his nose was flat, and his low slanting forehead was topped by a shock of the most scandalously red hair I ever looked at. When he rose from his stool I seen he was knock-kneed and when we came to the center of the ring to pretend to listen to instructions, I was disgusted to note that he was also cross-eyed. At first I thought he was counting the crowd, and it was slightly disconcerting to finally decide he was glaring at me!

WE WENT BACK to our corners, the gong sounded, the scrap started and I got another jolt.

Roach come out, right foot and right hand forward. He was left-handed! I was so disgusted I come near lighting in and giving him a good cussing. Red-headed, cross-eyed—and left-handed! And he was the first good port-sider I'd ever met in a ring.

I forgot to say our weights was 190 for me, and 193 for him. In addition, he was six feet three, or just three inches taller'n me, and he musta had a reach of anyways fifteen fathoms. We was still so far apart I didn't think he could reach me with a pole when—bam! his right licked out to my chin. I give a roar and plunged in, meaning to make it a quick fight. I wanted to crush this inhuman freak before the sight of him got on my nerves and rattled me.

But I was all at sea. A left-hander does everything backwards. He leads with his right and crosses his left. He side-steps to the left instead of the right ordinarily. This guy done everything a port-sider's supposed to do, and a lot more stuff he thought up for hisself. He had a fast hard straight right and a wicked left swing—oh boy, how he could hit with that left! Seemed like every time I did anything, I got that right in the eye or the mouth or on the nose, and whilst I was thinking about that, bam! come the left and nearly ripped my head clean off.

The long, lanky mutt—it looked like if I ever landed solid I'd bust him in two. But I couldn't get past that long straight right. My swings were all short and his straight right beat my left hook every time. When I tried trading jabs with him, his extra reach ruint that—anyway, I'm a natural hooker. My straight left is got force, but it ain't as accurate as it should be.

At the end of the first round my right ear was nearly mangled. In the second frame he half closed my eye with a sizzling right hook, and opened a deep gash on my forehead. At the beginning of the third he dropped me for no-count with a left hook to the body that nearly caved me in. The *Ruffian's* crew was getting crazier every second and the *Sea Girl's* gang was yelling bloody murder. But I wasn't worried. I'm used to more punishment than I was getting and I wasn't weakening any.

But dawg-gone it, it did make me mad not to be able to hit Roach. To date I hadn't landed a single solid punch. He was a clever boxer in his way, and his style woulda made Dempsey look like a one-armed paperhanger carryin' a bucket.

He managed to keep me at long range, and he belted me plenty, but it wasn't his speed nor his punch that kept me all at sea; it was his cruel and unusual appearance! Dawg-gone—them eyes of his nearly had me batty. I couldn't keep from looking at 'em. I tried to watch his waist-line or his feet, but every time my gaze wouldst wander back to his distorted optics. They had a kinda fatal attraction for me. Whilst I wouldst be trying to figure out where they was looking—wham! would come that left winging in from a entirely unexpected direction—and this continued.

WELL, AFTER ARISING from that knock-down in the third frame, I was infuriated. And after chasing him all around the ring, and getting only another black eye for my pains, I got desperate. With the round half a minute to go, I wowed the audience by closing both my eyes and tearing in, swinging wild and regardless.

He was pelting me plenty, but I didn't care; that visage of his wasn't upsetting all my calculations as long as I couldn't see it, and in a second I felt my left crash against what I knew to be a human jaw. Instantly the crowd went into hystericals and I opened my eyes and looked for the corpse.

My eyes rested on a recumbent figure, but it was not Red Roach. To my annoyance I realized that one of my blind swings had connected with the referee. At the same instant Roach's swinging left crashed against my jaw and I hit the canvas. But even as I went down I swung a wild dying effort right which sunk in just above Red's waistline. The round ended with all three of us on the canvas.

Our respective handlers dragged us to our corners, and somebody throwed a bucket of water on the referee, who was able to answer the gong with us battlers by holding on to the ropes.

Well, as I sat in my corner sniffing the smelling salts and watching Red's handlers massaging his suffering belly, I thought deeply, a very rare habit of mine while fighting. I do not believe in too much thinking; it gives a fighter the head-ache. Still and all, with my jaw aching from Red's left and my eyes getting strained from watching his unholy face, I rubbed the nose Mike stuck into my glove, and meditated. A left-hander is a right-hander backwards. Nine times out of ten his straight right will beat your left jab.

If you lead your right to a right-hander, he'll beat you to the punch with his left; but you can lead your right to a left-hander, because his left has as far to travel as your right.

So when we come out for the fourth round, instead of tearing in, I went in cautious-like for me, ignoring the yells of the *Ruffian's* crew that I was getting scared of their man. Red feinted with his right so clumsy even I knowed it was a feint and instantly shot my right with everything I had behind it. It beat his left swing and landed solid, but high. He staggered and I dropped him to his all fours with a whistling left hook under the heart. He was up at "Nine" and caught me with a wild left swing as I rushed in. It dizzied me but I kept coming, and every time he made a motion with his left I shot my right. Sometimes I landed first and sometimes he did, and sometimes we landed simultaneous, but my smashes had the most kick behind them. Like most port-siders when they're groggy, he'd clean forgot he had a right hand and was staking everything on his left swing.

I battered him back across the ring, and he rallied and smashed over a sledge-hammer left hook that rocked me to my heels and made the blood spatter, but I bored right in with a sizzling left hook under the heart. He gasped, his knees buckled, then he steadied hisself and shot over his left just as I crashed in with a right. Bam! Something exploded in my head, and then I heard the referee counting. To my chagrin I found I was on the canvas, but Roach was there too.

The still weaving and glassy-eyed referee was holding onto the ropes with one hand and counting over us both, but I managed to reel up at "Six!" Me and Red had landed square to the button at just the same second, but my jaw was just naturally tougher than his. He hadn't twitched at "Ten" and they had to carry him to his dressing room to bring him to.

Well, a few minutes' work on me with smelling salts, ammonia, sponges and the like made me as good as new. I couldn't hardly wait for Bill to dress my cuts with collodion, but the minute I got my clothes on and collected my winnings and bets from the bartender, who'd come to the ring under escort from both ships, I ducked out the back way. I even left Mike with Bill because he's always scrapping with some other dog on the streets and I was in a big hurry.

I was on my way to see if Gloria had followed my advice, also something else. One hundred and fifty bucks I won; with what I had that made three hundred. I got a hundred and fifty for the fracas. Altogether I had four hundred and fifty dollars all in greenbacks of large denomination in my jacket pocket. And I was going to give Gloria every cent of it, if she'd take it, so she could go back to New Jersey and the cows. This sure wasn't no place for a nice girl to be in, and I'll admit I indulged in some dreams as I hurried along—about the time I'd retire from the sea and maybe go into the dairy farming business in New Jersey.

I WAS HEADED for the Striped Cat, but on my way I passed Salana's gym, and I noticed that they was a light in one of the small rooms which served as a kind of office. As I passed the door I distinctly heard a voice I knowed was Gloria's. I stopped short and started to knock on the door, then something made me steal up close and listen—though I ain't a eavesdropper by nature. From the voices five people was in the room—Gloria, Salana, Abe Gold, Joe Cromwell, and Tony.

"Don't hand us no line, sister," Gold was saying in his nasty rasping voice. "You said leave it to you. Yeah, we did! And look what it got us! You was goin' to keep Costigan outa the way, so's we could run Tony in at the last minute. You know the promoter at the American was all set to match Tony with Roach when Costigan's ship docked and the big cheese changed his mind and matched the Mick instead, because the fool sailors wanted the scrap.

"Roach woulda been a spread for Tony, because the wop eats these port-siders up. The town sports know that, and they woulda sunk heavy on Tony. We was goin' to bet our shirts on Roach, and Tony would flop along about the third. Then we

coulda all left this dump and gone to Australia.

"Well, we left it up to you to get rid of Costigan. And what does he do, I ask you? He walks in as big as you please, just when Tony was fixing to go in for him. I ask you!"

"Well, don't rag me," said Gloria in a voice which startled me, it was that hard, "I did my best. I got hold of a Swede aboard the *Sea Girl* and primed the big stiff proper. I stirred him up and sent him down to climb Costigan, thinking he'd bung the mick up so he couldn't come on tonight, or that Costigan would at least break his hands on him.

"But the harp flattened him without even spraining a thumb, and the first thing I knew, he was waiting for me outside the cabaret. I thought he'd come to smack me down for sicking the Swede on him, but the big slob had just come to tell me the square-head couldn't keep his date. Can you feature that? Well, he fell for me right off, naturally, and I got him into the gym here, intending to lay him cold and lock him up till after the fight. But say! That big mick must have a skull made of reinforced battleship steel! I shattered a five-pound Indian club over his dome without even making him bat his eyes!

"Well, I hope I never have a half-minute like that again! When I failed to even stagger him with that clout, I thought I was a gone goose! I had visions of him twisting my head off and feeding it to that ugly cannibal he calls his bulldog.

"But you can't tell about those tough looking sluggers like him. He didn't even offer to lay a hand on me, and when I got my second wind, I spun him a yarn about having a kid brother that needed this fight to get back home. He fell for it so easy that I thought I could coax him to run out on his own accord, but he balked there. All he'd do was to advise me to bet on him, and then all at once he said it was time for him to be at the stadium, and he busted right out through the door and took it on the lam, making some crack about coming back after the fight."

"A fine mess you've made!" sneered Salana. "You've gummed things up proper! We had everything set for a killing—"

"A high class brand of sports you are!" she snapped. "I'm ashamed to be seen with you, you cheap grafters! A big killing! You don't know what one is. Anyway, what do you want me to do, cry?"

"We want you to give back that hundred we paid you in advance," snarled Salana, "and if you don't, you'll cry plenty."

"And I guess you think I risk my life for such cheap welchers as you for nothing?" she sneered. "Not one cent—"

There was the sound of a blow and Gloria give a short, sharp cry which was cut short in a sort of gasp.

"Give her the works, Joe," Salana snarled. "You can't cross me, you little—!"

NEVER MIND WHAT he called her. I'd have half killed him for that alone. I tore the door clean off the hinges as I went through it, and I seen a sight that made a red mist wave in front of me so everything in that room looked bloody and grim.

Salana had Gloria down on a chair and was twisting both her arms up behind her back till it looked like they'd break. Joe Cromwell had the fingers of his left hand sunk deep in her white throat and his right drawed back to smash in her face. Tony and Abe Gold was looking on with callous, contemptuous sneers.

They all turned to look as the door crashed in, and I saw Salana go white as I give one roar and went into action. He turned loose of the girl, but before he could get his hands up, I crashed him with a left-hander that crushed his nose and knocked out four teeth, and my next smash tore Joe Cromwell's ear loose and left it hanging by a shred. Another of the same sort stood him on his head in a corner with a cracked jaw-bone, and almost simultaneous Abe Gold barely missed me with a pair of brass knuckles, and Tony landed hard on my ear. But I straightened with a right-hander that dropped Gold across Salana with three broken ribs, and missed a left swing that wouldst of decapitated Tony hadst it landed.

I ain't one of these fellows which has to be crazy mad to put up a good fight, but when I am crazy mad, they's no limit to the destruction I can hand out. Maybe in the ring, under ordinary circumstances, Tony could of cut me to ribbons, but here he never had a chance. I didn't even feel the punches he was raining on me, and after missing a flock of swings in a row, I landed under his jaw with a hay-making right-hander that I brought up from the floor. Tony turned a complete somersault in the air, and when he come down his head hit the wall with a force that laid his scalp open and wouldst of knocked him cold, if he hadn't already been unconscious before he landed.

Maybe a minute and a half after I busted through the door, I stood alone in the middle of the carnage, panting and glaring down at the four silent figures which littered the room. All I craved was for all the other yeggs in Honolulu to come busting in. Pretty soon I looked around for Gloria and saw her cringing in a corner like she was trying to flatten herself out against the wall. She was white-faced and her eyes was blazing with terror.

She give a kind of hunted cry when I looked at her. "Don't! Please, don't!"

"Please don't what?" I snapped in some irritation. "Ain't you learned by this time that I don't clout frails? I come in here to rescue you from these gypes, and you insult me!"

"Forgive me," she begged. "I can't help but be a little afraid of you—you look so much like a gorilla—"

"What!"

"I mean you're such a terrible fighter," she hastily amended. "Come on—let's get out of here before these welchers come to."

"Would that they wouldst," I brooded. "What I done to 'em was just a sample of what I'm goin' to do to 'em. Dawg-gone it, some of these days somebody's goin' to upset my temper, then I'll lose control of myself and hurt somebody."

Well, we went out on the street, which was mostly deserted and rather dimly lighted, and Gloria said pretty soon: "Thank you for rescuing me. If my brother had been there—"

"Gloria," I said wearily, "ain't you ever goin' to stop lyin'? I was outside the door and heard it all."

"Oh," said she.

"Well," I said, "I reckon I'm a fool when it comes to women. I thought I was stuck on you, and didn't have sense enough to know you was stringin' me. Why, I even brung the four hundred and fifty bucks I won, intendin' to give it to you."

And so saying I threw out the wad of bills, waved it reproachfully in front of her eyes and replaced it in my jacket pocket. All at once she started crying.

"Oh, Steve, you make me ashamed of myself! You're so fine and noble—"

"Well," I said with my quiet dignity, "I know it, but I can't help it. It's just my nature."

"I'm so ashamed," she sobbed.

"There's no use lying; Salana paid me a hundred dollars to get you out of the way. But, Steve, I'm changing my ways right here! I'm not asking you to forgive me, because I guess it's too much to ask, and you've done enough for me. But I'm going home tomorrow. That stuff I told you about the dairy farm in New Jersey was the only thing I told you that wasn't a lie. I'm going home and live straight, and I want to kiss you, just once, because you've showed me the error of my ways."

And so saying, she threw her arms around me and kissed me vigorously—and me not objectin' in no manner.

"I'm going back to the old, pure simple life," she said. "Back to the green meadows and babbling cows!"

And she made off down the street at a surprising rate of speed. I watched her go and a warm glow spread over me. After all, I thought, I do know women, and the hardest of them is softened by the influence of a strong, honest, manly heart like mine.

She vanished around a corner and I turned back toward the Hibernian Bar, at the same time reaching for my bank roll. Then I give a yell that woke up everybody in that section of Honolulu with cold sweat standing out on them. Now I knowed why she wanted to put her arms around me. My money was gone! She loved me—she loved me not!

CHAMP *of the* FORECASTLE.

ALTERNATE TITLE: CHAMP OF THE SEVEN SEAS.

This short story was first published in the November 1930 issue of Fight Stories *magazine.*

I DON'T HAVE to have a man tell me he craves war. I can tell it by the set of his jaw, the glare in his eyes. So, when Sven Larson raised his huge frame on his bunk and accused me of swiping his tobaccer, I knowed very well what his idee was. But I didn't want to fight Sven. Havin' licked the big cheese three or four times already, I seen no need in mauling him any

more. So somewhat to the surprise of the rest of the crew, I said:

"Sven, that's purty crude. You didn't need to think up no lie to pick a fight with me. I know you crave to be champion of the *Sea Girl*, but they ain't a chance, and I don't want to hurt you—"

I got no further, because with a bull's beller he heaved hisself offa his bunk and come for me like a wild man. Gosh, what a familiar scene that was—the fierce, hard faces ringing us, the rough bunks along the wall, the dim light of the lantern swinging overhead, and me standing in the middle, barefooted and stripped to the waist, holding my only title against all comers! They ain't a inch of that forecastle floor that I ain't reddened with my blood. They ain't a edge of a upper bunk that I ain't had my head smashed against. And since I been a man grown they ain't a sailor on the Seven Seas that can say he stood up to me in that forecastle and beat me down.

The lurching of the ship and the unsteady footing don't bother me none, nor the close space and foul, smoke-laden air. That's my element, and if I couldst fight in the ring like I can in the forecastle, with nothing barred, I'd be champion of something besides a tramp wind-jammer.

Well, Sven come at me with his old style—straight up, wide open, with a wild swinging right. I ducked inside it and smashed my left under his heart, following instantly with a blasting right hook to the jaw as he sagged. He started falling and a lurch of the ship throwed him half under a opposite bunk. They's no mercy ast, give or expected in a forecastle fight; it's always to the finish. I was right after him, and no sooner hadst he got to his feet than I smashed him down again before he could get his hands up.

"Let's call it a day, Sven," I growled. "I don't want to punch you no more."

But he come weaving up, spitting blood and roaring in his own tongue. He tried to clinch and gouge, but another right hook to the jaw sent him down and out. I shook the sweat outa my eyes and glared down at him in some irritation, which was mixed with the satisfaction of knowing that again I hadst proved my right to the title of champion of the toughest ship afloat. Maybe you think that's a mighty small thing, but it's the only title I got and I'm proud of it.

But I couldn't get onto Sven. Me and him was good friends ordinarily, but ever so often he'd get the idee he couldst lick me. So the next day I looked him up between watches and found him sulking and brooding. I looked over his enormous frame and shook my head in wonder to think that I hadst gotten no further in the legitimate ring than I have, when I can lay out such incredible monsters as Sven so easy.

Six feet four he was in his socks, and his two hundred and forty-five pounds was all muscle. I can bend coins between my fingers, tear up decks of cards and twist horseshoes in two, but Sven's so much stronger'n me they's no comparison. But size and strength ain't everything.

"Sven," said I, "how come you forever got to be fightin' me?"

Well, at first he wouldn't say, but at last it come out.

"AYE BANE GOT girl at Stockholm. She bane like me purty good, but they bane another faller. His name bane Olaf Ericson and he own fishing smack. Always when Aye go out with my girl, he bane yump on me and he always lick me. Aye tank if Aye ever lick you, Aye can lick Olaf."

"So you practice on me, hey?" I said. "Well, Sven, you never will lick me nor Olaf nor any man which can use his hands unless you change your style. Oh, uh course, you're a bear-cat when it comes to fightin' ignorant dock-wallopers and deck-hands which never seen a glove and can't do nothin' but bite and gouge. But you see what happens when you get up against a real fightin' man. Sven," said I on a sudden impulse, like I usually do, "far be it from me to see a deep water seaman get beat up regular by a Baltic fish-grabber. It's a reflection on the profession and on the ship. Sven," said I, "I'm goin' to train you to lick this big cheese."

Well, I hadn't never give much thought to Sven before, only in a general way—you can't pay close attention to every square-head which comes and goes aboard a trading ship—but in the weeks which followed I done my best to make a fighting man of him. I rigged up a punching bag for him and sparred with him between watches. When him or me wasn't doing our trick at the wheel or holystoning the deck, or scraping the cable or hauling on a rope, or trimming sail or exchanging insults with the mates, I tried to teach him all I knowed.

Understand, I didn't try to make no boxing wizard outa him. The big slob couldn't of learned even if I could of taught him. And I didn't know how myself. I ain't a clever boxer. I'm a rough and willing mixer in the ring, but compared to such rough-house scrappers as Sven, I'm a wonder. The simple ducking, slipping and blocking, which even the crudest slugger does in the ring, is beyond the ken of the average untrained man, and as for scientific hitting, they never heard of it. They just draw back the right and let it go without any aim, timing nor nothing. Well, I just taught Sven the fundamentals—to stand with his left foot forward and not get his legs crossed, to lead with his left and to time and aim a little. I got him outa the habit of swinging wild and wide open with his right all the time, and by constant drilling I taught him the knack of hooking and hitting straight. I also give him a lot of training to harden his body muscles, which was his weak spot.

Well, the big Swede took to it like a duck takes to water, and after I'd explained each simple move upwards of a thousand times, he'd understand it and apply it and he wouldn't forget. Like lots of square-heads, he was slow to learn, but once he had learned, he remembered what he'd learned. And his great size and strength was a big asset.

Bill O'Brien says, "Steve, you're trainin' the big sap to take your title away from you." But I merely laughed with great merriment at the idee.

Sven had a wallop like a mule's kick in either hand, and when he learned to use it, he was dangerous to any man. He was pretty tough, too, or got so before I got through with him. He wasn't very fast, and I taught him a kind of deep defensive crouch like Jeffries used. He took to it natural and developed a surprising left for the body.

After six months of hard work on him, I felt sure that he could lick the average alley-fighter easy. And about this time we was cruising Baltic waters and headed for Stockholm.

As we approached his native heath, Sven grew impatient and restless. He had a lot more self-confidence now and he craved another chance at Olaf, the demon rival. Sven wasn't just a big unwieldy slob no more. Constant sparring with me and Bill O'Brien had taught him how to handle hisself and how to use his bulk and strength. A few days outa Stockholm he had a row with Mushy Hansen, which was two hundred pounds of fighting man, and he knocked the Dane so cold it took us a hour and a half to bring him to.

Well, that cheered Sven up considerable and when we docked, he said to me: "Aye go see Segrida, my girl, and find out if Olaf bane in port. He bane hang out at dey Fisherman's Tavern. Aye go past with Segrida and he come out and yump on me, like usual. Only diss time Aye bane lick him."

Well, at the appointed time me and Bill and Mushy was loafing around the Fisherman's Tavern, a kind of bar where a lot of tough Swedish fishermen hung out, and pretty soon, along come Sven.

He had his girl with him, all right, a fine, big blonde girl—one of these tall, slender yet well-built girls which is overflowing with health and vitality. She was so pretty I was plumb astounded as to what she seen in a big boob like Sven. But women is that way. They fall for the dubs and pass up the real prizes—like me, for instance.

Segrida looked kind of worried just now and as they neared the Tavern, she cast a apprehensive eye that way. Well, they was abreast of the door when a kind of irritated roar sounded from within and out bulged what could of been nobody but Olaf the Menace, hisself, in person.

THERE WAS A man for you! He was fully as tall as Sven, though not as heavy. Tall, lithe and powerful he was, like a big, blond tiger. He was so handsome I couldst easily see why Segrida hesitated between him and Sven—or rather I couldn't see why she hesitated at all! Olaf looked like one of these here Vikings you read about which rampaged around in old times, licking everybody. But he had a hard, cruel eye, which I reckon goes with that kind of nature.

He had some fellers with him, but they stayed back in the doorway while he swaggered out and stopped square in front of Sven. He had a most contemptuous sneer and he said something which of course I couldn't understand, but as Mushy later translated the conversation to me, I'll give it like Mushy told to me and Bill.

"Well, well," said Olaf, "looking for another licking, eh? Your deep sea boy friend is back in port looking for his usual trouncing, eh, Segrida?"

"Olaf, please," said Segrida, frightened. "Don't fight, please!"

"I warned you what would happen to him," said Olaf, "if you went out with him—"

At this moment Sven, who had said nothing, shocked his bold rival by growling: "Too much talk; put up your hands!"

Olaf, though surprised, immediately done so, and cut Sven's lip with a flashing straight left before the big boy couldst get in position. Segrida screamed but no cops was in sight and the battle was on.

Olaf had learned boxing some place, and was one of the fastest men for his size I ever seen. For the first few seconds he plastered Sven plenty, but from the way the big fellow hunched his shoulders and surged in, I hadst no doubt about the outcome.

Sven dropped into the deep, defensive crouch I'd taught him, and I seen Olaf was puzzled. He hisself fought in the straight-up English sparring position and this was the first time he'd ever met a man who fought American style, I could see. With Sven's crouch protecting his body and his big right arm curved around his jaw, all Olaf couldst see to hit was his eyes glaring over the arm.

He battered away futilely at Sven's hard head, doing no damage whatever, and then Sven waded in and drove his ponderous left to the wrist in Olaf's midriff. Olaf gasped, went white, swayed and shook like a leaf. He sure couldn't take it there and I yelled for Sven to hit him again in the same place, but the big dumb-bell tried a heavy swing for the jaw, half straightening out of his crouch as he swung and Olaf ducked and staggered him with a sizzling right to the ear. Sven immediately went back into his shell and planted another battering-ram left under Olaf's heart.

Olaf broke ground gasping and his knees trembling, but Sven kept right on top of him in his plodding sort of way. Olaf jarred him with a dying-effort swing to the jaw, but them months of punching hadst toughened Sven and the big fellow shook his head and leaned on a right to the ribs.

That finished Olaf; his knees give way and he started falling, grabbing feebly at Sven as he done so. But Sven, with one of the few laughs I ever heard him give, pushed him away and crashed a tremendous right-hander to his jaw. Olaf straightened out on the board-walk and he didn't even quiver.

A LOW RUMBLE of fury warned us and we turned to see Olaf's amazed but wrathful cronies surging towards the victor. But me and Bill and Mushy and Mike kind of drifted in between and at the sight of three hard-eyed American seamen and a harder-eyed Irish bulldog, they stopped short and signified their intention of merely taking Olaf into the Tavern and bringing him to.

At this Sven, grinning placidly and turning to Segrida with open arms, got the shock of his life. Instead of falling on to his manly bosom, Segrida, who hadst stood there like she was froze, woke up all at once and bust into a perfect torrent of speech. I would of give a lot to understand it. Sven stood gaping with his mouth wide open and even the rescue party which had picked up Olaf, stood listening. Then with one grand burst of oratory, she handed Sven a full-armed, open-handed slap that cracked like a bull-whip, and busting into tears, she run forward to help with Olaf. They vanished inside the Tavern.

"What'd she say? What's the idee?" I asked, burnt up with curiosity.

"She say she bane through with me," Sven answered dazedly. "She say Aye bane a brute. She say she ain't bane want to see me no more."

"Well, keel-haul me," said I profanely. "Can ya beat that? First she wouldn't choose Sven because he got licked by Olaf all the time; now she won't have him because he licked Olaf. Women are all crazy."

"Never mind, old timer," said Bill, slapping the dejected Sven on the back. "Anyway, you licked Olaf to a fare-you-well. Come along, and we'll buy you a drink."

But Sven just shook his head sullen-like and moped off by hisself; so after arguing with him unsuccess-fully, me and Bill and Mushy betook ourselves to a place where we couldst get some real whiskey and not the stuff they make in them Scandinavian countries. The barkeep kicked at first because I give my white bulldog, Mike, a pan-full of beer on the floor, but we overcome that objection and fell to talking about Sven.

"I don't savvy dames," I said. "If she gives Sven the bounce for beatin' up Olaf, whyn't she give Olaf the bounce long ago for beatin' up Sven so much?"

"It's Olaf she really loves," said Mushy.

"Maybe," said Bill. "And maybe he's just persistent. But women is kind-hearted. They pities a poor boob which has just got punched in the nose, and as long as Sven was gettin' licked all the time, he got all her pity. But now her pity and affec-tions is transferred to Olaf, naturally."

Well, we didn't see no more of Sven till kind of late that night, when in come one of our square-head ship-mates named Fritz to the bar where me and Bill and Mushy was, and said he: "Steve, Sven he say maybeso you bane come down to a place on Hjolmer Street; he bane got something to show you."

"Now what could that Swede want now?" said Bill testily, but I said, "Oh well, we got nothin' else to do." So we went to Hjolmer Street, a kind of narrow street just out of the waterfront section. It wasn't no particularly genteel place—kind of dirty and dingy for a Swedish street, with little crumby shops along the way, all closed up and deserted that time of night. The square-head, Fritz, led us to a place which was lighted up, though the shutters was closed. He knocked on the door and a short fat Swede opened it and closed it behind us.

To my surprise I seen the place was a kind of third-rate gymnasium. They was a decrepit punching bag, a horizontal bar and a lot of bar-bells, dumb-bells, kettle bells—in fact, all the lifting weights you couldst imagine. They was also a rastling mat and, in the middle of the floor, a canvas covered space about the size of a small ring. And in the middle of this stood Sven, in fighting togs and with his hands taped.

"Who you goin' to fight, Sven?" I asked curiously.

He scowled slightly, flexed his mighty arms kind of embarrassed-like, swelled out his barrel chest and said: "You!"

You could of bowled me over with a jib boom.

"Me?" I said in amazement. "What kind of joke is this?"

"It bane no yoke," he answered stolidly. "Mine friend Knut bane own diss gym and teach rastlin' and weight liftin'. He bane let us fight here."

Knut, a stocky Swede with the massive arms and pot belly of a retired weight lifter, give me a kind of apologetic look, but I glared at him.

"But what you want to fight me for?" I snarled in perplexity. "Ain't I taught you all you know? Didn't I teach you to lick Olaf? You ungrateful—"

"Aye ain't got no grudge for you, Steve," the big cheese answered placidly. "But Aye tank Aye like be champion of dass *Sea Girl*. Aye got to lick you to be it, ain't it? Sure!"

Bill and Mushy was looking at me expectantly, but I was all at sea. After you've worked six months teaching a man your trade and built him up and made something outa him, you don't want to undo it all by rocking him to sleep.

"Why're you so set on bein' champ of the *Sea Girl?*" I asked irritably.

"Well," said the overgrown heathen, "Aye tank Aye lick you and then Aye can lick Olaf, and Segrida she like me. But Aye lick Olaf, and Segrida she give me dass gate. Dass bane your fault, for teach me to lick Olaf. But Aye ain't blame you. Aye like you fine, Steve, but now Aye tank Aye be champ of dass *Sea Girl*. Aye ain't got no girl no more, so Aye got to be something. Aye lick Olaf so Aye can lick you. Aye lick you and be champ and we be good friends, ya?"

"But I don't want to fight you, you big mutton-head!" I snarled in wrathful perplexity.

"Then Aye fight you on the street or the fo'c's'le or wherever Aye meet you," he said cheerfully.

At that my small stock of temper was plumb exhausted. With a blood thirsty howl I ripped off my shirt. "Bring on the gloves, you square-headed ape!" I roared. "If I got to batter some sense into your solid ivory skull I might as well start now!"

A FEW MINUTES later I was clad in a dingy pair of trunks which Knut dragged out of somewhere for me, and we was donning the gloves a set lighter than the standard weight, which Knut hadst probably got as a present from John L. Sullivan or somebody.

We agreed on Bill as referee, but Sven being afraid of Mike, made me agree to have Mushy hold him, though I assured him Mike wouldn't interfere in a glove fight. They was no ropes around the canvas space, no stools nor gong. However, as it happened, they wasn't needed.

As we advanced toward each other I realized more'n ever how much of a man Sven was. Six feet

four—245 pounds—all bone and muscle. He towered over me like a giant, and I musta looked kinda small beside him, though I'm six feet tall and weigh 190 pounds. Under his white skin the great muscles rolled and billowed like flexible iron, and his chest looked more like a gorilla's than a human's.

But size ain't everything. Old Fitz used to flatten men which outweighed him over a hundred pounds, and lookit what Dempsey and Sharkey used to do to such like giants—and I'm as tough as Sharkey and can hit as hard as either of them other palookas, even if I ain't quite as accurate or scientific.

No, I hadst no worries about Sven, but I'd got over being mad at him and I seen his point of view. Sven wasn't sore at me, nor nothing. He just wanted to be champ of his ship, which was a natural wish. Since his girl give him the air, he wanted to more'n ever to kind of soothe his wounded vanity, as they say.

No, I cooled down and kind of sympathized with Sven's point of view which is a bad state of mind to enter into any kind of a scrap. They ain't nothing more helpful than a good righteous anger and a feeling like the other bird is a complete rascal and absolutely in the wrong.

As we come together, Sven said: "No rounds, Steve; we fight to dass finish, yes?"

"All right," I said with very little enthusiasm. "But, Sven, for the last time—have you just got to fight me?"

His reply was a left which he shot for my jaw so sudden like I just barely managed to slip it. I come back with a slashing right which he blocked, clumsy but effective. He then dropped into the deep crouch I'd taught him and rammed his left for my wind. But I knowed the counter to that, having seen pictures of the second Fitzsimmons-Jeffries riot. I stepped around and inside his ramming left, slapping a left uppercut inside the crook of his right arm, to his jaw, cracking his teeth together and rocking his head up and back for a right hook which I opened a gash on his temple with.

He give a deafening roar and immediately abandoned his defensive posture and come for me like a mad bull. I figured, here's where I end this scrap quick, like always. But in half a second I seen my error.

Sven didn't rush wide open, flailing wild, like he used to. He come plunging in, bunched in a compact bulk of iron muscles and fighting fury; he hooked and hit straight, and he kept his chin clamped down on his hairy chest and his shoulders hunched to guard it, half crouching to protect his body. Even the rudiments of boxing science he'd learned, coupled with his enormous size and strength made him plenty formidable to any man.

I don't know how to tin-can and back pedal. If Jeffries hisself was to rush me, all I'd know to do wouldst be to stand up to him and trade punches until I went out cold. I met Sven with a right smash that was high, but stopped him in his tracks. Blood spattered and he swayed like a big tree about to crash, but before I could follow up, he plunged in again, hitting with both hands. He hit and he hit—and—he—hit!

He throwed both hands as fast as he could drive one after the other and every blow had all his weight behind it. Outa the depths of his fighting fit he'd conjured up amazing speed. It happens some time. I never seen a man his size hit that fast before or since. It was just like being in a rain of sledge-hammers that never quit coming. All I couldst see was his glaring eyes, his big shoulders hunched and rocking as he hit—and a perfect whirlwind of big glove-covered clubs.

He wasn't timing or aiming much—hitting too fast for that. But even when he landed glancing-like, he shook me, with that advantage of fifty-five pounds. And he landed solid too often to suit me.

Try as I would, I couldn't get in a solid smash under the heart, or on the jaw. He kept his head down, and my vicious uppercuts merely glanced off his face, too high to do much good. Black and blue bruises showed on his ribs and shoulders, but his awkward half crouch kept his vitals protected.

It's mighty hard to hammer a giant like him out of position—especially when you're trying to keep him from tearing off your head at the same time. I bored in close, letting

Sven's blows go around my neck while I blasted away with both hands. No—they was little science used on either side. It was mostly a wild exchange of sledge-hammer wallops.

In one of our rare clinches, Sven lifted me off my feet and throwed me the full width of the room where I hit the wall—wham!—like I was going on through. This made Bill, as referee, very mad at Sven and he cussed him and kicked him heartily in the pants, but the big cheese never paid no attention.

I WAS LANDING the most blows and they rocked Sven from stem to stern, but they wasn't vital ones. Already his face was beef. One eye was closed, his lips were pulped and his nose was bleeding; his left side was raw, but, if anything, he seemed to be getting stronger. My training hadst toughened him a lot more than I'd realized!

Blim! A glancing slam on my jaw made me see plenty of stars. Wham! His right met the side of my head and I shot back half-way across the room to crash into the wall. Long ago we'd got off the canvas; we was fighting all over the joint.

Sven was after me like a mad bull, and I braced myself and stopped him in his tracks with a left hook that ripped his ear loose and made his knees sag for a second. But the Swede had worked hisself into one

of them berserk rages where you got to mighty near kill a man to stop him. His right, curving up from his hip, banged solid on my temple and I thought for a second my skull was caved in like an egg-shell.

Blood gushed down my neck when he drawed his glove back, and, desperate, I hooked my right to his body with everything I had behind it. I reckon that was when I cracked his rib, because I heard something snap and he kind of grunted.

Both of us was terrible looking by this time and kind of in a dream like, I saw Knut wringing his hands and begging Bill and Mushy and Fritz to stop it—I reckon he'd never saw a real glove battle before and it was so different from lifting weights! Naturally, they, who was clean goggle-eyed and yelling theirselves deaf and dumb, paid no attention to him at all, and so in a second Knut turned and run out into the street like he was going for the cops.

But I paid no heed. For the first time in many a day I was fighting with my back to the wall against one of my own crew. Sven was inhuman—it was like fighting a bull or an elephant. He was landing solid now, and even if them blows was clumsy, with 245 pounds of crazy Swede behind them, they was like the blows of a pile-driver.

He knowed only one kind of footwork—going forward. And he kept plunging and hitting, plunging and hitting till the world was blind and red. I shook my head and the blood flew like spray. The sheer weight of his plunges hurtled me back in spite of myself.

Once more I tried to rock his head up for a solid shot to the jaw. My left uppercut split his lips and rattled his teeth, but his bowed neck was like iron. In desperation I banged him square on the side of the head where his skull was hardest.

Blood spurted like I'd hit him with a hand spike, and he swayed drunkenly—then he dropped into a deep crouch and shot his left to my midriff with all his weight behind it. Judas! It was so unexpected I couldn't get away from it. I was standing nearly upright and that huge fist sank into my solar-plexus till I felt it banged against my spine. I dropped like a sack and writhed on the floor like a snake with a busted back, fighting for air. Bill said later I was purple in the face.

Like I was looking through a thick fog, I seen Bill, dazed and white-faced, counting over me. I dunno how I got up again. I was sick—I thought I was dying. But Sven was standing right over me, and looking up at him, a lot of thoughts surged through my numbed and battered brain in a kind of flash.

The new champion of the *Sea Girl*, I thought, after all these years I've held my title against all comers. After all the men I've fought and licked to hold the only title I got. All the cruel punishment I've took, all the blood I've spilt, now I lose my only title to this square-head that

I've licked half a dozen times. Like a dream it all come back—the dim-lighted, smelly, dingy forecastle, the yelling, cursing seamen—and me in the middle of it all—the bully of the forecastle. And now—never no more to defend my title—never to hear folks along the docks say: "That's Steve Costigan, champ of the toughest ship afloat!"

WITH A KIND of gasping sob, I grabbed Sven's legs and climbed up, up, till I was on my feet, leaning against him chest to chest, till he shook me off and smashed me down like he was driving a nail into the floor. I reeled up just as Bill began to count, and this time I ducked Sven's swing and clinched him with a grip even he couldn't break.

And as I held on and drew in air in great racking gasps, I looked over his straining shoulder and seen Knut come rushing in through the door with a white-faced girl behind him—Segrida. But I was too near out to even realize that Sven's ex-girl was there.

Sven pushed me away finally and dropped me once more with a punch that was more a push than anything else. This time I took the count of nine, resting, as my incredible vitality, the wonder of many the sporting scribe, began to assert itself.

I rose suddenly and beat Sven to the punch with a wild right that smashed his nose. Like most sluggers, I never lose my punch, no matter how badly beaten I am. I'm dangerous right to the last second, as better men than Sven Larson has found out.

Sven wasn't going so strong hisself as he had been. He moved stiff and mechanical and swung his arms awkwardly, like they was dead. He walked in stolidly and smashed a club-like right to my face. Blood spattered and I went back on my heels, but surged in and ripped my right under the heart, landing square there for the first time.

Another right smashed full on Sven's already battered mouth, and, spitting out the fragments of a tooth, he crashed a flailing left to my body, which I distinctly felt bend my ribs to the breaking point.

I ripped a left to his temple, and he flattened my ear with a swinging right, rocking drunkenly like a tall ship in the Trades with all sails set. Another right glanced offa the top of my head as I ducked and for the first time I seen his unguarded jaw as he loomed above me where I crouched.

I straightened, crashing my right from the hip, with every ounce of my weight behind it, and all the drive they was in leg, waist, shoulder and arm. I landed solid on the button with a jolt that burst my glove and numbed my whole arm—I heard a scream—I seen Sven's eyes go blank—I seen him sway like a falling mast—I seen him pitching forward—bang! The lights went out.

I WAS PROPPED up in a chair and Bill was sloshing me with water. I looked around at the dingy gym; then I remember. A queer, sad, cold feeling come over me. I felt old and worn out. After all, I wasn't a boy no more. All the hard, bitter years of fighting the sea and fighting men come over me and settled like a cold cloud on my shoulders. All the life kind of went out of me.

"Believe me, Steve," said Bill, slapping at me with his towel, "that fight sure set Sven solid with Segrida. Right now she's weepin' over his busted nose and black eye and the like, and huggin' him and kissin' him and vowin' everlastin' love. I knowed I was right all the time. Knut run after her to get her to stop the bout. Gosh, the Marines couldn't a stopped it! Mushy clean chawed Mike's collar in two, he was that excited! Say, would you uh thought a slob like Sven coulda made the fightin' man he has in six months?"

"Yeah," I said listlessly, scratching Mike's ear as he licked my hand. "Well, he had it comin'. He worked hard enough. And he was lucky havin' somebody to teach him. All I know, I learned for myself in cruel hard battles. But, Bill, I can't stay on the *Sea Girl* now; I just can't get used to bein' just a contender on a ship where I was champion."

Bill dropped his towel and glared at me: "What you talkin' about?"

"Why, Sven's the new champ of the *Sea Girl*, lickin' me this way.

Strange, what a come-back he made just as I thought he was goin' down."

"You're clean crazy!" snorted Bill. "By golly, a rap on the dome has a funny effect on some skates. Sven's just now comin' to. Mushy and Fritz and Knut has been sloshin' him with water for ten minutes. You knocked him stiff as a wedge with that last right hook."

I come erect with a bound! "What? Then I licked Sven? I'm still champion? But if he didn't knock me out, who did?"

Bill grinned. "Don't you know no man can hit you hard enough with his fist to knock you out? Swedish girls is impulsive. Segrida done that—with a iron dumb-bell!"

ALLEYS *of* PERIL.

ALTERNATE TITLE: LEATHER LIGHTNING.

This short story was first published in the January 1931 issue of Fight Stories *magazine.*

THE MINUTE I seen the man they'd picked to referee the fight between me and Red McCoy, I didn't like his looks. His name was Jack Ridley and he was first mate aboard the *Castleton*, one of them lines which acts very high tone, making their officers wear uniforms. Bah! The first cap'n I ever sailed with never wore nothing at sea but a pair of old breeches, a ragged undershirt and a month's growth of whiskers. He used to say uniforms was all right for navy admirals and bell-hops but they was a superflooity anywheres else.

Well, this Ridley was a young fellow, slim and straight as a spar, with cold eyes and a abrupt manner. I seen right off that he was a bucko which wouldn't even let his crew shoot craps on deck if he could help it. But I decided not to let his appearance get on my nerves, but to ignore him and knock McCoy stiff as quick

105

as possible so I couldst have the rest of the night to myself.

They is a old feud between the *Sea Girl* and McCoy's ship, the *Whale*. The minute the promoter of the Waterfront Fight Arena heard both our ships had docked, he rushed down and signed us up for a fifteen-round go—billed it as a grudge fight, which it wasn't nothing but, and packed the house.

The crews of both ships was holding down ringside seats and the special police was having a merry time keeping 'em from wrecking the place. The Old Man was rared back on the front row and ever few seconds he'd take a long swig out of a bottle, and yell: "Knock the flat-footed ape's lousy head off, Steve!" And then he'd shake his fist across at Cap'n Branner of the *Whale*, and the compliments them two old sea horses wouldst exchange wouldst have curled a Hottentot's hair.

You can judge by this that the Waterfront Fight Arena is kinda free and easy in its management. It is. It caters to a rough and ready class, which yearns for fast action, in the ring or out. Its performers is mostly fighting sailors and longshoremen, but, if you can stand the crowd that fills the place, you'll see more real mayhem committed there in one evening than you'll see in a year in the politer clubs of the world.

Well, it looked like every sailor in Hong Kong was there that night. Finally the announcer managed to make hisself heard above the howls of the mob, and he bellered: "The main attrackshun of the evenin'! Sailor Costigan, one hunnerd an' ninety pounds, of the *Sea Girl*—"

"The trimmest craft afloat!" roared the Old Man, heaving his empty bottle at Cap'n Branner.

"And Red McCoy, one hunnerd an' eighty-five pounds, of the *Whale*," went on the announcer, being used to such interruption. "Referee, First Mate Ridley of the steamship Castleton, the management havin' requested him to officiate this evenin'. Now, gents, this is a grudge fight, as you all know. You has seen both these boys perform, an'—"

"And if you don't shut up and give us some action we'll wreck the dump and toss your mangled carcass amongst the ruins!" screamed the maddened fans. "Start somethin' before we do!"

The announcer smiled gently, the gong sounded, and me and Red went together like a couple of wild-cats. He was a tough baby, one of them squat, wide-built fellows. I'm six feet; he was four inches shorter, but they wasn't much difference in our weight. He was tough and fast, with one of these here bulldog faces, and how that sawed-off brick-top could hit!

Well, nothing much of interest happened in the first three rounds. Of course, we was fighting hard, neither of us being clever, but both strong on mixing it. But we was both too tough to show much damage that early in the fight. He'd cut my lip and skinned my ear and loosened some teeth, and I'd dropped him for no-count a couple of times, but outside of that nothing much had happened.

We'd stood toe-to-toe for three rounds, flailing away right and left and neither giving back a step, but, just before the end of the third, my incessant body punching began to show even on that chunk of granite they called Red McCoy. For the first time he backed out of a mix-up, and just before the gong I caught him with a swinging right to the belly that made him grunt and bat his eyes.

S O I COME out for the fourth round full of snap and ginger and promptly run into a right hook that knocked me flat on my back. The crowd went crazy, and the *Whale's* men begun to kiss each other in their ecstasy, but I arose without a count and, ducking the cruel and unusual right swing McCoy tossed at me, I sunk my left to the wrist in his belly and crashed my right under his heart.

This shook Red from stem to stern and, realizing that my body blows was going to beat him if he didn't do something radical, he heaved over a hay-making right with everything he had behind it. It had murder writ all over it, and when it banged solid on my ear so you could hear it all over the house, the crowd jumped up and yelled: "There he goes!" But I'm a glutton for punishment if I do say so, and I merely

tittered amusedly, shook my head to clear it, and caressed Red with a left hook that broke his nose.

The baffled look on his face caused me to bust into hearty laughter, in the midst of which Red closed my left eye with a right-hander he started in Mesopotamia. Enraged for the first time that night, I rammed a blasting left hook to his midriff, snapped his head back between his shoulders with another left, and sank my terrible right mauler to the wrist in his belly just above the waist-line.

He immediately went to the canvas like he figured on staying there indefinitely, and his gang jumped up and yelled "Foul!" till I bet they was plainly heard in Bombay. They knowed it wasn't no foul, but when Red heard 'em, he immediately put both hands over his groin and writhed around like a snake with a busted back.

The referee came over, and as I stood smiling amusedly to hear them howl about fouls, I suddenly noticed he wasn't counting.

"Say, you, ain't you goin' to count this ham out?" I asked.

"Shut up, you cad!" he snapped to my utter amazement. "Get out of this ring. You're disqualified!"

And while I gaped at him, he helped Red to his feet and raised his hand.

"McCoy wins on a foul!" he shouted. The crowd sat speechless for a second and then went into hysterics. The Old Man went for the *Whale's* skipper, the two crews pitched in free and hearty, the rest of the crowd took sides and began to bash noses, and Red's handlers started working over him. The smug look he give me and the wink he wunk, drove me clean cuckoo. I grabbed Ridley's shoulder as he started through the ropes.

"You double-crossin' louse," I ground. "You can't get away with that! You know that wasn't no foul!"

"Take your hands off me," he snapped. "You deliberately hit low, Costigan."

"You're a liar!" I roared, maddened, and crack come his fist in my mouth quick as lightning, and I hit the canvas on the seat of my trunks. Before I could hop up, a bunch of men pounced on me and held me whilst I writhed and yelled and cussed till the air was blue.

"I'll get you for this!" I bellered. "I'll take you apart and scatter the pieces to the sharks, you gyppin', lyin', thievin' son of a skunk!"

He looked down at me very scornful. "A fine specimen of sportsmanship you are," he sneered, and his tongue cut me like a keen knife. "Keep out of my way, or I'll give you a belly-full of what you want. Let him loose—I'll handle him!"

"Handle him my eye!" said one of the fellows holding me. "Get outa here while gettin's good. They ain't but ten of us settin' on him and we're givin' out. Either beat it or get seven or eight other birds to help hold him!"

He laughed kind of short, and, climbing from the ring, strode out of the building between rassling, slugging and cursing groups of bellering fans, many of which was yellin' for his blood. Funny how some men can get by with anything. Here was hundreds of tough birds which was raving mad at Ridley, yet he just looked 'em in the eye and they give back and let him past. Good thing for him, though, that my white bulldog Mike was too busy licking Cap'n Branner's police dog to go for him.

WELL, EVENTUALLY THE cops had things quieted, separated the dogs and even pried the Old Man and Cap'n Branner apart, with their hands full of whiskers they had tore off each other.

I didn't take no part in the rough-house. As quick as I could get dressed and put some collodion on my cuts, I slipped out the back way by myself. I even left Mike with Bill O'Brien because I didn't want him interfering and chewing up my man; I wanted nobody but me to get hold of Mister Jack Ridley and beat him into a red hash. He wasn't going to cow me with the cold stare of his eyes, because I was going to close both of 'em.

Honest to cats, I dunno when I ever been so mad in my life. I was sure he'd deliberately jobbed me and throwed the fight to McCoy, and what was worse, he'd slugged me in the face and got away with it. A red haze swum in front of me and I growled deep black curses which made people stop and stare at me as I swaggered along the waterfront streets.

After a while I seen a barkeep I knowed and I asked him if he'd seen Ridley.

"No," said he, "but if you're after him, I'll give you a tip. Lay off him. He's a hard man to fool with."

That only made me madder. "I'll lay off him," I snarled, "after I've made hash for the fishes outa him, the dirty, double-crossin', thievin' rat! I'll—"

At this minute the barkeep commenced to shine glasses like he was trying for a record, and I turned around to see a girl standing just behind me. She was a white girl and she was a beauty. Her face very white, all except her red lips and her hair was blacker than mine. Her eyes was deep and a light gray, shaded by heavy lashes. And them eyes was the tip-off. At first glance she mighta been a ordinary American flapper, but no flapper ever had eyes like them. They was deep but they was hard. They was yellow sparks of light dancing in them, and I had a funny feeling that they'd shine in the dark like a cat's.

"You were speaking of Mr. Jack Ridley, of the Castleton?" she asked.

"Yeah, I was, Miss," I said, dragging off my ragged old cap.

"Who are you?"

"Steve Costigan, A. B. mariner

aboard the trader *Sea Girl*, outa San Francisco."

"You hate Ridley?"

"Well, to be frank, I ain't got no love for him," I said. "He just robbed me of a fight I won fair and square."

She eyed me for a minute. I ain't no beauty. In fact, I been told by my closest enemies that I look more like a gorilla than a human being. But she seemed plenty satisfied.

"Come into the back room," she said, and, to the bartender: "Send us a couple of whisky-and-sodas."

In the back room, as we sipped our drinks, she said, "You hate Ridley, eh? What would you do to him if you could?"

"Anything," I said bitterly. "Hangin's too good for a rat like him."

She rested her elbows on the table and her chin in her hands, and, looking into my eyes, she said, "Do you know who I am?"

"Yeah," I answered. "I ain't never seen you before, but you couldn't be nobody else but the girl the Chinese call the 'White Tigress.'"

Her narrow eyes glittered a little and she nodded.

"Yes. And would you like to know what drove a decent white girl into the shadows of the Orient—made an innocent, trusting child into one of a band of international criminals, and the leader of desperate tongmen? Well, I'll tell you in a few words. It was the heartlessness of a man—the man who took me from my home in England, lied to me, deceived me, and finally left me to the tender mercies of a yellow mandarin in interior China."

I shuffled my feet kind of restless; I felt sorry for her and didn't know what to say. She leaned toward me, her voice dropped almost to whisper, while her eyes burned into mine: "The man who betrayed and deserted me was the man who robbed you tonight—Jack Ridley!"

"Why, the low-down swine!" I ejaculated.

"I, too, want revenge," she breathed. "We can be useful to each other. I will send a note to Ridley asking him to come to a certain place in the Alley of Rats. He will come. There you will meet him. There will be no one to hold you this time."

I grinned—kinda wolfishly, I reckon. "Leave the rest to me."

"No one will ever know," she murmured, which kind of puzzled me. "Hong Kong's waterfront has many secrets and many mysteries. I will send a man with you to guide you to the place. Then, come to me here tomorrow night; I can use you. A man like you need not work away his life on a trading schooner."

She clapped her hands. A Chinaboy come in. She spoke to him in the language for a minute, and he bowed and beat it. She arose: "I am going now. In a few minutes your guide will come. Do as he says. Good luck to you; may you avenge us both."

S HE GLIDED OUT and left me sitting there sipping my licker and wondering what it was all about. I'd heard of the White Tigress; who in China ain't? A white girl who had more power amongst the yellow boys than the Chinese government did. Who was she? How come her to get so much pull? Them as knowed didn't say. That she was a international crook she'd just admitted. Some said she was a pirate on the sly; some said she was the secret wife of a big mandarin; some said she was a spy for a big European power. Anyway, nobody knowed for sure, but everybody agreed that anybody which crossed her was outa luck.

Well, I set there and guzzled my licker, and pretty soon in come the meanest, scrawniest looking piece uh humanity I ever seen. A ragged, dirty shrimp he was, with a evil, furtive face.

"Bli'me, mate," said he, "le's be up and doin'. It's a nice night's work we got ahead of us."

"Suits me," said I, and I follered him out of the saloon by a side door into the nasty, dimly lighted streets, and through twisty alleys which wasn't lighted at all. They stunk like sin and I couldst hear the stealthy rustling noises which always goes on in such places. Rats, maybe, but if a yellow-faced ghost hadda jumped around my neck, I wouldn'ta been surprised a bit.

Well, the cockney seemed to

know his way, though my sense of direction got clean bumfuzzled. At last he opened a door and I follered him into a squalid, ramshackle room which was as dark as the alleys. He struck a light and lit a candle on a rough table. They was chairs there, and he brought out a bottle. A door opened out of the room into some other part of the place, I guess; the windows was heavily barred and I saw a trap door in the middle of the floor. I could hear the slow, slimy waves sucking and lapping under us, and I knowed the house was built out over the water.

"Mate," said the Cockney, after we'd finished about half the bottle, "it comes to me that we're a couple o' blightin' idjits to be workin' for a skirt."

"What d'ya mean?" I asked, taking a pull at the bottle.

"Well, 'ere's us, two red-blooded 'e-men, takin' orders from a lousy little frail, 'andin' the swag h'over to 'er, and takin' wot she warnts to 'and us, w'en we could 'ave the 'ole lot. Take this job 'ere now—"

I stared at him. "I don't get you."

He glanced around furtive-like, and lowered his voice: "Mate, let's cop the sparkler for ourselves and shove out! We can get back to Hengland or the States and live like blurry lords for a while. Hi'm sick o' this bloody dump."

"Say, you," I snarled, "what'r you drivin' at? What sparkler?"

"W'y, lorlumme," said he, "the sparkler we takes off Mate Ridley afore we dumps his carcass through that trapdoor."

"Hold everything!" I was up on my feet, all in a muddle. "I didn't contract to do no murder."

"Wot!" said the Cockney. "Bli'me! The Tigress says as you was yearnin' for Ridley's gore!"

'Well, I am," I growled, "but she didn't get my meanin'. I didn't mean I wanted to kill him, though, come to think about it, it mighta sounded like it. But I ain't no murderer, though killin' is what he needs after the way he treated that poor kid. When he comes through that door, I'm goin' to hammer him within a inch of his life, understand, but they ain't goin' to be no murder done— not tonight. You can bump him later, if you want to. But you got to let me pound him first, and I ain't goin' to be in on no assassination."

"But we got to finish him," argued the Cockney, "or him and To Yan will have all the bobbies in the world after us."

"Say," I said, "the Tigress didn't say nothin' about no jewel nor no To Yan. What's they got to do with it? She said Ridley brung her into China and left her flat—"

"Banan orl!" sneered the Cockney. "She was spoofin' you proper, mate. Ridley never even seen 'er. Hi dunno 'ow she got into so much power in China myself, but she's got somethin' on a mandarin and a clique o' government officials. She's been a crook ever since she was big enough to steal the blinkin' paint orf 'er bloomin' cradle.

"Listen to me, mate, and we 'ands 'er the double-cross proper. I wasn't to spill this to you, y'understand. I was to cop the sparkler after you'd bumped Ridley, and say nuthin' to you about it, see? But Hi'm sick o' takin' orders orf the 'ussy.

"Old To Yan, the chief of the Yan Tong, 'as a great fancy to Ridley. Fact is, Ridley's old man and the old Chinee 'as been close friends for years. Right now, To Yan's oldest darter is in Hengland gettin' a Western eddication. Old To Yan's that progressive and hup to the times. Well, it's the yellow girl's birthday soon, and To Yan's sendin' 'er a birthday present as would make your heyes bug out. Bli'me! It's the famous Ting ruby, worth ten thousand pounds—maybe more. Old To Yan give it to Jack Ridley to take to the girl, bein' as Ridley's ship weighs anchor for Hengland tomorrer. I dunno 'ow the Tigress found hout habout it, but that's wot she's hafter."

"I see," said I, grinding my teeth. "I was the catspaw, hey? She handed me a line to rub me up to do her dirty work. She thought I wanted to bump Ridley, anyway. Why'n't she have some of her own thugs do it?"

"That's the blightin' smoothness o' 'er," said the Cockney. "Why risk one o' her own men on a job like that, w'en 'ere was a tough sailor sizzlin' for the blinkin' hopportunity? She really thought you was wantin' to bump Ridley; she didn't know you just warnted to beat 'im hup. If you'd

bumped 'im and got caught, she wouldn't a been connected with it, so's it could be proved, because you ain't one o' 'er regular men. She thought you was the right man for the job, anyway, because, mate, if Hi may say so, you looks like a natural-born murderer. But look 'ere—let's cross 'er, and do the trick hon our hown."

"Not a chance," I snapped. "Unlock that door and let me out!"

"Let you hout to squeal hon me," he whined, a red light beginning to gleam in his little rat eyes. "Not me, says you! Watch hout, you Yankee swine—!"

I saw the flash of his knife as he came at me, and I kicked a chair into his legs; and while he was spitting curses like a cat and trying to untangle hisself, I bent my right on his jaw and he took the count.

WITH SCARCELY A glance at his recumbent form, I twisted the lock off the door and stalked forth into the darkness. I groped around in a lot of twisty back alleys for a while, expecting any minute to get a knife in my back or fall into the bay, but finally I blundered into a narrow street which was dimly lit and soon found myself back in a more civilized portion of the waterfront. And a few minutes later who do I see emerging from a saloon but a man I recognized as a stoker aboard the Castleton.

"Hey, you," I accosted him

politely, "where is that lousy first mate of yours?"

"Try and find out, you bone-headed mick," he answered rudely. "What d'ya think uh that?"

"Chew on this awhile," I growled, clouting him heartily in the mush, and for a few seconds a merry time was had by all. But pretty quick I smashed a right hook under his heart that took all the fight out of him, along with his wind.

Having brung him to by a liberal deluge of water from a nearby horse trough, I said: "All right, if you got to be so stubborn you won't answer a civil question, I won't insist. But lemme tell you somethin', and you can pass it on to that four-flushin' mate—when I get my hands on him, I'm goin' make him eat that foul decision. And say, you better find him and tell him that if he keeps packin' around what To Yan give him, he's goin' to lose it, along with his life. He'll understand what I mean. And tell him to stay away from the Alley of Rats, if he ain't already gone there."

Well, it was mighty late by this time. The streets was nearly deserted, even them which usually has a crowd of revelers on 'em all night. I was sleepy, but knowing that the Castleton was sailing the next morning, I took one more stroll around, hoping to run onto the mate. I was sure he hadn't gone aboard yet, because he always spent his nights ashore when he could.

After hunting for maybe an hour or more, I was about to give it up. I was passing a dark alleyway when something come slipping out, looking like a slim white ghost. It was the White Tigress.

"Wait a minute, Costigan," she said, as friendly as you please. "May I speak to you just a moment?"

"You got a nerve, Miss," I said reproachfully, "after the bunk you handed me—"

"Ah, don't be angry at me," she cooed, patting my arm. "Forget it. I'll make it up to you, if you'll just come with me. You're the kind of a man I admire."

I'm the prize boob of the Asiatics. I follered her along the little, dark, smelly alley, through an arched doorway and into a kind of small court, lighted by smoky lamps. Then she turned on me and I got a chill.

Boy, all the cat-spirit in her eyes was up and blazing. Her face was whiter than ever, her red lips writhed into a snarl, and of all the concentrated venom I ever seen flaming out of a woman's eyes, it was there! Murder, destruction, torture, sudden death and damnation she looked at me.

"I reckon maybe I better be going Miss," I said, kind of nervous. "It's gettin' late and the Old Man'll be expectin' me back—"

"Stand where you are!" she said in a voice so low it was almost a whisper.

"But the cook may be drunk and I'll have to make breakfast for the crew!" I said wildly, beginning to get desperate.

"Shut up, you fool!" she exclaimed in a voice which plumb shook with passion. "I'll fix you, you dumb, imbecilic, boneheaded, double-crossing beast! It was you who warned Ridley, wasn't it? And he ditched the ruby and never showed up at the Alley of Rats. It was just by pure luck that we got him at all. But he'll tell what he did with the gem before we get through with him. And as for you—"

She stopped a minute and her eyes ran up and down my huge frame gloatingly; she actually licked her lips like a cat over a mouse.

"When I finish with you, you'll have learned not to interfere with my affairs," she added, taking a long, thin raw-hide whip from somewhere and flicking it through the air. "I'm going to lash you within an inch of your life," she announced. "You won't be the first, either. I'm going to flay you and cut you to pieces. I'm going to whip you until you're a blind, whimpering, writhing mass of raw flesh."

"Now listen, Miss," I said, with quiet dignity, "I like to oblige a lady but they is such a thing as carryin' curtesy too far. I ain't goin' to let you even touch me with that cat."

"I didn't suppose you would," she sneered, "so I provided for that." She clapped her hands and into the courtyard from nowhere come five big Chinese. They was big, too; the smallest was larger than me and the biggest looked more like a elephant than a man. They come for me from all sides like shadows.

"Grab him, boys," she snapped in English, and I give a wolfish grin. I was plumb at ease now I had men to deal with. They was reaching for me when I went into action. A trained fighter can clean up a roomful of white civilians—and a Chinee can't take a punch. Quick as a flash I threw my whole shoulder-weight behind the left I smashed into the yellow map of the one in front of me; blood spattered and he sagged down, out cold. The next instant the rest was on me like a pack of wolves, but I whirled, ducking under a pair of arms and dropping the owner with a right hook to the heart. For the next few seconds it was a kind of whirlwind of flailing arms and legs, with me as the center.

At first they tried to capture me alive, but, being convinced of the futility of this endeavor, they tried to kill me. A knife licked along my arm, and the sting of the wound maddened me. With a roar, I crashed my right down on the neck of the Chinee which had me around the legs, driving him against the ground so hard his face splattered like a tomato. Then, reaching back and getting a good hold on the yellow boy which was both strangling me from behind and trying to knife me, I tossed him over my head. He hit on his neck and didn't get up. I then ducked a hatchet swiped at me by the biggest of the gang, and, rising on my toes, I reached his jaw and crashed him with a torrid left hook. I didn't need to hit him again.

THE FIGHT HAD took maybe a minute and a half. I glanced scornfully at the prostrate figures of my victims, and then looked around for the Tigress. She was crouched back in a angle of the wall, with a kind of stunned look in her eyes, the whip dangling from her limp fingers. She give me one horrified look and shuddered and murmured something about a gorilla.

"Well," I said, kind of sarcastic, "it don't look like they is goin' to be no whippin' tonight—or have you got some more hatchet-men hid away somewheres? If you have, trot 'em out. Action is what I crave."

"Great heavens," she murmured, "are you human? Do you realize that you've just laid out five professional murderers? And—and—what are you going to do with me?"

Seeing that she was scared gave me a idea. Maybe I could make her tell something about Ridley.

"You come with me," I growled, and taking her arm, I marched her out of the courtyard by another way, until we come to another courtyard similar to the one we'd left, but open enough so I couldst see if anybody tried to slip up on me. Spite of what she'd did, I felt kind of ashamed of myself, because if I ever seen a scared girl, it was the White Tigress. Her knees knocked together and she

looked like she thought I'd eat her. When she thought I wasn't looking, she dropped the whip like it was hot, giving me a most guilty glance. I reckon she thought maybe I'd use it on her, and I felt clean insulted.

"Where's Jack Ridley?" I asked her, and she named a place I'd never heard of.

"Don't hit me," she begged, though I never hit a woman and hadst made not the slightest threatening motion at her. "I'll tell you about it. I sent the note to Ridley and waited for the Cockney to come and report to me. He had orders to hide you in a safe place after you'd turned the trick, and then come back and tell me about it. But after a while the Cockney turned up with a welt on his jaw, and said you'd balked on the job. He said you knew about the ruby somehow and that you proposed that you and he kill Ridley, take the stone and skip—"

"Aha," thought I to myself, "I bet he lied hisself into a jam!"

"—but I realized that you couldn't have known about it unless he told you, so I laid into him with the raw-hide and pretty soon he admitted that he let it slip about the ruby. But he said you wanted him to double-cross me, and he wouldn't do it, and you knocked him out and left. He said that after he came to he waited a while, intending to kill Ridley himself, but the mate never showed up. I knew the Cockney was lying about part of it, at least, but I believed him when he said that likely you had killed Ridley yourself and skipped. I started my gang out looking for you, but they caught Ridley instead. It was just by chance.

"They brought him to the hang-out and we searched him, but he didn't have the ruby on him and he wouldn't tell what he'd done with it. We did worm it out of him that he was on his way to the Alley of Rats in answer to the note he got, when a stoker on his ship met him and warned him to keep away. While we were getting ready to make him talk, one of my boys brought me word that he'd just seen you on the streets, and I thought I'd settle the score between us. I'm sorry; I'll never try it again. What are you going to do with me?"

"How do I know you're tellin' the truth?" I asked.

She shuddered. "I'd be afraid to lie to you. You're the only man I ever saw that I was afraid of. Don't be angry—but I saw a gorilla kill six or seven niggers on the West African Coast once, and, when you were fighting those China-boys, you looked just like him."

I was too offended to say anything for a second, and she kind of whimpered: "Please, what are you going to do with me? Please let me go!"

"I'm goin' to let you take me to where you got Jack Ridley," I growled, mopping the blood off my cut arm, and working it so it wouldn't get stiff. "I got a account to settle with the big cheese—and you ain't goin' to

torture no Americans while I can stand on my two feet. Lead the way!"

WELL, I'D OF been in a jamb if she'd refused, because I don't know what I coulda done to make her— it just ain't in me to be rough with no women—but my bluff worked. She didn't argue at all. She led me out of the courtyard, down three or four narrow, deserted streets, across a bunch of back alleys, and finally through a narrow doorway.

Here she stopped. The room was very dimly lighted by a street lamp that burned just outside and through the cracks in the wall I could see they was a light in the room beyond.

I had my hand on her arm, just so she wouldn't try to give me the slip, but I guess she thought I'd wring her neck if she crossed me, because she whispered: "Ridley's in there, but there's a gang of men with him."

"How many and who all are they?" I whispered.

"Smoky and Squint-Eye and Snake and the Dutchman; and then there's Wladek and—"

Just then I heard a nasty voice rise that I recognized as belonging to the said Smoky—a shady character but one which I hadn't known was mixed up in the Tigress game: "Orl right, you bloody Yank, we'll see wot you says after we've touched yer up a bit wiv a 'ot h'iron, eh, mates?"

I let go the girl's arm and slid to

the door, soft and easy. And then I found out the Tigress wasn't near as scared as she'd pretended, because she jumped back and yelled: "Look out, boys!"

Secrecy being now out of the question, the best thing was to get in the first punch. I hit that door like a typhoon and crashed right through it. I had a fleeting glimpse of a smoky lamp in a bracket on the wall, of a rope-wrapped figure on a bunk and a ring of startled, evil faces.

"Ow, murder!" howled somebody I seen was the Cockney. "It's that bloody sailor again!" And he dived through the nearest window.

In that room they was a Chinee, a Malay, a big Russian and six thugs which was a mixed mess of English, Dutch and American. As I come through the door, I slugged the big Russian on the jaw and finished him for the evening, and grabbing the Chinee and the Malay by their necks, I disposed of them by slammin' their heads together. Then the rest of the merry men rose up and come down on me like a wolf on the fold, and the real hilarity commenced.

It was just a whirlwind. Fists, boots, bottles and chairs! And a few knives and brass knuckles throwed in for good measure. We romped all over the room and busted the chairs and shattered the table, and it was while I was on the floor, on top of three of them while the other three was dancing a horn-pipe on me, that I got hold of a heavy chair-leg. Shaking off my assailants for a instant, I arose and smote Dutchy over the head with a joyous abandon that instantly reduced the number of my foes to five. Another swat broke Snake's arm, and at that moment a squint-eyed yegg ran in and knifed me in the ribs. I give a roar of irritation and handed him one that finished him and the chair-leg simultaneous.

At this moment a red-headed thug laid my scalp open with a pair of brass knuckles, and Smoky planted his hob-nailed boots in my ribs so hard it put me on my back again, where the survivors leaped on me with howls of delirious joy. But I was far from through, though rather breathless.

Biting a large hunk out of the thumb a scar-faced beachcomber tried to shove in my eyes, I staggered up again. Doing this meant lifting Smoky too, as he was on my back, industriously gnawing my ear. With a murmur of resentment, I shook him off and flattened him with a right-handed smash that broke three ribs; and, ducking the chair Scar-Face swung at me, I crashed him with a left that smashed his nose and knocked out all his front teeth.

Red-Head was still swinging at me with the brass knuckles, and he contrived to gash my jaw pretty deep before I broke his jaw with a hay-making right swing. As the poem says, the tumult and the clouting died, and, standing panting in the body-littered room, I shook the blood and sweat outa my eyes and glared around for more thugs to conquer.

But I was the only man on his feet. I musta been a sight. All my clothes was tore off except my pants, and they wasn't enough of them left to amount to anything. I was bleeding from a dozen cuts. I was bruised all over and I had another black eye to go with the one McCoy had give me earlier in the evening. I looked around for Ridley and seen him lying on the bunk where he was tied up, staring at me like he'd never seen a critter like me before. I looked for the Tigress but she was gone.

SO I WENT over and untied Ridley, and he never said a word; acted like he was kinda stunned. He worked his fingers and glanced at the victims on the floor, some of which was groaning and cussing, and some of which was slumbering peaceful.

"Gettin' the circulation back in your hands?" I asked, and he nodded.

"All right," said I, "Put up your mitts; I'm goin' to knock you into the middle of Kingdom Come."

"Good Lord, man," he cried, "you've saved my life—and you mean you want to fight me?"

"What the hell did you think?" I roared. "Think I come around to thank you for jobbin' me out of a rightful decision? I never fouled nobody in my life!"

"But you're in no shape to fight now!" he exclaimed. "You've just whipped a roomful of men and taken more punishment than I thought any human being could take, and live! You're bleeding like a stuck hog. Both your eyes are half-closed, your lips are pulped, your scalp's laid open, one of your ears is mangled, and you've got half a dozen knife cuts on you. I saw one of those fellows stab you in the ribs—"

"Aw, it just slid along 'em," I said. "If you think I'm marked up, you oughta seen me after I went fifteen rounds to a draw with Iron Mike Brennon. But listen, that ain't neither here nor there. You ain't as big as I am, but you got the reputation of a fighter. Now you put up your mitts like a man."

Instead, he dropped his hands to his sides. "I won't fight you. Not after what you've just done for me. Do you realize that you've burst into the secret den of the most dangerous crook in China—and cleaned up nine of her most desperate gangmen, practically bare-handed?"

"But what about that foul?" I asked petulantly.

"I was wrong," he said. "I was standing behind McCoy and didn't really get a good look at the blow you dropped him with. Honestly, it looked low to me, and when McCoy began to writhe around on the canvas, I thought you had fouled him. But if you did, it wasn't intentional. A man like you wouldn't deliberately hit another fighter low. You didn't even hit these thugs below the belt, though God knows you had every right. Now then, I apologize for that foul decision, and for hitting you, and for what I said to you. If you want to take a swing at me anyway, I won't blame you, but I'm not going to fight you."

He looked at me with steady eyes and I seen he wasn't afraid of me, or handing me no bluff. And, somehow, I was satisfied.

"Well," I said, mopping the blood off my scalp, "that's all right. I just wanted you to know I don't fight foul. Now let's get outa here. Say—the White Tigress was here with me—where'd she go, do you reckon?"

"I don't know. And I don't want to know. If I don't see her again, it will be soon enough. It must have been she who sent me that note earlier in the night."

"It was. And I don't understand, if you was goin' to do what it said, why it took you so long. You shoulda been at the Alley of Rats before the stoker had time to find you and give you my warnin'."

"Well," he said, "I hesitated for nearly an hour after getting the note, as to whether I'd go or not, but finally decided I would. But I left the To Yan ruby with the captain. On the way, the stoker met me and gave me your tip, which he didn't understand but thought I ought to know nevertheless. So I didn't go to the Alley of Rats, but later on a gang jumped me, tied me up and brought me here. And say, how is it that you're mixed up in all this?"

"It's a long story," I said, as we come out into one of the politer streets, "and—"

"And just now you need those cuts and bruises dressed. Come with me and I'll attend to that. You can tell me all about it while I bandage you."

"All right," I said, "but let's make it snappy 'cause I got business."

"Got a girl in this port, have you?"

"Naw," I said. "I think I can find the promoter of the Waterfront Fight Arena at his saloon about now, and I want to ask him to get Red McCoy to fight me at the Arena again tomorrow night."

The TNT PUNCH.

ALTERNATE TITLE: THE WATERFRONT WALLOP.

This short story was first published in the January 1931 issue of Action Stories *magazine.*

THE FIRST THING that happened in Cape Town, my white bulldog Mike bit a policeman and I had to come across with a fine of ten dollars, to pay for the cop's britches. That left me busted, not more'n an hour after the *Sea Girl* docked.

The next thing who should I come on to but Shifty Kerren, manager of Kid Delrano, and the crookedest leather-pilot which ever swiped the gate receipts. I favored this worthy with a hearty scowl, but he had the everlasting nerve to smile welcomingly and hold out the glad hand.

"Well, well! If it ain't Steve Costigan! Howdy, Steve!" said the infamous hypocrite. "Glad to see you. Boy, you're lookin' fine! Got good old Mike with you, I see. Nice dawg."

He leaned over to pat him.

"Grrrrrr!" said good old Mike, fixing for to chaw his hand. I pushed Mike away with my foot and said to

121

Shifty, I said: "A big nerve you got, tryin' to fraternize with me, after the way you squawked and whooped the last time I seen you, and called me a dub and all."

"Now, now, Steve!" said Shifty. "Don't be foolish and go holdin' no grudge. It's all in the way of business, you know. I allus did like you, Steve."

"Gaaahh!" I responded ungraciously. I didn't have no wish to hobnob none with him, though I figgered I was safe enough, being as I was broke anyway.

I've fought that palooka of his twice. The first time he outpointed me in a ten-round bout in Seattle, but didn't hurt me none, him being a classy boxer but kinda shy on the punch.

Next time we met in a Frisco ring, scheduled for fifteen frames. Kid Delrano give me a proper shellacking for ten rounds, then punched hisself out in a vain attempt to stop me, and blowed up. I had him on the canvas in the eleventh and again in the twelfth and with the fourteenth a minute to go, I rammed a right to the wrist in his solar plexus that put him down again. He had sense enough left to grab his groin and writhe around.

And Shifty jumped up and down and yelled: "Foul!" so loud the referee got scared and rattled and disqualified me. I swear it wasn't no foul. I landed solid above the belt line. But I officially lost the decision and it kinda rankled.

SO NOW I GLOWERED at Shifty and said: "What you want of me?"

"Steve," said Shifty, putting his hand on my shoulder in the old comradely way his kind has when they figger on putting the skids under you, "I know you got a heart of gold! You wouldn't leave no feller countryman in the toils, would you? Naw! Of course you wouldn't! Not good old Steve. Well, listen, me and the Kid is in a jam. We're broke—and the Kid's in jail.

"We got a raw deal when we come here. These Britishers went and disqualified the Kid for merely bitin' one of their ham-and-eggers. The Kid didn't mean nothin' by it. He's just kinda excitable thataway."

"Yeah, I know," I growled. "I got a scar on my neck now from the rat's fangs. He got excitable with me, too."

"Well," said Shifty hurriedly, "they won't let us fight here now, and we figgered on movin' upcountry into Johannesburg. Young Hilan is tourin' South Africa and we can get a fight with him there. His manager—er, I mean a promoter there—sent us tickets, but the Kid's in jail. They won't let him out unless we pay a fine of six pounds. That's thirty dollars, you know. And we're broke.

"Steve," went on Shifty, waxing eloquent, "I appeals to your national pride! Here's the Kid, a American like yourself, pent up in durance vile, and for no more reason than for just takin' up for his own country—"

"Huh!" I perked up my ears. "How's that?"

"Well, he blows into a pub where three British sailors makes slanderous remarks about American ships and seamen. Well, you know the Kid—just a big, free-hearted, impulsive boy, and terrible proud of his country, like a man should be. He ain't no sailor, of course, but them remarks was a insult to his countrymen and he wades in. He gives them limeys a proper drubbin' but here comes a host of cops which hauls him before the local magistrate which hands him a fine we can't pay.

"Think, Steve!" orated Shifty. "There's the Kid, with thousands of admirin' fans back in the States waitin' and watchin' for his triumphal return to the land of the free and the home of the brave. And here's him, wastin' his young manhood in a stone dungeon, bein' fed on bread and water and maybe beat up by the jailers, merely for standin' up for his own flag and nation. For defendin' the honor of American sailors, mind you, of which you is one. I'm askin' you, Steve, be you goin' to stand by and let a feller countryman languish in the 'thrallin' chains of British tyranny?"

"Not by a long ways!" said I, all my patriotism roused and roaring. "Let bygones be bygones!" I said.

It's a kind of unwritten law among sailors ashore that they should stand by their own kind. A kind of waterfront law, I might say.

"I ain't fought limeys all over the world to let an American be given the works by 'em now," I said. "I ain't got a cent, Shifty, but I'm goin' to get some dough.

"Meet me at the American Seamen's Bar in three hours. I'll have the dough for the Kid's fine or I'll know the reason why.

"You understand, I ain't doin' this altogether for the Kid. I still intends to punch his block off some day. But he's an American and so am I, and I reckon I ain't so small that I'll let personal grudges stand in the way of helpin' a countryman in a foreign land."

"Spoken like a man, Steve!" applauded Shifty, and me and Mike hustled away.

A short, fast walk brung us to a building on the waterfront which had a sign saying: "The South African Sports Arena." This was all lit up and yells was coming forth by which I knowed fights was going on inside.

The ticket shark told me the main bout had just begun. I told him to send me the promoter, "Bulawayo" Hurley, which I'd fought for of yore, and he told me that Bulawayo was in his office, which was a small room next to the ticket booth. So I went in and seen Bulawayo talking to a tall, lean gent the sight of which made my neck hair bristle.

"Hey, Bulawayo," said I, ignoring the other mutt and coming direct to the point, "I want a fight. I want to fight tonight—right now. Have you got anybody you'll throw in with me, or if not willya let me get up in your ring and challenge the house for a purse to be made up by the crowd?"

"By a strange coincidence," said Bulawayo, pulling his big mustache, "here's Bucko Brent askin' me the same blightin' thing."

Me and Bucko gazed at each other with hearty disapproval. I'd had dealings with this thug before. In fact, I built a good part of my reputation as a bucko-breaker on his lanky frame. A bucko, as you likely know, is a hard-case mate, who punches his crew around. Brent was all that and more. Ashore he was a prize-fighter, same as me.

Quite a few years ago I was fool enough to ship as A.B. on the *Elinor*, which he was mate of then. He's an Australian and the *Elinor* was an Australian ship. Australian ships is usually good crafts to sign up with, but this here *Elinor* was a exception. Her cap'n was a relic of the old hell-ship days, and her mates was natural-born bullies. Brent especially, as his nickname of "Bucko" shows. But I was broke and wanted to get to Makassar to meet the *Sea Girl* there, so I shipped aboard the *Elinor* at Bristol.

Brent started ragging me before we weighed anchor.

Well, I stood his hazing for a few days and then I got plenty and we went together. We fought the biggest part of one watch, all over the ship from the mizzen cross trees to the bowsprit. Yet it wasn't what

I wouldst call a square test of manhood because marlin spikes and belaying pins was used free and generous on both sides and the entire tactics smacked of rough house.

In fact, I finally won the fight by throwing him bodily offa the poop. He hit on his head on the after deck and wasn't much good the rest of the cruise, what with a broken arm, three cracked ribs and a busted nose. And the cap'n wouldn't even order me to scrape the anchor chain less'n he had a gun in each hand, though I wasn't figgering on socking the old rum-soaked antique.

Well, in Bulawayo's office me and Bucko now set and glared at each other, and what we was thinking probably wasn't printable.

"Tell you what, boys," said Bulawayo, "I'll let you fight ten rounds as soon as the main event's over with. I'll put up five pounds and the winner gets it all."

"Good enough for me," growled Bucko.

"Make it six pounds and it's a go," said I.

"Done!" said Bulawayo, who realized what a break he was getting, having me fight for him for thirty dollars.

Bucko give me a nasty grin.

"At last, you blasted Yank," said he, "I got you where I want you. They'll be no poop deck for me to slip and fall off this time. And you can't hit me with no hand spike."

"A fine bird you are, talkin' about

hand spikes," I snarled, "after tryin' to tear off a section of the main-rail to sock me with."

"Belay!" hastily interrupted Bulawayo. "Preserve your ire for the ring."

"Is they any *Sea Girl* men out front?" I asked. "I want a handler to see that none of this thug's henchmen don't dope my water bottle."

"Strangely enough, Steve," said Bulawayo, "I ain't seen a *Sea Girl* bloke tonight. But I'll get a handler for you."

WELL, THE MAIN EVENT went the limit. It seemed like it never would get over with and I cussed to myself at the idea of a couple of dubs like them was delaying the performance of a man like me. At last, however, the referee called it a draw and kicked the both of them outa the ring.

Bulawayo hopped through the ropes and stopped the folks who'd started to go, by telling them he was offering a free and added attraction—Sailor Costigan and Bucko Brent in a impromptu grudge bout. This was good business for Bulawayo. It tickled the crowd who'd seen both of us fight, though not ag'in each other, of course. They cheered Bulawayo to the echo and settled back with whoops of delight.

Bulawayo was right—not a *Sea Girl* man in the house. All drunk or in jail or something, I suppose. They was quite a number of thugs there

from the *Nagpur*—Brent's present ship—and they all rose as one and gimme the razz. Sailors is funny. I know that Brent hazed the liver outa them, yet they was rooting for him like he was their brother or something.

I made no reply to their jeers, maintaining a dignified and aloof silence only except to tell them that I was going to tear their pet mate apart and strew the fragments to the four winds, and also to warn them not to try no monkey-shines behind my back, otherwise I wouldst let Mike chaw their legs off. They greeted my brief observations with loud, raucous bellerings, but looked at Mike with considerable awe.

The referee was an Englishman whose name I forget, but he hadn't been outa the old country very long, and had evidently got his experience in the polite athletic clubs of London. He says: "Now understand this, you blighters, w'en H'I says break, H'I wants no bally nonsense. Remember as long as H'I'm in 'ere, this is a blinkin' gentleman's gyme."

But he got in the ring with us, American style.

Bucko is one of these long, rangy, lean fellers, kinda pale and rawboned. He's got a thin hatchet face and mean light eyes. He's a bad actor and that ain't no lie. I'm six feet and weigh one ninety. He's a inch and three-quarters taller'n me, and he weighed then, maybe, a pound less'n me.

BUCKO COME OUT STABBING with his left, but I was watching his right. I knowed he packed his T.N.T. there and he was pretty classy with it.

In about ten seconds he nailed me with that right and I seen stars. I went back on my heels and he was on top of me in a second, hammering hard with both hands, wild for a knockout. He battered me back across the ring. I wasn't really hurt, though he thought I was. Friends of his which had seen me perform before was yelling for him to be careful, but he paid no heed.

With my back against the ropes I failed to block his right to the body and he rocked my head back with a hard left hook.

"You're not so tough, you lousy mick—" he sneered, shooting for my jaw. Wham! I ripped a slungshot right uppercut up inside his left and tagged him flush on the button. It lifted him clean offa his feet and dropped him on the seat of his trunks, where he set looking up at the referee with a goofy and glassy-eyed stare, whilst his friends jumped up and down and cussed and howled: "We told you to be careful with that gorilla, you conceited jassack!"

But Bucko was tough. He kind of assembled hisself and was up at the count of "Nine," groggy but full of fight and plenty mad. I come in wide open to finish him, and run square into that deadly right. I thought for a instant the top of my head was tore off, but rallied and shook Bucko from stem to stern with a left hook under the heart. He tin-canned in a hurry, covering his retreat with his sharp-shooting left. The gong found me vainly follering him around the ring.

The next round started with the fans which was betting on Bucko urging him to keep away from me and box me. Them that had put money on me was yelling for him to take a chance and mix it with me.

But he was plenty cagey. He kept his right bent across his midriff, his chin tucked behind his shoulder and his left out to fend me off. He landed repeatedly with that left and brung a trickle of blood from my lips, but I paid no attention. The left ain't made that can keep me off forever. Toward the end of the round he suddenly let go with that right again and I took it square in the face to get in a right to his ribs.

Blood spattered when his right landed. The crowd leaped up, yelling, not noticing the short-armed smash I ripped in under his heart. But he noticed it, you bet, and broke ground in a hurry, gasping, much to the astonishment of the crowd, which yelled for him to go in and finish the blawsted Yankee.

Crowds don't see much of what's going on in the ring before their eyes, after all. They see the wild swings and haymakers but they miss most of the real punishing blows—the short, quick smashes landed in close.

Well, I went right after Brent,

concentrating on his body. He was too kind of long and rangy to take much there. I hunched my shoulders, sunk my head on my hairy chest and bulled in, letting him pound my ears and the top of my head, while I slugged away with both hands for his heart and belly.

A left hook square under the liver made him gasp and sway like a mast in a high wind, but he desperately ripped in a right uppercut that caught me on the chin and kinda dizzied me for a instant. The gong found us fighting out of a clinch along the ropes.

My handler was highly enthusiastic, having bet a pound on me to win by a knockout. He nearly flattened a innocent ringsider showing me how to put over what he called "The Fitzsimmons Smoker." I never heered of the punch.

Well, Bucko was good and mad and musta decided he couldn't keep me away anyhow, so he come out of his corner like a bounding kangaroo, and swarmed all over me before I realized he'd changed his tactics. In a wild mix-up a fast, clever boxer can make a slugger look bad at his own game for a few seconds, being as the cleverer man can land quicker and oftener, but the catch is, he can't keep up the pace. And the smashes the slugger lands are the ones which really counts.

THE CROWD WENT CLEAN crazy when Bucko tore into me, ripping both hands to head and body as fast as he couldst heave one after the other. It looked like I was clean swamped, but them that knowed me tripled their bets. Brent wasn't hurting me none—cutting me up a little, but he was hitting too fast to be putting much weight behind his smacks.

Purty soon I drove a glove through the flurry of his punches. His grunt was plainly heered all over the house. He shot both hands to my head and I come back with a looping left to the body which sunk in nearly up to the wrist.

It was kinda like a bull fighting a tiger, I reckon. He swarmed all over me, hitting fast as a cat claws, whilst I kept my head down and gored him in the belly occasionally. Them body punches was rapidly taking the steam outa him, together with the pace he was setting for hisself. His punches was getting more like slaps and when I seen his knees suddenly tremble, I shifted and crashed my right to his jaw with everything I had behind it. It was a bit high or he'd been out till yet.

Anyway, he done a nose dive and hadn't scarcely quivered at "Nine," when the gong sounded. Most of the crowd was howling lunatics. It looked to them like a chance blow, swung by a desperate, losing man, hadst dropped Bucko just when he was winning in a walk.

But the old-timers knowed better. I couldst see 'em lean back and wink at each other and nod like they was saying: "See, what did I tell you, huh?"

Bucko's merry men worked over him and brung him up in time for the fourth round. In fact, they done a lot of work over him. They clustered around him till you couldn't see what they was doing.

Well, he come out fairly fresh. He had good recuperating powers. He come out cautious, with his left hand stuck out. I noticed that they'd evidently spilt a lot of water on his glove; it was wet.

I glided in fast and he pawed at my face with that left. I didn't pay no attention to it. Then when it was a inch from my eyes I smelt a peculiar, pungent kind of smell! I ducked wildly, but not quick enough. The next instant my eyes felt like somebody'd throwed fire into 'em. Turpentine! His left glove was soaked with it!

I'd caught at his wrist when I ducked. And now with a roar of rage, whilst I could still see a little, I grabbed his elbow with the other hand and, ignoring the smash he gimme on the ear with his right, I bent his arm back and rubbed his own glove in his own face.

He give a most ear-splitting shriek. The crowd bellered with bewilderment and astonishment and the referee rushed in to find out what was happening.

"I say!" he squawked, grabbing hold of us, as we was all tangled up by then. "Wot's going on 'ere? I say, it's disgryceful—OW!"

By some mischance or other, Bucko, thinking it was me, or swinging blind, hit the referee right smack between the eyes with that turpentine-soaked glove.

Losing touch with my enemy, I got scared that he'd creep up on me and sock me from behind. I was clean blind by now and I didn't know whether he was or not. So I put my head down and started swinging wild and reckless with both hands, on a chance I'd connect.

Meanwhile, as I heered afterward, Bucko, being as blind as I was, was doing the same identical thing. And the referee was going around the ring like a race horse, yelling for the cops, the army, the navy or what have you!

THE CROWD WAS CLEAN off its nut, having no idee as to what it all meant.

"That blawsted blighter Brent!" howled the cavorting referee in response to the inquiring screams of the maniacal crowd. "'E threw vitriol in me blawsted h'eyes!"

"Cheer up, cull!" bawled some thug. "Both of 'em's blind too!"

"Ow can H'I h'officiate in this condition?" howled the referee, jumping up and down. "Wot's tyking plyce in the bally ring?"

"Bucko's just flattened one of his handlers which was climbin' into the ring, with a blind swing!" the crowd whooped hilariously. "The Sailor's gone into a clinch with a ring post!"

Hearing this, I released what I had thought was Brent, with some annoyance. Some object bumping into me at this instant, I took it to be Bucko and knocked it head over heels. The delirious howls of the multitude informed me of my mistake. Maddened, I plunged forward, swinging, and felt my left hook around a human neck. As the referee was on the canvas this must be Bucko, I thought, dragging him toward me, and he proved it by sinking a glove to the wrist in my belly.

I ignored this discourteous gesture, and, maintaining my grip on his neck, I hooked over a right with all I had. Having hold of his neck, I knowed about where his jaw oughta be, and I figgered right. I knocked Bucko clean outa my grasp and from the noise he made hitting the canvas I knowed that in the ordinary course of events, he was through for the night.

I groped into a corner and clawed some of the turpentine outa my eyes. The referee had staggered up and was yelling: "'Ow in the blinkin' 'Ades can a man referee in such a mad-'ouse? Wot's 'ere, wot's 'ere?"

"Bucko's down!" the crowd screamed. "Count him out!"

"W'ere is 'e?" bawled the referee, blundering around the ring.

"Three p'ints off yer port bow!" they yelled and he tacked and fell over the vaguely writhing figger of Bucko. He scrambled up with a howl of triumph and begun to count with the most vindictive voice I ever heered. With each count he'd kick Bucko in the ribs.

"—H'eight! Nine! Ten! H'and you're h'out, you blawsted, blinkin' blightin', bally h'assassinatin' pirate!" whooped the referee, with one last tremendjous kick.

I climb over the ropes and my handler showed me which way was my dressing-room. Ever have turpentine rubbed in your eyes? Jerusha! I don't know of nothing more painful. You can easy go blind for good.

But after my handler hadst washed my eyes out good, I was all right. Collecting my earnings from Bulawayo, I set sail for the American Seamen's Bar, where I was to meet Shifty Kerren and give him the money to pay Delrano's fine with.

IT WAS QUITE A BIT past the time I'd set to meet Shifty, and he wasn't nowhere to be seen. I asked the barkeep if he'd been there and the barkeep, who knowed Shifty, said he'd waited about half an hour and then hoisted anchor. I ast the barkeep if he knowed where he lived and he said he did and told me. So I ast him would he keep Mike till I got back and he said he would. Mike despises Delrano so utterly I was afraid I couldn't keep him away from the Kid's throat, if we saw him, and I figgered on going down to the jail with Shifty.

Well, I went to the place the

bartender told me and went upstairs to the room the landlady said Shifty had, and started to knock when I heard men talking inside. Sounded like the Kid's voice, but I couldn't tell what he was saying so I knocked and somebody said: "Come in."

I opened the door. Three men was sitting there playing pinochle. They was Shifty, Bill Slane, the Kid's sparring partner, and the Kid hisself.

"Howdy, Steve," said Shifty with a smirk, kinda furtive eyed, "whatcha doin' away up here?"

"Why," said I, kinda took aback, "I brung the dough for the Kid's fine, but I see he don't need it, bein' as he's out."

Delrano hadst been craning his neck to see if Mike was with me, and now he says, with a nasty sneer: "What's the matter with your face, Costigan? Some street kid poke you on the nose?"

"If you wanta know," I growled, "I got these marks on your account. Shifty told me you was in stir, and I was broke, so I fought down at The South African to get fine-money."

At that the Kid and Slane bust out into loud and jeering laughter—not the kind you like to hear. Shifty joined in, kinda nervous-like.

"Whatcha laughin' at?" I snarled. "Think I'm lyin'?"

"Naw, you ain't lyin'," mocked the Kid. "You ain't got sense enough to. You're just the kind of a dub that would do somethin' like that."

"You see, Steve," said Shifty, "the Kid—"

"Aw shut up, Shifty!" snapped Delrano. "Let the big sap know he's been took for a ride. I'm goin' to tell him what a sucker he's been. He ain't got his blasted bulldog with him. He can't do nothin' to the three of us."

DELRANO GOT UP AND stuck his sneering, pasty white face up close to mine.

"Of all the dumb, soft, bone-headed boobs I ever knew," said he, and his tone cut like a whip lash, "you're the limit. Get this, Costigan, I ain't broke and I ain't been in jail! You want to know why Shifty spilt you that line? Because I bet him ten dollars that much as you hate me and him, we could hand you a hard luck tale and gyp you outa your last cent.

"Well, it worked! And to think that you been fightin' for the dough to give me! Ha-ha-ha-ha-ha! You big chump! You're a natural born sucker! You fall for anything anybody tells you. You'll never get nowheres. Look at me—I wouldn't give a blind man a penny if he was starvin' and my brother besides. But you—oh, what a sap!

"If Shifty hadn't been so anxious to win that ten bucks that he wouldn't wait down at the bar, we'd had your dough, too. But this is good enough. I'm plenty satisfied just to know how hard you fell for our graft, and to see how you got beat up gettin' money to pay my fine! Ha-ha-ha!"

By this time I was seeing them

through a red mist. My huge fists was clenched till the knuckles was white, and when I spoke it didn't hardly sound like my voice at all, it was so strangled with rage.

"They's rats in every country," I ground out. "If you'd of picked my pockets or slugged me for my dough, I coulda understood it. If you'd worked a cold deck or crooked dice on me, I wouldn'ta kicked. But you appealed to my better nature, 'stead of my worst.

"You brung up a plea of patriotism and national fellership which no decent man woulda refused. You appealed to my natural pride of blood and nationality. It wasn't for you I done it—it wasn't for you I spilt my blood and risked my eyesight. It was for the principles and ideals you've mocked and tromped into the muck—the honor of our country and the fellership of Americans the world over.

"You dirty swine! You ain't fitten to be called Americans. Thank gosh, for everyone like you, they's ten thousand decent men like me. And if it's bein' a sucker to help out a countryman when he's in a jam in a foreign land, then I thanks the Lord I am a sucker. But I ain't all softness and mush—feel this here for a change!"

And I closed the Kid's eye with a smashing left hander. He give a howl of surprise and rage and come back with a left to the jaw. But he didn't have a chance. He'd licked me in the ring, but he couldn't lick me bare-handed, in a small room where he couldn't keep away from my hooks, not even with two men to help him. I was blind mad and I just kind of gored and tossed him like a charging bull.

If he hit at all after that first punch I don't remember it. I know I crashed him clean across the room with a regular whirlwind of smashes, and left him sprawled out in the ruins of three or four chairs with both eyes punched shut and his arm broke. I then turned on his cohorts and hit Bill Slane on the jaw, knocking him stiff as a wedge. Shifty broke for the door, but I pounced on him and spilled him on his neck in a corner with a open-handed slap.

I THEN STALKED FORTH in silent majesty and gained the street. As I went I was filled with bitterness. Of all the dirty, contemptible tricks I ever heered of, that took the cake. And I got to thinking maybe they was right when they said I was a sucker. Looking back, it seemed to me like I'd fell for every slick trick under the sun. I got mad. I got mighty mad.

I shook my fist at the world in general, much to the astonishment and apprehension of the innocent by-passers.

"From now on," I raged, "I'm harder'n the plate on a battleship! I ain't goin' to fall for nothin'! Nobody's goin' to get a blasted cent outa me, not for no reason what-the-some-ever—"

At that moment I heered a commotion going on nearby. I looked. Spite of the fact that it was late, a pretty good-sized crowd hadst gathered in front of a kinda third-class boarding-house. A mighty purty blonde-headed girl was standing there, tears running down her cheeks as she pleaded with a tough-looking old sister who stood with her hands on her hips, grim and stern.

"Oh, please don't turn me out!" wailed the girl. "I have no place to go! No job—oh, please. Please!"

I can't stand to hear a hurt animal cry out or a woman beg. I shouldered through the crowd and said: "What's goin' on here?"

"This hussy owes me ten pounds," snarled the woman. "I got to have the money or her room. I'm turnin' her out."

"Where's her baggage?" I asked.

"I'm keepin' it for the rent she owes," she snapped. "Any of your business?"

The girl kind of slumped down in the street. I thought if she's turned out on the street tonight they'll be hauling another carcass outa the bay tomorrer. I said to the landlady, "Take six pounds and call it even."

"Ain't you got no more?" said she.

"Naw, I ain't," I said truthfully.

"All right, it's a go," she snarled, and grabbed the dough like a sea-gull grabs a fish.

"All right," she said very harshly to the girl, "you can stay another week. Maybe you'll find a job by that time—or some other sap of a Yank sailor will come along and pay your board."

She went into the house and the crowd give a kind of cheer which inflated my chest about half a foot. Then the girl come up close to me and said shyly, "Thank you. I—I—I can't begin to tell you how much I appreciate what you've done for me."

Then all to a sudden she throwed her arms around my neck and kissed me and then run up the steps into the boarding-house. The crowd cheered some more like British crowds does and I felt plenty uplifted as I swaggered down the street. Things like that, I reflected, is worthy causes. A worthy cause can have my dough any time, but I reckon I'm too blame smart to get fooled by no shysters.

I COME INTO THE AMERICAN Seamen's Bar where Mike was getting anxious about me. He wagged his stump of a tail and grinned all over his big wide face and I found two American nickels in my pocket which I didn't know I had. I give one of 'em to the barkeep to buy a pan of beer for Mike. And whilst he was lapping it, the barkeep, he said: "I see Boardin'-house Kate is in town."

"Whatcha mean?" I ast him.

"Well," said he, combing his mustache, "Kate's worked her racket all over Australia and the West Coast of America, but this is the first time I ever seen her in South Africa. She lets some landlady of a cheap boardin'-house in on the scheme and this dame pretends to throw her out. Kate puts up a wail and somebody— usually some free-hearted sailor about like you—happens along and pays the landlady the money Kate's supposed to owe for rent so she won't kick the girl out onto the street. Then they split the dough."

"Uh huh!" said I, grinding my teeth slightly. "Does this here Boardin'-house Kate happen to be a blonde?"

"Sure thing," said the barkeep. "And purty as hell. What did you say?"

"Nothin'," I said. "Here. Give me a schooner of beer and take this nickel, quick, before somebody comes along and gets it away from me."

TEXAS FISTS.

ALTERNATE TITLE: SHANGHAIED MITTS.

This short story was first published in the May 1931 issue of Fight Stories *magazine.*

THE *Sea Girl* hadn't been docked in Tampico more'n a few hours when I got into a argument with a big squarehead off a tramp steamer. I forget what the row was about—sailing vessels versus steam, I think. Anyway, the discussion got so heated he took a swing at me. He musta weighed nearly three hundred pounds, but he was meat for me. I socked him just once and he went to sleep under the ruins of a table.

As I turned back to my beer mug in high disgust, I noticed that a gang of fellers which had just come in was gawping at me in wonder. They was cow-punchers, in from the ranges, all white men, tall, hard and rangy, with broad-brimmed hats, leather chaps, big Mexican spurs, guns an' everything; about ten of them, altogether.

"By the gizzard uh Sam Bass," said the tallest one, "I plumb believe we've found our man, hombres. Hey,

135

pardner, have a drink! Come on—set down at this here table. I wanta talk to you."

So we all set down and, while we was drinking some beer, the tall cow-puncher glanced admiringly at the squarehead which was just coming to from the bar-keep pouring water on him, and the cow-puncher said:

"Lemme introduce us: we're the hands of the Diamond J—old Bill Dornley's ranch, way back up in the hills. I'm Slim, and these is Red, Tex, Joe, Yuma, Buck, Jim, Shorty, Pete and the Kid. We're in town for a purpose, pardner, which is soon stated.

"Back up in the hills, not far from the Diamond J, is a minin' company, and them miners has got the fightin'est buckaroo in these parts. They're backin' him agin all comers, and I hates to say what he's did to such Diamond J boys as has locked horns with him. Them miners has got a ring rigged up in the hills where this gent takes on such as is wishful to mingle with him, but he ain't particular. He knocked out Joe, here, in that ring, but he plumb mopped up a mesquite flat with Red, which challenged him to a rough-and-tumble brawl with bare fists. He's a bear-cat, and the way them miners is puttin' on airs around us boys is somethin' fierce.

"We've found we ain't got no man on the ranch which can stand up to that grizzly, and so we come into town to find some feller which

could use his fists. Us boys is more used to slingin' guns than knuckles. Well, the minute I seen you layin' down that big Swede, I says to myself, I says, 'Slim, there's your man!'

"How about it, amigo? Will you mosey back up in the hills with us and flatten this big false alarm? We aim to bet heavy, and we'll make it worth yore while."

"And how far is this here ranch?" I asked.

"'Bout a day's ride, hossback—maybe a little better'n that."

"That's out," I decided. "I can't navigate them four-legged craft. I ain't never been on a horse more'n three or four times, and I ain't figgerin' on repeatin' the experiment."

"Well," said Slim, "we'll get hold of a auteymobeel and take you out in style."

"No," I said, "I don't believe I'll take you up; I wanta rest whilst I'm in port. I've had a hard voyage; we run into nasty weather and had one squall after another. Then the Old Man picked up a substitute second mate in place of our regular mate which is in jail in Melbourne, and this new mate and me has fought clean across the Pacific, from Melbourne to Panama, where he give it up and quit the ship."

The cow-punchers all started arguing at the same time, but Slim said:

"Aw, that's all right boys; I reckon the gent knows what he wants to do. We can find somebody else, I reckon.

No hard feelin's. Have another drink."

I kinda imagined he had a mysterious gleam in his eye, and it looked like to me that when he motioned to the bartender, he made some sort of a signal; but I didn't think nothing about it. The bar-keep brought a bottle of hard licker, and Slim poured it, saying: "What did you say yore name was, amigo?"

"Steve Costigan, A. B. on the sailing vessel *Sea Girl*," I answered. "I want you fellers to hang around and meet Bill O'Brien and Mushy Hanson, my shipmates, they'll be around purty soon with my bulldog Mike. I'm waitin' for 'em. Say, this stuff tastes funny."

"That's just high-grade tequila," said Slim. "Costigan, I shore wish you'd change yore mind about goin' out to the ranch and fightin' for us."

"No chance," said I. "I crave peace and quiet ... Say, what the heck ... ?"

I hadn't took but one nip of that funny-tasting stuff, but the bar-room had begun to shimmy and dance. I shook my head to clear it and saw the cowboys, kinda misty and dim, they had their heads together, whispering, and one of 'em said, kinda low-like: "He's fixin' to pass out. Grab him!"

At that, I give a roar of rage and heaved up, upsetting the table and a couple of cow-hands.

"You low-down land-sharks," I roared. "You doped my grog!"

"Grab him, boys!" yelled Slim, and three or four nabbed me. But I throwed 'em off like chaff and caught Slim on the chin with a clout that sprawled him on the back of his neck. I socked Red on the nose and it spattered like a busted tomater, and at this instant Pete belted me over the head with a gun-barrel.

With a maddened howl, I turned on him, and he gasped, turned pale and dropped the gun for some reason or other. I sunk my left mauler to the wrist in his midriff, and about that time six or seven of them cow-punchers jumped on my neck and throwed me by sheer weight of man-power.

I got Yuma's thumb in my mouth and nearly chawed it off, but they managed to sling some ropes around me, and the drug, from which I was already weak and groggy, took full effect about this time and I passed clean out.

I musta been out a long time. I kinda dimly remember a sensation of bumping and jouncing along, like I was in a car going over a rough road, and I remember being laid on a bunk and the ropes took off, but that's all.

I WAS WOKE up by voices. I set up and cussed. I had a headache and a nasty taste in my mouth, and, feeling the back of my head, I found a bandage, which I tore off with irritation. Keel haul me! As if a scalp cut like that gun-barrel had give me needed dressing!

I was sitting on a rough bunk in a kinda small shack which was built of heavy planks. Outside I heered Slim talking:

"No, Miss Joan, I don't dast let you in to look at him. He ain't come to, I don't reckon 'cause they ain't no walls kicked outa the shack, yet; but he might come to hisself whilst you was in there, and they's no tellin' what he might do, even to you. The critter ain't human, I'm tellin' you, Miss Joan."

"Well," said a feminine voice, "I think it was just horrid of you boys to kidnap a poor ignorant sailor and bring him away off up here just to whip that miner."

"Golly, Miss Joan," said Slim, kinda like he was hurt, "if you got any sympathy to spend, don't go wastin' it on that gorilla. Us boys needs yore sympathy. I winked at the bar-keep for the dope when I ordered the drinks, and, when I poured the sailor's, I put enough of it in his licker to knock out three or four men. It hit him quick, but he was wise to it and started sluggin'. With all them knockout drops in him, he near wrecked the joint! Lookit this welt on my chin—when he socked me I looked right down my own spine for a second. He busted Red's nose flat, and you oughta see it this mornin'. Pete lammed him over the bean so hard he bent the barrel of his forty-five, but all it done was make Costigan mad. Pete's still sick at his stummick from the sock the sailor give him. I tell you, Miss Joan, us

boys oughta have medals pinned on us; we took our lives in our hands, though we didn't know it at the start, and, if it hadn't been for the dope, Costigan would have destroyed us all. If yore dad ever fires me, I'm goin' to git a job with a circus, capturin' tigers and things. After that ruckus, it oughta be a cinch."

At this point, I decided to let folks know I was awake and fighting mad about the way I'd been treated, so I give a roar, tore the bunk loose from the wall and throwed it through the door. I heard the girl give a kind of scream, and then Slim pulled open what was left of the door and come through. Over his shoulder I seen a slim nice-looking girl legging it for the ranch-house.

"What you mean scarin' Miss Joan?" snarled Slim, tenderly fingering a big blue welt on his jaw.

"I didn't go to scare no lady," I growled. "But in about a minute I'm goin' to scatter your remnants all over the landscape. You think you can shanghai me and get away with it? I want a big breakfast and a way back to port."

"You'll git all the grub you want if you'll agree to do like we says," said Slim; "but you ain't goin' to git a bite till you does."

"You'd keep a man from mess, as well as shanghai him, hey?" I roared. "Well, lemme tell you, you long-sparred, leather-rigged son of a sea-cock, I'm goin' to—"

"You ain't goin' to do nothin'," snarled Slim, whipping out a long-barreled gun and poking it in my face.

"You're goin' to do just what I says or get the daylight let through you—"

Having a gun shoved in my face always did enrage me. I knocked it out of his hand with one mitt, and him flat on his back with the other, and, jumping on his prostrate frame with a blood-thirsty yell of joy, I hammered him into a pulp.

His wild yells for help brought the rest of the crew on the jump, and they all piled on me for to haul me off. Well, I was the center of a whirl-wind of fists, boots, and blood-curdling howls of pain and rage for some minutes, but they was just too many of them and they was too handy with them lassoes. When they finally had me hawg-tied again, the side wall was knocked clean out of the shack, the roof was sagging down and Joe, Shorty, Jim and Buck was out cold.

SLIM, LOOKING A lee-shore wreck, limped over and glared down at me with his one good eye whilst the other boys felt theirselves for broken bones and throwed water over the fallen gladiators.

"You snortin' buffalo," Slim snarled. "How I hones to kick yore ribs in! What do you say? Do you fight or stay tied up?"

The cook-shack was near and I could smell the bacon and eggs sizzling. I hadn't eat nothing since dinner the day before and I was hungry enough to eat a raw sea lion.

"Lemme loose," I growled. "I gotta have food. I'll lick this miner for you, and when I've did that, I'm going to kick down your bunkhouse and knock the block offa every man, cook and steer on this fool ranch."

"Boy," said Slim with a grin, spitting out a loose tooth, "does you lick that miner, us boys will each give you a free swing at us. Come on— you're loose now—let's go get it."

"Let's send somebody over to the Bueno Oro Mine and tell them mavericks 'bout us gittin' a slugger," suggested Pete, trying to work back a thumb he'd knocked outa place on my jaw.

"Good idee," said Slim. "Hey, Kid, ride over and tell 'em we got a man as can make hash outa their longhorn. Guess we can stage the scrap in about five days, hey, Sailor?"

"Five days my eye," I grunted. "The *Sea Girl* sails day after tomorrow and I gotta be on her. Tell 'em to get set for the go this evenin'."

"But, gee whiz!" expostulated Slim. "Don't you want a few days to train?"

"If I was outa trainin', five days wouldn't help me none," I said. "But I'm allus in shape. Lead on the mess table. I crave nutriment."

Well, them boys didn't hold no grudge at all account of me knocking 'em around. The Kid got on a broom-tailed bronc and cruised off across the hills, and the rest of us went for the cook-shack. Joe yelled after the

Kid: "Look out for Lopez the Terrible!" And they all laughed.

Well, we set down at the table and the cook brung aigs and bacon and fried steak and sour-dough bread and coffee and canned corn and milk till you never seen such a spread. I lay to and ate till they looked at me kinda bewildered.

"Hey!" said Slim, "ain't you eatin' too much for a tough scrap this evenin'?"

"What you cow-pilots know about trainin'?" I said. "I gotta keep up my strength. Gimme some more of them beans, and tell the cook to scramble me five or six more aigs and bring me in another stack of buckwheats. And say," I added as another thought struck me, "who's this here Lopez you-all was jokin' about?"

"By golly," said Tex, "I thought you cussed a lot like a Texan. 'You-all,' huh? Where was you born?"

"Galveston," I said.

"Zowie!" yelled Tex. "Put 'er there, pard; I aims for to triple my bets on you! Lopez? Oh, he's just a Mex bandit—handsome cuss, I'll admit, and purty mean. He ranges around in them hills up there and he's stole some of our stock and made a raid or so on the Bueno Oro. He's allus braggin' 'bout how he aims for to raid the Diamond J some day and ride off with Joan—that's old Bill Dornley's gal. But heck, he ain't got the guts for that."

"Not much he ain't," said Jim. "Say, I wish old Bill was at the ranch now, 'steada him and Miz Dornley visitin' their son at Zacatlan. They'd shore enjoy the scrap this evenin'. But Miss Joan'll be there, you bet."

"Is she the dame I scared when I called you?" I asked Slim.

"Called me? Was you callin' me?" said he. "Golly, I'd of thought a bull was in the old shack, only a bull couldn't beller like that. Yeah, that was her."

"Well," said I, "tell her I didn't go for to scare her. I just naturally got a deep voice from makin' myself heard in gales at sea."

Well, we finished breakfast and Slim says: "Now what you goin' to do, Costigan? Us boys wants to help you train all we can."

"Good," I said. "Fix me up a bunk; nothing like a good long nap when trainin' for a tough scrap."

"All right," said they. "We reckons you knows what you wants; while you git yore rest, we'll ride over and lay some bets with the Bueno Oro mavericks."

SO THEY SHOWED me where I couldst take a nap in their bunkhouse and I was soon snoozing. Maybe I should of kinda described the ranch. They was a nice big house, Spanish style, but made of stone, not 'dobe, and down to one side was the corrals, the cook-shack, the long bunk-house where the cowboys stayed, and a few Mexican huts. But they wasn't many Mexes working on the Diamond J. They's quite a few

TEXAS FISTS

ranches in Old Mexico owned and run altogether by white men. All around was big rolling country, rough ranges of sagebrush, mesquite, cactus and chaparral, sloping in the west to hills which further on became right good-sized mountains.

Well, I was woke up by the scent of victuals; the cook was fixing dinner. I sat up on the bunk and—lo, and behold—there was the frail they called Miss Joan in the door of the bunkhouse, staring at me wide-eyed like I was a sea horse or something.

I started to tell her I was sorry I scared her that morning, but when she seen I was awake she give a gasp and steered for the ranch-house under full sail.

I was bewildered and slightly irritated. I could see that she got a erroneous idee about me from listening to Slim's hokum, and, having probably never seen a sailor at close range before, she thought I was some kind of a varmint.

Well, I realized I was purty hungry, having ate nothing since breakfast, so I started for the cook-shack and about that time the cow-punchers rode up, plumb happy and hilarious.

"Hot dawg!" yelled Slim. "Oh, baby, did them miners bite! They grabbed everything in sight and we has done sunk every cent we had, as well bettin' our hosses, saddles, bridles and shirts."

"And believe me," snarled Red,

tenderly fingering what I'd made outa his nose, and kinda hitching his gun prominently, "you better win!"

"Don't go makin' no grandstand plays at me," I snorted. "If I can't lick a man on my own inisheyative, no gun-business can make me do it. But don't worry; I can flatten anything in these hills, includin' you and all your relatives. Let's get into that mess gallery before I clean starve."

While we ate, Slim said all was arranged; the miners had knocked off work to get ready and the scrap would take place about the middle of the evening. Then the punchers started talking and telling me things they hadst did and seen, and of all the triple-decked, full-rigged liars I ever listened to, them was the beatenest. The Kid said onst he come onto a mountain lion and didn't have no rope nor gun, so he caught rattlesnakes with his bare hands and tied 'em together and made a lariat and roped the lion and branded it, and he said how they was a whole breed of mountain lions in the hills with the Diamond J brand on 'em and the next time I seen one, if I would catch it and look on its flank, I would see it was so.

So I told them that once when I was cruising in the Persian Gulf, the wind blowed so hard it picked the ship right outa the water and carried it clean across Arabia and dropped it in the Mediterranean Sea; all the riggings was blown off, I said, and the masts outa her, so we caught sharks and hitched them to the bows

141

and made 'em tow us into port.

Well, they looked kinda weak and dizzy then, and Slim said: "Don't you want to work out a little to kinda loosen up your muscles?"

Well, I was still sore at them cow-wranglers for shanghaing me the way they done, so I grinned wickedly and said: "Yeah, I reckon I better; my muscles is purty stiff, so you boys will just naturally have to spar some with me."

Well they looked kinda sick, but they was game. They brung out a battered old pair of gloves and first Joe sparred with me. Whilst they was pouring water on Joe they argued some about who was to spar with me next and they drawed straws and Slim was it.

"By golly," said Slim looking at his watch, "I'd shore admire to box with you, Costigan, but it's gettin' about time for us to start dustin' the trail for the Bueno Oro."

"Heck, we got plenty uh time," said Buck.

Slim glowered at him. "I reckon the foreman—which is me—knows what time uh day it is," said Slim. "I says we starts for the mine. Miss Joan has done said she'd drive Costigan over in her car, and me and Shorty will ride with 'em. I kinda like to be close around Miss Joan when she's out in the hills. You can't tell; Lopez might git it into his haid to make a bad play. You boys will foller on your broncs."

WELL, THAT'S THE way it was. Joan was a mighty nice looking girl and she was very nice to me when Slim interjuced me to her, but I couldst see she was nervous being that close to me, and it offended me very much, though I didn't show it none.

Slim set on the front seat with her, and me and Shorty on the back seat, and we drove over the roughest country I ever seen. Mostly they wasn't no road at all, but Joan knowed the channel and didn't need no chart to navigate it, and eventually we come to the mine.

The mine and some houses was up in the hills, and about half a mile from it, on a kind of a broad flat, the ring was pitched. Right near where the ring stood, was a narrow canyon, leading up through the hills. We had to leave the car close to the mine and walk the rest of the way, the edge of the flat being too rough to drive on.

They was quite a crowd at the ring, which was set up in the open. I notice that the Bueno Oro was run by white men same as the ranch. The miners was all big, tough-looking men in heavy boots, bearded and wearing guns, and they was a considerable crew of 'em. They was still more cow-punchers from all the ranches in the vicinity, a lean, hard-bit gang, with even more guns on them than the miners had. By golly, I never seen so many guns in one place in my life!

They was quite a few Mexicans watching, men and women, but Joan was the only white woman I seen. All the men took their hats off to her, and I seen she was quite a favorite among them rough fellers, some of which looked more like pirates than miners or cowboys.

Well the crowd set up a wild roar when they seen me, and Slim yelled: "Well, you mine-rasslin' mavericks, here he is! I shudders to think what he's goin' to do to yore man."

All the cow-punchers yipped jubilantly and all the miners yelled mockingly, and up come the skipper of the mine—the guy that done the managing of it—a fellow named Menly.

"Our man is in his tent getting on his togs, Slim," said he. "Get your fighter ready—and we'd best be on the lookout. I've had a tip that Lopez is in the hills close by. The mine's unguarded. Everybody's here. And while there's no ore or money for him to swipe—we sent out the ore yesterday and the payroll hasn't arrived yet—he could do a good deal of damage to the buildings and machinery if he wanted to."

"We'll watch out, you bet," assured Slim, and steered me for what was to serve as my dressing room. They was two tents pitched one on each side of the ring, and they was our dressing rooms. Slim had bought a pair of trunks and ring shoes in Tampico, he said, and so I was rigged out shipshape.

As it happened, I was the first man in the ring. A most thunderous yell went up, mainly from the cow-punchers, and, at the sight of my manly physique, many began to pullout their watches and guns and bet them. The way them miners snapped up the wagers showed they had perfect faith in their man. And when he clumb in the ring a minute later they just about shook the hills with their bellerings. I glared and gasped.

"Snoots Leary or I'm a Dutchman!" I exclaimed.

"Biff Leary they call him," said Slim which, with Tex and Shorty and the Kid, was my handler. "Does you know him?"

"Know him?" said I. "Say, for the first fourteen years of my life I spent most of my time tradin' punches with him. They ain't a back-alley in Galveston that we ain't bloodied each other's noses in. I ain't seen him since we was just kids—I went to sea, and he went the other way. I heard he was mixin' minin' with fightin'. By golly, hadst I knowed this you wouldn't of had to shanghai me."

Well, Menly called us to the center of the ring for instructions and Leary gawped at me: "Steve Costigan, or I'm a liar! What you doin' fightin' for cow-wranglers? I thought you was a sailor."

"I am, Snoots," I said, "and I'm mighty glad for to see you here. You know, we ain't never settled the question as to which of us is the best man. You'll recollect in all the fights we had, neither of us ever really won;

we'd generally fight till we was so give out we couldn't lift our mitts, or else till somebody fetched a cop. Now we'll have it out, once and for all!"

"Good!" said he, grinning like a ogre. "You're purty much of a man, Steve, but I figger I'm more. I ain't been swingin' a sledge all this time for nothin'. And I reckon the nickname of 'Biff' is plenty descriptive."

"You always was conceited, Biff," I scowled. "Different from me. Do I go around tellin' people how good I am? Not me; I don't have to. They can tell by lookin' at me that I'm about the best two-fisted man that ever walked a forecastle. Shake now and let's come out fightin'."

Well, the referee had been trying to give us instructions, but we hadn't paid no attention to him, so now he muttered a few mutters under his breath and told us to get ready for the gong. Meanwhile the crowd was developing hydrophobia wanting us to get going. They'd got a camp chair for Miss Joan, but the men all stood up, banked solid around the ring so close their noses was nearly through the ropes, and all yelling like wolves.

"For cat's sake, Steve," said Slim as he crawled out of the ring, "don't fail us. Leary looks even meaner than he done when he licked Red and Joe."

I'll admit Biff was a hard looking mug. He was five feet ten to my six feet, and he weighed 195 to my 190. He had shoulders as wide as a door,

a deep barrel chest, huge fists and arms like a gorilla's. He was hairy and his muscles swelled like iron all over him, miner's style, and his naturally hard face hadst not been beautified by a broken nose and a cauliflower ear. Altogether, Biff looked like what he was—a rough and ready fighting man.

AT THE TAP of the gong he come out of his corner like a typhoon, and I met him in the center of the ring. By sheer luck he got in the first punch—a smashing left hook to the head that nearly snapped my neck. The crowd went howling crazy, but I come back with a sledge-hammer right hook that banged on his cauliflower ear like a gunshot. Then we went at it hammer and tongs, neither willing to take a back step, just like we fought when we was kids.

He had a trick of snapping a left uppercut inside the crook of my arm and beating my right hook. He'd had that trick when we fought in the Galveston alleys, and he hadn't forgot it. I never couldst get away from that peculiar smack. Again and again he snapped my head back with it—and I got a neck like iron, too; ain't everybody can rock my head back on it.

He wasn't neglecting his right either. In fact he was mighty fond of banging me on the ear with that hand. Meanwhile, I was ripping both hands to his liver, belly and heart, every now and then bringing up a left or right to his head. We slugged that round out without much advantage on either side, but just before the gong, one of them left uppercuts caught me square in the mouth and the claret started in streams.

"First blood, Steve," grinned Biff as he turned to his corner.

Slim wiped off the red stuff and looked kinda worried.

"He's hit you some mighty hard smacks, Steve," said he.

I snorted. "Think I been pattin' him? He'll begin to feel them body smashes in a round or so. Don't worry; I been waitin' for this chance for years."

At the tap of the gong for the second round we started right in where we left off. Biff come in like he aimed for to take me apart, but I caught him coming in with a blazing left hook to the chin. His eyes rolled, but he gritted his teeth and come driving in so hard he battered me back in spite of all I couldst do. His head was down, both arms flying, legs driving like a charging bull. He caught me in the belly with a right hook that shook me some, but I braced myself and stopped him in his tracks with a right uppercut to the head.

He grunted and heaved over a right swing that started at his knees, and I didn't duck quick enough. It caught me solid but high, knocking me back into the ropes.

The miners roared with joy and the cow-punchers screamed in dismay, but I wasn't hurt. With a supercilious sneer, I met Leary's rush with a straight left which snapped his head right back between his shoulders and somehow missed a slungshot right uppercut which had all my beef behind it.

Biff hooked both hands hard to my head and shot his right under my heart, and I paid him back with a left to the midriff which brung a grunt outa him. I crashed an overhand right for his jaw but he blocked it and was short with a hard right swing. I went inside his left to blast away at his body with both hands in close, and he throwed both arms around me and smothered my punches.

We broke of ourselves before Menly couldst separate us, and I hooked both hands to Leary's head, taking a hard drive between the eyes which made me see stars. We then stood head to head in the center of the ring and traded smashes till we was both dizzy. We didn't hear the gong and Menly had to jump in and haul us apart and shove us toward our corners.

The crowd was plumb cuckoo by this time; the cowboys was all yelling that I won that round and the miners was swearing that it was Biff's by a mile. I snickered at this argument, and I noticed Biff snort in disgust. I never go into no scrap figgering to win it on points. If I can't knock the other sap stiff, he's welcome to the decision. And I knowed Biff felt the same way.

Leary was in my corner for the next round before I was offa my stool, and he missed me with a most murderous right. I was likewise wild with a right, and Biff recovered his balance and tagged me on the chin with a left uppercut. Feeling kinda hemmed in, I went for him with a roar and drove him out into the center of the ring with a series of short, vicious rushes he couldn't altogether stop.

I shook him to his heels with a left hook to the body and started a right hook for his head. Up flashed his left for that trick uppercut, and I checked my punch and dropped my right elbow to block. He checked his punch too and crashed a most tremendous right to my unguarded chin. Blood splattered and I went back on my heels, floundering and groggy, and Biff, wild for the kill and flustered by the yells, lost his head and plunged in wide open, flailing with both arms.

I caught him with a smashing left hook to the jaw and he rolled like a clipper in rough weather. I ripped a right under his heart and cracked a hard left to his ear, and he grabbed me like a grizzly and hung on, shaking his head to get rid of the dizziness. He was tough—plenty tough. By the time the referee had broke us, his head had plumb cleared and he proved it by giving a roar of rage and smacking me square on the nose with a punch that made the blood fly.

Again the gong found us slugging head-to-head. Slim and the boys was so weak and wilted from excitement they couldn't hardly see straight enough to mop off the blood and give me a piece of lemon to suck.

Well, this scrap was to be to a finish and it looked like to me it wouldst probably last fifteen or twenty more rounds. I wasn't tired or weakened any, and I knowed Biff was like a granite boulder—nearly as tough as me. I figgered on wearing him down with body punishment, but even I couldn't wear down Biff Leary in a few shakes. Just like me, he won most of his fights by simply outlasting the other fellow.

Still, with a punch like both of us carried in each hand, anything might happen—and did, as it come about.

WE OPENED THE fourth like we had the others, and slugged our way through it, on even terms. Same way with the fifth, only in this I opened a gash on Biff's temple and he split my ear. As we come up for the sixth, we both showed some wear and tear. One of my eyes was partly closed, I was bleeding at the mouth and nose, and from my cut ear; Biff had lost a tooth, had a deep cut on his temple, and his ribs on the left side was raw from my body punches.

But neither of us was weakening. We come together fast and Biff ripped my lip open with a savage left hook. His right glanced offa my head and again he tagged me with his left uppercut. I sunk my right deep in his ribs and we both shot our lefts. His started a fraction of a second before mine, and he beat me to the punch; his mitt biffed square in my already closing eye, and for a second the punch blinded me.

His right was coming behind his left, swinging from the floor with every ounce of his beef behind it. Wham! Square on the chin that swinging mauler tagged me, and it was like the slam of a sledge-hammer. I felt my feet fly out from under me, and the back of my head hit the canvas with a jolt that kinda knocked the cobwebs outa my brain.

I shook my head and looked around to locate Biff. He hadn't gone to no corner but was standing grinning down at me, just back of the referee a ways. The referee was counting, the crowd was clean crazy, and Biff was grinning and waving his gloves at 'em, as much as to say what had he told 'em.

The miners was dancing and capering and mighty near kissing each other in their joy, and the cowboys was white-faced, screaming at me to get up, and reaching for their guns. I believe if I hadn't of got up, they'd of started slaughtering the miners. But I got up. For the first time I was good and mad at Biff, not because he knocked me down, but because he had such a smug look on his ugly map. I knowed I was the best man, and I was seeing red.

I come up with a roar, and Biff wiped the smirk offa his map quick and met me with a straight left. But I wasn't to be stopped. I bored into close quarters where I had the advantage, and started ripping away with both hands.

Quickly seeing he couldn't match me at infighting, Biff grabbed my shoulders and shoved me away by main strength, instantly swinging hard for my head. I ducked and slashed a left hook to his head. He ripped a left to my body and smashed a right to my ear. I staggered him with a left hook to the temple, took a left on the head, and beat him to the punch with a mallet-like right hander to the jaw. I caught him wide open and landed a fraction of a second before he did. That smash had all my beef behind it and Biff dropped like a log.

But he was a glutton for punishment. Snorting and grunting, he got to his all-fours, glassy-eyed but shaking his head, and, as Menly said "nine," Leary was up. But he was groggy; such a punch as I dropped him with is one you don't often land. He rushed at me and connected with a swinging left to the ribs that shook me some, but I dropped him again with a blasting left hook to the chin.

This time I seen he'd never beat the count, so I retired to the furtherest corner and grinned at Slim and the other cowboys, who was doing a Indian scalp-dance while the miners was shrieking for Biff to get up.

Menly was counting over him, and, just as he said "seven," a sudden rattle of shots sounded. Menly stopped short and glared at the mine, half a mile away. All of us looked. A gang of men was riding around the buildings and shooting in them. Menly give a yell and hopped out of the ring.

"Gang up!" he yelled. "It's Lopez and his men! They've come to do all the damage they can while the mine's unguarded! They'll burn the office and ruin the machinery if we don't stop 'em! Come a-runnin'!"

He grabbed a horse and started smoking across the flat, and the crowd followed him, the cowboys on horses, the rest on foot, all with their guns in their hands. Slim jumped down and said to Miss Joan: "You stay here, Miss Joan. You'll be safe here and we'll be back and finish this prize fight soon's we chase them Greasers over the hill."

WELL, I WAS plumb disgusted to see them mutts all streak off across the flat, leaving me and Biff in the ring, and me with the fight practically won. Biff shook hisself and snorted and come up slugging, but I stepped back and irritably told him to can the comedy.

"What's up?" said he, glaring around. "Why, where's Menly? Where's the crowd? What's them shots?"

"The crowd's gone to chase Lopez and his merry men," I snapped. "Just as I had you out, the fool referee quits countin'."

"Well, I'd of got up anyhow," said

Biff. "I see now. It is Lopez's gang, sure enough—"

The cow-punchers and miners had nearly reached the mine by this time, and guns was cracking plenty on both sides. The Mexicans was drawing off, slowly, shooting as they went, but it looked like they was about ready to break and run for it. It seemed like a fool play to me, all the way around.

"Hey, Steve," said Biff, "whatsa use waitin' till them mutts gits back? Let's me and you get our scrap over."

"Please don't start fighting till the boys come back," said Joan, nervously. "There's something funny about this. I don't feel just right. Oh—"

She give a kind of scream and turned pale. Outa the ravine behind the ring rode a Mexican. He was young and good-looking but he had a cruel, mocking face; he rode a fine horse and his clothes musta cost six months' wages. He had on tight pants which the legs flared at the bottoms and was ornamented with silver dollars, fine boots which he wore inside his pants legs, gold-chased spurs, a silk shirt and a jacket with gold lace all over it, and the costliest sombrero I ever seen. Moreover, they was a carbine in a saddle sheath, and he wore a Luger pistol at his hip.

"Murder!" said Biff. "It's Lopez the Terrible!"

"Greetings, senorita!" said he, with a flash of white teeth under his black mustache, swinging off his sombrero and making a low bow in his saddle. "Lopez keeps his word—have I not said I would come for you? Oho, I am clever. I sent my men to make a disturbance and draw the Americanos away. Now you will come with me to my lair in the hills where no gringo will ever find you!"

Joan was trembling and white-faced, but she was game. "You don't dare touch an American woman, you murderer!" she said. "My cowboys would hang you on a cactus."

"I will take the risk," he purred. "Now, senorita, come—"

"Get up here in the ring, Miss Joan," I said, leaning down to give her a hand. "That's it—right up with me and Biff. We won't let no harm come to you. Now, Mr. Lopez, if that's your name, I'm givin' you your sailin' orders—weigh anchor and steer for some other port before I bend one on your jaw."

"I echoes them sentiments," said Biff, spitting on his gloves and hitching at his trunks.

Lopez's white teeth flashed in a snarl like a wolf's. His Luger snaked into his hand.

"So," he purred, "these men of beef, these bruisers dare defy Lopez!" He reined up alongside the ring and, placing one hand on a post, vaulted over the ropes, his pistol still menacing me and Biff. Joan, at my motion, hadst retreated back to the other side of the ring. Lopez began to walk towards us, like a cat stalking a mouse.

"The girl I take," he said, soft and deadly. "Let neither of you move if you wish to live."

"Well, Biff," I said, tensing myself, "we'll rush him from both sides. He'll get one of us but the other'n'll git him."

"Oh, don't!" cried Joan. "He'll kill you. I'd rather—"

"Let's go!" roared Biff, and we plunged at Lopez simultaneous.

But that Mex was quicker than a cat; he whipped from one to the other of us and his gun cracked twice. I heard Biff swear and saw him stumble, and something that burned hit me in the left shoulder.

Before Lopez couldst fire again, I was on him, and I ripped the gun outa his hand and belted him over the head with it just as Biff smashed him on the jaw. Lopez the Terrible stretched out limp as a sail-rope, and he didn't even twitch.

"OH, YOU'RE SHOT, both of you!" wailed Joan, running across the ring toward us. "Oh, I feel like a murderer! I shouldn't have let you do it. Let me see your wounds."

Biff's left arm was hanging limp and blood was oozing from a neat round hole above the elbow. My own left was getting so stiff I couldn't lift it, and blood was trickling down my chest.

"Heck, Miss Joan," I said, "don't worry 'bout us. Lucky for us Lopez was usin' them steel-jacket bullets that make a clean wound and don't tear. But I hate about me and Biff not gettin' to finish our scrap—"

"Hey, Steve," said Biff hurriedly, "the boys has chased off the bandits and heered the shots, and here they come across the flat on the run! Let's us finish our go before they git here. They won't let us go on if we don't do it now. And we may never git another chance. You'll go off to your ship tomorrer and we may never see each other again. Come on. I'm shot through the left arm and you got a bullet through your left shoulder, but our rights is okay. Let's toss this mutt outa the ring and give each other one more good slam!"

"Fair enough, Biff," said I. "Come on, before we gets weak from losin' blood."

Joan started crying and wringing her hands.

"Oh, please, please, boys, don't fight each other any more! You'll bleed to death. Let me bandage your wounds—"

"Shucks, Miss Joan," said I, patting her slim shoulder soothingly, "me and Biff ain't hurt, but we gotta settle our argument. Don't you fret your purty head none."

We unceremoniously tossed the limp and senseless bandit outa the ring and we squared off, with our rights cocked and our lefts hanging at our sides, just as the foremost of the cow-punchers came riding up.

We heard the astounded yells of Menly, Slim and the rest, and Miss Joan begging 'em to stop us, and then we braced our legs, took a deep breath and let go.

We both crashed our rights at exactly the same instant, and we both landed—square on the button. And we both went down. I was up almost in a instant, groggy and dizzy and only partly aware of what was going on, but Biff didn't twitch.

The next minute Menly and Steve and Tex and all the rest was swarming over the ropes, yelling and hollering and demanding to know what it was all about, and Miss Joan was crying and trying to tell 'em and tend to Biff's wound.

"Hey!" yelled Yuma, outside the ring. "That was Lopez I seen ride up to the ring a while ago—here he is with a three-inch gash in his scalp and a fractured jawbone!"

"Ain't that what Miss Joan's been tellin' you?" I snapped. "Help her with Biff before he bleeds to death—naw, tend to him first—I'm all right."

Biff come to about that time and nearly knocked Menly's head off before he knowed where he was, and later, while they was bandaging us, Biff said: "I wanta tell you, Steve, I still don't consider you has licked me, and I'm figgerin' on lookin' you up soon's as my arm's healed up."

"Okay with me, Snoots," I grinned. "I gets more enjoyment outa fightin' you than anybody. Reckon there's fightin' Texas feud betwixt me and you."

"Well, Steve," said Slim, "we said we'd make it worth your while—what'll it be?"

"I wouldn't accept no pay for fightin' a old friend like Biff," said I.

"All I wantcha to do is get me back in port in time to sail with the *Sea Girl*. And, Miss Joan, I hope you don't feel scared of me no more."

Her answer made both me and Biff blush like school-kids. She kissed us.

The SIGN *of the* SNAKE.

This short story was first published in the June 1931 issue of Action Stories *magazine.*

I WAS READY for trouble. Canton's narrow waterfront streets were still and shadowy in that hour before dawn when I left the docks. The guttering street lamps gave little light. My bulldog, Bill, bristled suddenly and began to rumble in his throat. There was a rattle of feet on the cobblestones down an alley to the right. Then the sound of a heavy fall, scuffling, a strangled scream.

Plainly it was none of my business. But I quickened my pace and dashing around the corner, nearly fell over a writhing, struggling mass on the cobblestones. The dim light of a street lamp showed me what was going on. Two men fought there in deadly silence. One was a slim young Chinese in European clothes. Down on his back in the muck, he was. Kneeling on his chest was a slant-eyed devil in native riggings. He was big and lean, with a face like

153

a Taoist devil-mask. With one talon-like hand, he clutched the throat of the smaller man. A knife flashed in his other hand.

I recognized him for what he was—one of the bloody hatchet-men the big tongs and secret societies use for their dirty work. I followed my natural instinct and knocked him senseless with a smashing right hook behind the ear. He stretched out without a twitch and the young Chinese sprang up, gasping and wild eyed.

"Thank you, my friend," he gurgled in perfect English. "I owe my life to you. Here, take this ... " And he tried to stuff a wad of banknotes into my hand.

I drew back. "You owe me nothing," I growled. "I'd have done as much for any man."

"Then please accept my humble and sincere thanks," he exclaimed, seizing my hand. "You are an American, are you not? What is your name?"

"I'm Steve Costigan, first mate of the trading vessel *Panther*," I answered.

"I will not forget," he said. "I will repay you some day, as my name is Yotai T'sao. But now I must not linger. This is my one chance of escape. If I can get aboard the English ship that is anchored in the bay, I am safe. But I must go before this beast comes to. Best that you go too. May fortune attend you. But beware of the Yo Thans."

The next instant he was racing down the street at full speed. Watching him in amazement, I saw him sprint onto the docks and dive off, without the slightest pause. I heard the splash as he hit and a little later I saw, in the growing gray light, a widening ripple aiming toward the British *S. S. Marquis*, which lay out in the bay. I left off wondering what it could mean, when the hatchet-man scrambled uncertainly to his feet. More or less ironically, I said: "Well, my bully boy, give me the low-down on this business, will you?"

His answer was a look of such diabolic hatred as to almost send cold shivers down my spine. He limped away into the shadows. I dismissed the whole affair from my mind and went on down the street.

About sun-up I decided I would get a little sleep in preparation for the day. It was my first shore leave in weeks, and I was determined to make the most of it. I turned into a seamen's boarding house kept by a Eurasian called Diego, got a room and turned in.

I WAS WAKENED BY BILL'S growling. He was clawing at the locked door and looking up at the transom, which was open. Then I saw something lying on my chest—a piece of stiff paper, rolled into a dart-shaped wad. I unrolled it, but there were no words on it, either English or Chinese, just a picture portraying a coiled snake, somewhat resembling a cobra. That was all.

154

Somewhat puzzled, I rose and dressed and shouted for Diego. When he came I said: "Look, Diego. Someone threw this through the transom onto my chest. Do you know what the meaning of it is."

He took a single look. Then he leaped back with a shriek: "Yo Than. Death. It's the murder sign of the Yo Thans."

"What do you mean?" I growled. "Who are these Yo Thans?"

"A Chinese secret society," gasped Diego, white and shaking like a leaf. "International criminals—murderers. Three times have I seen men receive the sign of the snake. Each time he who received it dies before the sun rose again. Get back to your ship. Hide, stay aboard until she sails. Maybe you can escape."

"Skulk aboard my ship like a cringing rat?" I growled. "I, who am known as a fighting man in every Asiatic port? I've never run or hidden from any man yet. Tell me, who is Yotai T'sao?"

But Diego was gripped by the yellow hand of fear.

"I'll tell you nothing," he screamed. "I'm risking my life talking to you. Get out, quick. You mustn't stay here. I can't have another murder in my house. Go, please, Steve."

"All right," I snapped. "Don't burst a blood-vessel, Diego. I'm going."

In disgust, I stalked forth in quest of food. While I ate and Bill had his scoffings from a panikin on the floor, I reviewed the situation

and had the uncomfortable feeling that I had somehow blundered into the affairs of some mysterious gang of Oriental cut-throats. Under the bland outer surface of the Orient run dark and mysterious currents of plot and intrigue, unknown to white men—unless one unluckily goes beyond his depth in native affairs and is caught by some such deadly undertow.

In that case .... Well, it is no uncommon thing for a white man to disappear, to simply vanish as into thin air. Perhaps he is never heard of again. Perhaps his knife-riddled body is found floating in the river, or cast up on the beach. In either event, only silence rewards investigations. China never speaks. Like a vast, sleeping yellow giant she preserves her ancient and mysterious silence inviolate.

Finishing my meal, I sauntered out into the streets again, with their filth and glamor, sordidity and allure going hand in hand; throngs of Orientals buying and selling, bargaining in their monotonous sing-song, sailors of all nations rolling through the crowds ....

I began to have a queer feeling that I was being followed. Again and again I wheeled quickly and scanned the crowd, but in that teeming swarm of yellow slant-eyed faces it was impossible to tell whether anyone was trailing me. Yet the sensation persisted.

AS THE DAY WORE ON I found myself in Froggy Ladeau's American Bar, at the edge of the waterfront district. There I spied a man I knew—an Englishman named Wells, who had some sort of a government job. I sat down at his table. "Wells," I said, "did you ever hear of a man named Yotai T'sao?"

"That I have," he answered. "But I fear the blighter's been potted off. He's been working with the government trying to get evidence against a certain gang of dangerous criminals and last night he disappeared."

"He's all right," I replied. "I saw him swim out to an English ship which weighed anchor shortly after sun-up. But who are these criminals?"

"Bad blokes," said Wells, taking a long swig of ale. "An organized society. It's rumored their chief is a coral button mandarin. They specialize in murder and blackmail, to say nothing of smuggling, gun-running and jewel-stealing. Of late they've been tampering with bigger things—governmental secrets. The Yo Thans, they're called. The government would jolly well like to lay hands on them. But you've no idea what snaky customers they are. They're here, there and everywhere. We know they exist, but we can't nab the beggars. If the natives would talk—but they won't, and there's China for you. Even victims of the society won't blab. So what can we do?

"But the government has gotten a promise of assistance from the most Honorable and Eminent Yun Lai Kao. You've heard of him?"

"Sure," I nodded. "Sort of a wealthy Oriental recluse and philanthropist, isn't he?"

"That and more. The natives look on him as a sort of god. He has almost unbelievable power in Canton, though he's never bothered to wield it very much. He's a philosopher—too busy considering abstract ideals and principles to bother with material things. He seldom ever appears in public. It was the very deuce to get him interested enough in sordid reality to promise to help the government scotch a gang of thugs. That shows, too, how helpless the government really is in this matter, when it has to call on private individuals. The only argument that moved him was the assurance that the Yo Thans are swiftly assuming a political importance, and were likely to start a civil war in China."

"Is it that important?" I asked, startled.

"Believe me, it is. These things grow fast. The unknown power, the nameless man, directing the activities of these thugs, is ruthless and clever as the devil, quite capable of raising the red flag of anarchy if he gets a little more power. China is a powder keg, ready for some unscrupulous rogue to set it off. No conservative Chinese wants that to happen. That's why Yun Lai Kao agreed to help.

And with his power over the natives, I believe the government will lay the Yo Thans by the heels."

"What sort of a man is this mandarin, Yun Lai Kao?" I asked. "A venerable, white bearded patriarch, with ten-inch finger nails encased in gold and a load of Confucian epigrams?"

"Not by a long shot," answered Wells. "He doesn't look the type of a mystic at all. A clean-cut chap in middle life, he is, with a firm jaw and gimlet eyes—a graduate from Oxford too, by the way. Should have been a scientist or a soldier. Some queer quirk in his Oriental mind turned him to philosophy."

A COMMOTION BURST out in the bar. Ladeau was having some kind of a row with a big sailor. Suddenly the sailor hauled off and hit Froggy between the eyes. Ladeau crashed down on a table, with beer mugs and seltzer water bottles spilling all over him, and began yelling for Big John Clancy, his American bouncer. Hearing this, the sailor took to his heels. But Ladeau, floundering around in the ruins of the table with his eyes still full of stars, didn't see that. Big John came barging in and Froggy yelled: "Throw him out! Beat him up! Give him the bum's rush! Out with him, John!"

"Out with who?" roared Clancy, glaring around and doubling up his huge fists.

"That blasted sailor," bawled Froggy. Clancy then made a natural mistake. As it happened, I was the only sailor in the bar. I had just turned back to speak to Wells, when to my outraged amazement, I felt myself gripped by what appeared to be a gorilla.

"Out with you, my bully," growled Big John, hauling me out of my chair and trying to twist me around and get a hammerlock on my right arm.

I might have explained the situation, but my nerves were on edge already. And being mate on a tough tramp trader makes a man handier with his fists than with his tongue. I acted without conscious thought and jolted him loose from me with a left hook under the heart that nearly upset him. It would have finished an ordinary man, but Big John was built like a battleship. He gave a deafening roar and plunged headlong on me, locking both of his mighty arms around me. We went to the floor together, smashing a few chairs in our fall. As we cursed and wrestled, his superior weight enabled him to get on top of me.

At that instant my bulldog Bill landed square between Clancy's shoulders. By some chance his jaws missed Big John's bull neck, but ripped out the whole back of his coat. Big John gave a yell of fright and with a desperate heave of his enormous shoulders, shook Bill off and jumped up. I arose, too, and caught Bill just as he was soaring for Clancy's throat. I pushed him back, ordering him to keep out of it, and then turned toward Big John, who was snorting and blowing like a grampus in his wrath.

I was seeing red myself.

"Come on, you son-of-a-seahorse," I snarled. "If it's fighting you want, I'll give you a belly-full."

At that he gave a terrible howl and came for me, crazy-eyed. Ladeau ran between us, dancing and howling like a burnt cat.

"Git away, Froggy," bellowed Big John, swinging his huge arms like windmills. "Git outa the way! I'm goin' to smear this salt-water tramp all over the joint."

"Wait a minute, please, John," screamed Ladeau, pushing against Clancy's broad chest with both hands. "This here is Steve Costigan of the *Panther*."

"What do I care who he is?" roared Big John. "Git outa the way!"

"You can't fight in here," Froggy howled desperately. "If you two tangles here, you'll tear the joint down. I can't afford it. Anyway, he ain't the man that hit me."

"Well, he's the swine that hit me," rumbled Big John.

"Get aside, Froggy," I snapped. "Let us have it out. It's the only way."

"No, no!" shrieked Ladeau. "It cost me five hundred dollars to repair the place after you throwed Red McCoy out, John, and I seen Costigan lick Bully Dawson in a saloon in Hong Kong. They had to rebuild the joint. Come down on the beach, back of the Kago Tong warehouses and fight it out where you can't bust nothin' but each others' noses."

"A jolly good idea," put in Wells. "You fellows don't want to make a spectacle of yourselves here, in a respectable district, and have the police on you. If you must fight, why don't you do as Ladeau says?"

Big John folded his mighty arms and glared at me, as he growled: "Fair enough. I ain't the man to do useless damage. I'll be at the beach as quick as I can get there. Get some of your crew, Costigan, so as to have fair play all around. And get there as soon as you can."

"Good enough," I snapped. Turning on my heel, I left the bar. Oh, it seems foolish, no doubt, grown men fighting like school boys. But reputations grow. A man in the ordinary course of duty acquires the name of a fighter and before he knows it, his pride is forcing him into fights to maintain it.

HOPING TO FIND SOME of the *Panther's* crew, I went down the narrow waterfront streets. My efforts met with no success. As a last resort, I thought of a shop down a little side street in the native quarter, run by a Chinese named Yuen Lao, who sells trinkets such as sailors buy in foreign ports to give to their sweethearts.

With the thought that I might find some of my friends there, I turned into the obscure, winding street. I noticed that there were even fewer people traversing it than usual. An old man with a cage full of canary birds, a coolie pulling a cart, a fish peddler or so—that was all.

I saw the shop just ahead of me. Then, with a vicious zing—something came humming through the air. It hissed by my neck as I instinctively ducked. It thudded into the wall at my shoulder—a long thin bladed knife, stuck a good three inches into the hard boards and quivering from the force of the throw. Had it hit me, it would have gone clear through me.

I looked across the street, but all I could see was the blank fronts of a row of vacant shops. The windows all seemed to be boarded up, but I knew that the knife had come from one of them. The Chinese on the street paid no attention to me at all. They went about their affairs as if they seen nothing, not even me. Little use to ask them if they saw the knife-thrower. China never speaks.

And the thought of the Yo Thans came back to me with a shudder. It had been no idle threat, that cryptic sign of the snake. They had struck and missed, but they would strike again and again until they opened the Doors of Doom for Steve Costigan. Cold sweat broke out on me. This was like fighting a cobra in the dark.

I turned into Yuen Lao's shop, with its shelves of jade idols, coral jewelry and tiny ivory elephants. A bronze Buddha squatted on a raised dais, its inscrutable face veiled by the smoke of burning joss sticks. Only Yuen Lao, tall and lean, with a mask-like face, stood in the shop.

I turned to leave, when he came quickly from behind his counter.

"You are Costigan, mate of the *Panther*?" said he in good English. I nodded, and he continued in a lowered voice. "You are in danger. Do not ask me how I know. These things have a way of getting about among the Chinese. Listen to me. I would be your friend. And you need friends. Without my aid, you will be dead before dawn."

"Oh, I don't know," I growled, involuntarily tensing my biceps. "I've never been in a jam yet that I couldn't slug my way out of."

"Your strength will not help you." He shook his head. "Your shipmates cannot aid you. Your enemies will strike secretly and subtly. Their sign is the cobra. And, like the cobra, they kill swiftly, silently, giving their victim no chance to defend himself."

I began to feel wild and desperate, like a wolf in a trap, as the truth of his words came home to me.

"How am I going to fight men who won't come into the open?" I snarled, helplessly, knotting my fists until the knuckles showed white. "Get them in front of me and I'll battle the whole gang. But I can't smoke them out of their hives."

"You must listen to me," said Yuen Lao. "I will save you. I have no cause to love the Yo Thans."

"But why have they turned on me?" I asked in perplexity.

"You prevented their chief hatchet-man from slaying Yotai T'sao," said he. "Yotai T'sao was doomed, tried and sentenced by their most dread tribunal. He had intrigued his way into their secret meeting places and councils, to get evidence to use against them in the court. For he was a spy of the government. His life was forfeit and not even the government could save him from the vengeance of the Yo Thans. Last night he sought to escape and was trapped by Yaga, the hatchet-man who hunted him down and caught him almost on the wharves. There had Yotai T'sao died but for you. Today he is far at sea and safe. But the vengeance of the Yo Thans is turned upon you. And you are doomed."

"A nice mess," I muttered.

"But I am your friend," continued Yuen Lao. "And I hate the Yo Thans. I am more than I seem."

"Are you a government spy too?" I asked.

"Shh!" He laid his long finger to his lips and glanced around quickly and warily. "The very walls have ears in Canton. But I will tell you this. There is but one man in Canton who can save you, who will, if I ask him, speak the word that will make even the Yo Thans stay their hands."

"Yun Lai Kao," I muttered.

Yuen Lao started and peered at me intensely for an instant. Then he seemed to nod, almost imperceptibly.

"Tonight I will take you to—this—this man. Let him remain nameless, for the present. You must come alone, hinting your errand to no one. Trust me!"

"It's not many hours till sundown," I muttered. "When and where shall I meet you?"

"Come to me alone, in the Alley of Bats, as soon as it is well dark. And go now, quickly. We must not be seen too much together. And be wary, lest the Yo Thans strike again before we meet."

AS I LEFT THE SHOP I HAD a distinct feeling of relief. I had not been inclined to trust Yuen Lao's mere word, but his evident connection with the mighty and mysterious mandarin, Yun Lai Kao, together with what Wells had said of the mandarin, reassured me. If I could evade the hatred of the unknown murderers until dark ....

Suddenly, with a curse of annoyance, I remembered that at this very moment I was supposed to be on my way to the beach to fight Big John Clancy with my naked fists. Well, it must be done. Even if I died that night, I must keep that appointment. I could not go out with men thinking I dared not meet Big John in open fight. Besides, the thought came to me, that was the safest place in Canton for me—on the open beach, surrounded by men of my own race. The problem lay in getting there alive. I made no further attempts to find the crew, but set off at a rapid walk, keeping my eye alert and passing alleyways very warily. Bill sensed my caution and kept close to me, walking stiff-legged, rumbling deep and ominously in his throat.

But I arrived unharmed at the strip of open beach behind the big warehouses. Big John was already there, stripped to the waist, growling his impatience and flexing his mighty arms. Froggy Ladeau was there and half a dozen others, all friends of Clancy. Wells was not there. I couldn't help wondering about that.

"I couldn't find any of my friends, Clancy," I said abruptly. "But I'm not afraid of not getting fair play. I've always heard of you as a square shooter. My dog won't interfere. I'll make him understand that. But Froggy can hold him if you'd rather."

"You've kept me waitin'," growled Big John. "Let's get goin'."

It's like a dream now, that fight on the Kago Tong beach. Men still talk about it, from Vladivostok to Sumatra, wherever the roving brotherhood gathers to spin old yarns over their glasses.

"No kickin', gougin', or bitin'," Big John growled. "Let it be a white man's fight."

And a white man's fight it was, there on the naked beach, both of us stripped to the waist, with no weapons but our naked fists. What a man John Clancy was! I was six feet tall and weighed 190 pounds. He stood six feet one and three quarter inches and he weighed 230 pounds—all bone and muscle it was, with never an ounce of fat on him. His legs were like tree trunks, his arms looked as if they had been molded out of iron, and his chest was arching and broad as a door. A massive, corded neck upheld a lion-like head and a face like a Roman senator's.

I weighed my chances as we approached each other, I and this giant who had never known defeat. In sheer strength and bulk he had the edge. But I was strong, too, in those days, and I knew that I was the faster man and the more scientific boxer.

He came at me like a charging bull and I met him half-way. Mine was the skill or fortune to get in the first punch, a smashing left hook square to the jaw. It stopped him dead in his tracks. But he roared and came on again, shaking his lion-like head. I went under his gigantic swings to rip both hands to his body. I was fast enough and skilled enough to avoid his mightiest blows for a time, but let it not be thought that I back-pedalled and ran, or fought a merely defensive fight. Men do not fight that way on the beach—or anywhere in the raw edges of the world.

I stood up to him and he stood up to me. My head was singing with his blows and the blood trickled from my mouth. Blue welts showed on his ribs and one of his eyes was closing.

He loomed like a giant over me as I ducked his terrible swing. It whistled over my head and my glancing return tore the skin on his ribs. Gad, his right hand whistled past my face like a white hot brick, and when he landed he shook me from head to heel. But my battles with men and with the Seven Seas had toughened me into steel and whale-bone endurance. I stood up to it.

I was landing the more and cleaner blows. Again and again I had him floundering, but always he came back with a crashing, bone-crushing attack I could not altogether avoid. I bulled in close, ducking inside his wide looping smashes, and ripped both hands to body and head. I had the better at the infighting. But, staggering under a machine-gun fire of short hooks and uppercuts, he suddenly ripped up an uppercut of his own. Gad, my head snapped back as if my neck was broken. Only blind instinct made me fall into Big John and clinch before he could strike again. And I held on with a grizzly grip not even he could break, until my head cleared.

The onlookers had formed a tense ring about us. Their nails bit into their clenching palms and their breaths came in swift gasps. There was no other sound save the scruff of our feet on the beach, the thud and smash of savagely driven blows,

an occasional grunt, and Bill's low, incessant growling.

CLANCY'S HUGE FIST banged against my eye, half closing it. My right crashed full into his mouth and he spit out a shattered tooth.

My left hook was doing most of the damage. Big John was too fond of using his right. He drew it back too far before he let it go. Again and again I beat him to the punch with my left, and I made raw beef out of the right side of his jaw. Sometimes he would duck clumsily and my hook would smash on his ear, which was a beautiful cauliflower before the fight was over. But I was not unmarked.

Things floated in a red mist. I saw Big John's face before me, with the lips smashed and pulped, one eye closed and blood streaming from his nose. My arms were growing heavy, my feet slow. I stumbled as I side-stepped. The taste of blood was in my mouth. How long we had stood toe to toe, exchanging terrific smashes, I did not know. It seemed like ages. In chaotic, flashing glances, I saw the strained, white, tense faces of the onlookers.

From somewhere smashed Big John's thundering right hand. Square on the jaw it crashed. I felt myself falling into an abyss of blackness, shot with a million gleams and darts of light. I struck the beach hard, and the jolt of the fall jarred me back into my senses. I looked up, shaking the blood and sweat out of my eyes, and saw Big John looming above me. He was swaying, wide-braced on his mighty legs. His great, hairy chest was heaving as his breath came in panting gasps. I dragged myself to my feet. The knowledge that he was in as bad a way as I, nerved my weary muscles.

"You must be made outa iron," he croaked, lurching toward me. I took a deep breath and braced myself to meet his right. The blow was a glancing one and I blasted both hands under his heart. He reeled like a ship in rough weather, but came back with a left swing that staggered me. Again he swung his right, like a club. I ducked and straightened with a left hook that cracked on the side of his head. But it was high. I felt my knuckles crumple. His knees buckled and I put all I had behind my right. Like a swinging maul, it smashed on Big John Clancy's jaw. And he swayed and fell.

I felt men about me, heard their awed congratulations, felt Bill's cold wet nose shoved into my hand. Froggy was staring down at the senseless form of Big John in a sort of unbelieving horror.

Then came memory of Yuen Lao and the Yo Thans. I shook the blood and sweat from my eyes, pulling away from the men who were pawing over me. The sun was setting. If I expected to see that sun rise again, I must meet Yuen Lao and go with him to Yun Lai Kao.

Snatching up my clothes, I tore away from the amazed men and reeled drunkenly up the beach. Out of sight of the group, I dropped from sheer exhaustion. It was minutes before I could rise and go on.

My mind cleared as I walked, and my head ceased to sing from Big John's smashes. I was fiercely weary, sore and bruised. It seemed impossible for me to get my wind back. My left hand was swollen and sore, and the skin was torn on my right knuckles. One of my eyes was partly closed, my lips were smashed and cut, my ribs battered black and blue. But the cool wind from the sea helped me, and with the recuperative powers of youth and an iron frame, I regained my wind, shook off some of my weariness and felt fairly fit as I neared the Alley of Bats, in the growing darkness.

I FOUND TIME TO WONDER why the Yo Thans had not struck again. There was something unnatural about the whole business, it seemed to me. Since that knife had been flung at me earlier in the day, I had had no sign at all of the existence of that murderous gang.

I came unharmed to the narrow, stinking rat-den in the heart of the native quarter which the Chinese call, for some unknown reason, the Alley of Bats. It was pitch-dark there. I felt cold shivers creep up and down my spine. Suddenly a figure loomed up beside me and Bill snarled. In my nervousness I almost struck out at the figure, when Yuen Lao's voice halted me. He was like a ghost in the deep shadows. Bill growled savagely.

"Come with me," whispered Yuen Lao. And I groped after him. Down that alley he led me. Across another even darker and nastier. Through a wide shadowy courtyard. Down a narrow side street, deep in the heart of what I knew must be a mysterious native quarter seldom seen by white men. Down another alley and into a dimly lighted courtyard. He stopped before a heavy arched doorway.

As he rapped upon it, I realized the utter silence, eeriness and brooding mystery of the place. Truly, I was in the very heart of ancient and enigmatic China, as surely as if I had been five hundred miles in the interior. The very shadows seemed lurking perils. I shuddered involuntarily.

Three times Yuen Lao rapped. Then the door swung silently inward, to disclose a veritable well of darkness. I could not even see who had opened the door. Yuen Lao entered first, motioning me to follow. I stepped in, Bill crowding close after me. The door slammed between us, leaving the dog on the outside. I heard the click of a heavy lock. Bill was clawing and whining outside the door. And then the lights came on. While I blinked like a blinded owl, I heard a low throaty chuckle that sent involuntary shivers up and down my spine. My eyes

became accustomed to the light. I saw that I was in a big room, furnished in true Oriental style. The walls were covered with velvet and silken hangings, ornamented with silver dragons worked into the fabric. A faint scent of some Eastern incense or perfume pervaded the atmosphere.

Ranged about me were ten big, dark, wicked-faced men, naked except for loin-cloths. Malays they were, tougher and stronger than any Chinese. On a kind of tiger-skin covered dais across the room an unmistakable Chinaman sat on a lacquer-worked chair. He was clad in robes worked in dragons like those on the hangings, and his keen piercing eyes gleamed through holes in the mask which hid his features. But it was the figure which stood image-like beside the lacquered chair which drew and held my gaze. It was the hatchet-man from whom I had rescued Yotai T'sao on the wharfs that morning.

In a sickening instant I realized that I was trapped. Blind fool that I was, to walk into the snare. A child might have suspected that mask-faced snake of a Yuen Lao. He too was a Yo Than, I realized. And he had not brought me to the Honorable and Benevolent Yun Lai Kao. He had brought me before the nameless and mysterious chief of the Yo Thans, to die like a butchered sheep.

And there he stood before me, Yuen Lao, smiling evilly. I acted instinctively. Square into his mouth

I crashed my right before he could move. His teeth caved in and he dropped like a log.

The masked man on the dais laughed. And in his laughter sounded all the ancient and heartless cruelty of the Orient.

"The white barbarian is strong and fierce," he mocked. "But this night, my bold savage, you shall learn what it is to interfere with the plans of Kang Kian of the Yo Thans. Fool, to pit your paltry powers against mine. You, with the striding arrogance of your breed.

"Know, fool, before you die, that the ancient dragon that is China is waking slowly beneath the feet of the foreign dogs, and their doom is not far off. Soon I, Kang Kian, master of the Yo Thans, will come from the shadows, raise the dragon banner of revolution and mount again the ancient throne of my ancestors. Your fate will be the fate of all your race who oppose me. I laugh at you. Do you deem yourself important because the future emperor of China deigns to see personally to your removal? Bah! I merely crush you as I crush the gnat that annoys me."

Then he spoke shortly to the Malays: "Kill him."

THEY CLOSED IN ON me silently, drawing knives, strangling cords and loaded cudgels. It looked like trail's end for Steve Costigan. I, with two black eyes, ribs pounded black and blue, one hand broken, from one fierce fight, pitted against these trained killers. They approached warily. Bill, outside, sensing my peril, began to roar and hurl himself against the bolted door. I tensed myself for one last rush. The thought flashed through me that perhaps Bill would escape my fate. I hoped that it might be so.

I drew back, tensed and watchful as a hawk. The ring was closing in on me. The nearest Malay edged within reach. He raised his knife for the death leap. I smashed my heel to his knee and distinctly heard the bone snap. He went down. I leaped across him and hit that closing ring as a plunging fullback hits a line.

Cudgels swished past my head. I felt a knife lick along my ribs. Then I was through, bounding across the room and onto the dais.

Kang Kian screamed. He jerked a pistol from his robes. How he missed me at that range, I cannot say. The powder flash burned my face, but before he could fire again I knocked him head over heels with a blow that was backed with the power of desperation. The pistol flew out of reach.

The hatchet-man was on me like a clawing cat. He drove a long knife deep into my chest muscles. Then I got in a solid smash. His jaw was brittle. It crunched like an egg-shell. I swung his limp form up bodily above my head and hurled him into the clump of Malays who came leaping up on the dais, bowling over the front line like ten-pins. The rest came at me.

Carried beyond myself on a red wave of desperate battle fury, I caught up the lacquered chair and swung it with all my strength. Squarely it landed and I felt my victim's shoulder bone give way. But the chair flew into splinters. Then a whistling cudgel stroke laid my scalp open and knocked me to my knees. The whole pack piled on me, hacking and slashing. But their very numbers hindered them. Somehow, I managed to shake them off momentarily and stagger up.

A big Chinaman I had not seen before bobbed up from nowhere and got a bone-breaking wrestling hold on my right arm. A giant Malay was thrusting for my life. I could not wrench my right free. So, setting my teeth, I slugged him with my broken left. I went sick and dizzy from the pain of it, but the Malay dropped like a sack.

But they downed me again, as my berserk fighting frenzy waned. They swarmed over me and forced me down by sheer weight of man-power. I heard Kang Kian yelling to them with the rage of a fiend in his voice, and a big dark-skinned devil raised his knife and drove it down for my heart. Somehow, I managed to throw up my left arm and take the blade through it. That arm felt like I'd bathed in molten lead.

Then I heard the door crash and splinter. A familiar voice roared like a high sea. And something like a white cannon-ball hit the clump of natives on top of me.

The press slackened as the group flew apart. I reeled up, sick, dizzy and weak from loss of the blood that was spurting from me in half a dozen places. As in a daze, I saw Bill leaping and tearing at dark, howling figures which fell over each other trying to get away. And I saw a white giant ploughing through them as a battle-ship goes through breakers.

Big John Clancy!

I saw him seize a Malay in each hand, by the neck, crack their heads together and throw them into a corner. A dusky giant ran in, lunging upward with a stroke meant to disembowel, only to be stretched senseless by one blow of Big John's mighty fist. The big Chinaman—a wrestler, by his looks—got a head-lock on Clancy. But Big John broke the hold, wheeled and threw the wrestler clear over his shoulders, head over heels. The Chinaman hit on his head and he didn't get up.

That was enough for the Yo Thans. They scattered like a flock of birds, all except Kang Kian, the masked lord. He sprang for the fallen pistol. Before he could reach it, Bill, jaws already streaming red, dragged him down. One fearful scream broke from the Yo Than's yellow lips and then Bill's iron jaws tore out his throat.

B IG JOHN CAME QUICKLY toward me. "By golly, Costigan," he rumbled, "you look like you been through a sawmill. Here, lemme tie up some of them stabs before you bleed to death. You've lost a gallon of blood already. We got to git you where you can git dressed right. But for the time bein' we'll see can we stop the bleedin'."

He ripped strips from his shirt and began to bandage me. Bill climbed all over me, wagging his stump of a tail and licking my hand.

I gazed at Big John in amazement. I had thought my own vitality unusual, but Big John's endurance was beyond belief. He looked as if he'd been mauled by a gorilla. I was astounded to realize the extent to which I had punished him in our battle. Yet he seemed almost as fresh and fit as ever. My smashes which had blackened his eyes, smashed his lips, ripped his ears, shattered some of his teeth and laid open his jaw, had battered him down and out, but had not sapped the vast reservoir of his vitality. I had merely weakened him momentarily and knocked him out, that was all, and accomplishing that feat had taken more of my strength than it had his.

"I supposed you'd be laid up for a week after our fight," I said bluntly.

He snorted. "You must think I'm effeminate. I wasn't out but a few minutes. And when I'd got back my breath, I was ready to go on with the fight. Of course I'm kinda stiff and sore and tired-like, right now, but that amounts to nothing.

"When I'd got my bearin's I looked around for you. Froggy and them had a hard time convincin' me that I'd been licked, for the first time in my life. I'll swear, I still don't see how it could of happened. Anyway, I started right out to find you and take you apart, because I was mighty near blind mad. A coolie had seen you go into the Alley of Bats and I followed, not long behind you. I know Canton better'n most white men, but I got clean tangled up in all them alley-ways and courtyards.

"Then I heard your dog makin' a big racket. I knowed it was yours, because they ain't but one dog in China with a voice like his. So I come and found him roarin' and plungin' at the door and I heard the noise inside. So knowin' you must be in some kind of a jam, I just up and busted in. Who was them thugs, anyhow?"

I told him quickly about Yotai T'sao and the Yo Thans. He growled: "I mighta knowed it. I've heard of 'em. I bet they won't put no snake sign on no more Americans very soon. Come on, let's get outa here."

"I don't know how to thank you, Clancy," I said. "You certainly saved my hide ...."

"Aw, don't thank me," he grunted. "I couldn't see them mutts bump off a white man. And you'd sure give 'em a tussle by yourself. Naw, don't thank me. Remember I was lookin' for you to beat you up."

"Well," said I, "I hate to fight a man who's saved my life, but if you're set on it ... "

He laughed gustily and slapped me on the back. "Thunderation, Steve, I wouldn't hit a man which has just stopped as many knives as you have. Anyway, I'm beginnin' to like you. Who's this?"

A tall man in European clothes stepped suddenly into the doorway, with a revolver in one hand.

"Wells!" I exclaimed. "What are you doing here?"

"Following a tip-off I got earlier in the evening," he said crisply. "I got wind of a secret session of the Yo Thans to be held here."

"So you are a Secret Service man after all," I said slowly. "If I'd known that, I might not have all these knife-stabs in my hide."

"I've been trailing the Yo Thans for some time," he answered. "Working with special powers invested in me by British and Chinese authorities. Who's this dead man?"

"He called himself Kang Kian and boasted that he was the mysterious lord of the Yo Thans and the next emperor of China," I answered, with an involuntary shudder, as I glanced at the grisly havoc Bill's ripping fangs had wrought.

Wells' eyes blazed. He stepped forward and tore away the blood stained mask, revealing the smooth yellow face and clean-cut aristocrat features of a middle-aged China-man.

Wells recoiled with an exclamation.

"My word! Can it be possible! No wonder he delayed the aid he promised the government, and only promised, I can see now, to avert suspicion. And no wonder he was able to keep his true identity a secret. Clancy, Costigan, this is the Honorable and Eminent Yun Lai Kao."

"What, the philosopher and philanthropist?" Clancy, who knew Canton, was even more amazed than I.

Wells nodded slowly. "What strange quirk in his nature led him along this path?" he said half to himself. "What a mind he had. What heights he might have risen to, but for that one twist in his soul. Who can explain it?"

Clancy, who knew the Orient, seemed to be groping for words to frame a thought.

"China," he said, "is China. And there's no use in a white man tryin' to figger her out."

Aye, China is China—vast, aloof, inscrutable, the Sphynx of the nations.

The HOUSE *of* PERIL.

ALTERNATE TITLE: BLOW THE CHINKS DOWN.

This short story was first published in the October 1931 issue of Action Stories *magazine.*

A FAMILIAR STOCKY SHAPE, stood with a foot on the brass rail, as I entered the American Bar, in Hong Kong. I glared at the shape disapprovingly, recognizing it as Bill McGlory of the *Dutchman*. That is one ship I enthusiastically detest, this dislike being shared by all the bold lads aboard the *Sea Girl*, from the cap'n to the cook.

I shouldered up along the bar. Ignoring Bill, I called for a whisky straight.

"You know, John," said Bill, addressing hisself to the bartender, "you got no idee the rotten tubs which calls theirselves ships that's tied up to the wharfs right now. Now then, the *Sea Girl* for instance. An' there's a guy named Steve Costigan—"

"You know, John," I broke in, addressing myself to the bartender, "it's clean surprisin' what goes around on their hind laigs callin' theirselves sailor-men, these days. A baboon got outa the zoo at Brisbane and they just now spotted it on the wharfs here in Hong Kong."

"You don't say," said John the bar-keep. "Where'd it been?"

"To sea," I said. "It'd shipped as A.B. mariner on the *Dutchman* and was their best hand."

With which caustic repartee, I stalked out in gloating triumph, leaving Bill McGlory gasping and strangling as he tried to think of something to say in return. To celebrate my crushing victory over the enemy I swaggered into the La Belle Cabaret and soon seen a good looking girl setting alone at a table. She was toying with her cigaret and drink like she was bored, so I went over and set down.

"Evenin', Miss," I says, doffing my cap. "I'm just in from sea and cravin' to toss my money around. Do you dance?"

She eyed me amusedly from under her long, drooping lashes and said: "Yes, I do, on occasion. But I don't work here, sailor."

"Oh, excuse me, Miss," I said, getting up. "I sure beg your pardon."

"That's all right," she said. "Don't run away. Let's sit here and talk."

"That's fine," I said, setting back down again, when to my annoyance a sea-going figger bulked up to the table.

"Even', Miss," said Bill McGlory, fixing me with a accusing stare. "Is this walrus annoyin' you?"

"Listen here, you flat-headed mutt—" I begun with some heat, but the girl said: "Now, now, don't fight, boys. Sit down and let's all talk sociably. I like to meet people from the States in this heathen land. My name is Kit Worley and I work for Tung Yin, the big Chinese merchant."

"Private secretary or somethin'?" says Bill.

"Governess to his nieces," said she. "But don't let's talk about me. Tell me something about yourselves. You boys are sailors, aren't you?"

"I am," I replied meaningly. Bill glared at me.

"Do tell me about some of your voyages," said she hurriedly. "I just adore ships."

"Then you'd sure like the *Dutchman*, Miss Worley," beamed Bill. "I don't like to brag, but for trim lines, smooth rig, a fine figger and speed, they ain't a sailin' craft in the China trade can hold a candle to her. She's a dream. A child could steer her."

"Or anybody with a child's mind," I says. "And does—when you're at the wheel."

"Listen here, you scum of the Seven Seas," said Bill turning brick color. "You layoff the *Dutchman*. I'd never have the nerve to insult a sweet ship like her if I sailed in a wormy, rotten-timbered, warped-decked, crank-ruddered, crooked-keeled, crazy-rigged tub like the *Sea Girl*."

"You'll eat them words with a sauce of your own blood," I howled.

"Boys!" said Miss Worley. "Now, boys."

"Miss Worley," I said, getting up and shedding my coat, "I'm a law-abidin' and peaceful man, gentle and generous to a fault. But they's times when patience becomes a vice and human kindness is a stumblin' block on the road of progress. This baboon in human form don't understand no kind of moral suasion but a bust on the jaw."

"Come out in the alley," squalled Bill, bounding up like a jumping-jack.

"Come on," I said. "Let's settle this here feud once and for all. Miss Worley," I said, "wait here for the victor. I won't be gone long."

Out in the alley, surrounded by a gang of curious coolies, we squared off without no more ado. We was well matched, about the same height and weighing about 190 pounds each. But as we approached each other with our fists up, a form stepped between. We stopped and glared in outraged surprise. It was a tall, slender Englishman with a kind of tired, half humorous expression.

"Come, come, my good men," he said. "We can't have this sort of thing, you know. Bad example to the natives and all that sort of thing. Can't have white men fighting in the alleys these days. Times too unsettled, you know. Must uphold the white man's standard."

"Well, by golly," I said. "I've had a hundred fights in Hong-kong and nobody yet never told me before I was settin' a bad example to nobody."

"Bad tactics, just the same," he said. "And quite too much unrest now. If the discontented Oriental sees white men bashing each other's bally jaws, the white race loses just that much prestige, you see."

"But what right you got buttin' into a private row?" I complained.

"Rights vested in me by the Chinese government, working with the British authorities, old topper," said the Englishman. "Brent is the name."

"Sir Peter Brent of the Secret Service, hey?" I grunted. "I've heard tell of you. But I dunno what you could do if we was to tell you to go chase yourself."

"I could summon the bally police and throw you in jail, old thing," he said apologetically. "But I don't want to do that."

"Say," I said, "You got any idee how many Chinee cops it'd take to lug Steve Costigan and Bill McGlory to the hoosegow?"

"A goodly number, I should judge," said he. "Still if you lads persist in this silly feud, I shall have to take the chance. I judge fifty would be about the right number."

"Aw, hell," snorted Bill, hitching up his britches. "Let's rock him to sleep and go on with the fray. He can't do nothin'."

But I balked. Something about the slim Britisher made me feel mad and ashamed too. He was so frail looking alongside us sluggers.

"Aw, let it slide for the time bein'," I muttered. "We'd have to lay him out first before he'd let us go on, and he's too thin to hit. We might bust him in half. Let it go, if he's so plumb set on it. We got the whole world to fight in."

"You're gettin' soft and sentimental," snorted Bill. And with that he swaggered off in high disgust.

I eyed him morosely.

"Now he'll probably think I was afraid to fight him," I said gloomily. "And it's all your fault."

"Sorry, old man," said Sir Peter. "I'd have liked to have seen the mill myself, by jove. But public duty comes first, you know. Come, forget about it and have a drink."

"I ain't a-goin' to drink with you," I said bitterly. "You done spoilt my fun and made me look like a coward."

And disregarding his efforts to conciliate me, I shoved past him and wandered gloomily down the alley. I didn't go back to the La Belle. I was ashamed to admit to Miss Worley that they wasn't no fight. But later on I got to thinking about it and wondering what Bill told her in case he went back to her. It would be just like him to tell her I run out on him and refused to fight, I thought, or that he flattened me without getting his hair ruffled. He wasn't above punching a wall or something and telling her he skinned them knuckles on my jaw.

So I decided to look Miss Worley up and explain the whole thing to her—also take her to a theater or something if she'd go. She was a very pretty girl, refined and

educated—anybody could tell that—yet not too proud to talk with a ordinary sailorman. Them kind is few and far betweenst.

I asked a bar-keep where Tung Yin lived and he told me. "But," he added, "you better keep away from Tung Yin. He's a shady customer and he don't like whites."

"You're nuts," I said. "Any man which Miss Kit Worley works for is bound to be okay."

"Be that as it may," said the bar-keep. "The cops think that Tung Yin was some way mixed up in the big diamond theft."

"What big diamond theft?" I said.

"Gee whiz," he said. "Didn't you hear about the big diamond theft last month?"

"Last month I was in Australia," I said impatiently.

"Well," he said, "somebody stole the Royal Crystal—that's what they called the diamond account of a emperor of China once usin' it to tell fortunes, like the gypsies use a crystal ball, y'know. Somebody stole it right outa the government museum. Doped the guards, hooked the stone and got clean away. Slickest thing I ever heard of in my life. That diamond's worth a fortune. And some think that Tung Yin had a hand in it. Regular international ruckus. They got Sir Peter Brent, the big English detective, workin' on the case now."

"Well," I said, "I ain't interested. Only I know Tung Yin never stole it, because Miss Worley wouldn't work for nobody but a gent."

S O I WENT TO TUNG YIN'S place. It was a whopping big house, kinda like a palace, off some distance from the main part of the city. I went in a 'ricksha and got there just before sundown. The big house was set out by itself amongst groves of orange trees and cherry trees and the like, and I seen a airplane out in a open space that was fixed up like a landing field. I remembered that I'd heard tell that Tung Yin had a young Australian aviator named Clanry in his employ. I figgered likely that was his plane.

I started for the house and then got cold feet. I hadn't never been in a rich Chinee's dump before and I didn't know how to go about it. I didn't know whether you was supposed to go up and knock on the door and ask for Miss Kit Worley, or what. So I decided I'd cruise around a little and maybe I'd see her walking in the garden. I come up to the garden, which had a high wall around it, and I climbed up on the wall and looked over. They was lots of flowers and cherry trees and a fountain with a bronze dragon, and over near the back of the big house they was another low wall, kind of separating the house from the garden. And I seen a feminine figger pass through a small gate in this wall.

Taking a chance it was Miss Worley, I dropped into the garden,

hastened forward amongst the cherry trees and flowers, and blundered through the gate into a kind of small court. Nobody was there, but I seen a door just closing in the house so I went right on through and come into a room furnished in the usual Chinese style, with tapestries and screens and silk cushions and them funny Chinese tea tables and things. A chorus of startled feminine squeals brung me up standing and I gawped about in confusion. Miss Worley wasn't nowhere in sight. All I seen was three or four Chinese girls which looked at me like I was a sea serpent.

"What you do here?" asked one of them.

"I'm lookin' for the governess," I said, thinking that maybe these was Tung Yin's nieces. Though, by golly, I never seen no girls which had less of the schoolgirl look about 'em.

"Governor?" she said. "You crazee? Governor him live along Nanking."

"Naw, naw," I said. "Gover-ness, see? The young lady which governesses the big boy's nieces—Tung Yin's nieces."

"You crazee," she said decisively. "Tung Yin him got no fool nieces."

"Say, listen," I said. "We ain't gettin' nowhere. I can't speak Chinee and you evidently can't understand English. I'm lookin' for Miss Kit Worley, see?"

"Ooooh!" she understood all right and looked at me with her slant eyes widened. They all got together and whispered while I got nervouser and nervouser. I didn't like the look of things, somehow. Purty soon she said: "Mees Worley she not live along here no more. She gone."

"Well," I said vaguely, "I reckon I better be goin'." I started for the door, but she grabbed me. "Wait," she said. "You lose your head, suppose you go that way."

"Huh?" I grunted, slightly shocked and most unpleasantly surprised. "What? I ain't done nothin'."

She made a warning gesture and turning to one of the other girls said: "Go fetch Yuen Tang."

The other girl looked surprised: "Yuen Tang?" she said kind of dumb-like, like she didn't understand. The first girl snapped something at her in Chinee and give her a disgusted push through the door. Then she turned to me.

"Tung Yin no like white devils snooping around," she said with a shake of her head. "Suppose he find you here, he cut your head off—snick," she said dramatically, jerking her finger acrost her throat.

I will admit cold sweat bust out on me.

"Great cats," I said plaintively. "I thought this Tung Yin was a respectable merchant. I ain't never heard he was a mysterious mandarin or a brigand or somethin'. Stand away from that door, sister. I'm makin' tracks."

Again she shook her head and laying a finger to her lips cautiously, she beckoned me to look through the door by which I'd entered. The gate opening into the garden from the courtyard was partly open.

What I seen made my hair stand up. It was nearly dark. The garden looked shadowy and mysterious, but it was still light enough for me to make out the figgers of five big coolies sneaking along with long curved knives in their hands.

"They look for you," whispered the girl. "Tung Yin fear spies. They know somebody climb the wall. Wait, we hide you."

THEY GRABBED ME AND pushed me into a kind of closet and shut the door, leaving me in total darkness. How long I stood there sweating with fear and nervousness, I never knowed. I couldn't hear much in there and what I did hear was muffled, but it seemed like they was a lot of whispering and muttering going on through the house. Once I heard a kind of galloping like a lot of men running, then they was some howls and what sounded like a voice swearing in English.

Then at last the door opened. A Chinaman in the garb of a servant looked in and I was about to bust him one, when I seen the Chinese girl looking over his shoulder.

"Come out cautiously," he said, in his hissing English. "I am your friend and would aid you to escape, but if you do not follow my directions exactly, you will not live to see the sunrise. Tung Yin will butcher you."

"Holy cats," I said vaguely. "What's he got it in for me for? I ain't done nothin'."

"He mistrusts all men," said the Chinaman. "I am Yuen Tang and I hate his evil ways, though circumstances have forced me to do his bidding. Come."

That was a nice mess for a honest seaman to get into, hey? I followed Yuen Tang and the girl, sweating profusely, and they led me through long, deserted corridors and finally stopped before a heavy barred door.

"Through this door lies freedom," hissed Yuen Tang. "To escape from the house of Tung Yin you must cross the chamber which lies beyond this portal. Once through, you will come to an outer door and liberty. Here." He shoved a small but wicked looking pistol into my hand.

"What's that for?" I asked nervously, recoiling. "I don't like them things."

"You may have to shoot your way through," he whispered. "No man knows the guile of Tung Yin. In the darkness of the chamber he may come upon you with murder in his hand."

"Oh gosh," I gasped wildly. "Ain't they no other way out?"

"None other," said Yuen Tang. "You must take your chance."

I felt like my legs was plumb turning to taller. And then I got mad. Here was me, a peaceful, law-abiding sailorman, being hounded and threatened by a blame yellow-belly I hadn't never even seen.

"Gimme that gat," I growled. "I ain't never used nothin' but my fists in a fray, but I ain't goin' to let no Chinee carve me up if I can help it."

"Good," purred Yuen Tang. "Take the gun and go swiftly. If you hear a sound in the darkness, shoot quick and straight."

So, shoving the gun into my sweaty fingers, him and the girl opened the door, pushed me through and shut the door behind me. I turned quick and pushed at it. They'd barred it on the other side and I could of swore I heard a sort of low snicker.

I strained my eyes trying to see something. It was as dark as anything. I couldn't see nothing nor hear nothing. I started groping my way forward, then stopped short. Somewhere I heard a door open stealthily. I started sweating. I couldn't see nothing at all, but I heard the door close again, a bolt slid softly into place and I had the uncanny sensation that they was somebody in that dark room with me.

CUSSING FIERCELY TO myself because my hand shook so, I poked the gun out ahead of me and waited. A stealthy sound came to me from the other side of the chamber and I pulled the trigger wildly. A flash of fire stabbed back at me and I heard the lead sing past my ear as I ducked wildly. I was firing blindly, as fast as I could jerk the trigger, figgering on kind of swamping him with the amount of lead I was throwing his way. And he was shooting back just as fast. I seen the flash spitting in a continual stream of fire and the air was full of lead, from the sound. I heard the bullets sing past my ears so close they nearly combed my hair, and spat on the wall behind me. My hair stood straight up, but I kept on jerking the trigger till the gun was empty and no answering shots came.

Aha, I thought, straightening up. I've got him. And at that instant, to my rage and amazement, there sounded a metallic click from the darkness. It was incredible I should miss all them shots, even in the dark. But it must be so, I thought wrathfully. He wasn't laying on the floor full of lead; his gun was empty too. I knowed that sound was the hammer snapping on a empty shell.

And I got real mad. I seen red. I throwed away the gun and, cussing silently, got on my all-fours and begun to crawl stealthily but rapidly acrost the floor. If he had a knife, this mode of attack would give me some advantage.

That was a blame big chamber. I judge I'd traversed maybe half the distance across it when my head come into violent contact with what I instinctively realized was a human skull. My opponent had got the same idee I had. Instantly we throwed ourselves ferociously on each other and there begun a most desperate battle in the dark. My unseen foe didn't seem to have no knife, but he was a bearcat in action. I was doing my best, slugging, kicking, rassling and ever and anon sinking my fangs into his hide, but I never see the Chinaman that could fight like this 'un fought. I never seen one which could use his fists, but this 'un could.

I heard 'em swish past my head in the dark and purty soon I stopped one of them fists with my nose. Whilst I was trying to shake the blood and stars outa my eyes, my raging opponent clamped his teeth in my ear and set back. With a maddened roar, I hooked him in the belly with such heartiness that he let go with a gasp and curled up like a angle-worm. I then climbed atop of him and set to work punching him into a pulp, but he come to hisself under my very fists, as it were, pitched me off and got a scissors hold that nearly caved my ribs in.

Gasping for breath, I groped around and having found one of his feet, got a toe-hold and started twisting it off. He give a ear-piercing and bloodthirsty yell and jarred me loose with a terrific kick in the neck.

We arose and fanned the air with wild swings, trying to find each other in the dark. After nearly throwing our arms out of place missing haymakers, we abandoned this futile and aimless mode of combat and having stumbled into each other, we got each other by the neck with our lefts and hammered away with our rights.

A minute or so of this satisfied my antagonist, who, after a vain attempt to find my right and tie it up, throwed hisself blindly and bodily at me. We went to the floor together. I got a strangle hold on him and soon had him gurgling spasmodically. A chance swat on the jaw jarred me loose, but I come back with a blind swing that by pure chance crunched solidly into his mouth. Again we locked horns and tumbled about on the floor.

"**D**ERN YOUR YELLER hide," said the Chinaman between gasps. "You're the toughest Chinee I ever fit in my life, but I'll get you yet!"

"Bill McGlory," I said in disgust. "What you doin' here?"

"By golly," said he. "If I didn't know you was Tung Yin, I'd swear you was Steve Costigan."

"I am Steve Costigan, you numb-skull," I said impatiently, hauling him to his feet.

"Well, gee whiz," he said. "Them girls told me I might have to shoot Tung Yin to make my getaway, but they didn't say nothin' about you. Where is the big shot?"

"How should I know?" I snapped. "Yuen Tang and a girl told me Tung Yin was goin' to chop my head off. And they gimme a gun and pushed me in here. What you doin' anyway?"

"I come here to see Miss Worley," he said. "She'd done left when I went back to the La Belle. I looked around the streets for her, then I decided I'd come out to Tung Yin's and see her."

"And who told you you could come callin' on her?" I snarled.

"Well," he said smugly, "anybody could see that girl had fell for me. As far as that goes, who told you to come chasin' after her?"

"That's entirely different," I growled. "Go ahead with your story."

"Well," he said, "I come and knocked on the door and a Chinaman opened it and I asked for Miss Worley and he slammed the door in my face. That made me mad, so I prowled around and found a gate unlocked in the garden wall and come in, hopin' to find her in the garden. But a gang of tough lookin' coolies spotted me and though I tried to explain my peaceful intentions, they got hard and started wavin' knives around.

"Well, Steve, you know me. I'm a peaceful man but I ain't goin' be tromped on. I got rights, by golly. I hauled off and knocked the biggest one as cold as a wedge. Then I lit out and they run me clean through the garden. Every time I made for the wall, they headed me off, so I run through the courtyard into the house and smack into Tung Yin hisself. I knowed him by sight, you see. He had a golden pipe-case which he was lookin' at like he thought it was a million dollars or somethin'. When he seen me, he quick stuck it in his shirt and give a yelp like he was stabbed.

"I tried to explain, but he started yelling to the coolies in Chinese and they bust in after me. I run through a door ahead of 'em and slammed it in their faces and bolted it, and whilst I was holding it on one side and they was tryin' to kick it down on the other side, up come a Chinagirl which told me in broken English that she'd help me, and she hid me in a closet. Purty soon her and a coolie come and said that Tung Yin was huntin' me in another part of the house, and that they'd help me escape. So they took me to a door and gimme a gun and said if I could get through the room I'd be safe. Then they shoved me in here and bolted the door behind me. The next thing I knowed, bullets was singin' past my ears like a swarm of bees. You sure are a rotten shot, Steve."

"You ain't so blamed hot yourself," I sniffed. "Anyway, it looks to me like we been took plenty, and you sure are lucky to be alive. For some reason or other Tung Yin wanted to get rid of us and he seen a good way to do it without no risk to his own hide, by gyppin' us into bumpin' each other off. Wait, though—looks to me like that mutt Yuen Tang engineered this deal. Maybe Tung Yin didn't know nothin' about it."

"Well, anyway," said Bill, "they's somethin' crooked goin' on here that these Chinese don't want known.

They think we're government spies, I betcha."

"Well, let's get outa here," I said.

"I bet they think we're both dead," said Bill. "They told me these walls was sound-proof. I bet they use this for a regular murder room. I been hearin' a lot of dark tales about Tung Yin. I'm surprised a nice girl like Miss Worley would work for him."

"Aw," I said, "we musta misunderstood her. She don't work here. The Chinagirls told me so. He ain't got no nieces. It musta been somebody else."

"Well let's get out and argy later," Bill said. "Come on, let's feel around and find a door."

"Well," I said, "what good'll that do? The doors is bolted, ain't they?"

"Well, my gosh," he said, "can't we bust 'em down? Gee whiz, you'd stop to argy if they was goin' to shoot you."

We felt around and located the walls and we hadn't been groping long before I found what I knowed was bound to be a door. I told Bill and he come feeling his way along the wall. Then I heard something else.

"Easy, Bill," I whispered. "Somebody's unboltin' this door from the other side."

STANDING THERE SILENTLY, we plainly heard the sound of bolts being drawn. Then the door began opening and a crack of light showed. We flattened ourselves on either side of the door and waited, nerves tense and jumping.

Right then my white bulldog, Mike, could 'a' been able to help, if he hadn't been laid up with distemper.

The door opened. A Chinaman stuck his head in, grinning nastily. He had a electric torch in his hand and he was flashing it around over the floor—to locate the corpses, I reckon.

Before he had time to realize they wasn't no corpses, I grabbed him by the neck and jerked him headlong into the room. Bill connected a heavy right swing with his jaw. The Chinee stiffened, out cold. I let him fall careless-like to the floor. He'd dropped the light when Bill socked him. It went out when it hit the floor, but Bill groped around, and found it and flashed it on.

"Let's go," said Bill, so we went into the dark corridor outside and shut the door and bolted it. Bill flashed his light around, for it was dark in the corridor. We went along it and come through a door. Lights was on in that chamber, and in them adjoining it, but everything was still and deserted. We stole very warily through the rooms but we seen nobody, neither coolies, servants nor girls.

The house was kind of disheveled and tumbled about. Some of the hangings and things was gone. Things was kind of jerked around like the people had left all of a sudden, taking part of their belongings with 'em.

"By golly," said Bill. "This here's uncanny. They've moved out and left it with us."

I was opening a door and started to answer, then stopped short. In the room beyond, almost within arm's length, as I seen through the half open door, was Yuen Tang. But he wasn't dressed in servant's clothes no more. He looked like a regular mandarin. He had a golden pipe case in his hands and he was gloating over it like a miser over his gold.

"There's Yuen Tang," I whispered.

"Yuen Tang my pet pig's knuckle," snorted Bill. "That's Tung Yin hisself."

The Chinaman heard us and his head jerked up. His eyes flared and then narrowed wickedly. He stuck the case back in his blouse, quick but fumbling, like anybody does when they're in a desperate hurry to keep somebody from seeing something.

His other hand went inside his waist-sash and come out with a snub-nosed pistol. But before he could use it, me and Bill hit him simultaneous, one on the jaw and one behind the ear. Either punch woulda settled his hash. The both of 'em together dropped him like a pole-axed steer. The gun flew outa his hand and he hit the floor so hard the golden pipe case dropped outa his blouse and fell open on the floor.

"Let's get going before he comes to," said I impatiently, but Bill had stopped and was stooping with his hands on his knees, eying the pipe case covetously.

"Boy, oh boy," he said. "Ain't that some outfit? I betcha it cost three or four hundred bucks. I wisht I was rich. Them Chinee merchant princes sure spread theirselves when it comes to elegance."

I looked into the case which laid open on the floor. They was a small pipe with a slender amber stem and a ivory bowl, finely carved and yellow with age, some extra stems, a small silver box of them funny looking Chinese matches, and a golden rod for cleaning the pipe.

"By golly," said Bill, "I always wanted one of them ivory pipes."

"Hey," I said, "You can't hook Tung Yin's pipe. He ain't a-goin' to like it."

"Aw, it won't be stealin'," said Bill. "I'll leave him mine. 'Course it's made outa bone instead of ivory, but it cost me a dollar'n a half. Wonder you didn't bust it while ago when we was fightin'. I'll change pipes with him and he won't notice it till we're outa his reach."

"Well, hustle, then," I said impatiently. "I don't hold with no such graft, but what can you expect of a mutt from the Dutchman? Hurry up, before Tung Yin comes to and cuts our heads off."

So Bill took the ivory pipe and put his pipe in the case and shut the case up and stuck it back in Tung Yin's blouse. And we hustled. We come out into the courtyard. They

wasn't no lanterns hanging there, or if they was they wasn't lighted, but the moon had come up and it was bright as day.

AND WE RAN RIGHT SMACK into Miss Kit Worley. There she was, dressed in flying togs and carrying a helmet in her hand. She gasped when she seen us.

"Good heavens," she said. "What are you doing here?"

"I come here to see you, Miss Worley," I said. "And Tung Yin made out like he was a servant tryin' to save me from his master, and gimme a gun and sent me into a dark room and, meanwhile, Bill had come buttin' in where he hadn't no business and they worked the same gag on him and we purty near kilt each other before we found out who we was."

She nodded, kind of bewildered, and then her eyes gleamed.

"I see," she said. "I see." She stood there twirling her helmet a minute, kind of studying, then she laid her hands on our shoulders and smiled very kindly and said: "Boys, I wish you'd do me a favor. I'm leaving in a few minutes by plane and I have a package that must be delivered. Will you boys deliver it?"

"Sure," we said. So she took out a small square package and said: "Take this to the Red Dragon. You know where that is? Sure you would. Well, go in and give it to the proprietor, Kang Woon. Don't give it to anyone else. And when you hand it to him, say, 'Tung Yin salutes you.' Got that straight?"

"Yeah," said Bill. "But gee whiz, Miss Worley, we can't leave you here to the mercy of them yellow-skinned cut-throats."

"Don't worry." She smiled. "I can handle Tung Yin. Go now, please. And thank you."

Well, she turned and went on in the house. We listened a minute and heard somebody howling and cussing in Chinese, and knowed Tung Yin had come to. We was fixing to go in and rescue Miss Worley, when we heard her talking to him, sharp and hard-like. He quieted down purty quick, so we looked at each other plumb mystified, and went on out in the garden and found the gate Bill come in at and went through it. We hadn't gone but a few yards when Bill says: "Dern it, Steve, I've lost that pipe I took offa Tung Yin."

"Well, gee whiz," I said disgustedly. "You ain't goin' back to look for it."

"I had it just before we come outa the garden," he insisted. So I went back with him, though highly disgusted, and he opened the gate and said: "Yeah, here it is. I musta dropped it as I started through the gate. Got a hole in my pocket."

About that time we seen three figgers in the moonlight crossing the garden—Miss Worley, Tung Yin and a slim, dark young fellow I knowed must be Clanry, the Australian aviator. All of 'em was dressed for flying, though Tung Yin looked like he'd just dragged on his togs recent. He looked kind of disrupted generally. As we looked we seen Miss Worley grab his arm and point and as Tung Yin turned his head, Clanry hit him from behind, hard, with a blackjack. For the second time that night the merchant prince took the count.

Miss Worley bent over him, tore his jacket open and jerked out that same golden pipe case. Then her and Clanry ran for a gate on the opposite side of the garden. They went through, leaving it open in their haste and then we saw 'em running through the moonlight to the plane, which lay amongst the orange groves. They reached it and right away we heard the roar of the propeller. They took off perfect and soared away towards the stars and outa sight.

As we watched, we heard the sound of fast driving autos. They pulled up in front of the place. We heard voices shouting commands in English and Chinese. Then Tung Yin stirred and staggered up, holding his head. From inside the house come the sound of doors being busted open and a general ruckus. Tung Yin felt groggily inside his blouse, then tore his hair, shook his fists at the sky, and run staggeringly across the garden to vanish through the other gate.

"What you reckon this is all about?" wondered Bill. "How come Miss Worley wanted Tung Yin's pipe, you reckon?"

"How should I know?" I replied. "Come on. This ain't any of our business. We got to deliver this package to Kang Woon."

So we faded away. And as we done so a backward look showed men in uniform ransacking the house and estate of Tung Yin.

No 'rickshas being available, we was purty tired when we come to the Red Dragon, in the early hours of morning. It was a low class dive on the waterfront which stayed open all night. Just then, unusual activity was going on. A bunch of natives was buzzing around the entrance and some Chinese police was shoving them back.

"Looks like Kang Woon's been raided," I grunted.

"That's it," said Bill. "Well, I been expectin' it, the dirty rat. I know he sells opium and I got a good suspicion he's a fence, too."

W E WENT UP TO THE DOOR and the Chinese cops wasn't going to let us in. We was about to haul off and sock 'em, when some autos drove up and stopped and a gang of soldiers with a Chinese officer and a English officer got out. They had a battered looking Chinaman with 'em in handcuffs. He was the one me and Bill socked and locked up in the murder room. They all went in and we fell in behind 'em and was in the dive before the cops knowed what we was doing.

It was a raid all right. The place was full of men in the uniform of the Federal army and the Chinese constabulary. Some of 'em—officers, I reckon—was questioning the drunks and beggars they'd found in the place. Over on one side was a cluster of Chinamen in irons, amongst them Kang Woon, looking like a big sullen spider. He was being questioned, but his little beady black eyes glinted dull with murder and he kept his mouth shut.

"There's the mutt which butted in on our fight," grunted Bill in disgust.

One of the men questioning Kang Woon was Sir Peter Brent; the others was a high rank Chinese officer and a plain clothes official of some sort.

The British officer we'd followed in saluted and said: "I regret to report, Sir Peter, that the birds have flown the bally coop. We found the house deserted and showing signs of a recent and hurried evacuation. We found this Chinaman lying unconscious in an inner chamber which was locked from the outside, but we've gotten nothing out of him. We heard a plane just as we entered the house and I greatly fear that the criminals have escaped by air. Of Tung Yin and the others we found no trace at all, and though we made a careful search of the premises, we did not discover the gem."

"We did not spring the trap quick enough," said Sir Peter. "I should have suspected that they would be warned."

Well, while they was talking, me and Bill went up to Kang Woon and handed him the package. He shrunk back and glared like we was trying to hand him a snake, but we'd been told to give it to him, so we dropped it into his lap and said: "Tung Yin salutes you," just like Miss Worley had told us. The next minute we was grabbed by a horde of cops and soldiers.

"Hey," yelled Bill wrathfully. "What kinda game is this?" And he stood one of 'em on the back of his neck with a beautiful left hook.

I'm a man of few words and quick action. I hit one of 'em in the solar plexus and he curled up like a snake. We was fixing to wade through them deluded heathens like a whirlwind through a cornfield when Sir Peter sprang forward.

"Hold hard a bit, lads," he ordered. "Let those men go."

They fell away from us and me and Bill faced the whole gang belligerently, snorting fire and defiance.

"I know these men." he said. "They're honest American sailors."

"But they gave this to the prisoner," said the Chinese official, holding up the package.

"I know," said Sir Peter. "But if they're mixed up in this affair, I'm certain it's through ignorance rather than intent. They're rather dumb, you know."

Me and Bill was speechless with rage. The official said: "I'm not so sure."

THE OFFICIAL OPENED the package and said: "Ah, just as I suspected. The very case in which the gem was stolen."

He held it up and it was a jewel case with the arms of the old Chinese empire worked on it in gold. Kang Woon glowered at it and his eyes was Hell's fire itself.

"Now look." The official opened it and we all gasped. Inside was a large white gem which sparkled and glittered like ice on fire. The handcuffed Chinaman gave a howl and kind of collapsed.

"The Royal Crystal," cried the official in delight. "The stolen gem itself. Who gave you men this package?"

"None of your blamed business," I growled and Bill snarled agreement.

"Arrest them," exclaimed the official, but Sir Peter interposed again. "Wait." And he said to us: "Now, lads, I believe you're straight, but you'd best come clean, you know."

We didn't say nothing and he said: "Perhaps you don't know the facts of the case. This stone—which is of immense value—was stolen from the governmental museum. We know that it was stolen by a gang of international thieves who have been masquerading as honest merchants and traders. This gang consisted of Tung Yin, Clanry the aviator, a number of lesser crooks who pretended to be in Tung Yin's employ, and a girl called Clever Kit Worley."

"Hey, you," said Bill. "You lay offa Miss Worley."

"Aha," said Sir Peter, "I fancied I'd strike fire there. Now come, lads, didn't Clever Kit give you that stone?"

We still didn't say nothing. About that time the Chinaman the soldiers had brung with them hollered: "I'll tell. I'll tell it all. They've betrayed me and left me to go to prison alone, have they? Curse them all!"

He was kind of hysterical, but talked perfect English—was educated at Oxford, I learned later. Everybody looked at him and he spilled the beans so fast his words tripped over each other: "Tung Yin, Clanry and the Worley woman stole the Royal Crystal. They were equal partners in all the crimes they committed. We—the coolies, the dancing girls and I—were but servants, doing their bidding, getting no share of the loot, but being paid higher salaries than we could have earned honestly. Oh, it was a business proposition, I tell you.

"Tonight we got the tip that the place was to be raided—Tung Yin has plenty of spies. No sooner had we received this information than these sailors came blundering in, hunting Kit Worley, who had charmed them as she has so many men. The woman and Clanry were not in the house. They were preparing the plane for a hurried flight. Tung Yin supposed these men to be spies of the government, so he sent some of his servants to beguile the one, while he donned a disguise of menial garments and befooled the other. We sent them into a dark chamber to slay each other. And, meanwhile, we hurried our plans for escape.

"Clanry, the Worley woman and Tung Yin were planning to escape in the plane, and they promised to take me with them. Tung Yin told the coolies and dancing girls to save themselves as best they could. They scattered, looting the house as they fled. Then Tung Yin told me to look into the death chamber and see if the two foreign devils had killed each other. I did so—and was knocked senseless. What happened then I can only guess, but that Tung Yin, Clanry and Kit Worley escaped in the plane, I am certain, though how these men came to have the gem is more than I can say."

"I believe I can answer that," said Sir Peter. "I happen to know that Kang Woon here has been handling stolen goods for the Tung Yin gang. That's why we raided him tonight at the same time we sent a squad to nab the others at Tung Yin's place. But as you've seen, we were a bit too late. Kang Woon had advanced them quite a bit of money already for the privilege of handling the stone for them—the amount to be added to his commission when the gem was sold. The sale would have made them all rich, even though they found it necessary to cut it up and sell it in smaller pieces. They dared not skip without sending this stone to Kang Woon, for he knew too much. But watch."

He laid the gem on a table and hit it with his pistol butt and smashed it into bits. Everybody gawped. Kang Woon gnashed his teeth with fury.

"A fake, you see," said Sir Peter. "I doubt if any but an expert could have told the difference. I happen to have had quite a bit of experience in that line, don't you know. Yes, Tung Yin and Kit Worley and Clanry planned to double-cross Kang Woon. They sent him this fake, knowing that they would be out of his reach before he learned of the fraud. He's an expert crook, but not a jewel expert, you know. And now I suppose Tung Yin and his pals are safely out of our reach with the Royal Crystal."

WHILE WE WAS LISTENING Bill took out the pipe he'd stole from Tung Yin and began to cram tobaccer in it. He cussed disgustedly.

"Hey, Steve," said he. "What you think? Somebody's gone and crammed a big piece of glass into this pipe bowl." He was trying to work it loose.

"Gimme that pipe," I hollered and jerked it outa his hands. Disregarding his wrathful protests, I opened my knife and pried and gouged at the pipe bowl until the piece of glass rolled into my hand. I held it up and it caught the candle

lights with a thousand gleams and glittering sparkles.

"The Royal Crystal," howled the Chinese. And Sir Peter grabbed it.

"By Jove," he exclaimed. "It's the real gem, right enough. Where did you get it?"

"Well," I said, "I'll tell you. Seein' as how Miss Worley is done got away and you can't catch her and put her in jail—and I don't mind tellin' you I'm glad of it, 'cause she mighta been a crook but she was nice to me. I see now why she and Clanry wanted that pipe case. It was a slick place to hide the gem in, but nothin's safe from one of them thieves offa the *Dutchman*. Tung Yin was goin' to double-cross Kang Woon and Clanry and Miss Worley double-crossed Tung Yin, but I betcha they look funny when they open that golden pipe case and find nothin' in it but Bill's old pipe."

"Aw," said Bill, "I betcha she keeps it to remember me by. I betcha she'll treasure it amongst her dearest sooverneats."

Sir Peter kind of tore his hair and moaned: "Will you blighters tell us what it's all about and how you came by that gem?"

"Well," I said, "Tung Yin evidently had the gem in his pipe and Bill stole his pipe. And ... Well, it's a long story."

"Well, I'll be damned," said Sir Peter. "The keenest minds in the secret service fail and a pair of blundering bone-headed sailors succeed without knowing what it's all about."

"Well," said Bill impatiently, "if you mutts are through with me and Steve, we aims for to go forth and seek some excitement. Up to now this here's been about the tiresomest shore leave I've had yet."

BREED *of* BATTLE.

ALTERNATE TITLE: THE FIGHTIN'EST PAIR.

This short story was first published in the November 1931 issue of Action Stories *magazine.*

M E AND MY WHITE BULLDOG Mike was peaceably taking our beer in a joint on the waterfront when Porkey Straus come piling in, plumb puffing with excitement.

"Hey, Steve!" he yelped. "What you think? Joe Ritchie's in port with Terror."

"Well?" I said.

"Well, gee whiz," he said, "you mean to set there and let on like you don't know nothin' about Terror, Ritchie's fightin' brindle bull? Why, he's the pit champeen of the Asiatics. He's killed more fightin' dogs than—"

"Yeah, yeah," I said impatiently. "I know all about him. I been listenin' to what a bear-cat he is for the last year, in every Asiatic port I've touched."

"Well," said Porkey, "I'm afraid we ain't goin' to git to see him perform."

"Why not?" asked Johnnie Blinn, a shifty-eyed bar-keep.

"Well," said Porkey, "they ain't a dog in Singapore to match ag'in' him. Fritz Steinmann, which owns the pit and runs the dog fights, has scoured the port and they just ain't no canine which their owners'll risk ag'in' Terror. Just my luck. The chance of a lifetime to see the fightin'est dog of 'em all perform. And they's no first-class mutt to toss in with him. Say, Steve, why don't you let Mike fight him?"

"Not a chance," I growled. "Mike gets plenty of scrappin' on the streets. Besides, I'll tell you straight, I think dog fightin' for money is a dirty low-down game. Take a couple of fine, upstandin' dogs, full of ginger and fightin' heart, and throw 'em in a concrete pit to tear each other's throats out, just so a bunch of four-flushin' tin-horns like you, which couldn't take a punch or give one either, can make a few lousy dollars bettin' on 'em."

"But they likes to fight," argued Porkey. "It's their nature."

"It's the nature of any red-blooded critter to fight. Man or dog!" I said. "Let 'em fight on the streets, for bones or for fun, or just to see which is the best dog. But pit-fightin' to the death is just too dirty for me to fool with, and I ain't goin' to get Mike into no such mess."

"Aw, let him alone, Porkey," sneered Johnnie Blinn nastily. "He's too chicken-hearted to mix in them rough games. Ain't you, Sailor?"

"Belay that," I roared. "You keep a civil tongue in your head, you wharfside rat. I never did like you nohow, and one more crack like that gets you this." I brandished my huge fist at him and he turned pale and started scrubbing the bar like he was trying for a record.

"I wantcha to know that Mike can lick this Terror mutt," I said, glaring at Porkey. "I'm fed up hearin' fellers braggin' on that brindle murderer. Mike can lick him. He can lick any dog in this lousy port, just like I can lick any man here. If Terror meets Mike on the street and gets fresh, he'll get his belly-full. But Mike ain't goin' to get mixed up in no dirty racket like Fritz Steinmann runs and you can lay to that." I made the last statement in a voice like a irritated bull, and smashed my fist down on the table so hard I splintered the wood, and made the decanters bounce on the bar.

"Sure, sure, Steve," soothed Porkey, pouring hisself a drink with a shaky hand. "No offense. No offense. Well, I gotta be goin'."

"So long," I growled, and Porkey cruised off.

UP STROLLED A MAN WHICH had been standing by the bar. I knowed him—Philip D'Arcy, a man whose name is well known in all parts of the world. He was a tall, slim, athletic fellow, well dressed, with bold gray eyes and a steel-trap jaw. He was one of them gentleman adventurers, as they call 'em, and he'd did everything from running a revolution in South America and flying a war plane in a Balkan brawl, to exploring in the Congo. He was deadly with a six-gun, and as dangerous as a rattler when somebody crossed him.

"That's a fine dog you have, Costigan," he said. "Clean white. Not a speck of any other color about him. That means good luck for his owner."

I knowed that D'Arcy had some pet superstitions of his own, like lots of men which live by their hands and wits like him.

"Well," I said, "anyway, he's about the fightin'est dog you ever seen."

"I can tell that," he said, stooping and eying Mike close. "Powerful jaws—not too undershot—good teeth—broad between the eyes—deep chest—legs that brace like iron. Costigan, I'll give you a hundred dollars for him, just as he stands."

"You mean you want me to sell you Mike?" I asked kinda incredulous.

"Sure. Why not?"

"Why not!" I repeatedly indignantly. "Well, gee whiz, why not ask a man to sell his brother for a hundred dollars? Mike wouldn't stand for it. Anyway, I wouldn't do it."

"I need him," persisted D'Arcy. "A white dog with a dark man—it means luck. White dogs have always been lucky for me. And my luck's been running against me lately. I'll give you a hundred and fifty."

"D'Arcy," I said, "you couldst stand there and offer me money all day long and raise the ante every hand, but it wouldn't be no good. Mike ain't for sale. Him and me has knocked around the world together too long. They ain't no use talkin'."

His eyes flashed for a second. He didn't like to be crossed in any way. Then he shrugged his shoulders.

"All right. We'll forget it. I don't blame you for thinking a lot of him. Let's have a drink."

So we did and he left.

I WENT AND GOT ME A shave, because I was matched to fight some tramp at Ace Larnigan's Arena and I wanted to be in shape for the brawl. Well, afterwards I was walking down along the docks when I heard somebody go: "Hssst!"

I looked around and saw a yellow hand beckon me from behind a stack of crates. I sauntered over, wondering what it was all about, and there was a Chinese boy hiding there. He put his finger to his lips. Then quick he handed me a folded piece of paper, and beat it, before I couldst ask him anything.

I opened the paper and it was a note in a woman's handwriting which read:

> *Dear Steve.*
>
> *I have admired you for a long time at a distance, but have been too timid to make myself known to you. Would it be too much to ask you to give me an opportunity to tell you my emotions by*

word of mouth? If you care at all, I will meet you by the old Manchu House on the Tungen Road, just after dark.

An affectionate admirer.

P.S. Please, oh please be there! You have stole my heart away!

"Mike," I said pensively, "ain't it plumb peculiar the strange power I got over wimmen, even them I ain't never seen? Here is a girl I don't even know the name of, even, and she has been eatin' her poor little heart out in solitude because of me. Well—" I hove a gentle sigh—"it's a fatal gift, I'm afeared."

Mike yawned. Sometimes it looks like he ain't got no romance at all about him. I went back to the barber shop and had the barber to put some ile on my hair and douse me with perfume. I always like to look genteel when I meet a feminine admirer.

Then, as the evening was waxing away, as the poets say, I set forth for the narrow winding back street just off the waterfront proper. The natives call it the Tungen Road, for no particular reason as I can see. The lamps there is few and far between and generally dirty and dim. The street's lined on both sides by lousy looking native shops and hovels. You'll come to stretches which looks clean deserted and falling to ruins.

Well, me and Mike was passing through just such a district when I heard sounds of some kind of a fracas in a dark alley-way we was passing.

Feet scruffed. They was the sound of a blow and a voice yelled in English: "Halp! Halp! These Chinese is killin' me!"

"Hold everything," I roared, jerking up my sleeves and plunging for the alley, with Mike at my heels. "Steve Costigan is on the job."

It was as dark as a stack of black cats in that alley. Plunging blind, I bumped into somebody and sunk a fist to the wrist in him. He gasped and fell away. I heard Mike roar suddenly and somebody howled bloody murder. Then wham! A blackjack or something like it smashed on my skull and I went to my knees.

"That's done yer, yer blawsted Yank," said a nasty voice in the dark.

"You're a liar," I gasped, coming up blind and groggy but hitting out wild and ferocious. One of my blind licks musta connected because I heard somebody cuss bitterly. And then wham, again come that black-jack on my dome. What little light they was, was behind me, and whoever it was slugging me, couldst see me better'n I could see him. That last smash put me down for the count, and he musta hit me again as I fell.

I COULDN'T OF BEEN OUT but a few minutes. I come to myself lying in the darkness and filth of the alley and I had a most splitting headache and dried blood was clotted on a cut in my scalp. I groped around and found a match in my pocket and struck it.

The alley was empty. The ground was all tore up and they was some blood scattered around, but neither the thugs nor Mike was nowhere to be seen. I run down the alley, but it ended in a blank stone wall. So I come back onto the Tungen Road and looked up and down but seen nobody. I went mad.

"Philip D'Arcy!" I yelled all of a sudden. "He done it. He stole Mike. He writ me that note. Unknown admirer, my eye. I been played for a sucker again. He thinks Mike'll bring him luck. I'll bring him luck, the double-crossin' son-of-a-sea-cook. I'll sock him so hard he'll bite hisself in the ankle. I'll bust him into so many pieces he'll go through a sieve—"

With these meditations, I was running down the street at full speed, and when I busted into a crowded thoroughfare, folks turned and looked at me in amazement. But I didn't pay no heed. I was steering my course for the European Club, a kind of ritzy place where D'Arcy generally hung out. I was still going at top-speed when I run up the broad stone steps and was stopped by a pompous looking doorman which sniffed scornfully at my appearance, with my clothes torn and dirty from laying in the alley, and my hair all touseled and dried blood on my hair and face.

"Lemme by," I gritted, "I gotta see a mutt."

"Gorblime," said the doorman. "You cawn't go in there. This is a very exclusive club, don't you know. Only gentlemen are allowed here. Cawn't have a blawsted gorilla like you bursting in on the gentlemen. My word! Get along now before I call the police."

There wasn't time to argue.

With a howl of irritation I grabbed him by the neck and heaved him into a nearby goldfish pond. Leaving him floundering and howling, I kicked the door open and rushed in. I dashed through a wide hallway and found myself in a wide room with big French winders. That seemed to be the main club room, because it was very scrumptiously furnished and had all kinds of animal heads on the walls, alongside of crossed swords and rifles in racks.

They was a number of Americans and Europeans setting around drinking whiskey-and-sodas, and playing cards. I seen Philip D'Arcy setting amongst a bunch of his club-members, evidently spinning yarns about his adventures. And I seen red.

"D'Arcy!" I yelled, striding toward him regardless of the card tables I upset. "Where's my dog?"

PHILIP D'ARCY SPRANG UP with a kind of gasp and all the club men jumped up too, looking amazed.

"My word!" said a Englishman in a army officer's uniform. "Who let this boundah in? Come, come, my man, you'll have to get out of this."

"You keep your nose clear of this or I'll bend it clean outa shape," I howled, shaking my right mauler under the aforesaid nose. "This ain't none of your business. D'Arcy, what you done with my dog?"

"You're drunk, Costigan," he snapped. "I don't know what you're talking about."

"That's a lie," I screamed, crazy with rage. "You tried to buy Mike and then you had me slugged and him stole. I'm on to you, D'Arcy. You think because you're a big shot and I'm just a common sailorman, you can take what you want. But you ain't gettin' away with it. You got Mike and you're goin' to give him back or I'll tear your guts out. Where is he? Tell me before I choke it outa you."

"Costigan, you're mad," snarled D'Arcy, kind of white. "Do you know whom you're threatening? I've killed men for less than that."

"You stole my dog!" I howled, so wild I hardly knowed what I was doing.

"You're a liar," he rasped. Blind mad, I roared and crashed my right to his jaw before he could move. He went down like a slaughtered ox and laid still, blood trickling from the corner of his mouth. I went for him to strangle him with my bare hands, but all the club men closed in between us.

"Grab him," they yelled. "He's killed D'Arcy. He's drunk or crazy.

Hold him until we can get the police."

"Belay there," I roared, backing away with both fists cocked. "Lemme see the man that'll grab me. I'll knock his brains down his throat. When that rat comes to, tell him I ain't through with him, not by a dam' sight. I'll get him if it's the last thing I do."

And I stepped through one of them French winders and strode away cursing between my teeth. I walked for some time in a kind of red mist, forgetting all about the fight at Ace's Arena, where I was already due. Then I got a idee. I was fully intending to get ahold of D'Arcy and choke the truth outa him, but they was no use trying that now. I'd catch him outside his club some time that night. Meanwhile, I thought of something else. I went into a saloon and got a big piece of white paper and a pencil, and with much labor, I printed out what I wanted to say. Then I went out and stuck it up on a wooden lamp-post where folks couldst read it. It said:

I WILL PAY ANY MAN FIFTY DOLLARS ($50) THAT CAN FIND MY BULDOG MIKE WHICH WAS STOLE BY A LO-DOWN SCUNK. STEVE COSTIGAN.

I was standing there reading it to see that the words was spelled right when a loafer said: "Mike stole? Too bad, Sailor. But where you goin' to git the fifty to pay the reward?

Everybody knows you ain't got no money."

"That's right," I said. So I wrote down underneath the rest:

P. S. I AM GOING TO GET FIFTY DOLLARS FOR LICKING SOME MUTT AT ACE'S AREENER THAT IS WHERE THE REWARD MONEY IS COMING FROM.

S. C.

I then went morosely along the street wondering where Mike was and if he was being mistreated or anything. I moped into the Arena and found Ace walking the floor and pulling his hair.

"Where you been?" he howled. "You realize you been keepin' the crowd waitin' a hour? Get into them ring togs."

"Let 'em wait," I said sourly, setting down and pulling off my shoes. "Ace, a yellow-livered son-of-a-skunk stole my dog."

"Yeah?" said Ace, pulling out his watch and looking at it. "That's tough, Steve. Hustle up and get into the ring, willya? The crowd's about ready to tear the joint down."

I CLIMBED INTO MY trunks and bathrobe and mosied up the aisle, paying very little attention either to the hisses or cheers which greeted my appearance. I clumb into the ring and looked around for my opponent.

"Where's Grieson?" I asked Ace.

"'E 'asn't showed up yet," said the referee.

"Ye gods and little fishes!" howled Ace, tearing his hair. "These bone-headed leather-pushers will drive me to a early doom. Do they think a pummoter's got nothin' else to do but set around all night and pacify a ragin' mob whilst they play around? These thugs is goin' to lynch us all if we don't start some action right away."

"Here he comes," said the referee as a bath-robed figger come hurrying down the aisle. Ace scowled bitterly and held up his hands to the frothing crowd.

"The long delayed main event," he said sourly. "Over in that corner, Sailor Costigan of the *Sea Girl*, weight 190 pounds. The mutt crawlin' through the ropes is 'Limey' Grieson, weight 189. Get goin'—and I hope you both get knocked loop-legged."

The referee called us to the center of the ring for instructions and Grieson glared at me, trying to scare me before the scrap started—the conceited jassack. But I had other things on my mind. I merely mechanically noted that he was about my height—six feet—had a nasty sneering mouth and mean black eyes, and had been in a street fight recent. He had a bruise under one ear.

We went back to our corners and I said to the second Ace had give me: "Bonehead, you ain't seen nothin' of nobody with my bulldog, have you?"

"Naw, I ain't," he said, crawling through the ropes. "And beside ... Hey, look out."

I hadn't noticed the gong sounding and Grieson was in my corner before I knowed what was happening. I ducked a slungshot right as I turned and clinched, pushing him outa the corner before I broke. He nailed me with a hard left hook to the head and I retaliated with a left to the body, but it didn't have much enthusiasm behind it. I had something else on my mind and my heart wasn't in the fight. I kept unconsciously glancing over to my corner where Mike always set, and when he wasn't there, I felt kinda lost and sick and empty.

Limey soon seen I wasn't up to par and began forcing the fight, shooting both hands to my head. I blocked and countered very slouchily and the crowd, missing my rip-roaring attack, began to murmur. Limey got too cocky and missed a looping right that had everything he had behind it. He was wide open for a instant and I mechanically ripped a left hook under his heart that made his knees buckle, and he covered up and walked away from me in a hurry, with me following in a sluggish kind of manner.

After that he was careful, not taking many chances. He jabbed me plenty, but kept his right guard high and close in. I ignores left jabs at all times, so though he was outpointing

me plenty, he wasn't hurting me none. But he finally let go his right again and started the claret from my nose. That irritated me and I woke up and doubled him over with a left hook to the guts which wowed the crowd. But they yelled with rage and amazement when I failed to foller up. To tell the truth, I was fighting very absent-mindedly.

AS I WALKED BACK TO my corner at the end of the first round, the crowd was growling and muttering restlessly, and the referee said: "Fight, you blasted Yank, or I'll throw you h'out of the ring." That was the first time I ever got a warning like that.

"What's the matter with you, Sailor?" said Bonehead, waving the towel industriously. "I ain't never seen you fight this way before."

"I'm worried about Mike," I said. "Bonehead, where-all does Philip D'Arcy hang out besides the European Club?"

"How should I know?" he said. "Why?"

"I wanta catch him alone some place," I growled. "I betcha—"

"There's the gong, you mutt," yelled Bonehead, pushing me out of my corner. "For cat's cake, get in there and FIGHT. I got five bucks bet on you."

I wandered out into the middle of the ring and absent-mindedly wiped Limey's chin with a right that dropped him on his all-fours. He bounced up without a count, clearly addled, but just as I was fixing to polish him off, I heard a racket at the door.

"Lemme in," somebody was squalling. "I gotta see Meest Costigan. I got one fellow dog belong along him."

"Wait a minute," I growled to Limey, and run over to the ropes, to the astounded fury of the fans, who rose and roared.

"Let him in, Bat," I yelled and the feller at the door hollered back: "Alright, Steve, here he comes."

And a Chinese kid come running up the aisle grinning like all get-out, holding up a scrawny brindle bull-pup.

"Here that one fellow dog, Mees Costigan," he yelled.

"Aw heck," I said. "That ain't Mike. Mike's white. I thought everybody in Singapore knowed Mike—"

At this moment I realized that the still groggy Grieson was harassing me from the rear, so I turned around and give him my full attention for a minute. I had him backed up ag'in' the ropes, bombarding him with lefts and rights to the head and body, when I heard Bat yell: "Here comes another'n, Steve."

"Pardon me a minute," I snapped to the reeling Limey, and run over to the ropes just as a grinning coolie come running up the aisle with a white dog which might of had three or four drops of bulldog blood in him.

"Me catchum, boss," he chortled.

"Heap fine white dawg. Me catchum fifty dolla?"

"You catchum a kick in the pants," I roared with irritation. "Blame it all, that ain't Mike."

At this moment Grieson, which had snuck up behind me, banged me behind the ear with a right hander that made me see about a million stars. This infuriated me so I turned and hit him in the belly so hard I bent his back-bone. He curled up like a worm somebody'd stepped on and while the referee was counting over him, the gong ended the round.

They dragged Limey to his corner and started working on him. Bonehead, he said to me: "What kind of a game is this, Sailor? Gee whiz, that mutt can't stand up to you a minute if you was tryin'. You shoulda stopped him in the first round. Hey, lookit there."

I glanced absent-mindedly over at the opposite corner and seen that Limey's seconds had found it necessary to take off his right glove in the process of reviving him. They was fumbling over his bare hand.

"They're up to somethin' crooked," howled Bonehead. "I'm goin' to appeal to the referee."

"HERE COMES SOME MORE mutts, Steve," bawled Bat and down the aisle come a Chinese coolie, a Jap sailor, and a Hindoo, each with a barking dog. The crowd had been seething with bewildered rage, but this seemed to somehow hit 'em in the funny bone and they begunst to whoop and yell and laugh like a passel of hyenas. The referee was roaming around the ring cussing to hisself and Ace was jumping up and down and tearing his hair.

"Is this a prize-fight or a dog-show," he howled. "You've rooint my business. I'll be the laughin' stock of the town. I'll sue you, Costigan."

"Catchum fine dawg, Meest' Costigan," shouted the Chinese, holding up a squirming, yowling mutt which done its best to bite me.

"You deluded heathen," I roared, "that ain't even a bull dog. That's a chow."

"You clazee," he hollered. "Him fine blull dawg."

"Don't listen," said the Jap. "Him bull dog." And he held up one of them pint-sized Boston bull-terriers.

"Not so," squalled the Hindoo. "Here is thee dog for you, sahib. A pure blood Rampur hound. No dog can overtake him in thee race—"

"Ye gods!" I howled. "Is everybody crazy? I oughta knowed these heathens couldn't understand my reward poster, but I thought—"

"Look out, sailor," roared the crowd.

I hadn't heard the gong. Grieson had slipped up on me from behind again, and I turned just in time to get nailed on the jaw by a sweeping right-hander he started from the canvas. Wham! The lights went out and I hit the canvas so hard it jolted

some of my senses back into me again.

I knowed, even then, that no ordinary gloved fist had slammed me down that way. Limey's men hadst slipped a iron knuckle-duster on his hand when they had his glove off. The referee sprung forward with a gratified yelp and begun counting over me. I writhed around, trying to get up and kill Limey, but I felt like I was done. My head was swimming, my jaw felt dead, and all the starch was gone outa my legs. They felt like they was made outa taller.

My head reeled. And I could see stars over the horizon of dogs.

" ... Four ... " said the referee above the yells of the crowd and the despairing howls of Bonehead, who seen his five dollars fading away. " ... Five ... Six ... Seven ..."

"There," said Limey, stepping back with a leer. "That's done yer, yer blawsted Yank."

Snap! went something in my head. That voice. Them same words. Where'd I heard 'em before? In the black alley offa the Tungen Road. A wave of red fury washed all the grogginess outa me.

I FORGOT ALL ABOUT MY taller legs. I come off the floor with a roar which made the ring lights dance, and lunged at the horrified Limey like a mad bull. He caught me with a straight left coming in, but I didn't even check a instant. His arm bent and I was on top of him and sunk my right mauler so deep into his ribs I felt his heart throb under my fist. He turned green all over and crumbled to the canvas like all his bones hadst turned to butter. The dazed referee started to count, but I ripped off my gloves and pouncing on the gasping warrior, I sunk my iron fingers into his throat.

"Where's Mike, you gutter rat?" I roared. "What'd you do with him? Tell me, or I'll tear your windpipe out."

"'Ere, 'ere," squawked the referee. "You cawn't do that. Let go of him, I say. Let go, you fiend."

He got me by the shoulders and tried to pull me off. Then, seeing I wasn't even noticing his efforts, he started kicking me in the ribs. With a wrathful beller, I rose up and caught him by the nape of the neck and the seat of the britches and throwed him clean through the ropes. Then I turned back on Limey.

"You Limehouse spawn," I bellered. "I'll choke the life outa you."

"Easy, mate, easy," he gasped, green-tinted and sick. "I'll tell yer. We stole the mutt? Fritz Steinmann wanted him—"

"Steinmann?" I howled in amazement.

"He warnted a dorg to fight Ritchie's Terror," gasped Limey. "Johnnie Blinn suggested he should 'ook your Mike. Johnnie hired me and some strong-arms to turn the trick—Johnnie's gel wrote you that note—but how'd you know I was into it—"

"I oughta thought about Blinn," I raged. "The dirty rat. He heard me and Porkey talkin' and got the idee. Where is Blinn?"

"Somewheres gettin' sewed up," gasped Grieson. "The dorg like to tore him to ribbons afore we could get the brute into the bamboo cage we had fixed."

"Where is Mike?" I roared, shaking him till his teeth rattled.

"At Steinmann's, fightin' Terror," groaned Limey. "Ow, lor'—I'm sick. I'm dyin'."

I riz up with a maddened beller and made for my corner. The referee rose up outa the tangle of busted seats and cussing fans and shook his fist at me with fire in his eye.

"Steve Costigan," he yelled. "You lose the blawsted fight on a foul."

"So's your old man," I roared, grabbing my bathrobe from the limp and gibbering Bonehead. And just at that instant a regular bedlam bust loose at the ticket-door and Bat come down the aisle like the devil was chasing him. And in behind him come a mob of natives—coolies, 'ricksha boys, beggars, shopkeepers, boatmen and I don't know what all—and every one of 'em had at least one dog and some had as many as three or four. Such a horde of chows, Pekineses, terriers, hounds and mongrels I never seen and they was all barking and howling and fighting.

"Meest' Costigan," the heathens howled, charging down the aisles: "You payum flifty dolla for dogs. We catchum."

The crowd rose and stampeded, trompling each other in their flight and I jumped outa the ring and raced down the aisle to the back exit with the whole mob about a jump behind me. I slammed the door in their faces and rushed out onto the sidewalk, where the passers-by screeched and scattered at the sight of what I reckon they thought was a huge and much battered maniac running at large in a red bathrobe. I paid no heed to 'em.

Somebody yelled at me in a familiar voice, but I rushed out into the street and made a flying leap onto the running board of a passing taxi. I ripped the door open and yelled to the horrified driver: "Fritz Steinmann's place on Kang Street— and if you ain't there within three minutes I'll break your neck."

WE WENT CAREENING through the streets and purty soon the driver said: "Say, are you an escaped criminal? There's a car followin' us."

"You drive," I yelled. "I don't care if they's a thousand cars follerin' us. Likely it's a Chinaman with a pink Pomeranian he wants to sell me for a white bull dog."

The driver stepped on it and when we pulled up in front of the innocent-looking building which was Steinmann's secret arena, we'd left the mysterious pursuer clean outa sight. I jumped out and raced down a short flight of stairs which led from the street down to a side entrance, clearing my decks for action by shedding my bathrobe as I went. The door was shut and a burly black-jowled thug was lounging outside. His eyes narrowed with surprise as he noted my costume, but he bulged in front of me and growled: "Wait a minute, you. Where do you think you're goin'?"

"In!" I gritted, ripping a terrible right to his unshaven jaw.

Over his prostrate carcass I launched myself bodily against the door, being in too much of a hurry to stop and see if it was unlocked. It crashed in and through its ruins I catapulted into the room.

It was a big basement. A crowd of men—the scrapings of the waterfront—was ganged about a deep pit sunk in the concrete floor from which come a low, terrible, worrying sound like dogs growling through a mask of torn flesh and bloody hair— like fighting dogs growl when they have their fangs sunk deep.

The fat Dutchman which owned the dive was just inside the door and he whirled and went white as I crashed through. He threw up his hands and screamed, just as I caught him with a clout that smashed his nose and knocked six front teeth down his throat. Somebody yelled: "Look out, boys! Here comes Costigan! He's on the kill!"

The crowd yelled and scattered like chaff before a high wind as I come ploughing through 'em like a typhoon, slugging right and left and dropping a man at each blow. I was so crazy mad I didn't care if I killed all of 'em. In a instant the brink of the pit was deserted as the crowd stormed through the exits, and I jumped down into the pit. Two dogs was there, a white one and a big brindle one, though they was both so bloody you couldn't hardly tell their original color. Both had been savagely punished, but Mike's jaws had locked in the death-hold on Terror's throat and the brindle dog's eyes was glazing.

Joe Ritchie was down on his knees working hard over them and his face was the color of paste. They's only two ways you can break a bull dog's death-grip; one is by deluging him with water till he's half drowned and opens his mouth to breathe. The other'n is by choking him off. Ritchie was trying that, but Mike had such a bull's neck, Joe was only hurting his fingers.

"For gosh sake, Costigan," he gasped. "Get this white devil off. He's killin' Terror."

"Sure I will," I grunted, stooping over the dogs. "Not for your sake, but for the sake of a good game dog." And I slapped Mike on the back and said: "Belay there, Mike; haul in your grapplin' irons."

Mike let go and grinned up at me with his bloody mouth, wagging his stump of a tail like all get-out and pricking up one ear. Terror had clawed the other'n to rags. Ritchie picked up the brindle bull and clumb

outa the pit and I follered him with Mike.

"You take that dog to where he can get medical attention and you do it pronto," I growled. "He's a better man than you, any day in the week, and more fittin' to live. Get outa my sight."

He slunk off and Steinmann come to on the floor and seen me and crawled to the door on his all-fours before he dast to get up and run, bleeding like a stuck hawg. I was looking over Mike's cuts and gashes, when I realized that a man was standing nearby, watching me.

I wheeled. It was Philip D'Arcy, with a blue bruise on his jaw where I'd socked him, and his right hand inside his coat.

"D'ARCY," I SAID, WALKING up to him. "I reckon I done made a mess of things. I just ain't got no sense when I lose my temper, and I honestly thought you'd stole Mike. I ain't much on fancy words and apologizin' won't do no good. But I always try to do what seems right in my blunderin' blame-fool way, and if you wanta, you can knock my head off and I won't raise a hand ag'in' you." And I stuck out my jaw for him to sock.

He took his hand outa his coat and in it was a cocked six-shooter.

"Costigan," he said, "no man ever struck me before and got away with it. I came to Larnigan's Arena tonight to kill you. I was waiting for you outside and when I saw you run out of the place and jump into a taxi, I followed you to do the job wherever I caught up with you. But I like you. You're a square-shooter. And a man who thinks as much of his dog as you do is my idea of the right sort. I'm putting this gun back where it belongs—and I'm willing to shake hands and call it quits, if you are."

"More'n willin'," I said heartily. "You're a real gent." And we shook. Then all at once he started laughing.

"I saw your poster," he said. "When I passed by, an Indian babu was translating it to a crowd of natives and he was certainly making a weird mess of it. The best he got out of it was that Steve Costigan was buying dogs at fifty dollars apiece. You'll be hounded by canine-peddlers as long as you're in port."

"The *Sea Girl's* due tomorrer, thank gosh," I replied. "But right now I got to sew up some cuts on Mike."

"My car's outside," said D'Arcy. "Let's take him up to my rooms. I've had quite a bit of practice at such things and we'll fix him up ship-shape."

"It's a dirty deal he's had," I growled. "And when I catch Johnnie Blinn I'm goin' kick his ears off. But," I added, swelling out my chest seven or eight inches, "I don't reckon I'll have to lick no more saps for sayin' that Ritchie's Terror is the champeen of all fightin' dogs in the Asiatics. Mike and me is the fightin'est pair of scrappers in the world."

CIRCUS FISTS.

ALTERNATE TITLE: SLUGGER BAIT

This short story was first published in the December 1931 issue of Fight Stories *magazine.*

ME AND THE Old Man had a most violent row whilst the *Sea Girl* was tied up at the docks of a small seaport on the West Coast. Somebody put a pole-cat in the Old Man's bunk, and he accused me of doing it. I denied it indignantly, and asked him where he reckoned I would get a pole-cat, and he said well, it was a cinch somebody had got a pole-cat, because there it was, and it was his opinion that I was the only man of the crew which was low-down enough to do a trick like that.

This irritated me, and I told him he oughta know it wasn't me, because I had the reputation of being kind to animals, and I wouldn't put a decent skunk where it would have to associate with a critter like the Old Man.

This made him so mad that he busted a bottle of good rye whiskey over my head. Annoyed at such wanton waste of good licker, I grabbed the old walrus and soused him in a horse-trough—us being on the docks at the time.

The Old Man ariz like Neptune from the deep, and, with whiskers dripping, he shook his fists at me and yelled, "Don't never darken my decks again, Steve Costigan. If you ever try to come aboard the *Sea Girl*, I'll fill you fulla buckshot, you mutineerin' pirate!"

"Go set on a marlin-spike," I sneered. "I wouldn't sail with you again for ten bucks a watch and plum duff every mess. I'm through with the sea, anyhow. You gimme a bad taste for the whole business. A landman's life is the life for me, by golly. Me and Mike is goin' to fare forth and win fame and fortune ashore."

And so saying, I swaggered away with my white bulldog, follered clean outa sight by the Old Man's sincere maledictions.

Casting about for amusement, I soon come onto a circus which was going full blast at the edge of town. I seen a side-show poster which said, Battling Bingo, Champion of the West Coast. So I went in and they was considerable of a crowd there and a big dumb-looking mutt in tights standing up in a ring, flexing his arms and showing off his muscles.

"Gents," yelled the barker, a flashy-dressed young feller with a diamond horse-shoe stick-pin, "the management offers fifty dollars to any man which can stay four rounds with this tiger of the ring! Five minutes ago I made the same offer on the platform outside, and some gent took me up. But now he seems to have got cold feet, and is nowhere to be found. So here and now I again make the original proposition—fifty round, bright iron men to any guy which can stay four rounds with this man-killin' terror, this fire-breathin' murderer, this iron-fisted man-mountain, Battling Bingo, the Terror of the Rockies!"

The crowd whooped, and three or four fellers made a move like they was going to take up the challenge, but I brushed 'em scornfully aside and bellered, "I'll take that dough, mate!"

I bounced into the ring, and the barker said, "You realize that the management ain't responsible for life or limb?"

"Aw, stow that guff and gimme them gloves," I roared, ripping off my shirt. "Get ready, champeen. I'm goin' to knock your crown off!"

The gong sounded, and we went for each other. They wasn't no canvas stretched across the back of the ring where Bingo couldst shove me up against to be blackjacked by somebody behind it, so I knowed very well he had a iron knuckle-duster on one of his hands, and, from the way he dangled his right, I knowed that was the hand. So I watched his right, and, when he throwed it, I stepped inside of his swing and banged him on the whiskers with a left and a right hook which tucked him away for the evening.

The crowd roared in huge approval, and I jerked the wad of greenbacks outa the barker's hand and started away when he stopped me.

"Say," he said, "I reckernize you now. You're Sailor Costigan. How'd you like to take this tramp's place? We'll pay you good wages."

"All I got to do is flatten jobbies?" I said, and he said it was. So that's how I come to start working in Flash Larney's Gigantic Circus and Animal Show.

Each night I'd appear in fighting tights before the multitude, and the barker, Joe Beemer, wouldst go through the usual ballyhoo, and then all I had to do was to knock the blocks offa the saps which tried to collect the fifty. I wouldn't use the knuckle-duster. I wouldn't of used it even if I'd of needed it, which I didn't. If I can't sock a palooka to sleep, fair and above-board, with my own personal knuckles, then they ain't no use in trying to dint him with a load of iron.

W
E WORKED UP and down the West Coast and inland, and it was mostly easy. The men which tried to lick me was practically all alley-fighters—big strong fellers, but they didn't know nothing. Mostly farmers, blacksmiths, sailors, long-shoremen, miners, cowpunchers, bar-room bouncers. All I had to do was to hit 'em. More'n once I knocked out three or four men in one night.

I always got action because the crowd was always against me, just like they was against Battling Bingo when I flattened him. A crowd is always against the carnival fighter, whether they know his opponent or not. And when the opponent is some well-known local boy, they nearly have hydrophobia in their excitement.

You oughta heered the cheers they'd give their home-town pride, and the dirty remarks they'd yell at me. No matter how hard I was fighting, I generally found time to reply to their jeers with choice insults I had picked up all over the seven seas, with the result that the maddened mob wouldst spew forth more raging sluggers to be slaughtered. Some men can't fight their best when the crowd's against 'em, but I always do better, if anything. It makes me mad, and I take it out on my opponent.

When I wasn't performing in the ring, I was driving stakes, setting up or taking down tents, and fighting with my circus-mates. Larney's outfit had the name of being the toughest on the Coast, and it was. The fights I had in the ring wasn't generally a stitch to them I had on the lot.

Well, I always makes it a point to be the champeen of whatever outfit I'm with, and I done so in this case. The first day I was with the show I licked three razor-backs, the lion-tamer and a side-show barker, and from then on it was a battle practically every day till them mutts realized I was the best man on the lot.

Fighting all the time like I was, I got so hard and mean I surprised myself. They wasn't a ounce of flesh on me that wasn't like iron, and I believe I could of run ten miles at top speed without giving out. The Dutch weight-lifter figgered to give me a close scrimmage, but he was way too slow. The toughest scrap I had was with a big Japanese acrobat. We fought all over the lot one morning, and everybody postponed the parade for a hour to watch. I was about all in when I finally put the heathen away, but, with my usual recuperative powers, I was able to go on that night as usual, and flatten a farm-hand, a piano-mover and a professional football player.

Some trouble was had with Mike, which always set in my corner and bit anybody which tried to hit me through the ropes, as often happened when the local boy started reeling. Larney wanted to shave him and tattoo him and put him in a sideshow.

"The tattooed dog!" said Larney. "That would draw 'em! A novelty! Can't you see the crowds flockin' through the gates for a look at him?"

"I can see me bustin' you in the snoot," I growled. "You let Mike alone."

"Well," said Larney, "we got to make him more presentable. He

looks kinda crude and uncultured alongside our trained poodles."

So the lion-trainer bathed Mike and combed him and perfumed him, and put on a little fool dog-blanket with straps and gilt buckles, and tied a big bow ribbon on his stump tail. But Mike seen himself in a mirror and tore off all that rigging and bit the lion-tamer.

Well, they had a old decrepit lion by the name of Oswald which didn't have no teeth, and Mike got to sleeping in his cage. So they fixed a place where Mike couldst get in and out without Oswald getting out, and made a kind of act out of it.

Larney advertised Mike as the dog which laid down with the lion, and wouldst have Mike and Oswald in the cage together, and spiel about how ferocious Oswald was, and how unusual it was for a friendship to spring up between such natural enemies. But the reason Mike slept in the cage was that they put more straw in it than they did in the other cages on account of Oswald being old and thin-blooded, and Mike liked a soft bed.

Larney was afraid Mike would hurt Oswald, but the only critters Mike couldn't get along with was Amir, a big African leopard which had already kilt three men, and Sultan, the man-eating tiger. They was the meanest critters in the show, and was always trying to get out and claw Mike up. But he wasn't afeard of 'em.

WELL, I WAS having a lot of fun. I thrives in a rough environment like that, though I'll admit I sometimes got kinda homesick for the *Sea Girl* and the sea, and wondered what Bill O'Brien and Mushy Hanson and Red O'Donnell was doing. But I got my pride, and I wouldn't go back after the Old Man had pratically kicked me out to shift for myself.

Anyway, it was a lot of fun. I'd stand out on the platform in front of the tent with my massive arms folded and a scowl on my battered face, whilst Joe Beemer wouldst cock his derby back on his head and start the ballyhoo.

He'd whoop and yell and interjuice me to the crowd as "Sailor Costigan, the Massive Man-mauler of the Seven Seas!" And I'd do strong-man stunts—twisting horseshoes in two and bending coins between my fingers and etc. Then he'd rare back and holler, "Is they any man in this fair city courageous enough to try and stay four rounds with this slashin' slugger? Take a chance, boys—he's been drivin' stakes all day and maybe he's tired and feeble—heh! heh! heh!"

Then generally some big ham wouldst jump outa the crowd and roar, "I'll fight the so-and-so." And Joe wouldst rub his hands together and say under his breath, "Money, roll in! I need groceries!" And he'd holler, "Right this way, gents! Right through the door to the left. Ten cents admission—one dime! See the battle of the century! Don't crowd, folks. Don't crowd."

The tent was nearly always packed with raging fans which hollered at the top of their voices for their local hope to knock my iron skull off. However small a tank-town might be, it generally had at least one huge roughneck with a reputation of some kind.

One time we hit a town in the throes of a rassling carnival. Nobody couldst be found to box with me, but a big Polack came forward claiming to be the rassling champeen of the West—I ain't never seen a rassler which wasn't champeen of something—and wanted me to rassle him. Beemer refused, and the crowd hissed, and the rassler said I was yeller.

I seen red and told him I wasn't no rassler but I'd give him more'n he could tote home. He figgered I was easy, but he got fooled. I don't know a lot about scientific rassling, but I know plenty rough-and-tumble, and I was so incredibly hard and tough, and played so rough that I broke his arm and dislocated his shoulder. And after that nobody ast me to rassle.

IT WASN'T LONG after that when we blowed into a mining town by the name of Ironville, up in the Nevada hills, and from the looks of the populace I figgered I'd have plenty of competition that night. I wasn't fooled none, neither, believe me.

Long before we was ready to start the show, a huge crowd of tough-looking mugs in boots and whiskers was congregated around the athaletic tent, which wasn't showing no interest whatever in the main-top nor the freaks nor the animals.

Joe hadn't hardly got started on his ballyhoo when through the crowd come a critter which looked more like a grizzly than a man—a big black-headed feller with shoulders as broad as a door, and arms like a bear's paw. From the way the crowd all swarmed around him, I figgered he was a man of some importance in Ironville.

I was right.

"You don't need to say no more, pard," he rumbled in a voice like a bull. "I'll take a whirl at yore tramp!"

Joe looked at the black-browed giant, and he kinda got cold feet for the first time in his career.

"Who are you?" he demanded, uneasily.

The big feller grinned wolfishly and said, "Who, me? Oh, I'm just a blacksmith around here." And the crowd all whooped and yelled and laughed like he'd said something very funny.

"Somethin's fishy about this, Steve," whispered Joe to me. "I don't like the looks of it."

About that time the crowd begun to hiss and boo, and the big feller said nastily, "Well, what's the matter—you hombres gettin' yeller?"

I seen red. "Get into this tent,

you black-muzzled palooka!" I roared. "I'll show you who's yeller! Shut up, Joe. Ain't I always said I barred nobody? What's the matter with you, anyhow?"

"I tell you, Steve," he said, wiping his forehead with his bandanner, "I seen this big punk somewheres, and if he's a simple blacksmith I'm a Bohemian!"

"Gahhh!" I snorted disgustfully. "When I get through with him, he'll look like a carpet. Have I lost you a penny since I joined the show? Naw! Come on!"

And so saying, I swaggered into the tent and bounded into the ring while the crowd gathered around, packing the place solid, applauding their man and howling insults at me, which I returned with interest, that being a game at which I ain't no amateur myself.

JOE STARTED TO lead the big feller to the dressing-room which was partitioned off with a curtain in one corner of the tent, but he snorted and began ripping off his clothes then and there, revealing ring togs under 'em. Ah, thought I, he come here with the intention of going on with me. Some local battler, no doubtless.

When he clumb into the ring, they was several men with him—one a tall cold-faced man which looked like a high-class gambler, and who they called Brelen, and three or four tough mugs which was to act as seconds. They had the game writ all over their flat noses and tin ears. In fact, it looked to me like the big feller had a right elaborate follering, even if he was a local white hope.

"Who referee's?" asked Brelen, the poker-faced gent.

"Oh, I referee," said Joe.

"Not this time you don't," said Brelen. "The crowd chooses a referee who'll give my boy a square deal, see?"

"It's against the rules of the management—" began Joe, and the crowd rumbled and begun to surge forward. "All right, all right," said Joe, hurriedly. "It's okay with me."

Brelen grinned kinda thin-like, and turned to the crowd and said, "Well, boys, who do you want to referee?"

"Honest Jim Donovan!" they roared, and pushed forward a bald-headed old sea-lion which had the crookedest face I ever seen on a human. Joe give him a look and clasped his head and groaned. The crowd was nasty—itching for trouble. Joe was kinda white around the gills, and my handlers was uneasy. I was glad I'd locked Mike up in Oswald's cage before the show started, being suspicious of the customers. Mike ain't got much discretion; when the crowd starts throwing things at me, he's likely to go for 'em.

"Gents," yelled Joe, who, being a natural-born barker, couldn't keep his mouth shut if he swung for it, "you are now about to witness the battle of the centu-ree, wherein the Fighting Blacksmith of your fair city endeavors to stay four actual rounds with Sailor Costigan, the Terror of the Seven Seas—"

"Aw, shut up and get out of this ring," snarled Brelen. "Let the massacre commence!"

THE GONG SOUNDED and the Blacksmith come swinging outa his corner. Jerusha, he was a man! He stood six feet one and a quarter and weighed not less than two hundred and ten pounds to my six feet and one ninety. With a broad chest matted with black hair, arms knotted with muscles like full-sized cables, legs like trees, a heavy jutting jaw, a broad fighting face with wicked gray eyes glittering from under thick black brows, and a shock of coarse black hair piled up on top of his low, broad forehead—I wanta tell you I ain't never seen a more formidable-looking fighter in my life!

We rushed together like a pair of mad bulls. Bang! In a shower of stars I felt myself flying through the air, and I landed on my shoulders with a jolt that shook the ring. Zowie! I sprawled about, almost petrified with dumfoundment. The crowd was whooping and cheering and laughing like all get-out.

I glared in wild amazement at the black-headed giant which was standing almost over me, with a nasty grin on his lips. A light dawned.

"Blacksmith my eye!" I roared,

leaping up at him. "They ain't but one man in the world can hit a lick like that—Bill Cairn!"

I heard Joe's despairing howl as I slashed into my foe. Wham! Wham! I was on the resin again before I even got a chance to connect. The yells sounded kinda jumbled this time, and I shook my head violently, cussing fervently as I got my feet under me. Ironville. I oughta knowed—Bill Cairn, which they called the Ironville Blacksmith, the hardest hitter in the game! This was his home town, and this was him!

Fighting mad, I bounded up, but Cairn was so close to me that he reached me with one of his pile-driving left hooks before I was balanced, and down I went again. Now the yelling was kinda dim and the lights was quaking and rocking. I crouched, taking a count which Honest Jim was reeling off a lot faster than necessary. Bill Cairn! The kayo king of the heavyweights, with thirty or forty knockouts in a row, and never been socked off his feet, himself. He was in line for a crack at the champ—and I was supposed to flatten this grizzly in four rounds!

I was up at nine, and, ducking a savage drive for the face, I clinched. By golly, it was like tying up a grizzly. But I ain't no chicken myself. I gripped him in a desperate bear-hug whilst him and the referee cussed and strained, and the crowd begged him to shake me loose and kill me.

"You side-show rat!" he gritted between his teeth. "Leggo whilst I rip yore head off! How can I show my best stuff with you hangin' on like a leech?"

"This is cheap stuff for a head-liner like you!" I snarled, red-eyed.

"Givin' my home town folks a free show," he grinned, nastily. "It was just my luck to have a mug like you blow in whilst I was visitin' back home."

Oh, I see the idee all right. It was a big joke with him to knock me off and give his friends a treat—show off before the home-folks! He was laughing at me and so was all them Ironville lubbers. Well, I thought, grinding my teeth with red rage, they's many a good man punched hisself into fistic oblivion on my iron jaw.

I let go of Cairn and throwed my right at his jaw like it was a hammer. He pulled away from it and—bang! It mighta been a left hook to the head. It felt like a hand-spike. And the next instant, whilst my eyes was still full of stars, I felt another jolt like a concentrated earthquake.

Purty soon I heered somebody say, "Seven!" and I instinctively clumb up and looked about for my foe. I didn't locate him, as he was evidently standing behind me, but I did locate a large gloved mauler which crashed under my ear and nearly unjinted my neck. I done a beautiful dive, ploughing my nose vigorously into the resin, whilst the crowd wept with delight, and then I heered a noise like a sleigh-bell and was aware of being dragged to my corner.

A SNIFTER OF ammonia brung me to myself, and I discovered I was propped on my stool and being worked over by my handlers and Joe, who was bleeding from a cut over the temple.

"How'd you get that?" I asked groggily.

"One of these eggs hit me with a bottle," he said. "They claim I jerked the gong too soon. Listen at 'em! Toughest crowd I ever seen."

They sure was. They was rumbling and growling, just seething for a scrap, but stopping now and then to cheer Cairn, which was bowing and smirking in his corner.

"I knew I'd seen him," said Joe, "and Ace Brelen, his manager. The lousy chiselers! You ain't got a chance, Steve—"

At this moment a rough-whiskered mug stuck his head through the ropes and waved a coil of rope at Joe.

"We're on to you, you rat!" he bellered. "None of your side-show tricks, understand? If you try anything dirty, we'll stretch your neck. And that goes for you, too, you tin-eared gorilla!"

"So's your old man!" I roared, kicking out with all my might. My heel crunched solid on his jaw, and he shot back into the first row amongst a tangle of busted seats and cussing customers, from which he emerged bleeding at the mouth and screaming with rage. He was fumbling for a gun in his shirt, but just then the gong sounded and me and Cairn went for each other.

I come in fast, and figgered on beating him to the punch, but he was too quick for me. He wasn't so clever, but he moved like a big cat, and the very power of his punches was a swell defense. No man couldst keep his balance under them thundering smashes, even if they didn't land on no vital spot. Just trying to block 'em numbed my arms.

Zip! His left whizzed past my jaw like a red-hot brick. Zinggg! His right burned my ear as it went by. I seen a opening and shot my right with everything I had. But I was too eager; my arm looped over his shoulder and he banged his left into my ribs, which I distinctly felt bend almost to the breaking point as my breath went outa me in a explosive grunt.

I throwed my arms about him in a vain effort to clinch, but he pushed me away and slammed a full-armed right to my jaw. Crash! I felt myself turning a complete somersault in the air, and I landed on my belly with my head sticking out under the ropes and ogling glassily down at the ecstatic customers. One of these riz up and slashed his thigh with his hat and, sticking his face almost into mine, yelled, "Well, you carnival punk, how do you like those?"

"Like this!" I roared, catching him on the whiskers with a

unexpected bash that sunk his nose in the sawdust. I then rolled over on my back and, observing that the referee had rapidly counted up to nine, I ariz and, abandoning my scanty boxing skill, started slugging wild and ferocious in the hope of landing a haymaker.

But that was Cairn's game; he blocked my punches for a second or so, then bang! he caught me square on the chin with one of them thunderbolt rights which shot me back into the ropes, and I rebounded from 'em square into a whistling left hook that dropped me face-down in the resin.

I couldst dimly hear the crowd yelling like wolves. When the average man falls face-first he's through, but nobody never accused me of being a average man. At nine I was up as usual, reeling, and Cairn approached me with a look of disgust on his brutal face.

"Will you stay down?" he gritted, and, measuring me with a left, he crashed his right square into my mouth, and I went down like a pole-axed ox.

"That finishes him!" I heered somebody yelp, and evidently Cairn thought so too, because he give a scornful laugh and started toward his corner where his manager was getting his bathrobe ready. But I got my legs under me and at nine I staggered up, as is my habit.

"Come back here, you big sissy!" I roared groggily, spitting out fragments of a tooth. "This fight ain't

over by a devil of a ways!"

The mob screamed with amazement, and Cairn, swearing ferociously, turned and rushed at me like a tiger. But though I reeled on buckling knees, I didn't go down under his smashing left hooks.

"Why don't you get a ax, you big false-alarm?" I sneered, trying to shake the blood outa my eyes. "What you got in them gloves—powder puffs?"

At that he give a roar which made the ring lights shimmy, and brought one up from the canvas which hung me over the top rope just as the gong sounded. Joe and his merry men untangled my limp carcass and held me on the stool while they worked despairingly over me.

"Drop it, Steve," urged Joe. "Cairn will kill you."

"How many times was I on the canvas that round?" I asked.

"How should I know?" he returned, peevishly, wringing the gore out of my towel. "I ain't no adding machine."

"Well, try to keep count, willya?" I requested. "It's important; I can tell how much he's weakenin' if you check up on the knockdowns from round to round."

Joe dropped the sponge he was fixing to throw into the ring.

"Ye gods! Are you figgerin' on continuin' the massakree?"

"He can't keep this pace all night," I growled. "Lookit Brelen talkin' to his baby lamb!"

Ace was gesticulating purty emphatic, and Cairn was growling back at him and glaring at me and kneading his gloves like he wisht it was my goozle. I knowed that Brelen was telling him this scrap was getting beyond the point of a joke, and that it wasn't helping his reputation none for me to keep getting up on him, and for him to make it another quick kayo. Ha, ha, thought I grimly, shaking the blood outa my mangled ear, let's see how quick a kayo Bill Cairn can make where so many other iron-fisted sluggers has failed.

At the gong I was still dizzy and bleeding copiously, but that's a old story to me.

CAIRN, INFURIATED AT not having finished me, rushed outa his corner and throwed over a terrible right, which I seen coming like a cannonball, and ducked. His arm looped over my shoulder and his shoulder rammed into my neck with such force that we both crashed to the canvas.

Cairn untangled hisself with a snarl of irritation, and, assisted by the fair-minded referee, arose, casually kicking me in the face as he done so. I ariz likewise, and, enraged by my constant position on the canvas, looped a whistling left at his head that would of undoubtedly decapitated him hadst it landed—but luck was against me as usual. My foot slipped in a smear of my own blood, my swing was wild, and I run smack into his ripping right.

I fell into Cairn, ignoring an uppercut which loosened all my lower teeth, and tied him up.

"Leggo, you tin-eared baboon!" he snarled, heaving and straining. "Try to show me up, wouldja? Try to make a monkey outa me, wouldja?"

"Nature's already attended to that, you lily-fingered tap-dancer," I croaked. "A flapper with a powderpuff couldst do more damage than you can with them chalk-knuckled bread-hooks."

"So!" he yelled, jerking away and crashing his right to my jaw with every ounce of his huge frame behind it. I revolved in the air like a spinwheel, felt the ropes scrape my back, and realized that I was falling through space. Crash! My fall was cushioned by a mass of squirming, cussing fans, else I would of undoubtedly broke my back.

I looked up, and high above me, it seemed, I seen the referee leaning over the ropes and counting down at me. I began to kick and struggle, trying to get up, and a number of willing hands—and a few hob-nailed boots—hoisted me offa the squawking fans, and I grabbed the ropes and swung up.

Somebody had a grip on my belt, and I heard a guy growl. "You're licked, you fool! Take the count. Do you want to get slaughtered?"

"Leggo!" I roared, kicking out furiously. "I ain't never licked!"

I tore loose and crawled through the ropes—it looked like I'd never make it—and hauled myself up just as the referee was lifting his arm to bring it down on "Ten!" Cairn didn't rush this time; he was scowling, and I noticed that sweat was streaming down his face, and his huge chest was heaving.

Some of the crowd yelled, "Stop it!" but most of 'em whooped, "Now you got him, Bill. Polish him off!"

Cairn measured me, and smashed his right into my face. The top-rope snapped as I crashed back against it, but I didn't fall. Cairn swore in amazement, and drawed back his right again, when the gong sounded. He hesitated, then lemme have it anyway—a pile-driving smash that nearly lifted me offa my feet. And the crowd cheered the big egg. My handlers jostled him aside and, as they pulled me offa the ropes, Cairn sneered and walked slowly to his corner.

S UPPORTED ON MY stool, I seen Joe pick up a sponge stealthily.

"Drop that sponge!" I roared, and Joe, seeing the baleful light in my one good eye, done so like it was red-hot.

"Lemme catch you throwin' a sponge in for me!" I growled. "Gimme ammonia! Dump that bucket of water over me! Slap the back of my neck with a wet towel! One more round to go, and I gotta save that fifty bucks!"

Swearing dumfoundedly, my handlers did as they was bid, and I felt better and stronger every second. Even they couldn't understand how I couldst take such a beating and come back for more. But any slugger which depends on his ruggedness to win his fights understands it. We got to be solid iron—and we are.

Besides, my recent rough-and-ready life hadst got me into condition such as few men ever gets in, even athaletes. This, coupled with my amazing recuperative powers, made me just about unbeatable. Cairn could, and had, battered me from pillar to post, knocked me down repeatedly, and had me groggy and glassy-eyed, but he hadn't sapped the real reservoir of my vitality. Being groggy and being weak is two different things. Cairn hadn't weakened me. The minute my head cleared under the cold water and ammonia, I was as good as ever. Well, just about, anyhow.

So I come out for the fourth round raring to go. Cairn didn't rush as usual. In fact, he looked a little bit sick of his job. He walked out and lashed at my head with his left. He connected solid, but I didn't go down. And for the first time I landed squarely. Bang. My right smashed under his ear, and his head rocked on his bull's neck.

With a roar of fury, he come back with a thundering right to the head, but it only knocked me to my knees, and I was up in a instant. I was out-lasting him! His blows was losing their dynamite! This realization electrified me, and I bored in, slashing with both hands.

A left to the face staggered but didn't stop me, and I ripped a terrific left hook under his heart. He grunted and backed away. He wasn't near as good at taking punishment as he was at handing it out. I slashed both hands to his head, and the blood flew. With a deafening roar, he sunk his right mauler clean outa sight in my belly.

I thought for a second that my spine was broke, as I curled up on the canvas, gasping. The referee sprang forward and began counting, and I looked for Cairn, expecting to see him standing almost astraddle of me, as usual, waiting to slug me down as I got up. He wasn't; but was over against the ropes, holding onto 'em with one mitt whilst he wiped the blood and sweat outa his eyes with the other'n. And I seen his great chest heaving, his belly billowing out and in, and his leg muscles quivering.

Grinning wolfishly, I drawed in great gulps of air and beat the count by a second. Cairn lurched offa the ropes at me, swinging a wide left, but I went under it and crashed my right to his heart. He rolled like a ship in a heavy gale, and I knowed I had him. That last punch which had floored me had been his dying effort. He'd fought hisself clean out on me, as so many a man had didst. Strategy, boy, strategy!

I went after him like a tiger after a bull, amid a storm of yells and curses and threats. The crowd, at first

dumfounded, was now leaping up and down and shaking their fists and busting chairs and threatening me with torture and sudden death if I licked their hero. But I was seeing red. Wait'll you've took the beating I'd took and then get a chance to even it up! I ripped both hands to Cairn's quivering belly and swaying head, driving him to the ropes, off of which he rolled drunkenly.

I HEERED A gong sounding frantically; Brelen hadst knocked the time-keeper stiff with a blackjack and was trying to save his man. Also the referee was grabbing at me, trying to push me away. But I give no heed. A left and right under the heart buckled Cairn's knees, and a blazing right to the temple glazed his eyes. He reeled, and a trip-hammer left hook to the jaw that packed all my beef sent him crashing to the canvas, just as the crowd come surging into the ring, tearing down the ropes. I seen Joe take it on the run, ducking out under the wall of the tent, and yelling, "Hey, Rube!"

Then me and the handlers was engulfed. Half a hundred hands grabbed at me, and fists, boots and chairs swung for me. But I ducked, ripping off my gloves, and come up fighting like a wild man.

I swung my fists like they was topping-mauls, and ribs snapped and noses and jaw-bones cracked, whilst through the melee I caught glimpses of Brelen and his men carrying out their battered gladiator. He was still limp.

Just as the sheer number of maddened citizens was dragging me down, a gang of frothing razor-backs come through the tent like a whirl-wind, swinging pick handles and tent-stakes.

Well, I ain't seen many free-for-alls to equal that 'un! The circus war-whoop of "Hey, Rube!" mingled with the blood-thirsty yells of the customers. The Iron-villians outnumbered us, but we give 'em a bellyful. In about three seconds the ring was tore to pieces and the storm of battle surged into the tent-wall, which collapsed under the impact.

Knives was flashing and a few guns barking, and all I wonder is that somebody wasn't kilt. The athaletic tent was literally ripped plumb to ribbons, and the battle surged out onto the grounds and raged around the other tents and booths.

Then a wild scream went up: "Fire!" And over everything was cast a lurid glow. Somehow or other the main top hadst caught in the melee—or maybe some fool set it on fire. A strong wind was fanning the flames, which mounted higher each second. In a instant the fight was abandoned. Everything was in a tumult, men running and yelling, children squalling, women screaming. The circus-people was running and hauling the cages and wagons outa the animal tent, which was just catching. The critters was bellering and howling in a most hair-raising way, and I remembered Mike in Oswald's cage. I started for there on the run, when there riz a most fearful scream above all the noise: "The animals are loose!"

EVERYBODY HOLLERED AND tore their hair and ran, and here come the elephants like a avalanche! They crashed over wagons and cages and booths, trumpeting like Judgment Day, and thundered on into the night. How they got loose nobody never exactly knowed. Anything can happen in a fire. But, in stampeding, they'd bumped into and busted open some more cages, letting loose the critters inside.

And here they come roaring— Sultan, the tiger, and Amir, the leopard, killers both of 'em. A crowd of screaming children rushed by me, and right after them come that striped devil, Sultan, his eyes blazing. I grabbed up a heavy tent-stake and leaped betweenst him and the kids. He roared and leaped with his talons spread wide, and I braced my feet and met him in mid-air with a desperate smash that had every ounce of my beef behind it. The impact nearly knocked me offa my feet, and the stake splintered in my hand, but Sultan rolled to the ground with a shattered skull.

And almost simultaneously a terrible cry from the people made me wheel just in time to see Amir racing toward me like a black shadder with balls of fire for eyes. And, just as I turned, he soared from the ground straight at my throat. I didn't have time to do nothing. He crashed full on my broad breast, and his claws ripped my hide as the impact dashed me to the earth. And at the same instant I felt another shock which knocked him clear of me.

I scrambled up to see a squat white form tearing and worrying at the limp body of the big cat. Again Mike had saved my worthless life. When Amir hit me, he hit Amir and broke his neck with one crunch of his iron jaws. He'd squoze out between the bars of Oswald's cage and come looking for me.

He lolled out his tongue, grinning, and vibrated his stump tail, and all to once I heered my name called in a familiar voice. Looking around, I seen a battered figger crawl out from under the ruins of a bandwagon, and, in the lurid light of the burning tents, I reckernized him.

"Jerusha!" I said. "The Old Man! What you doin' under that wagon?"

"I crawled under there to keep from bein' trampled by the mob," he said, working his legs to see if they was broke. "And it was a good idee, too, till a elephant run over the wagon. By gad, if I ever get safe to sea once more I'll never brave the perils of the land again, I wanta tell ya!"

"Did you see me lick Bill Cairn?" I asked.

"I ain't see nothin' but a passel of luneyticks," he snapped. "I arrived just as the free-for-all was ragin'. I don't mind a rough-house, but when they drags in a fire and a stampede of jungle-critters, I'm ready to weigh anchor! And you!" he added, accusingly. "A merry chase you've led me, you big sea-lion! I've come clean from Frisco, and it looked for a while like I wouldn't never find this blame circus."

"What you wanta find it for?" I growled, the thought of my wrongs renewing itself.

"Steve," said the Old Man, "I done you a injustice! It was the cabin-boy which put that pole-cat in my bunk—I found it out after he jumped ship. Steve, as champeen of the old *Sea Girl*, I asks you—let bygones be gone-byes! Steve, me and the crew has need of your mallet-like fists. At Seattle, a few weeks ago, I shipped on a fiend in human form by the name of Monagan, which immediately set hisself up as the bully of the fo'c'le. I had to put in Frisco because of shortage of hands. Even now, Mate O'Donnell, Mushy Hanson and Jack Lynch lies groanin' in their bunks from his man-handlin', and he has likewise licked Bill O'Brien, Maxie Heimer and Sven Larsen. He has threatened to hang me on my own bow-sprit by my whiskers. I dast not fire him, for fear of my life. Steve!" the Old Man's voice trembled with emotion, "I asks you—forgive and forget! Come back to the *Sea Girl* and demonstrate the eternal brotherhood of man by knockin' the devil outa this demon Monagan before he destroys us all!

Show the monster who's the real champeen of the craft!"

"Well," I said, "I got some money comin' to me from Larney—but let it go. He'll need it repairin' his show. Monagan, of Seattle—bah! I hammered him into a pulp in Tony Vitello's poolroom three years ago, and I can do it again. Calls hisself champeen of the *Sea Girl*, huh? Well, when I kick his battered carcass onto the wharf, he'll know who's champeen of the craft. They never was, and they ain't now, and they never will be but one champeen of her, and that's Steve Costigan, A.B. Let's go! I wasn't never cut out for no peaceful landlubber's existence, nohow."

DARK SHANGHAI.

ALTERNATE TITLE: ONE SHANGHAI NIGHT.

This short story was first published in the January 1932 issue of Action Stories *magazine.*

THE FIRST MAN I MET, when I stepped offa my ship onto the wharfs of Shanghai, was Bill McGlory of the *Dutchman*, and I should of took this as a bad omen because that gorilla can get a man into more jams than a Chinese puzzle. He says: "Well, Steve, what do we do for entertainment—beat up some cops or start a free-for-all in a saloon?"

I says: "Them amusements is low. The first thing I am goin' to do is to go and sock Ace Barlow on the nose. When I was in port six months ago somebody drugged my grog and lifted my wad, and I since found out it was him."

"Good," said Bill. "I don't like Ace neither and I'll go along and see it's well done."

So we went down to the Three Dragons Saloon and Ace come out from behind the bar grinning like a

217

crocodile, and stuck out his hand and says: "Well, well, if it ain't Steve Costigan and Bill McGlory! Glad to see you, Costigan."

"And I'm glad to see you, you double-crossin' polecat," I says, and socked him on the nose with a peach of a right. He crashed into the bar so hard he shook the walls and a demijohn fell off a shelf onto his head and knocked him stiff, and I thought Bill McGlory would bust laughing.

Big Bess, Ace's girl, give a howl like a steamboat whistle.

"You vilyun!" she squalled. "You've killed Ace. Get out of here, you murderin' son of a skunk!" I don't know what kind of knife it was she flashed, but me and Bill left anyway. We wandered around on the water-front most of the day and just about forgot about Ace, when all of a sudden he hove in view again, most unexpectedly. We was bucking a roulette wheel in Yin Song's Temple of Chance, and naturally was losing everything we had, including our shirts, when somebody tapped me on the shoulder. I turned around and it was Ace. I drawed back my right mauler but he said: "Nix, you numb-skull—I wanta talk business with you."

His nose was skinned and both his eyes was black, which made him look very funny, and I said: "I bet you went and blowed your nose— you shouldn't never do that after bein' socked."

"I ain't here to discuss my appearance," he said annoyedly. "Come on out where we can talk without bein' overheard."

"Foller you out into the alley?" I asked. "How many thugs you got out there with blackjacks?"

At this moment Bill lost his last dime and turned around and seen Ace and he said: "Wasn't one bust on the snoot enough?"

"Listen, you mugs," said Ace, waving his arms around like he does when excited, "here I got a scheme for makin' us all a lot of dough and you boneheads stand around makin' smart cracks."

"You're goin' to fix it so we make dough, hey?" I snorted. "I may be dumb, Ace Barlow, but I ain't that dumb. You ain't no pal of our'n."

"No, I ain't!" he howled. "I despises you! I wisht you was both in Davy Jones's locker! But I never lets sentiment interfere with busi-ness, and you two saps are the only men in Shanghai which has got guts enough for the job I got in mind."

I LOOKED AT BILL AND Bill looked at me, and Bill says: "Ace, I trusts you like I trusts a rattlesnake—but lead on. Them was the honestest words I ever heard you utter."

Ace motioned us to foller him, and he led us out of the Temple of Chance into the back of his grog-shop, which wasn't very far away. When we had set down and he had poured us some licker, taking some hisself, to show us it was on the level, he said: "Did you mutts ever hear of a man by the name of John Bain?"

"Naw," I said, but Bill scowled: "Seems like I have—naw—I can't place the name—"

"Well," said Ace, "he's a eccentric milyunaire, and he's here in Shanghai. He's got a kid sister, Catherine, which he's very fond of—"

"I see the point," I snapped, getting up and sticking the bottle of licker in my hip pocket. "That's out, we don't kidnap no dame for you. C'mon, Bill."

"That's a dirty insult!" hollered Ace. "You insinyouatin' I'd stoop so low as to kidnap a white woman?"

"It wouldn't be stoopin' for you," sneered Bill. "It would be a step upwards."

"Set down, Costigan," said Ace, "and put back that bottle, les'n you got money to pay for it .... Boys, you got me all wrong. The gal's already been kidnapped, and Bain's just about nuts."

"Why don't he go to the police?" I says.

"He has," said Ace, "but when could the police find a gal the Chineeses has stole? They'd did their best but they ain't found nothin'. Now listen—this is where you fellers come in. I know where the gal is!"

"Yeah?" we said, interested, but only half believing him.

"I guess likely I'm the only white man in Shanghai what does," he said. "Now I ask you—are you thugs ready to take a chance?"

"On what?" we said.

"On the three-thousand-dollar reward John Bain is offerin' for the return of his sister," said Ace. "Now listen—I know a certain big Chinee had her kidnapped outa her 'rickshaw out at the edge of the city one evenin'. He's been keepin' her prisoner in his house, waitin' a chance to send her up-country to some bandit friends of his'n; then they'll be in position to twist a big ransome outa John Bain, see? But he ain't had a chance to slip her through yet. She's still in his house. But if I was to tell the police, they'd raid the place and get the reward theirselves. So all you boys got to do is go get her and we split the reward three ways."

"Yeah," said Bill bitterly, "and git our throats cut while doin' it. What you goin' to do?"

"I give you the information where she is," he said. "Ain't that somethin'? And I'll do more—I'll manage to lure the big Chinee away from his house while you go after the gal. I'll fake a invitation from a big merchant to meet him somewheres—I know how to work it. An hour before midnight I'll have him away from that house. Then it'll be pie for you."

ME AND BILL MEDITATED.

"After all," wheedled Ace, "she's a white gal in the grip of the yeller devils."

"That settles it," I decided. "We ain't goin' to leave no white woman at the mercy of no Chinks."

"Good," said Ace. "The gal's at Yut Lao's house—you know where that is? I'll contrive to git him outa the house. All you gotta do is walk in and grab the gal. I dunno just where in the house she'll be, of course; you'll have to find that out for yourselves. When you git her, bring her to the old deserted ware-house on the Yen Tao wharf. I'll be there with John Bain. And listen—the pore gal has likely been mistreated so she don't trust nobody. She may not wanta come with you, thinkin' you've come to take her up-country to them hill-bandits. So don't stop to argy—just bring her along anyhow."

"All right," we says and Ace says, "Well, weigh anchor then, that's all."

"That ain't all, neither," said Bill. "If I start on this here expedition I gotta have a bracer. Gimme that bottle."

"Licker costs money," complained Ace as Bill filled his pocket flask.

"Settin' a busted nose costs money, too," snapped Bill, "so shut up before I adds to your expenses. We're in this together for the money, and I want you to know I don't like you any better'n I ever did."

Ace gnashed his teeth slightly at this, and me and Bill set out for Yut Lao's house. About half a hour to midnight we got there. It was a big house, set amongst a regular rat-den of narrow twisty alleys and native hovels. But they was a high wall around it, kinda setting it off from the rest.

"Now we got to use strategy," I said, and Bill says, "Heck, there you go makin' a tough job outa this. All we gotta do is walk up to the door and when the Chinks open it, we knock 'em stiff and grab the skirt and go."

"Simple!" I said sourcastically. "Do you realize this is the very heart of the native quarters, and these yell-er-bellies would as soon stick a knife in a white man as look at him?"

"Well," he said, "if you're so smart, you figger it out."

"Come on," I said, "we'll sneak over the wall first. I seen a Chinee cop snoopin' around back there a ways and he give us a very suspicious look. I bet he thinks you're a burglar or somethin'."

Bill shoved out his jaw. "Does he come stickin' his nose into our business, I bends it into a true-lover's knot."

"This takes strategy," I says annoyedly. "If he comes up and sees us goin' over the wall, I'll tell him we're boardin' with Yut Lao and he forgot and locked us out, and we lost our key."

"That don't sound right, somehow," Bill criticized, but he's always jealous, because he ain't smart like me, so I paid no heed to him, but told him to foller me.

WELL, WE WENT DOWN a narrow back-alley which run right along by the wall, and just as we started climbing over, up bobbed the very Chinese cop I'd mentioned. He musta been follering us.

"Stop!" he said, poking at me with his night-stick. "What fella monkey-business catchee along you?"

And dawgoned if I didn't clean forget what I was going to tell him!

"Well," said Bill impatiently, "speak up, Steve, before he runs us in."

"Gimme time," I said snappishly, "don't rush me—lemme see now—Yut Lao boards with us and he lost his key—no, that don't sound right—"

"Aw, nuts!" snorted Bill and before I could stop him he hit the Chinee cop on the jaw and knocked him stiff.

"Now you done it!" said I. "This will get us six months in the jug."

"Aw, shut up and git over that wall," growled Bill. "We'll git the gal and be gone before he comes to. Then with that reward dough, I'd like to see him catch us. It's too dark here for him to have seen us good."

So we climbed into the garden, which was dark and full of them funny-looking shrubs the Chineeses grows and trims into all kinds of shapes like ships and dragons and ducks and stuff. Yut Lao's house looked even bigger from inside the wall and they was only a few lights in it. Well, we went stealthily through the garden and come to a arched door which led into the house. It was locked but we jimmied it pretty easy

with some tools Ace had give us—he had a regular burglar's kit, the crook. We didn't hear a sound; the house seemed to be deserted.

We groped around and Bill hissed, "Steve, here's a stair. Let's go up."

"Well," I said, "I don't hardly believe we'll find her upstairs or nothin'. They proberly got her in a underground dunjun or somethin'."

"Well," said Bill, "this here stair don't go no ways but up and we can't stand here all night."

So we groped up in the dark and come into a faintly lighted corridor. This twisted around and didn't seem like to me went nowheres, but finally come onto a flight of stairs going down. By this time we was clean bewildered—the way them heathens builds their houses would run a white man nuts. So we went down the stair and found ourselves in another twisting corridor on the ground floor. Up to that time we'd met nobody. Ace had evidently did his job well, and drawed most everybody outa the house.

All but one big coolie with a meat cleaver.

WE WAS JUST CONGRATULATING ourselves when swish! crack! A shadow falling acrost me as we snuck past a dark nook was all that saved my scalp. I ducked just as something hummed past my head and sunk three inches deep into the wall. It was a meat cleaver in the hand of a big Chinee, and before he could wrench it loose, I tackled him around the legs like a fullback bucking the line and we went to the floor together so hard it knocked the breath outa him. He started flopping and kicking, but I would of had him right if it hadn't of been for Bill's carelessness. Bill grabbed a lacquered chair and swung for the Chinee's head, but we was revolving on the floor so fast his aim wasn't good. Wham! I seen a million stars. I rolled offa my victim and lay, kicking feebly, and Bill used what was left of the chair to knock the Chinaman cold.

"You dumb bonehead," I groaned, holding my abused head on which was a bump as big as a goose-egg. "You nearly knocked my brains out."

"You flatters yourself, Steve," snickered Bill. "I was swingin' at the Chinee—and there he lays. I always gits my man."

"Yeah, after maimin' all the innocent bystanders within reach," I snarled. "Gimme a shot outa that flask."

We both had a nip and then tied and gagged the Chinee with strips tore from his shirt, and then we continued our explorations. We hadn't made as much noise as it might seem; if they was any people in the house they was all sound asleep. We wandered around for a while amongst them dark or dim lighted corridors, till we seen a light shining under a crack of a door, and peeking through the keyhole, we seen what we was looking for.

On a divan was reclining a mighty nice-looking white girl, reading a book. I was plumb surprised; I'd expected to find her chained up in a dunjun with rats running around. The room she was in was fixed up very nice indeed, and she didn't look like her captivity was weighing very heavy on her; and though I looked close, I seen no sign of no chain whatever. The door wasn't even locked.

I opened the door and we stepped in quick. She jumped up and stared at us.

"Who are you?" she exclaimed. "What are you doing here?"

"Shhhhh!" I said warningly. "We has come to rescue you from the heathen!"

To my shocked surprise, she opened her mouth and yelled, "Yut Lao!" at the top of her voice.

I GRABBED HER AND CLAPPED my hand over her mouth, whilst goose-flesh riz up and down my spine.

"Belay there!" I said in much annoyance. "You wanta get all our throats cut? We're your friends, don't you understand?"

Her reply was to bite me so viciously that her teeth met in my thumb. I yelped involuntarily and let her go, and Bill caught hold of her and said soothingly, "Wait,

Miss—they's no need to be scared—ow!" She hauled off and smacked him in the eye with a right that nearly floored him, and made a dart for the door. I pounced on her and she yanked out my hair in reckless handfuls.

"Grab her feet, Bill," I growled. "I come here to rescue this dame and I'm goin' to do it if we have to tie her hand and foot."

Well, Bill come to my aid and in the end we had to do just that—tie her up, I mean. It was about like tying a buzz-saw. We tore strips offa the bed-sheets and bound her wrists and ankles, as gentle as we could, and gagged her likewise, because when she wasn't chawing large chunks out of us, she would screech like a steamboat whistle. If they'd been anybody at large in the house they'd of sure heard. Honest to gosh, I never seen anybody so hard to rescue in my life. But we finally got it done and laid her on the divan.

"Why Yut Lao or anybody else wants this wildcat is more'n I can see," I growled, setting down and wiping the sweat off and trying to get my wind back. "This here's gratitude—here we risks our lives to save this girl from the clutches of the Yeller Peril and she goes and bites and kicks like we was kidnappin' her ourselves."

"Aw, wimmen is all crazy," snarled Bill, rubbing his shins where she had planted her French heels. "Dawgone it, Steve, the cork is come outa my flask in the fray and alt my licker is spillin' out."

"Stick the cork back in," I urged. And he said, "You blame fool, what you think I'd do? But I can't find the cork."

"Make a stopper outa some paper," I advised, and he looked around and seen a shelf of books. So he took down a book at random, tore out the fly-leaf and wadded it up and stuck it in the flask and put the book back. At this moment I noticed that I'd carelessly laid the girl down on her face and she was kicking and squirming, so I picked her up and said, "You go ahead and see if the way's clear; only you gotta help me pack her up and down them stairs."

"No need of that," he said. "This room's on the ground floor, see? Well, I bet this here other door opens into the garden." He unbolted it and sure enough it did.

"I bet that cop's layin' for us," I grunted.

"I bet he ain't," said Bill, and for once he was right. I reckon the Chinee thought the neighborhood was too tough for him. We never seen him again.

WE TOOK THE OPPOSITE side from where we come in at, and maybe you think we had a nice time getting that squirming frail over the wall. But we finally done it and started for the old deserted warehouse with her. Once I started to untie her and explain we was her friends, but the instant I started taking off the gag, she sunk her teeth into my neck. So I got mad and disgusted and gagged her again.

I thought we wouldn't never get to the warehouse. Tied as she was, she managed to wriggle and squirm and bounce till I had as soon try to carry a boa-constrictor, and I wisht she was a man so I could sock her on the jaw. We kept to back alleys and it ain't no uncommon sight to see men carrying a bound and gagged girl through them twisty dens at night, in that part of the native quarters, so if anybody seen us, they didn't give no hint. Probably thought we was a couple of strong-arm gorillas stealing a girl for some big mandarin or something.

Well, we finally come to the warehouse, looming all silent and deserted on the rotting old wharf. We come up into the shadder of it and somebody went, "Shhhh!"

"Is that you, Ace?" I said, straining my eyes—because they wasn't any lamps or lights of any kind anywheres near and everything was black and eery, with the water sucking and lapping at the piles under our feet.

"Yeah," came the whisper, "right here in this doorway. Come on—this way—I got the door open."

We groped our way to the door and blundered in, and he shut the door and lit a candle. We was in a small room which must have been a kind of counting or checking room once when the warehouse was in use. Ace looked at the girl and didn't seem a bit surprised because she was tied up.

"That's her, all right," he says. "Good work. Well, boys, your part's did. You better scram. I'll meet you tomorrer and split the reward."

"We'll split it tonight," I growled. "I been kicked in the shins and scratched and bit till I got tooth-marks all over me, and if you think I'm goin' to leave here without my share of the dough, you're nuts."

"You bet," said Bill. "We delivers her to John Bain, personal."

ACE LOOKED INCLINED to argy the matter, but changed his mind and said, "All right, he's in here—bring her in."

So I carried her through the door Ace opened, and we come into a big inner room, well lighted with candles and fixed up with tables and benches and things. It was Ace's secret hangout. There was Big Bess and a tall, lean feller with a pale poker-face and hard eyes. And I felt the girl stiffen in my arms and kind of turn cold.

"Well, Bain," says Ace jovially, "here she is!"

"Good enough," he said in a voice like a steel rasp. "You men can go now."

"We can like hell," I snapped. "Not till you pay us."

"How much did you promise them?" said Bain to Ace.

"A grand apiece," muttered Ace, glancing at us kind of uneasy, "but I'll tend to that."

"All right," snapped Bain, "don't bother me with the details. Take off her gag."

I done so, and untied her, watching her nervously so I could duck if she started swinging on me. But it looked like the sight of her brother wrought a change in her. She was white and trembling.

"Well, my dear," said John Bain, "we meet again."

"Oh, don't stall!" she flamed out. "What are you going to do to me?"

Me and Bill gawped at her and at each other, but nobody paid no attention to us.

"You know why I had you brought here," said Bain in a tone far from brotherly. "I want what you stole from me."

"And you stole it from old Yuen Kiang," she snapped. "He's dead—it belongs to me as much as it does to you!"

"You've hidden from me for a long time," he said, getting whiter than ever, "but it's the end of the trail Catherine, and you might as well come through. Where's that formula?"

"Where you'll never see it!" she said, very defiant.

"No?" he sneered. "Well, there are ways of making people talk—"

"Give her to me," urged Big Bess with a nasty glint in her eyes.

"I'll tell you nothing!" the girl raged, white to the lips. "You'll pay for persecuting an honest woman this way—"

John Bain laughed like a jackal barking. "Fine talk from you, you snake-in-the-grass! Honest? Why, the police of half a dozen countries are looking for you right now!"

John Bain jumped up and grabbed her by the wrist, but I throwed him away from her with such force he knocked over a table and fell across it.

"Hold everything!" I roared. "What kind of a game is this?"

JOHN BAIN PULLED HISSELF up and his eyes was dangerous as a snake's.

"Get out of here and get quick!" he snarled. "Ace can settle with you for this job out of the ten thousand I'm paying him. Now get out, before you get hurt!"

"Ten thousand!" howled Bill. "Ace is gettin' ten thousand? And us only a measly grand apiece?"

"Belay everything!" I roared. "This is too blame complicated for me. Ace sends us to rescue Bain's sister from the Chinks, us to split a three-thousand-dollar reward—now it comes out that Ace gets ten thousand—and Bain talks about his sister robbin' him—"

"Oh, go to the devil!" snapped Bain. "Barlow, when I told you to get a couple of gorillas for this job, I didn't tell you to get lunatics."

"Don't you call us looneyticks," roared Bill wrathfully. "We're as good as you be. We're better'n you, by golly! I remember you now—you ain't no more a milyunaire than I am! You're a adventurer—that's what old Cap'n Hurley called you—you're a gambler and a smuggler and a crook in general. And I don't believe this gal is your sister, neither."

"Sister to that swine?" the girl yelped like a wasp had stung her. "He's persecuting me, trying to get a valuable formula which is mine by rights, in case you don't know it—"

"That's a lie!" snarled Bain. "You stole it from me—Yuen Kiang gave it to me before he got blown up in that experiment in his laboratory—"

"Hold on," I ordered, slightly dizzy, "lemme get this straight—"

"Aw, it's too mixed up," growled Bill. "Let's take the gal back where we got her, and bust Ace on the snoot."

"Shut up, Bill," I commanded. "Leave this to me—this here's a matter which requires brains. I gotta get this straight. This girl ain't Bain's brother—I mean, he ain't her sister. Well, they ain't no kin. She's got a formula—whatever that is—and he wants it. Say, was you hidin' at Yut Lao's, instead of him havin' you kidnapped?"

"Wonderful," she sneered. "Right, Sherlock!"

"Well," I said, "we been gypped into doin' a kidnappin' when we thought we was rescuin' her; that's why she fit so hard. But why did Ace pick us?"

"I'll tell you, you flat-headed gorilla!" howled Big Bess. "It was to get even with you for that poke on the nose. And what you goin' to do about it, hey?"

"I'll tell you what we're goin' to do!" I roared. "We don't want your dirty dough! You're all a gang of thieves! This girl may be a crook, too, but we're goin' to take her back to Yut Lao's! An' right off."

Catherine caught her breath and whirled on us.

"Do you mean that?" she cried.

"You bet," I said angrily. "We may look like gorillas but we're gents. They gypped us, but they ain't goin' to harm you none, kid."

"But it's my formula," snarled John Bain. "She stole it from me."

"I don't care what she stole!" I roared. "She's better'n you, if she stole the harbor buoys! Get away from that door! We're leavin'!"

THE REST WAS KIND OF like a explosion—happened so quick you didn't have much time to think. Bain snatched up a shotgun from somewhere but before he could bring it down I kicked it outa his hands and closed with him. I heard Bill's yelp of joy as he lit into Ace, and Catherine and Big Bess went together like a couple of wildcats.

Bain was all wire and spring-steel. He butted me in the face and started the claret in streams from my nose, he gouged at my eye and he drove his knee into my belly all before I could get started. But I finally lifted him bodily and slammed him head-first onto the floor, though, and that finished Mr. John Bain for the evening. He kind of spread out and didn't even twitch.

Well, I looked around and seen Bill jumping up and down on Ace with both feet, and I seen Catherine was winning her scrap, too. Big Bess had the advantage of weight but she was yeller. Catherine sailed into her, fist and tooth and nail, and inside of a minute Big Bess was howling for mercy.

"What I want to know," gritted Catherine, sinking both hands into her hair and setting back, "is why you and that mutt Barlow are helping Bain!"

"Ow, leggo!" squalled Big Bess. "Ace heard that Bain was lookin' for you, and Ace had found out you was hidin' at Yut Lao's. Bain promised us ten grand to get you into his hands— Bain stood to make a fortune outa the formula—and we figgered on gyppin' Costigan and McGlory into doin' the dirty work and then we was goin' to skip on the early mornin' boat and leave 'em holdin' the bag!"

"So!" gasped Catherine, getting up and shaking back her disheveled locks, "I guess that settles that!"

I looked at Bain and Ace and Big Bess, all kind of strewn around on the floor, and I said I reckon it did.

"You men have been very kind to me," she said. "I understand it all now."

"Yeah," I said, "they told us Yut Lao had you kidnapped."

"The skunks!" she said. "Will you do me just one more favor and keep these thugs here until I get a good start? If I can catch that boat that sails just at dawn, I'll be safe."

"You bet," I said, "but you can't go through them back-alleys alone. I'll go back with you to Yut Lao's and Bill can stay here and guard these saps."

"Good," she said. "Let me peek outside and see that no one's spying."

So she slipped outside and Bill picked up the shotgun and said, "Hot dawg, will I guard these babies! I hope Ace will try to jump me so I can blow his fool head off!"

"Hey!" I hollered, "be careful with that gun, you sap!"

"Shucks," he says, very scornful, "I cut my teeth on a gun—"

Bang! Again I ducked complete extinction by such a brief hair's breadth that that charge of buckshot combed my hair.

"You outrageous idjit!" I says, considerably shooken. "I believe you're tryin' to murder me. That's twice tonight you've nearly kilt me."

"Aw don't be onreasonable, Steve," he urged. "I didn't know it had a hair-trigger—I was just tryin' the lock, like this, see—"

I took the death-trap away from him and throwed it into the corner.

"Gimme a nip outa the flask," I said. "I'll be a rooin before this night's over."

I took a nip which just about emptied the flask, and Bill got to looking at the wadded-up fly-leaf which was serving as a stopper.

"Lookit, Mike," he said, "this leaf has got funny marks on it, ain't it?"

I glanced at it, still nervous from my narrer escape; it had a lot of figgers and letters and words which didn't mean nothing to me.

"That's Chinese writin'," I said peevishly. "Put up that licker; here comes Miss Deal."

She run in kind of breathless. "What was that shot?" she gasped.

"Ace tried to escape and I fired to warn him," says Bill barefacedly.

I told Bill I'd be back in a hour or so and me and the girl went out into those nasty alleys. I said, "It ain't none of my business, but would you mind tellin' me what this formula-thing is?"

"It's a new way to make perfume," she said.

"Perfume?" I snift. "Is that all?"

"Do you realize millions of dollars are spent each year on perfume?" she said. "Some of it costs hundreds of dollars an ounce. The most expensive kind is made from ambergris. Well, old Yuen Kiang, a Chinese chemist, discovered a process by which a certain chemical could be substituted for ambergris, producing the same result at a fraction of the cost. The perfume company that gets this formula will save millions. So they'll bid high.

"Outside of old Yuen Kiang, the only people who knew of its existence were John Bain, myself, and old Tung Chin, the apothecary who has that little shop down by the docks. Old Yuen Kiang got blown up in some kind of an experiment, he didn't have any people, and Bain stole the formula. Then I lifted it off of Bain, and have been hiding ever since, afraid to venture out and try to sell it. I've been paying Yut Lao plenty to let me stay in his house, and keep his mouth shut. But now it's all rosy! I don't know how much I can twist out of the perfume companies for the formula, but I know it'll run up into the hundred thousands!"

We'd reached Yut Lao's house and I went in through a side-gate— she had a key—and went into her room the same way me and Bill had brung her out.

"I'm going to pack and make that boat," she said. "I haven't much time. Steve—I trust you—I'm going to show you the formula. Yut Lao knows nothing about it—I wouldn't have trusted him if he'd known why I was hiding—he thinks I've murdered somebody.

"The simplest place to hide anything is the best place. I destroyed the original formula after copying it on the flyleaf of a book, and put the book on this shelf, in plain sight. No one would ever think to look there— they'd tear up the floor and the walls first—"

And blamed if she didn't pull down the very book Bill got to make his stopper! She opened it and let out a howl like a lost soul.

"It's gone!" she screeched. "The

leaf's been torn out! I'm robbed!"

At this moment a portly Chinee appeared at the door, some flustered.

"What catchee?" he squalled. "Too much monkey-business!"

"You yellow-bellied thief!" she screamed. "You stole my formula!"

And she went for him like a cat after a sparrow. She made a flying leap and landed right in his stummick with both hands locked in his pig-tail. He squalled like a fire-engine as he hit the floor, and she began grabbing his hair by the handfuls.

A BIG CLAMOR RIZ in some other part of the house. Evidently all Yut Lao's servants had returned too. They was jabbering like a zoo-full of monkeys and the clash of their knives turned me cold.

I grabbed Catherine by the slack of her dress and lifted her bodily offa the howling Yut Lao which was a ruin by this time. And a whole passel of coolies come swarming in with knives flashing like the sun on the sea-spray. Catherine showed some inclination of going to the mat with the entire gang—I never see such a scrapping dame in my life—but I grabbed her up and racing across the room, plunged through the outer door and slammed it in their faces.

"Beat it for the wall while I hold the door!" I yelled, and Catherine after one earful of the racket inside, done so with no more argument. She raced acrost the garden and begun

to climb the wall. I braced myself to hold the door and crash! a hatchet blade ripped through the wood a inch from my nose.

"Hustle!" I yelled in a panic and she dropped on the other side of the wall. I let go and jumped back; the door crashed outwards and a swarm of Chineeses fell over it and piled up in a heap of squirming yeller figgers and gleaming knives. The sight of them knives lent wings to my feet, as the saying is, and I wish somebody had been timing me when I went acrost that garden and over that wall, because I bet I busted some world's speed records.

Catherine was waiting for me and she grabbed my hand and shook it.

"So long, sailor," she said. "I've got to make that boat now, formula or not. I've lost a fortune, but it's been lots of fun. I'll see you some day, maybe."

"Not if I see you first, you won't," I said to myself, as she scurried away into the dark, then I turned and run like all get-out for the deserted warehouse.

I was thinking of the fly-leaf Bill McGlory tore out to use for a stopper. Them wasn't Chinese letters—them was figgers—technical symbols and things! The lost formula! A hundred thousand dollars! Maybe more! And since Bain stole it from Yuen Kiang which was dead and had no heirs, and since Catherine stole it from Bain, then it was as much mine and Bill's as it was anybody's. Catherine hadn't seen Bill tear out the sheet; she was lying face down on the divan.

I gasped as I run and the sweat poured off me. A fortune! Me and Bill was going to sell that formula to some perfume company and be rich men!

I didn't keep to the back-alleys this time, but took the most direct route; it was just getting daylight. I crossed a section of the waterfront and I seen a stocky figger careening down the street, bellering, "Abel Brown the sailor." It was Bill.

"Bill McGlory." I said sternly, "you're drunk!"

"If I wasn't I'd be a wonder!" he whooped hilariously. "Steve, you old sea-horse, this here's been a great night for us!"

"Where's Ace and them?" I demanded.

"I let 'em go half an hour after you left," he said. "I got tired settin' there doin' nothin'."

"Well, listen, Bill," I said, "where abouts is that—"

"Haw! Haw! Haw!" he roared, bending over and slapping his thighs. "Lemme tell you somethin'! Steve, you'll die laughin'! You knew old Tung Chin which runs a shop down on the waterfront, and stays open all night? Well, I stopped there to fill my flask and he got to lookin' at that Chineese writin' on that paper I had stuffed in it. He got all excited and what you think? He gimme ten bucks for it!"

"Ten bucks!" I howled. "You sold that paper to Tung Chin?"

"For ten big round dollars!" he whooped. "And boy, did I licker up! Can you imagine a mutt payin' good money for somethin' like that? What you reckon that sap wanted with that fool piece of paper? Boy, when I think how crazy them Chineese is—"

And he's wondering to this day why I hauled off and knocked him stiffer than a red-brick pagoda.

VIKINGS *of the* GLOVE.

ALTERNATE TITLE: INCLUDING THE SCANDINAVIAN.

This short story was first published in the February 1932 issue of Fight Stories *magazine.*

NO SOONER HAD the *Sea Girl* docked in Yokohama than Mushy Hansen beat it down the water-front to see if he couldst match me at some good fight club. Purty soon he come back and said: "No chance, Steve. You'd have to be a Scandinavian to get a scrap right now."

"What you mean by them remarks?" I asked, suspiciously.

"Well," said Mushy, "the sealin' fleet's in, and so likewise is the whalers, and the port's swarmin' with squareheads."

"Well, what's that got to do—?"

"They ain't but one fight club on the waterfront," said Mushy, "and it's run by a Dutchman named Neimann. He's been puttin' on a series of elimination contests, and, from what I hear, he's been cleanin' up. He matches Swedes against Danes, see? Well, they's hundreds of squareheads in port, and naturally

231

each race turns out to support its countryman. So far, the Danes is ahead. You ever hear of Hakon Torkilsen?"

"You bet," I said. "I ain't never seen him perform, but they say he's the real goods. Sails on the *Viking*, outa Copenhagen, don't he?"

"Yeah. And the *Viking's* in port. Night before last, Hakon flattened Sven Tortvigssen, the Terrible Swede, in three rounds, and tonight he takes on Dirck Jacobsen, the Gotland Giant. The Swedes and the Danes is fightin' all over the waterfront," said Mushy, "and they're bettin' their socks. I sunk a few bucks on Hakon myself. But that's the way she stands, Steve. Nobody but Scandinavians need apply."

"Well, heck," I complained, "how come I got to be the victim of race prejerdice? I need dough. I'm flat broke. Wouldn't this mug Neimann gimme a preliminary scrap? For ten dollars I'll fight any three square-heads in port—all in the same ring."

"Naw," said Mushy, "they ain't goin' to be no preliminaries. Neimann says the crowd'll be too impatient to set through 'em. Boy, oh boy, will they be excitement! Whichever way it goes, they's bound to be a rough-house."

"A purty lookout," I said bitterly, "when the *Sea Girl*, the fightenest ship on the seven seas, ain't repre-sented in the melee. I gotta good mind to blow in and bust up the whole show—"

At this moment Bill O'Brien hove in sight, looking excited.

"Hot dawg!" he yelled. "Here's a chance for us to clean up some dough!"

"Stand by to come about," I advised, "and give us the lay."

"Well," Bill said, "I just been down along the waterfront listening to them squareheads argy—and, boy, is the money changin' hands! I seen six fights already. Well, just now they come word that Dirck Jacobsen had broke his wrist, swinging for a sparrin' partner and hittin' the wall instead. So I run down to Neimann's arena to find out if it was so, and the Dutchman was walkin' the floor and tearin' his hair. He said he'd pay a hundred bucks extra, win or lose, to a man good enough to go in with Torkilsen. He says if he calls the show off, these squareheads will hang him. So I see where we can run a *Sea Girl* man in and cop the jack!"

"And who you think we can use?" I asked skeptically.

"Well, there's Mushy," began Bill. "He was raised in America, of course, but—"

"Yeah, there's Mushy!" snapped Mushy, bitterly. "You know as well as I do that I ain't no Swede. I'm a Dane myself. Far from wantin' to fight Hakon, I hope he knocks the block offa whatever fool Swede they finds to go against him."

"That's gratitude," said Bill, scathingly. "How can a brainy man like me work up anything big when I gets opposition from all quarters? I lays awake nights studyin' up plans for the betterment of my mates, and what do I get? Argyments! Wisecracks! Opposition! I tellya—"

"Aw, pipe down," I said. "There's Sven Larson—he's a Swede."

"That big ox would last about fifteen seconds against Hakon," said Mushy, with gloomy satisfaction. "Besides, Sven's in jail. He hadn't been in port more'n a half hour when he got jugged for beatin' up a cop."

Bill fixed a gloomy gaze on me, and his eyes lighted.

"Hot dawg!" he whooped. "I got it! Steve, you're a Swede!"

"Listen here, you flat-headed dogfish," I began, in ire, "me and you ain't had a fight in years, but by golly—"

"Aw, try to have some sense," said Bill. "This is the idee: You ain't never fought in Yokohama before. Neimann don't know you, nor anybody else. We'll pass you off for Swede—"

"Pass him off for a Swede?" gawped Mushy.

"Well," said Bill, "I'll admit he don't look much like a Swede—"

"Much like a Swede!" I gnashed, my indignation mounting. "Why, you son of a—"

"Well, you don't look nothin' like a Swede then!" snapped Bill, disgustedly, "but we can pass you off for one. I reckon if we tell 'em you're a Swede, they can't prove you ain't. If they dispute it, we'll knock the daylights outa 'em."

I thought it over.

"Not so bad," I finally decided.

"We'll get that hundred extra—and, for a chance to fight somebody, I'd purtend I was a Eskimo. We'll do it."

"Good!" said Bill. "Can you talk Swedish?"

"Sure," I said. "Listen: Yimmy Yackson yumped off the Yacobladder with his monkey-yacket on. Yimminy, what a yump!"

"Purty good," said Bill. "Come on, we'll go down to Neimann's and sign up. Hey, ain't you goin', Mushy?"

"No, I ain't," said Mushy sourly. "I see right now I ain't goin' to enjoy this scrap none. Steve's my shipmate but Hakon's my countryman. Whichever loses, I won't rejoice none. I hope it's a draw. I ain't even goin' to see it."

Well, he went off by hisself, and I said to Bill, "I gotta good mind not to go on with this, since Mushy feels that way about it."

"Aw, he'll get over it," said Bill. "My gosh, Steve, this here's a matter of business. Ain't we all busted? Mushy'll feel all right after we split your purse three ways and he has a few shots of hard licker."

"Well, all right," I said. "Let's get down to Neimann's."

SO ME AND Bill and my white bulldog, Mike, went down to Neimann's, and, as we walked in, Bill hissed, "Don't forget to talk Swedish."

A short, fat man, which I reckoned was Neimann, was setting and looking over a list of names, and now and then he'd take a long pull out of a bottle, and then he'd cuss fit to curl your toes, and pull his hair.

"Well, Neimann," said Bill, cheerfully, "what you doin'?"

"I got a list of all the Swedes in port which think they can fight," said Neimann, bitterly. "They ain't one of 'em would last five seconds against Torkilsen. I'll have to call it off."

"No you won't," said Bill. "Right here I got the fightin'est Swede in the Asiatics!"

Neimann faced around quick to look at me, and his eyes flared, and he jumped up like he'd been stung.

"Get outa here!" he yelped. "You should come around here and mock me in my misery! A sweet time for practical jokes—"

"Aw, cool off," said Bill. "I tell you this Swede can lick Hakon Torkilsen with his right thumb in his mouth."

"Swede!" snorted Neimann. "You must think I'm a prize sucker, bringin' this black-headed mick around here and tellin' me—"

"Mick, baloney!" said Bill. "Lookit them blue eyes—"

"I'm lookin' at 'em," snarled Neimann, "and thinkin' of the lakes of Killarney all the time. Swede? Ha! Then so was Jawn L. Sullivan. So you're a Swede, are you?"

"Sure," I said. "Aye bane Swedish, Mister."

"What part of Sweden?" he barked.

"Gotland," I said, and simultaneous Bill said, "Stockholm," and we glared at each other in mutual irritation.

"Cork, you'd better say," sneered Neimann.

"Aye am a Swede," I said, annoyed. "Aye want dass fight."

"Get outa here and quit wastin' my valuable time," snarled Neimann. "If you're a Swede, then I'm a Hindoo Princess!"

At this insulting insinuation I lost my temper. I despises a man that's so suspicious he don't trust his feller men. Grabbing Neimann by the neck with a viselike grip, and waggling a huge fist under his nose, I roared, "You insultin' monkey! Am I a Swede or ain't I?"

He turned pale and shook like an aspirin-leaf.

"You're a Swede," he agreed, weakly.

"And I get the fight?" I rumbled.

"You get it," he agreed, wiping his brow with a bandanner. "The squareheads may stretch my neck for this, but maybe, if you keep your mouth shut, we'll get by. What's your name?"

"Steve—"I began, thoughtlessly, when Bill kicked me on the shin and said, "Lars Ivarson."

"All right," said Neimann, pessimistically, "I'll announce it that I got a man to fight Torkilsen."

"How much do I—how much Aye bane get?" I asked.

"I guaranteed a thousand bucks to the fighters," he said, "to be split seven hundred to the winner and three hundred to the loser."

"Give me das loser's end now," I demanded. "Aye bane go out and bet him, you betcha life."

So he did, and said, "You better keep offa the street; some of your countrymen might ask you about the folks back home in dear old Stockholm." And, with that, he give a bitter screech of raucous and irritating laughter, and slammed the door; and as we left, we heered him moaning like he had the bellyache.

"I don't believe he thinks I'm a Swede," I said, resentfully.

"Who cares?" said Bill. "We got the match. But he's right. I'll go place the bets. You keep outa sight. Long's you don't say much, we're safe. But, if you go wanderin' around, some squarehead'll start talkin' Swedish to you and we'll be sunk."

"All right," I said. "I'll get me a room at the sailor's boardin' house we seen down Manchu Road. I'll stay there till it's time for the scrap."

SO BILL WENT off to lay the bets, and me and Mike went down the back alleys toward the place I mentioned. As we turned out of a side street into Manchu Road, somebody come around the corner moving fast, and fell over Mike, who didn't have time to get outa the way.

The feller scrambled up with a wrathful roar. A big blond bezark he was, and he didn't look like a sailor. He drawed back his foot to kick Mike, as if it was the dog's fault. But

I circumvented him by the simple process of kicking him severely on the shin.

"Drop it, cull," I growled, as he begun hopping around, howling wordlessly and holding his shin. "It wasn't Mike's fault, and you hadn't no cause to kick him. Anyhow, he'd of ripped yore laig off if you'd landed—"

Instead of being pacified, he gave a bloodthirsty yell and socked me on the jaw. Seeing he was one of them bull-headed mugs you can't reason with, I banged him once with my right, and left him setting dizzily in the gutter picking imaginary violets.

Proceeding on my way to the seamen's boardin's house, I forgot all about the incident. Such trifles is too common for me to spend much time thinking about. But, as it come out, I had cause to remember it.

I got me a room and stayed there with the door shut till Bill come in, jubilant, and said the crew of the *Sea Girl* hadst sunk all the money it could borrow at heavy odds.

"If you lose," said he, "most of us will go back to the ship wearin' barrels."

"Me lose?" I snorted disgustedly. "Don't be absurd. Where's the Old Man?"

"Aw, I seen him down at that dive of antiquity, the Purple Cat Bar, a while ago," said Bill. "He was purty well lit and havin' some kind of a argyment with old Cap'n Gid Jessup. He'll be at the fight all right. I didn't say nothin' to him; but he'll be there."

"He'll more likely land in jail for fightin' old Gid," I ruminated. "They hate each other like snakes. Well, that's his own lookout. But I'd like him to see me lick Torkilsen. I heered him braggin' about the squarehead the other day. Seems like he seen him fight once some place."

"Well," said Bill, "it's nearly time for the fight. Let's get goin'. We'll go down back alleys and sneak into the arena from the rear, so none of them admirin' Swedes can get ahold of you and find out you're really a American mick. Come on!"

So we done so, accompanied by three Swedes of the *Sea Girl's* crew who was loyal to their ship and their shipmates. We snuck along alleys and slunk into the back rooms of the arena, where Neimann come in to us, perspiring freely, and told us he was having a heck of a time keeping Swedes outa the dressing-room. He said numbers of 'em wanted to come in and shake hands with Lars Ivarson before he went out to uphold the fair name of Sweden. He said Hakon was getting in the ring, and for us to hustle.

So we went up the aisle hurriedly, and the crowd was so busy cheering for Hakon that they didn't notice us till we was in the ring. I looked out over the house, which was packed, setting and standing, and square-heads fighting to get in when they wasn't room for no more. I never knowed they was that many Scandinavians in Eastern waters. It

looked like every man in the house was a Dane, a Norwegian, or a Swede—big, blond fellers, all roaring like bulls in their excitement. It looked like a stormy night.

NEIMANN WAS WALKING around the ring, bowing and grinning, and every now and then his gaze wouldst fall on me as I set in my corner and he wouldst shudder viserbly and wipe his forehead with his bandanner.

Meanwhile, a big Swedish sea captain was acting the part of the announcer, and was making quite a ceremony out of it. He wouldst boom out jovially, and the crowd wouldst roar in various alien tongues, and I told one of the Swedes from the *Sea Girl* to translate for me, which he done so in a whisper, while pertending to tie on my gloves.

This is what the announcer was saying: "Tonight all Scandinavia is represented here in this glorious forthcoming struggle for supremacy. In my mind it brings back days of the Vikings. This is a Scandinavian spectacle for Scandinavian sailors. Every man involved in this contest is Scandinavian. You all know Hakon Torkilsen, the pride of Denmark!" Whereupon, all the Danes in the crowd bellered. "I haven't met Lars Ivarson, but the very fact that he is a son of Sweden assures us that he will prove no mean opponent for Denmark's favored son." It was the Swedes' turn to roar. "I now present the referee, Jon Yarssen, of Norway! This is a family affair. Remember, whichever way the fight goes, it will lend glory to Scandinavia!"

Then he turned and pointed toward the opposite corner and roared, "Hakon Torkilsen, of Denmark!"

Again the Danes thundered to the skies, and Bill O'Brien hissed in my ear. "Don't forget when you're interjuiced say 'Dis bane happiest moment of my life!' The accent will convince 'em you're a Swede."

The announcer turned toward me and, as his eyes fell on me for the first time, he started violently and blinked. Then he kind of mechanically pulled hisself together and stammered, "L a r s Ivarson—of—of—Sweden!"

I riz, shedding my bathrobe, and a gasp went up from the crowd like they was thunderstruck or something. For a moment a sickening silence reigned, and then my Swedish shipmates started applauding, and some of the Swedes and Norwegians took it up, and, like people always do, got louder and louder till they was lifting the roof.

Three times I started to make my speech, and three times they drowned me out, till I run outa my short stock of patience.

"Shut up, you lubbers!" I roared, and they lapsed into sudden silence, gaping at me in amazement. With a menacing scowl, I said, "Dis bane happiest moment of my life, by thunder!"

They clapped kind of feebly and dazedly, and the referee motioned us to the center of the ring. And, as we faced each other, I gaped, and he barked, "Aha!" like a hyena which sees some critter caught in a trap. The referee was the big cheese I'd socked in the alley!

I didn't pay much attention to Hakon, but stared morbidly at the referee, which reeled off the instructions in some Scandinavian tongue. Hakon nodded and responded in kind, and the referee glared at me and snapped something and I nodded and grunted, "Ja!" just as if I understood him, and turned back toward my corner.

He stepped after me, and caught hold of my gloves. Under cover of examining 'em he hissed, so low my handlers didn't even hear him, "You are no Swede! I know you. You called your dog 'Mike.' There is only one white bulldog in the Asiatics by that name! You are Steve Costigan, of the *Sea Girl*."

"Keep it quiet," I muttered nervously.

"Ha!" he snarled. "I will have my revenge. Go ahead—fight your fight. After the bout is over, I will expose you as the imposter you are. These men will hang you to the rafters."

"Gee whiz," I mumbled, "what you wanta do that for? Keep my secret and I'll slip you fifty bucks after the scrap."

He merely snorted, "Ha!" in disdain, pointing meaningly at the black eye which I had give him, and stalked back to the center of the ring.

"What did that Norwegian say to you?" Bill O'Brien asked.

I didn't reply. I was kinda wool-gathering. Looking out over the mob, I admit I didn't like the prospects. I hadst no doubt that them infuriated squareheads would be maddened at the knowledge that a alien had passed hisself off as one of 'em—and they's a limit to the numbers that even Steve Costigan can vanquish in mortal combat! But about that time the gong sounded, and I forgot everything except the battle before me.

FOR THE FIRST time I noticed Hakon Torkilsen, and I realized why he had such a reputation. He was a regular panther of a man—a tall, rangy, beautifully built young slugger with a mane of yellow hair and cold, steely eyes. He was six feet one to my six feet, and weighed 185 to my 190. He was trained to the ounce, and his long, smooth muscles rippled under his white skin as he moved. My black mane musta contrasted strongly with his golden hair.

He come in fast and ripped a left hook to my head, whilst I come back with a right to the body which brung him up standing. But his body muscles was like iron ridges, and I knowed it wouldst take plenty of pounding to soften him there, even though it was me doing the pounding.

Hakon was a sharpshooter, and he begunst to shoot his left straight and fast. All my opponents does, at first, thinking I'm a sucker for a left jab. But they soon abandons that form of attack. I ignores left jabs. I now walked through a perfect hail of 'em and crashed a thundering right under Hakon's heart which brung a astonished grunt outa him. Discarding his jabbing offensive, he started flailing away with both hands, and I wanta tell you he wasn't throwing no powder-puffs!

It was the kind of scrapping I like. He was standing up to me, giving and taking, and I wasn't called on to run him around the ring like I gotta do with so many of my foes. He was belting me plenty, but that's my style, and, with a wide grin, I slugged merrily at his body and head, and the gong found us in the center of the ring, banging away.

The crowd give us a roaring cheer as we went back to our corners, but suddenly my grin was wiped off by the sight of Yarssen, the referee, cryptically indicating his black eye as he glared morbidly at me.

I determined to finish Torkilsen as quick as possible, make a bold break through the crowd, and try to get away before Yarssen had time to tell 'em my fatal secret. Just as I started to tell Bill, I felt a hand jerking at my ankle. I looked down into the bewhiskered, bewildered and bleary-eyed face of the Old Man.

"Steve!" he squawked. "I'm in a terrible jam!"

Bill O'Brien jumped like he was

stabbed. "Don't yell 'Steve' thataway!" he hissed. "You wanta get us all mobbed?"

"I'm in a terrible jam!" wailed the Old Man, wringing his hands. "If you don't help me, I'm a rooined man!"

"What's the lay?" I asked in amazement, leaning through the ropes.

"It's Gid Jessup's fault," he moaned. "The serpent got me into a argyment and got me drunk. He knows I ain't got no sense when I'm soused. He hornswoggled me into laying a bet on Torkilsen. I didn't know you was goin' to fight—"

"Well," I said, "that's tough, but you'll just have to lose the bet."

"I can't!" he howled.

Bong! went the gong, and I shot outa my corner as Hakon ripped outa his.

"I can't lose!" the Old Man howled above the crowd. "I bet the *Sea Girl!*"

"What!" I roared, momentarily forgetting where I was, and half-turning toward the ropes. Bang! Hakon nearly tore my head off with a free-swinging right. Bellering angrily, I come back with a smash to the mush that started the claret, and we went into a slug-fest, flailing free and generous with both hands.

That Dane was tough! Smacks that would of staggered most men didn't make him wince. He come ploughing in for more. But, just before the gong, I caught him off balance with a blazing left hook that

knocked him into the ropes, and the Swedes arose, whooping like lions.

BACK ON MY stool I peered through the ropes. The Old Man was dancing a hornpipe.

"What's this about bettin' the *Sea Girl?*" I demanded.

"When I come to myself a while ago, I found I'd wagered the ship," he wept, "against Jessup's lousy tub, the *Nigger King*, which I find is been condemned by the shippin' board and wouldn't clear the bay without goin' to the bottom. He took a unfair advantage of me! I wasn't responsible when I made that bet!"

"Don't pay it," I growled, "Jessup's a rat!"

"He showed me a paper I signed while stewed," he groaned. "It's a contrack upholdin' the bet. If it weren't for that, I wouldn't pay. But if I don't, he'll rooin my reputation in every port of the seven seas. He'll show that contrack and gimme the name of a welsher. You got to lose!"

"Gee whiz!" I said, badgered beyond endurance. "This is a purty mess—"

Bong! went the gong, and I paced out into the ring, all upset and with my mind elsewhere. Hakon swarmed all over me, and drove me into the ropes, where I woke up and beat him off, but, with the Old Man's howls echoing in my ears, I failed to follow up my advantage, and Hakon come back strong.

The Danes raised the roof as he

battered me about the ring, but he wasn't hurting me none, because I covered up, and again, just before the gong, I snapped outa my crouch and sent him back on his heels with a wicked left hook to the head.

The referee gimme a gloating look, and pointed at his black eye, and I had to grit my teeth to keep from socking him stiff. I set down on my stool and listened gloomily to the shrieks of the Old Man, which was getting more unbearable every minute.

"You got to lose!" he howled. "If Torkilsen don't win this fight, I'm rooined! If the bet'd been on the level, I'd pay—you know that. But, I been swindled, and now I'm goin' to get robbed! Lookit the rat over there, wavin' that devilish paper at me! It's more'n human flesh and blood can stand! It's enough to drive a man to drink! You got to lose!"

"But the boys has bet their shirts on me," I snarled, fit to be tied with worry and bewilderment. "I can't lay down! I never throwed a fight. I don't know how—"

"That's gratitood!" he screamed, busting into tears. "After all I've did for you! Little did I know I was warmin' a serpent in my bosom! The poorhouse is starin' me in the face, and you—"

"Aw, shut up, you old sea horse!" said Bill. "Steve—I mean Lars—has got enough to contend with without you howlin' and yellin' like a maneyack. Them squareheads is gonna get suspicious if you and him

keep talkin' in English. Don't pay no attention to him, Steve—I mean Lars. Get that Dane!"

Well, the gong sounded, and I went out all tore up in my mind and having just about lost heart in the fight. That's a most dangerous thing to have happen, especially against a man-killing slugger like Hakon Torkilsen. Before I knowed what was goin' on, the Swedes rose with a scream of warning and about a million stars bust in my head. I realized faintly that I was on the canvas, and I listened for the count to know how long I had to rest.

I heered a voice droning above the roar of the fans, but it was plumb meaningless to me. I shook my head, and my sight cleared. Jon Yarssen was standing over me, his arm going up and down, but I didn't understand a word he said! He was counting in Swedish!

Not daring to risk a moment, I heaved up before my head had really quit singing an' Hakon come storming in like a typhoon to finish me.

But I was mad clean through and had plumb forgot about the Old Man and his fool bet. I met Hakon with a left hook which nearly tore his head off, and the Swedes yelped with joy. I bored in, ripping both hands to the wind and heart, and, in a fast mix-up at close quarters, Hakon went down—more from a slip than a punch. But he was wise and took a count, resting on one knee.

I watched the referee's arm so as to familiarize myself with the sound of the numerals—but he wasn't counting in the same langwidge as he had over me! I got it, then; he counted over me in Swedish and over Hakon in Danish. The langwidges is alike in many ways, but different enough to get me all mixed up, which didn't know a word in either tongue, anyhow. I seen then that I was going to have a enjoyable evening.

Hakon was up at nine—I counted the waves of the referee's arm—and he come up at me like a house afire. I fought him off half-heartedly, whilst the Swedes shouted with amazement at the change which had come over me since that blazing first round.

Well, I've said repeatedly that a man can't fight his best when he's got his mind on something else. Here was a nice mess for me to worry about. If I quit, I'd be a yeller dog and despize myself for the rest of my life, and my shipmates would lose their money, and so would all the Swedes which had bet on me and was now yelling and cheering for me just like I was their brother. I couldn't throw 'em down. Yet if I won, the Old Man would lose his ship, which was all he had and like a daughter to him. It wouldst beggar him and break his heart. And, as a minor thought, whether I won or lost, that scut Yarssen was going to tell the crowd I wasn't no Swede, and get me mobbed. Every time I looked at him over Hakon's shoulder in a clinch, Yarssen wouldst touch his black eye meaningly. I was bogged down in gloom, and I wished I could evaporate or something.

Back on my stool, between rounds, the Old Man wept and begged me to lay down, and Bill and my handlers implored me to wake up and kill Torkilsen, and I thought I'd go nuts.

I WENT OUT for the fourth round slowly, and Hakon, evidently thinking I'd lost my fighting heart, if any, come with his usual tigerish rush and biffed me three times in the face without a return.

I dragged him into a grizzly-like clinch which he couldn't break, and as we rassled and strained, he spat something at me which I couldn't understand, but I understood the tone of it. He was calling me yellow! Me, Steve Costigan, the terror of the high seas!

With a maddened roar, I jerked away from him and crashed a murderous right to his jaw that nearly floored him. Before he couldst recover his balance, I tore into him like a wild man, forgetting everything except that I was Steve Costigan, the bully of the toughest ship afloat.

Slugging right and left, I rushed him into the ropes, where I pinned him, while the crowd went crazy. He crouched and covered up, taking most of my punches on the gloves and elbows, but I reckoned it looked to the mob like I was beating him to death. All at once, above the roar, I heered the Old Man screaming, "Steve, for cats' sake, let up! I'll go on the beach, and it'll be your fault!"

That unnerved me. I involuntarily dropped my hands and recoiled, and Hakon, with fire in his eyes, lunged outa his crouch like a tiger and crashed his right to my jaw.

Bang! I was on the canvas again, and the referee was droning Swedish numerals over me. Not daring to take a count, and maybe get counted out unknowingly, I staggered up, and Hakon come lashing in. I throwed my arms around him in a grizzly hug, and it took him and the referee both to break my hold.

Hakon drove me staggering into the ropes with a wild-man attack, but I'm always dangerous on the ropes, as many a good man has found out on coming to in his dressing room. As I felt the rough strands against my back, I caught him with a slung-shot right uppercut which snapped his head right back betwixt his shoulders, and this time it was him which fell into a clinch and hung on.

Looking over his shoulder at that sea of bristling blond heads and yelling faces, I seen various familiar figgers. On one side of the ring—near my corner—the Old Man was dancing around like he was on a red-hot hatch, shedding maudlin tears and pulling his whiskers; and, on the other side, a skinny,

shifty-eyed old seaman was whooping with glee and waving a folded paper. Cap'n Gid Jessup, the old cuss! He knowed the Old Man would bet anything when he was drunk—even bet the *Sea Girl*, as sweet a ship as ever rounded the Horn, against that rotten old hulk of a *Nigger King*, which wasn't worth a cent a ton. And, near at hand, the referee, Yarssen, was whispering tenderly in my ear, as he broke our clinch, "Better let Hakon knock you stiff—then you won't feel so much what the crowd does to you when I tell them who you are!"

Back on my stool again, I put my face on Mike's neck and refused to listen either to the pleas of the Old Man or to the profane shrieks of Bill O'Brien. By golly, that fight was like a nightmare! I almost hoped Hakon would knock my brains out and end all my troubles.

I went out for the fifth like a man going to his own hanging. Hakon was evidently puzzled. Who wouldn't of been? Here was a fighter—me—who was performing in spurts, exploding in bursts of ferocious battling just when he appeared nearly out, and sagging half heartedly when he looked like a winner.

He come in, lashed a vicious left to my mid-section, and dashed me to the canvas with a thundering overhand right. Maddened, I arose and dropped him with a wild roundhouse swing he wasn't expecting. Again the crowd surged to its feet, and the referee got flustered and started counting over Hakon in what sounded like Swedish.

Hakon bounded up and slugged me into the ropes, offa which I floundered, only to slip in a smear of my own blood on the canvas, and again, to the disgust of the Swedes, I found myself among the resin.

I looked about, heard the Old Man yelling for me to stay down, and saw Old Cap'n Jessup waving his blame-fool contrack. I arose, only half aware of what I was doing, and bang! Hakon caught me on the ear with a hurricane swing, and I sprawled on the floor, half under the ropes.

Goggling dizzily at the crowd from this position, I found myself staring into the distended eyes of Cap'n Gid Jessup, which was standing up, almost touching the ring. Evidently froze at the thought of losing his bet—with me on the canvas—he was standing there gaping, his arm still lifted with the contrack which he'd been waving at the Old Man.

With me, thinking is acting. One swoop of my gloved paw swept that contrack outa his hand. He yawped with suprise and come lunging half through the ropes. I rolled away from him, sticking the contrack in my mouth and chawing as fast as I could. Cap'n Jessup grabbed me by the hair with one hand and tried to jerk the contrack outa my jaws with the other'n, but all he got was a severely bit finger.

At this, he let go of me and begun to scream and yell. "Gimme back that paper, you cannibal! He's eatin' my contrack! I'll sue you—!"

MEANWHILE, THE DUMBFOUNDED referee, overcome with amazement, had stopped counting, and the crowd, not understanding this by-play, was roaring with astonishment. Jessup begun to crawl through the ropes, and Yarssen yelled something and shoved him back with his foot. He started through again, yelling blue murder, and a big Swede, evidently thinking he was trying to attack me, swung once with a fist the size of a caulking mallet, and Cap'n Jessup bit the dust.

I arose with my mouth full of paper, and Hakon promptly banged me on the chin with a right he started from his heels. Ow, Jerusha! Wait'll somebody hits you on the jaw when you're chawing something! I thought for a second every tooth in my head was shattered, along with my jaw-bone. But I reeled groggily back into the ropes and begun to swaller hurriedly.

Bang! Hakon whanged me on the ear. "Gulp!" I said. Wham! He socked me in the eye. "Gullup!" I said. Blop! He pasted me in the stummick. "Oof—glup!" I said. Whang! He took me on the side of the head. "Gulp!" I swallered the last of the contrack, and went for that Dane with fire in my eyes.

I banged Hakon with a left that

sunk outa sight in his belly, and nearly tore his head off with a paralyzing right before he realized that, instead of being ready for the cleaners, I was stronger'n ever and ra'ring for action.

Nothing loath, he rallied, and we went into a whirlwind of hooks and swings till the world spun like a merry-go-round. Neither of us heered the gong, and our seconds had to drag us apart and lead us to our corners.

"Steve," the Old Man was jerking at my leg and weeping with gratitude, "I seen it all! That old pole-cat's got no hold on me now. He can't prove I ever made that fool bet. You're a scholar and a gent—one of nature's own noblemen! You've saved the *Sea Girl*!"

"Let that be a lesson to you," I said, spitting out a fragment of the contrack along with a mouthful of blood. "Gamblin' is sinful. Bill, I got a watch in my pants pocket. Get it and bet it that I lay this squarehead within three more rounds."

And I come out for the sixth like a typhoon. "I'm going to get mobbed by the fans as soon as the fight's over and Yarssen spills the beans," I thought, "but I'll have my fun now."

For once I'd met a man which was willing and able to stand up and slug it out with me. Hakon was as lithe as a panther and as tough as spring-steel. He was quicker'n me, and hit nearly as hard. We crashed together in the center of the ring,

throwing all we had into the storm of battle.

Through a red mist I seen Hakon's eyes blazing with a unearthly light. He was plumb berserk, like them old Vikings which was his ancestors. And all the Irish fighting madness took hold of me, and we ripped and tore like tigers.

We was the center of a frenzied whirlwind of gloves, ripping smashes to each other's bodies which you could hear all over the house, and socks to each other's heads that spattered blood all over the ring. Every blow packed dynamite and had the killer's lust behind it. It was a test of endurance.

At the gong, we had to be tore apart and dragged to our corners by force, and, at the beginning of the next round, we started in where we'd left off. We reeled in a blinding hurricane of gloves. We slipped in smears of blood, or was knocked to the canvas by each other's thundering blows.

The crowd was limp and idiotic, drooling wordless screeches. And the referee was bewildered and muddled. He counted over us in Swedish, Danish and Norwegian alike. Then I was on the canvas, and Hakon was staggering on the ropes, gasping, and the befuddled Yarssen was counting over me. And, in the dizzy maze, I recognized the langwidge. He was counting in Spanish!

"You ain't no Norwegian!" I said, glaring groggily up at him.

"Four!" he said, shifting into

English. "—As much as you're a Swede! Five! A man's got to eat. Six! They wouldn't have given me this job—seven!—if I hadn't pretended to be a Norwegian. Eight! I'm John Jones, a vaudeville linguist from Frisco. Nine! Keep my secret and I'll keep yours."

THE GONG! OUR handlers dragged us off to our corners and worked over us. I looked over at Hakon. I was marked plenty—a split ear, smashed lips, both eyes half closed, nose broken—but them's my usual adornments. Hakon wasn't marked up so much in the face—outside of a closed eye and a few gashes—but his body was raw beef from my continuous body hammering. I drawed a deep breath and grinned gargoylishly. With the Old Man and that fake referee offa my mind, I couldst give all my thoughts to the battle.

The gong banged again, and I charged like a enraged bull. Hakon met me as usual, and rocked me with thundering lefts and rights. But I bored in, driving him steadily before me with ripping, bone-shattering hooks to the body and head. I felt him slowing up. The man don't live which can slug with me!

Like a tiger scenting the kill, I redoubled the fury of my onslaught, and the crowd arose, roaring, as they foresaw the end. Nearly on the ropes, Hakon rallied with a dying burst of ferocity, and momentarily had me reeling under a fusillade of desperate swings. But I shook my head doggedly and plowed in under his barrage, ripping my terrible right under his heart again and again, and tearing at his head with mallet-like left hooks.

Flesh and blood couldn't stand it. Hakon crumpled in a neutral corner under a blasting fire of left and right hooks. He tried to get his legs under him, but a child couldst see he was done.

The referee hesitated, then raised my right glove, and the Swedes and Norwegians came roaring into the ring and swept me offa my feet. A glance showed Hakon's Danes carrying him to his corner, and I tried to get to him to shake his hand, and tell him he was as brave and fine a fighter as I ever met—which was the truth and nothing else—but my delirious followers hadst boosted both me and Mike on their shoulders and were carrying us toward the dressing-room like a king or something.

A tall form come surging through the crowd, and Mushy Hansen grabbed my gloved hand and yelled, "Boy, you done us proud! I'm sorry the Danes had to lose, but, after a battle like that, I can't hold no grudge. I couldn't stay away from the scrap. Hooray for the old *Sea Girl*, the fightin'est ship on the seven seas!"

And the Swedish captain, which had acted as announcer, barged in front of me and yelled in English,

"You may be a Swede, but if you are, you're the most unusual looking Swede I ever saw. But I don't give a whoop! I've just seen the greatest battle since Gustavus Adolphus licked the Dutch! Skoal, Lars Ivarson!"

And all the Swedes and Norwegians thundered, "Skoal, Lars Ivarson!"

"They want you to make a speech," said Mushy.

"All right," I said. "Dis bane happiest moment of my life!"

"Louder," said Mushy. "They're makin' so much noise they can't understand you, anyhow. Say somethin' in a foreign langwidge."

"All right," I said, and yelled the only foreign words I couldst think of, "Parleyvoo Francais! Vive le Stockholm! Erin go bragh!"

And they bellered louder'n ever. A fighting man is a fighting man in any langwidge!

NIGHT *of* BATTLE.

ALTERNATE TITLE: SHORE LEAVE FOR A SLUGGER.

This short story was first published in the March 1932 issue of Fight Stories *magazine.*

I'M BEGINNING TO believe that Singapore is a jinx for me. Not that I don't always get a fight there; I do. But it looks, by golly, like a lot of dirty luck is always throwed in with the fight.

Rumination of them sort was in my mind as I clumb the rickety stairs of the Seaman's Deluxe Boarding House and entered my room, tightly gripping the fifty bucks which constituted my whole wad.

I'd just been down to see Ace Larnigan, manager of the Arena, and had got matched with Black Jack O'Brien for ten rounds or less, that night. And I was wondering where I could hide my roll. I had the choice of taking it with me and getting it stole outa my britches whilst I was in the ring, or leaving it in my room and getting it hooked by the Chino servants from which you couldn't hide nothing.

I set on my ramshackle bed and meditated, and I had about decided to let my white bulldog, Mike, hold the roll in his mouth while I polished off Black Jack, with a good chance of him swallering it in his excitement, when all of sudden I heered sounds of somebody ascending the stairs about six steps at a jump, and then running wildly down the hall.

I paid no heed; guests of the Deluxe is always being chased into the dump or out of it by the cops. But instead of running into his own room and hiding under the bed, as was the usual custom, this particular fugitive blundered headlong against my door, blowing and gasping like a grampus. Much to my annoyance, the door was knocked violently open, and a disheveled shape fell all over the floor.

I riz with dignity. "What kind of a game is this?" I asked, with my instinctive courtesy. "Will you get outa my room or will I throw you out on your ear?"

"Hide me, Steve!" the shape gasped. "Shut the door! Hide me! Give me a gun! Call the cops! Lemme under the bed! Look out the window and see if you see anybody chasing me!"

"Make up your mind what you want me to do; I ain't no magician," I said disgustedly, recognizing the shape as Johnny Kyelan, a good-hearted but soft-headed sap of a kid which should of been jerking soda back home instead of trying to tend bar in a tough waterfront joint in Singapore. Just one of them fool kids which is trying to see the world.

He grabbed me with hands that shook, and I seen the sweat standing out on his face.

"You got to help me, Steve!" he babbled. "I came here because I didn't know anybody else to go to. If you don't help me, I'll never live to see another sunrise. I've stumbled onto something I wasn't looking for. Something that it's certain death to know about. Steve, I've found out who The Black Mandarin is!"

I grunted. This is serious.

"You mean you know who it is that's been committin' all these robberies and murders, dressed up in a mask and Chinee clothes?"

"The same!" he exclaimed, trembling and sweating. "The worst criminal in the Orient!"

"Then why in heck don't you go to the police?" I demanded.

He shook like he had aggers. "I don't dare! I'd never live to get to the police station. They're watching for me—it isn't one man who's been doing all these crimes; it's a criminal organization. One man is the head, but he has a big gang. They all dress the same way when they're robbing and looting."

"How'd you get onto this?" I asked.

"I was tending bar," he shuddered. "I went into the cellar to get some wine—it's very seldom I go there. By pure chance, I came onto a group of them plotting over a table by a candle-light. I recognized them and heard them talking—the fellow who owns the saloon where I work is one of them—and I never had an inkling he was a crook. I was behind a stack of wine-kegs, and listened till I got panicky and made a break. Then they saw me. They chased me in and out among those winding alleys till I thought I'd die. I shook them off just a few minutes ago, and reached here. But I don't dare stir out. I don't think they saw me coming in, but they're combing the streets, and they'd see me going out."

"Who is the leader?" I asked.

"They call him the Chief," he said.

"Yeah, but who is he?" I persisted, but he just shook that much more.

"I don't dare tell." His teeth was chattering with terror. "Somebody might be listening."

"Well, gee whiz," I said, "you're in bad with 'em already—"

But he was in one of them onreasoning fears, and wouldn't tell me nothing.

"You'd never in the world guess," he said. "And I just don't dare. I get goose-pimples all over when I think about it. Let me stay with you till tomorrow morning, Steve," he begged, "then we'll get in touch with Sir Peter Brent, the Scotland Yard guy. He's the only man of authority I trust. The police have proven themselves helpless—nobody ever recognized one of that Mandarin gang and lived to tell about it. But Sir Peter will protect me and trap these fiends."

"Well," I said, "why can't we get him now?"

"I don't know where to reach him," said Johnny. "He's somewhere in Singapore—I don't know where. But in the morning we can get him at his club; he's always there early in the morning. For heavens' sake, Steve, let me stay!"

"Sure, kid," I said. "Don't be scairt. If any them Black Mandarins comes buttin' in here, I'll bust 'em on the snoot. I was goin' to fight Black Jack O'Brien down at the Arena tonight, but I'll call it off and stick around with you."

"No, don't do that," he said, beginning to get back a little of his nerve. "I'll lock the door and stay here. I don't think they know where I am; and, anyway, with the door locked they can't get in to me without making a noise that would arouse the whole house. You go ahead and fight Black Jack. If you didn't show up, some of that gang might guess you were with me; they're men who know us both. Then that would get you into trouble. They know you're the only friend I've got."

"Well," I said, "I'll leave Mike here to purteck you."

"No! No!" he said. "That'd look just as suspicious, if you showed up without Mike. Besides, they'd only shoot him if they came. You go on, and, when you come back, knock on the door and tell me who it is. I'll know your voice and let me in."

"Well, all right," I said, "if you think you'll be safe. I don't think them Mandarins would have sense enough to figger out you was with me, just because I didn't happen to show up at the Arena—but maybe you know. And say, you keep this fifty bucks for me. I was wonderin' what to do with it. If I take it to the Arena, some dip will lift it offa me."

So Johnny took it, and me and Mike started for the Arena, and, as we went down the stairs, I heered him lock the door behind us. As I left the Deluxe, I looked sharp for any slinking figgers hanging around watching the house, but didn't see none, and went on down the street.

THE ARENA WAS just off the waterfront, and it was crowded like it always is when either me or Black Jack fights. Ace had been wanting to get us together for a long time, but this was the first time we happened to be in port at the same time. I was in my dressing-room putting on my togs when in stormed a figger I knowed must be my opponent. I've heered it said me and Black Jack looked enough alike to be brothers; he was my height, six feet, weighed same as me, and had black hair and smoldering blue eyes. But I always figgered I was better looking than him.

I seen he was in a wicked mood, and I knowed his recent fight with Bad Bill Kearney was still rankling him. Bad Bill was a hard-boiled egg which run a gambling hall in the toughest waterfront district of Singapore and fought on the side. A few weeks before, him and O'Brien

had staged a most vicious battle in the Arena, and Black Jack had been knocked cold in the fifth round, just when it looked like he was winning. It was the only time he'd ever been stopped, and, ever since, he'd been frothing at the mouth and trying to get Bad Bill back in the ring with him.

He give a snarling, blood-thirsty laugh as he seen me.

"Well, Costigan," he said, "I guess maybe you think you're man enough to stow me away tonight, eh? You slant-headed goriller!"

"I may not lick you, you black-jowled baboon," I roared, suspecting a hint of insult in his manner, "but I'll give you a tussle your great-grand-children will shudder to hear about!"

"How strong do you believe that?" he frothed.

"Strong enough to kick your brains out here and now," I thundered.

Ace got in between us.

"Hold it!" he requested. "I ain't goin' to have you boneheads rooin'in' my show by massacreein' each other before the fight starts."

"What you got there?" asked O'Brien, suspiciously, as Ace dug into his pockets.

"Your dough," said Ace sourly, bringing out a roll of bills. "I guar-anteed you each fifty bucks, win, lose or draw."

"Well," I said, "we don't want it now. Give it to us after the mill."

"Ha!" sneered Ace. "Keep it and get my pockets picked? Not me! I'm givin' it to you now. You two can take the responsibility. Here—take it! Now I've paid you, and you got no kick comin' at me if you lose it. If the dips get it offa you, that ain't my lookout."

"All right, you white-livered land-shark," sneered Black Jack, and turned to me. "Costigan, this fifty says I lays you like a carpet."

"I takes you!" I barked. "My fifty says you leaves that ring on a shutter. Who holds stakes?"

"Not me," said Ace, hurriedly.

"Don't worry," snapped Black Jack, "I wouldn't trust a nickel of my dough in your greasy fingers. Not a nickel. Hey Bunger!"

At the yell, in come a bewhiskered old wharf-rat which exuded a strong smell of trader's rum.

"What you want?" he said. "Buy me a drink, Black Jack."

"I'll buy you a raft of drinks later," growled O'Brien. "Here, hold these stakes, and if you let a dip get 'em, I'll pull out all your whiskers by the roots."

"They won't get it offa me," promised old Bunger. "I know the game, you bet."

Which he did, having been a dip hisself in his youth; but he had one virtue—when he was sober, he was as honest as the day is long with them he considered his friends. So he took the two fifties, and me and O'Brien, after a few more mutual insults, slung on our bathrobes and strode up the aisle, to the applause of the multitude, which cheered a long-looked-for melee.

The *Sea Girl* wasn't in port—in fact, I'd come to Singapore to meet her, as she was due in a few days. So, as they was none of my crew to second me, Ace had provided a couple of dumb clucks.

He'd also give Black Jack a pair of saps, as O'Brien's ship, the *Watersnake*, wasn't in port either.

THE GONG WHANGED, the crowd roared, and the dance commenced. We was even matched. We was both as tough as nails, and aggressive. What we lacked in boxing skill, we made up for by sheer ferocity. The Arena never seen a more furious display of hurricane battling and pile-driving punching; it left the crowd as limp as a rag and yammering gibberish.

At the tap of each gong we just rushed at each other and started slugging. We traded punches 'til everything was red and hazy. We stood head to head and battered away, then we leaned on each other's chest and kept hammering, and then we kept our feet by each resting his chin on the other's shoulder, and driving away with short-arm jolts to the body. We slugged 'til we was both blind and deaf and dizzy, and kept on battering away, gasping and drooling curses and weeping with sheer fighting madness.

At the end of each round our handlers would pull us apart and guide us to our corners, where they wouldst sponge off the blood and sweat and tears, and douse us with ice-water, and give us sniffs of ammonia, whilst the crowd watched, breathless, afeared neither of us would be able to come up for the next round. But with the marvelous recuperating ability of the natural-born slugger, we would both revive under the treatments, and stiffen on our stool, glaring red-eyed at each other, and, with the tap of the gong, it would begin all over again. Boy, that was a scrap, I'm here to tell you!

Time and again either him or me would be staggering on the ragged edge of a knockout, but would suddenly rally in a ferocious burst of battling which had the crowd delirious. In the eighth he put me on the canvas with a left hook that nearly tore my head off, and the crowd riz, screaming. But at "eight" I come up, reeling, and dropped him with a right hook under the heart that nearly cracked his ribs. He lurched up just before the fatal "ten," and the gong sounded.

The end of the ninth found us both on the canvas, but ten rounds was just too short a time for either of us to weaken sufficient for a knockout. But I believe, if it had gone five more rounds, half the crowd would of dropped dead. The finish found most of 'em feebly flapping their hands and croaking like frogs. At the final gong we was standing head to head in the middle of the ring, trading smashes you couldst hear all over the house, and the referee pulled us apart by main strength and lifted both our hands as an indication that the fight was a draw.

DRAWING ON HIS bathrobe, Black Jack come over to my corner, spitting out blood and the fragments of a tooth, and he said, grinning like a hyena, "Well, you owe me fifty bucks which you bet on lickin' me."

"And, by the same token, you owe me fifty," I retorted. "Your bet was you'd flatten me. By golly, I don't know when I ever enjoyed a scrap more! I don't see how Bad Bill licked you."

O'Brien's face darkened like a thunder-cloud.

"Don't mention that egg to me," he snapped. "I can't figger it out myself. You hit me tonight a lot harder'n he ever did. I'd just battered him clean across the ring, and he was reelin' and rockin'—then it happened. All I know is that he fell into me, and we in a sort of half-clinch—then bing! The next thing I knowed, they was pourin' water on me in my dressin'-room. They said he socked me on the jaw as we broke, but I never seen the punch—or felt it."

"Well," I said, "forget it. Let's get our dough from old Bunger and go get a drink. Then I gotta go back to my room."

"What you turnin' in so soon for?" he scowled. "The night's young. Let's see if we can't shake up some fun. They's a couple of tough bouncers down at Yota Lao's I been layin' off to lick a long time—"

"Naw," I said, "I got business at the Deluxe. But we'll have a drink, first."

So we looked around for Bunger, and he wasn't nowhere to be seen. We went back to our dressing-rooms, and he wasn't there either.

"Now, where is the old mutt?" inquired Black Jack, fretfully. "Here's us famishin' with thirst, and that old wharf-rat—"

"If you mean old Bunger," said a lounger, "I seen him scoot along about the fifth round."

"Say," I said, as a sudden suspicion struck me, "was he drunk?"

"If he was, I couldn't tell it," said Black Jack.

"Well," I said, "I thought he smelt of licker."

"He always smells of licker," answered O'Brien, impatiently. "I defies any man to always know whether the old soak's drunk or sober. He don't ack no different when he's full, except you can't trust him with dough."

"Well," I growled, "he's gone, and likely he's blowed in all our money already. Come on; let's go hunt for him."

So we donned our street clothes, and went forth. Our mutual battering hadn't affected our remarkable vitalities none, though we both had black eyes and plenteous cuts and bruises. We went down the street and glanced in the dives, but we didn't see Bunger, and purty soon we was in the vicinity of the Deluxe.

"Come on up to my room," I said. "I got fifty bucks there. We'll get it and buy us a drink. And listen, Johnny Kyelan's up there, but you keep your trap shut about it, see?"

"Okay," he said. "If Johnny's in a jam, I ain't the man to blab on him. He ain't got no sense, but he's a good kid."

SO WE WENT up to my room; everybody in the house was either asleep or had gone out some place. I knocked cautious, and said, "Open up, kid; it's me, Costigan."

They wasn't no reply. I rattled the knob impatiently and discovered the door wasn't locked. I flang it open, expecting to find anything. The room was dark, and, I switched on the light. Johnny wasn't nowhere to be seen. The room wasn't mussed up nor nothing, and though Mike kept growling deep down in his throat, I couldn't find a sign of anything suspicious. All I found was a note on the table. I picked it up and read, "Thanks for the fifty, sucker! Johnny."

"Well, of all the dirty deals!" I snarled. "I took him in and perteckted him, and he does me outa my wad!"

"Lemme see that note," said Black Jack, and read it and shook his head. "I don't believe this here's Johnny's writin'," he said.

"Sure it is," I snorted, because I was hurt deep. "It's bad to lose your dough; but it's a sight worse to find out that somebody you thought was your friend is nothing but a cheap crook. I ain't never seen any of his writin' before, but who else would of writ it? Nobody but him knowed about my wad. Black Mandarins my eye!"

"Huh?" Black Jack looked up quick, his eyes glittering; that phrase brung interest to anybody in Singapore. So I told him all about what Johnny had told me, adding disgustedly, "I reckon I been took for a sucker again. I bet the little rat had got into a jam with the cops, and he just seen a chance to do me out of my wad. He's skipped; if anybody'd got him, the door would be busted, and somebody in the house would of heered it. Anyway, the note wouldn't of been here. Dawggonit, I never thought Johnny was that kind."

"Me neither," said Black Jack, shaking his head, "and you don't figger he ever saw them Black Mandarins."

"I don't figger they is any Black Mandarins," I snorted, fretfully.

"That's where you're wrong," said O'Brien. "Plenty of people has seen 'em—and others saw 'em and didn't live to tell who they was. I said all the time it was more'n any one man which was doin' all these crimes. I thought it was a gang—"

"Aw, ferget it," I said. "Come on. Johnny's stole my wad, and old Bunger has gypped the both of us. I'm a man of action. I'm goin' to find the old buzzard if I have to take Singapore apart."

"I'm with you," said Black Jack, so we went out into the street and started hunting old Bunger, and, after about a hour of snooping into low-class dives, we got wind of him.

"Bunger?" said a bartender, twisting his flowing black mustaches. "Yeah, he was here earlier in the evenin'. He had a drink and said he was goin' to Kerney's Temple of Chance. He said he felt lucky."

"Lucky?" gnashed Black Jack. "He'll feel sore when I get through kickin' his britches up around his neck. Come on, Steve. I oughta thought about that before. When he's lit, he always thinks he can beat that roulette wheel at Kerney's."

SO WE WENT into the mazes of the waterfront till we come to Kerney's Temple, which was as little like a temple as a critter couldst imagine. It was kinda underground, and, to get to it, you went down a flight of steps from the street.

We went in, and seen a number of tough-looking eggs playing the various games or drinking at the bar. I seen Smoky Rourke, Wolf McGernan, Red Elkins, Shifty Brelen, John Lynch, and I don't know how many more—all shady characters. But the hardest looking one of 'em was Bad Bill hisself—one of these square-set, cold-eyed thugs which sports flashy clothes, like a gorilla in glad rags. He had a thin, sneering gash of a mouth, and his big, square, hairy hands glittered with diamonds. At the sight of his enemy, Black Jack growled deep in his throat and quivered with rage.

Then we seen old Bunger, leaning disconsolately against the bar, watching the clicking roulette wheel. Toward him we strode with a beller of rage, and he started to run, but seen he couldn't get away.

"You old mud-turtle!" yelled Black Jack. "Where's our dough?"

"Boys," quavered old Bunger, lifting a trembling hand, "don't jedge me too harsh! I ain't spent a cent of that jack."

"All right," said Black Jack, with a sigh of relief. "Give it to us."

"I can't," he sniffled, beginning to cry. "I lost it all on this here roulette wheel!"

"What!" our maddened beller made the lights flicker.

"It was this way, boys," he whimpered. "Whilst I was watchin' you boys fight, I seen a dime somebody'd dropped on the floor, and I grabbed it. And I thought I'd just slip out and get me a drink and be back before the scrap was over. Well, I got me the drink, and that was a mistake. I'd already had a few, and this'n kinda tipped me over the line. When I got some licker in me, I always get the gamblin' craze. Tonight I felt onusual lucky, and I got the idea in my head that I'd beat it down to Kerney's, double or triple this roll, and be that much ahead. You boys would get back your dough, and I'd be in the money, too. It looked like a great idea, then. And I was lucky for a while, if I'd just knowed when to quit. Once I was a hundred and forty-five dollars ahead, but the tide turned, and, before I knowed it, I was cleaned."

"Dash-blank-the-blank-dash!" said Black Jack, appropriately. "This here's a sweet lay! I oughta kick you in the pants, you white-whiskered old mutt!"

"Aw," I said, "I wouldn't care, only that was all the dough I had, except my lucky half-dollar."

"That's me," snarled O'Brien. "Only I ain't got no half-dollar."

About this time up barged Bad Bill.

"What's up, boys?" he said, with a wink at the loafers.

"You know what's up, you louse!" snarled Black Jack. "This old fool has just lost a hundred bucks on your crooked roulette game."

"Well," sneered Bad Bill, "that ain't no skin offa your nose, is it?"

"That was our money," howled Black Jack. "And you gotta give it back!"

Kerney laughed in his face. He took out a roll of bills and fluttered the edges with his thumb.

"Here's the dough he lost," said Kerney. "Mebbe it was yours, but it's mine now. What I wins, I keeps— onless somebody's man enough to take it away from me, and I ain't never met anybody which was. And what you goin' to do about it?"

BLACK JACK WAS so mad he just strangled, and his eyes stood out. I said, losing my temper, "I'll tell you what we're goin' to do, Kerney, since you wanta be tough. I'm goin' to knock you stiff and take that wad offa your senseless carcass."

"You are, hey?" he roared, blood-thirstily. "Lemme see you try it, you black-headed sea-rat! Wanta fight, eh? All right. Lemme see how much man you are. Here's the wad. If you can lick me, you can have it back. I won it fair and square, but I'm a sport. You come around here cryin' for your money back—all right, we'll see if you're men enough to fight for it!"

I growled deep and low, and lunged, but Black Jack grabbed me.

"Wait a minute," he yelped. "Half that dough's mine. I got just as much right to sock this polecat as you has, and you know it."

"Heh! Heh!" sneered Kerney, jerking off his coat and shirt. "Settle it between yourselves. If either one of you can lick me, the dough's yours. Ain't that fair, boys?"

All the assembled thugs applauded profanely. I seen at a glance they was all his men—except old Bunger, which didn't count either way.

"It's my right to fight this guy," argued Black Jack.

"We'll flip a coin," I decided, bringing out my lucky half-dollar. "I'll take—"

"I'll take heads," busted in Black Jack, impatiently.

"I said it first," I replied annoyedly.

"I didn't hear you," he said.

"Well, I did," I answered pettishly. "You'll take tails."

"All right, I'll take tails," he snorted in disgust. "Gwan and flip."

So I flopped, and it fell heads.

"Didn't I say it was my lucky piece?" I crowed jubilantly, putting the coin back in my pocket and tearing off my shirt, whilst Black Jack ground his teeth and cussed his luck something terrible.

"Before I knock your brains out," said Kerney, "you got to dispose of that bench-legged cannibal."

"If you mean Mike, you foul-mouthed skunk," I said, "Black Jack can hold him."

"And let go of him so he can tear my throat out just as I got you licked," sneered Kerney. "No, you don't. Take this piece of rope and tie him up, or the scrap's off."

So, with a few scathing remarks which apparently got under even Bad Bill's thick hide, to judge from his profanity, I tied one end of the rope to Mike's collar and the other'n to the leg of a heavy gambling table. Meanwhile, the onlookers had cleared away a space between the table and the back wall, which was covered by a matting of woven grass. To all appearances, the back wall was solid, but I thought they must be a lot of rats burrowing in there, because every now and then I heered a kind of noise like something moving and thumping around.

WELL, ME AND Kerney approached each other in the gleam of the gas-lights. He was a big, black-browed brute, with black hair matted on his barrel chest and on his wrists, and his hands was like sledge-hammers. He was about my height, but heavier.

I started the scrap like I always do, with a rush, slugging away with both hands. He met me, nothing loath. The crowd formed a half-circle in front of the stacked-up tables and chairs, and the back wall was behind us. Above the thud and crunch of blows I couldst hear Mike growling as he strained at his rope, and Black Jack yelling for me to kill Kerney.

Well, he was tough and he could hit like a mule kicking. But he was fighting Steve Costigan. There, under the gas-lights, with the mob yelling, and my bare fists crunching on flesh and bone, I was plumb in my element. I laughed at Bad Bill as I took the best he could hand out, and come plunging in for more.

I worked for his belly, repeatedly sinking both hands to the wrists, and he began to puff and gasp and go away from me. My head was singing from his thundering socks, and the taste of blood was in my mouth, but that's a old, old story to me. I caught him on the ear and blood spattered. Like a flash, up come his heavy boot for my groin, but I twisted aside and caught him with a terrible right-hander under the heart. He groaned

and staggered, and a ripping left hook to the body sent him down, but he grabbed my belt as he fell and dragged me with him.

On the floor he locked his gorilla arms around me, and spat in my eye, trying to pull my head down where he could sink his fangs in my ear. But my neck was like iron, and I pulled back, fighting mad, and, getting a hand free, smashed it savagely three times into his face. With a groan, he went slack. And just then a heavy boot crashed into my back, purty near paralyzing me, and knocking me clear of Kerney.

It was John Lynch which had kicked me, and even as I snarled up at him, trying to get up, I heered Black Jack roar, and I heered the crash of his iron fist under Lynch's jaw, and the dirty yegg dropped amongst the stacked-up tables and lay like a empty sack.

The thugs surged forward with a menacing rumble, but Black Jack turned on 'em like a maddened tiger, his teeth gleaming in a snarl, his eyes blazing, and they hesitated. And then I climbed on my feet, the effecks of that foul lick passing. Kerney was slavering and cursing and trying to get up, and I grabbed him by his hair and dragged him up.

"Stand on your two feet and fight like as if you was a man," I snarled disgustedly, and he lunged at me sudden and unexpected, trying to knee me in the groin. He fell into me, and, as I pulled out of a half-clinch, I heered Black Jack yell suddenly, "Look out, Steve! That's the way he got me!"

And simultaneous I felt Kerney's hand at the side of my neck. Instinctively, I jerked back, and as I did, Kerney's thumb pressed cunning and savage into my neck just below the ear. Jiu-jitsu! Mighty few white men know that trick—the Japanese death-touch, they call it. If I hadn't been going away from it, so he didn't hit the exact nerve he was looking for, I'd of been temporarily paralyzed. As it was, my heavy neck muscles saved me, though for a flashing instant I staggered, as a wave of blindness and agony went all over me.

Kerney yelled like a wild beast, and come for me, but I straightened and met him with a left hook that ripped his lip open from the corner of his mouth to his chin, and sent him reeling backward. And, clean maddened by the dirty trick he had tried on me, I throwed every ounce of my beef into a thundering right swing that tagged him square on the jaw.

It was just a longshoreman's haymaker with my whole frame behind it, and it lifted him clean offa his feet and catapulted him bodily against the back wall. Crash! The matting tore, the wood behind it splintered, and Kerney's senseless form smashed right on through!

THE FORCE OF my swing throwed me headlong after Kerney, and I landed with my head and forearms through the hole he'd made. The back wall wasn't solid! They was a secret room beyond it. I seen Kerney lying in that room with his feet projecting through the busted partition, and beyond I seen another figger— bound and gagged and lying on the floor.

"Johnny!" I yelled, scrambling up, and behind me rose a deep, ominous roar. Black Jack yelled, "Look out, Steve!" and a bottle whizzed past my ear and crashed against the wall. Simultaneous come the thud of a sock and the fall of a body, as Black Jack went into action, and I wheeled as Kerney's thugs come surging in on me.

Black Jack was slugging right and left, and men were toppling like ten-pins, but they was a whole room full of 'em. I saw old Bunger scooting for the exit, and I heered Mike roaring, lunging against his rope. I caught the first thug with a smash that near broke his neck, and then they swarmed all over me, and I cracked Red Elkins' ribs with my knee as we went to the floor.

I heered Black Jack roaring and battling, and I shook off my attackers and riz, fracturing Shifty Brelen's skull, and me and Black Jack stiffened them deluded mutts till we was treading on a carpet of senseless yeggs, but still they come, with bottles and knives and chair-legs, till we was both streaming blood.

Black Jack hadst just been felled with a table-leg, and half a dozen of 'em was stomping on my prostrate form, whilst I was engaged in gouging and strangling three or four I had under me, when Mike's rope broke under repeated gnawings and lunges. I heered him beller, and I heered a yegg yip as Mike's iron fangs met in his meat. The clump on me bust apart, and I lurched up, roaring like a bull and shaking the blood in a shower from my head.

Black Jack come up with the table-leg he'd been floored with, and he hit Smoky Rourke so hard they had to use a pulmotor to bring Smoky to. The battered mob staggered dizzily back, and scattered as Mike plunged and raged amongst them.

Spang! Wolf McGernan had broke away from the melee and was risking killing some of his mates to bring us down. They run for cover, screeching. Black Jack throwed the table-leg, but missed, and the three of us—him and Mike and me—rushed McGernan simultaneous.

His muzzle wavered from one to the other as he tried to decide quick which to shoot, and then crack! Wolf yelped and dropped his gun; he staggered back against the wall, grabbing his wrist, from which blood was spurting.

The yeggs stopped short in their head-long fight for the exit, and me and Black Jack wheeled. A dozen policemen was on the stairs with drawed guns and one of them guns was smoking.

THE THUGS BACKED against the wall, their hands up, and I run into the secret room and untied Johnny Kyelan.

All he could say was, "Glug ug glug!" for a minute, being nearly choked with fear and excitement and the gag. But I hammered him on the back, and he said, "They got me, Steve. They sneaked into the hall and knocked on the door. When I stooped to look through the key-hole, as they figgered I'd do—its a natural move—they blew some stuff in my face that knocked me clean out for a few minutes. While I was lying helpless, they unlocked the door with a skeleton key and came in. I was coming to myself, then, but they had guns on me and I didn't dare yell for help.

"They searched me, and I begged them to leave your fifty dollars on the table because I knew it was all the money you had, but they took it, and wrote a note to make it look like I'd skipped out with the money. Then they blew some more powder in my face, and the next thing I knew I was in a car, being carried here.

"They were going to finish me before daylight. I heard the Chief Mandarin say so."

"And who's he?" we demanded.

"I don't mind telling you now," said Johnny, looking at the yeggs which was being watched by the cops, and at Bad Bill, who was just beginning to come to on the floor. "The Chief of the Mandarins is Bad

Bill Kerney! He was a racketeer in the States, and he's been working the same here."

An officer broke in: "You mean this man is the infamous Black Mandarin?"

"You're darn tootin'," said Johnny, "and I can prove it in the courts."

WELL, THEM COPS pounced on the dizzy Kerney like gulls on a fish, and in no time him and his gang, such as was conscious, was decorated with steel bracelets. Kerney didn't say nothing, but he looked black murder at all of us.

"Hey, wait!" said Black Jack, as the cops started leading them out. "Kerney's got some dough which belongs to us."

So the cop took a wad offa him big enough to choke a shark, and Black Jack counted off a hundred and fifty bucks and give the rest back. The cops led the yeggs out, and I felt somebody tugging at my arm. It was old Bunger.

"Well, boys," he quavered, "don't you think I've squared things? As soon as the roughhouse started, I run up into the street screamin' and yellin' till all the cops within hearin' come on the run!"

"You've done yourself proud, Bunger," I said. "Here's a ten spot for you."

"And here's another'n," said Black Jack, and old Bunger grinned all over.

"Thank you, boys," he said,

ruffling the bills in his eagerness. "I gotta go now—they's a roulette wheel down at Spike's I got a hunch I can beat."

"Let's all get outa here," I grunted, and we emerged into the street and gazed at the street-lamps, yellow and smoky in the growing daylight.

"Boy, oh, boy!" said Johnny. "I've had enough of this life. It's me for the old U.S.A. just as soon as I can get there."

"And a good thing," I said gruffly, because I was so glad to know the boy wasn't a thief and a cheat that I felt kinda foolish. "Snappy kids like you got no business away from home."

"Well," said Black Jack, "let's go get that drink."

"Aw, heck," I said, disgustedly, as I shoved my money back in my pants, "I lost my good-luck half-dollar in the melee."

"Maybe this is it," said Johnny, holding it out. "I picked it up off the floor as we were coming out."

"Gimme it," I said, hurriedly, but Black Jack grabbed it with a startled oath.

"Good luck piece?" he yelled. "Now I see why you was so insistent on takin' heads. This here blame half-dollar is a trick coin, and it's got heads on both sides! Why, I hadn't a chance. Steve Costigan, you did me out of a fight, and I resents it! You got to fight me."

"All right," I said. "We'll fight again tonight at Ace's Arena. And now let's go get that drink."

"Good heavens," said Johnny, "It's nearly sun-up. If you fellows are going to fight again tonight, hadn't you better get some rest? And some of those cuts you both got need bandaging."

"He's right, Steve," said Black Jack. "We'll have a drink and then we'll get sewed up, and then we'll eat breakfast, and after that we'll shoot some pool."

"Sure," I said, "that's a easy, restful game, and we oughta take things easy so we can be in shape for the fight tonight. After we shoot some pool, we'll go to Yota Lao's and lick some bouncers you was talkin' about."

ALLEYS *of* DARKNESS.

This short story was first published in the January 1934 issue of Magic Carpet *magazine. To avoid trouble with the publishers of* Fight Stories *and* Action Stories, *the names of most of the characters were changed, including that of Steve Costigan, who appears in this tale under the alias "Dennis Dorgan."*

W HEN THE GONG ended my fight with Kid Leary in the Sweet Dreams Fight Club, Singapore, I was tired but contented. The first seven rounds had been close, but the last three I'd plastered the Kid all over the ring, though I hadn't knocked him out like I'd did in Shanghai some months before, when I flattened him in the twelfth round. The scrap in Singapore was just for ten; another round and I'd had him.

But anyway, I'd shaded him so thoroughly I knowed I'd justified the experts which had made me a three to one favorite. The crowd was applauding wildly, the referee was approaching, and I stepped forward and held out my glove hand—when to my utter dumfoundment, he brushed past me and lifted the glove of the groggy and bloody Kid Leary!

A instant's silence reigned, shattered by a nerve-racking scream from the ringside. The referee, Jed Whithers, released Leary, who collapsed into the rosin, and Whithers ducked through the ropes like a rabbit. The crowd riz bellowing, and recovering my frozen wits, I gave vent to lurid langwidge and plunged outa the ring in pursuit of Whithers. The fans was screaming mad, smashing benches, tearing the ropes offa the ring and demanding the whereabouts of Whithers, so's they could hang him to the rafters. But he had disappeared, and the maddened crowd raged in vain.

I found my way dazedly to my dressing-room, where I set down on a table and tried to recover from the shock. Bill O'Brien and the rest of the crew was there, frothing at the mouth, each having sunk his entire wad on me. I considered going into Leary's dressing-room and beating him up again, but decided he'd had nothing to do with the crooked decision. He was just as surprised as me when Whithers declared him winner.

Whilst I was trying to pull on my clothes, hindered more'n helped by my raging shipmates, whose langwidge was getting more appalling every instant, a stocky bewhiskered figger come busting through the mob, and done a fantastic dance in front of me. It was the Old Man,

with licker on his breath and tears in his eyes.

"I'm rooint!" he howled. "I'm a doomed man! Oh, to think as I've warmed a sarpint in my boozum! Dennis Dorgan, this here's the last straw!"

"Aw, pipe down!" snarled Bill O'Brien. "It wasn't Denny's fault. It was that dashety triple-blank thief of a referee—"

"To think of goin' on the beach at my age!" screamed the Old Man, wringing the salt water outa his whiskers. He fell down on a bench and wept at the top of his voice. "A thousand bucks I lost—every cent I could rake, scrape and borrer!" he bawled.

"Aw, well, you still got your ship," somebody said impatiently.

"That's just it!" the Old Man wailed. "That thousand bucks was dough owed them old pirates, McGregor, McClune & McKile. Part of what I owe, I mean. They agreed to accept a thousand as part payment, and gimme more time to raise the rest. Now it's gone, and they'll take the ship! They'll take the *Python!* All I got in the world! Them old sharks ain't got no more heart than a Malay pirate. I'm rooint!"

The crew fell silent at that, and I said: "Why'd you bet all that dough?"

"I was lickered up," he wept. "I got no sense when I'm full. Old Cap'n Donnelly, and McVey and them got to raggin' me, and the first thing I knowed, I'd bet 'em the thousand, givin' heavy odds. Now I'm rooint!"

He threw back his head and bellered like a walrus with the belly-ache.

I just give a dismal groan and sunk my head in my hands, too despondent to say nothing. The crew bust forth in curses against Whithers, and sallied forth to search further for him, hauling the Old Man along with them, still voicing his woes in a voice like a steamboat whistle.

PRESENTLY I RIZ with a sigh and hauled on my duds. They was no sound outside. Apparently I was alone in the building except for Spike, my white bulldog. All at once I noticed him smelling of a closed locker. He whined, scratched at it, and growled. With a sudden suspicion I strode over and jerked open the door. Inside I seen a huddled figger. I jerked it rudely forth and set it upright. It was Jed Whithers. He was pale and shaking, and he had cobwebs in his hair. He kind a cringed, evidently expecting me to bust into loud cusses. For once I was too mad for that. I was probably as pale as he was, and his eyes dilated like he seen murder in mine.

"Jed Whithers," I said, shoving him up against the wall with one hand whilst I knotted the other'n into a mallet, "this is one time in my life when I'm in the mood for killin'."

"For God's sake, Dorgan," he gurgled, "you can't murder me!"

"Can you think of any reason why I shouldn't put you in a wheel-chair for the rest of your life?" I demanded. "You've rooint my friends and all the fans which bet on me, lost my skipper his ship—"

"Don't hit me, Dorgan!" he begged, grabbing my wrist with shaking fingers. "I had to do it; honest to God, Sailor, I *had* to do it! I know you won—won by a mile. But it was the only thing I could do!"

"What you mean?" I demanded suspiciously.

"Lemme sit down!" he gasped.

I reluctantly let go of him, and he slumped down onto a near-by bench. He sat there and shook, and mopped the sweat offa his face. He was trembling all over.

"Are the customers all gone?" he asked.

"Ain't nobody here but me and my man-eatin' bulldog," I answered grimly, standing over him. "Go on—spill what you got to say before I start varnishin' the floor with you."

"I was forced to it, Sailor," he said. "There's a man who has a hold on me."

"What you mean, a hold?" I asked suspiciously.

"I mean, he's got me in a spot," he said. "I have to do like he says. It ain't myself I have to think of—Dorgan, I'm goin' to trust you. You got the name of bein' a square shooter. I'm goin' to tell you the whole thing.

"Sailor, I got a sister named Constance, a beautiful girl, innocent as a newborn lamb. She trusted a man, Sailor, a dirty, slimy snake in human form. He tricked her into signin' a document—Dorgan, that paper was a confession of a crime he'd committed himself!"

Whithers here broke down and sobbed with his face in his hands. I shuffled my feet uncertainly, beginning to realize they was always more'n one side to any question.

He raised up suddenly and said: "Since then, that man's been holdin' that faked confession over me and her like a club. He's forced me to do his filthy biddin' time and again. I'm a honest man by nature, Sailor, but to protect my little sister"—he kinda choked for a instant—"I've stooped to low deeds. Like this tonight. This man was bettin' heavy on Leary, gettin' big odds—"

"Somebody sure was," I muttered. "Lots of Leary money in sight."

"Sure!" exclaimed Whithers eagerly. "That was it; he made me throw the fight to Leary, the dirty rat, to protect his bets."

I begun to feel new wrath rise in my gigantic breast.

"You mean this low-down polecat has been blackmailin' you on account of the hold he's got over your sister?" I demanded.

"Exactly," he said, dropping his face in his hands. "With that paper he can send Constance to prison, if he takes the notion."

"I never heered of such infermy," I growled. "Whyn't you bust him on the jaw and take that confession away from him?"

"I ain't no fightin' man," said Whithers. "He's too big for me. I wouldn't have a chance."

"Well, *I* would," I said. "Listen, Whithers, buck up and quit cryin'. I'm goin' to help you."

His head jerked up and he stared at me kinda wild-eyed.

"You mean you'll help me get that paper?"

"You bet!" I retorted. "I ain't the man to stand by and let no innercent girl be persecuted. Besides, this mess tonight is his fault."

Whithers just set there for a second, and I thought I seen a slow smile start to spread over his lips, but I mighta been mistook, because he wasn't grinning when he held out his hand and said tremulously: "Dorgan, you're all they say you are!"

A remark like that ain't necessarily a compliment; some of the things said about me ain't flattering; but I took it in the spirit in which it seemed to be give, and I said: "Now tell me, who is this rat?"

He glanced nervously around, then whispered: "Ace Bissett!"

I grunted in surprise. "The devil you say! I'd never of thought it."

"He's a fiend in human form," said Whithers bitterly. "What's your plan?"

"Why," I said, "I'll go to his Diamond Palace and demand the confession. If he don't give it to me, I'll maul him and take it away from him."

"You'll get shot up," said Whithers. "Bissett is a bad man to fool with. Listen, I got a plan. If we can get him to a certain house I know about, we can search him for the paper. He carries it around with him, though I don't know just where. Here's my plan—"

I listened attentively, and as a result, perhaps a hour later I was heading through the narrer streets with Spike, driving a closed car which Whithers had produced kinda mysteriously. Whithers wasn't with me; he was gone to prepare the place where I was to bring Bissett to.

I driv up the alley behind Ace's big new saloon and gambling-hall, the Diamond Palace, and stopped the car near a back door. It was a very high-class joint. Bissett was friends with wealthy sportsmen, officials, and other swells. He was what they call a soldier of fortune, and he'd been everything, everywhere— aviator, explorer, big game hunter, officer in the armies of South America and China—and what have you.

A native employee stopped me at the door, and asked me what was my business, and I told him I wanted to see Ace. He showed me into the room which opened on the alley, and went after Bissett—which could not of suited my plan better.

Purty soon a door opened, and Bissett strode in—a tall, broad-shouldered young fellow, with steely eyes and wavy blond hair. He was in a dress suit, and altogether looked like

he'd stepped right outa the social register. And as I looked at him, so calm and self-assured, and thought of poor Whithers being driv to crime by him, and the Old Man losing his ship on account of his crookedness, I seen red.

"Well, Dorgan, what can I do for you?" he asked.

I said nothing. I stepped in and hooked my right to his jaw. It caught him flat-footed, with his hands down. He hit the floor full length, and he didn't twitch.

I bent over him, run my hands through his clothes, found his six-shooter and throwed it aside. Music and the sounds of revelry reached me through the walls, but evidently nobody had seen or heard me slug Bissett. I lifted him and histed him onto my shoulders—no easy job, because he was as big as me, and limp as a rag.

But I done it, and started for the alley. I got through the door all right, which I was forced to leave open, account of having both hands full, and just as I was dumping Ace into the back part of the car, I heered a scream. Wheeling, I seen a girl had just come into the room I'd left, and was standing frozen, staring wildly at me. The light from the open door shone full on me and my captive. The girl was Glory O'Dale, Ace Bissett's sweetheart. I hurriedly slammed the car door shut and jumped to the wheel, and as I roared off down the alley, I was vaguely aware that Glory had rushed out of the building after me, screaming blue murder.

IT WAS PURTY late, and the route I took they wasn't many people abroad. Behind me I begun to hear Bissett stir and groan, and I pushed Spike over in the back seat to watch him. But he hadn't fully come to when I drawed up in the shadows beside the place Whithers had told me about—a ramshackle old building down by a old rotting, deserted wharf. Nobody seemed to live anywheres close around, or if they did, they was outa sight. As I clum outa the car, a door opened a crack, and I seen Whithers' white face staring at me.

"Did you get him, Sailor?" he whispered.

For answer I jerked open the back door, and Bissett tumbled out on his ear and laid there groaning dimly. Whithers started back with a cry.

"Is he dead?" he asked fearfully.

"Would he holler like that if he was?" I asked impatiently. "Help me carry him in, and we'll search him."

"Wait'll I tie him up," said Whithers, producing some cords, and to my disgust, he bound the unconscious critter hand and foot.

"It's safer this way," Whithers said. "He's a devil, and we can't afford to take chances."

We then picked him up and carried him through the door, into a very dimly lighted room, across

that 'un, and into another'n which was better lit—the winders being covered so the light couldn't be seen from the outside. And I got the surprise of my life. They was five men in that room. I wheeled on Whithers. "What's the idee?" I demanded.

"Now, now, Sailor," said Whithers, arranging Bissett on the bench where we'd laid him. "These are just friends of mine. They know about Bissett and my sister."

I heered what sounded like a snicker, and I turned to glare at the assembled "friends." My gaze centered on a fat, flashy-dressed bird smoking a big black cigar; diamonds shone all over his fingers, and in his stick-pin. The others was just muggs.

"A fine lot of friends you pick out!" I said irritably to Whithers. "Diamond Joe Galt is been mixed up in every shady deal that's been pulled in the past three years. And if you'd raked the Seven Seas you couldn't found four dirtier thugs than Limey Teak, Bill Reynolds, Dutch Steinmann, and Red Partland."

"Hey, you—" Red Partland riz, clenching his fists, but Galt grabbed his arm.

"Stop it, Red," he advised. "Easy does it. Sailor," he addressed me with a broad smile which I liked less'n I'd liked a scowl, "they's no use in abuse. We're here to help our pal Whithers get justice. That's all. You've done your part. You can go now, with our thanks."

"Not so fast," I growled, and just

then Whithers hollered: "Bissett's come to!"

We all turned around and seen that Bissett's eyes was open, and blazing.

"Well, you dirty rats," he greeted us all and sundry, "you've got me at last, have you?" He fixed his gaze on me, and said: "Dorgan, I thought you were a man. If I'd had any idea you were mixed up in this racket, you'd have never got a chance to slug me as you did."

"Aw, shut up," I snarled. "A fine nerve you've got, talkin' about men, after what you've did!"

Galt pushed past me and stood looking down at Bissett, and I seen his fat hands clenched, and the veins swell in his temples.

"Bissett," he said, "we've got you cold and you know it. Kick in—where's that paper?"

"You cursed fools!" Bissett raved, struggling at his cords till the veins stood out on his temples too. "I tell you, the paper's worthless."

"Then why do you object to givin' it to us?" demanded Whithers.

"Because I haven't got it!" raged Bissett. "I destroyed it, just as I've told you before."

"He's lyin'," snarled Red Partland. "He wouldn't never destroy such a thing as that. It means millions. Here, I'll make him talk—"

He shouldered forward and grabbed Bissett by the throat. I grabbed Red in turn, and tore him away.

"Belay!" I gritted. "He's a rat, but just the same I ain't goin' to stand by and watch no helpless man be tortured."

"Why, you—" Red bellered, and swung for my jaw.

I ducked and sunk my left to the wrist in his belly and he dropped like his legs had been cut out from under him. The others started forward, rumbling, and I wheeled towards 'em, seething with fight. But Galt got between us and shoved his gorillas back.

"Here," he snapped. "No fightin' amongst ourselves! Get up, Red. Now, Sailor," he begun to pat my sleeves in his soothing way, which I always despises beyond words, "there ain't no need for hard feelin's. I know just how you feel. But we got to have that paper. You know that, Sailor—"

Suddenly a faint sound made itself evident. "What's that?" gasped Limey, going pale.

"It's Spike," I said. "I left him in the car, and he's got tired of settin' out there, and is scratchin' at the front door. I'm goin' to go get him, but I'll be right back, and if anybody lays a hand on Bissett whilst I'm gone, I'll bust him into pieces. We'll get that paper, but they ain't goin' to be no torturin'."

I strode out, scornful of the black looks cast my way. As I shut the door behind me, a clamor of conversation bust out, so many talking at wunst I couldn't understand much, but every now and then Ace Bissett's voice riz above the din in accents of anger and not pain, so I knowed they wasn't doing nothing to him. I crossed the dim outer room, opened the door and let Spike in, and then, forgetting to bolt it—I ain't used to secrecy and such—I started back for the inner room.

BEFORE I REACHED the other door, I heered a quick patter of feet outside. I wheeled—the outer door bust violently open, and into the room rushed Glory O'Dale. She was panting hard, her dress was tore, her black locks damp, and her dark eyes was wet and bright as black jewels after a rain. And she had Ace's six-shooter in her hand.

"You filthy dog!" she cried, throwing down on me.

I looked right into the muzzle of that .45 as she jerked the trigger. The hammer snapped on a faulty cartridge, and before she could try again, Spike launched hisself from the floor at her. I'd taught him never to bite a woman. He didn't bite Glory. He throwed hisself bodily against her so hard he knocked her down and the gun flew outa her hand.

I picked it up and stuck it into my hip pocket. Then I started to help her up, but she hit my hand aside and jumped up, tears of fury running down her cheeks. Golly, she was a beauty!

"You beast!" she raged. "What have you done with Ace? I'll kill you if you've harmed him! Is he in that room?"

"Yeah, and he ain't harmed," I said, "but he oughta be hung—"

She screamed like a siren. "Don't you dare! Don't you touch a hair of his head! Oh, Ace!"

She then slapped my face, jerked out a handful of hair, and kicked both my shins.

"What I can't understand is," I said, escaping her clutches, "is why a fine girl like you ties up with a low-down rat like Bissett. With your looks, Glory—"

"To the devil with my looks!" she wept, stamping on the floor. "Let me past; I know Ace is in that room—I heard his voice as I came in."

They wasn't no noise in the inner room now. Evidently all of them was listening to what was going on out here, Ace included.

"You can't go in there," I said. "We got to search Ace for the incriminatin' evidence he's holdin' against Jed Whithers' sister—"

"You're mad as a March hare," she said. "Let me by!"

And without no warning she back-heeled me and pushed me with both hands. It was so unexpected I ignominiously crashed to the floor, and she darted past me and throwed open the inner door. Spike drove for her, and this time he was red-eyed, but I grabbed him as he went by.

Glory halted an instant on the threshold with a cry of mingled triumph, fear and rage. I riz, cussing beneath my breath and dusting off my britches. Glory ran across the room, eluding the grasping paws of Joe Galt, and threw herself with passionate abandon on the prostrate form of Ace Bissett. I noticed that Ace, which hadn't till then showed the slightest sign of fear, was suddenly pale and his jaw was grim set.

"It was madness for you to come, Glory," he muttered.

"I saw Dorgan throw you into the car," she whimpered, throwing her arms around him, and tugging vainly at his cords. "I jumped in another and followed—blew out a tire a short distance from here—lost sight of the car I was following and wandered around in the dark alleys on foot for awhile, till I saw the car standing outside. I came on in—"

"Alone? My God!" groaned Ace.

"Alone?" echoed Galt, with a sigh of relief. He flicked some dust from his lapel, stuck his cigar back in his mouth at a cocky angle, and said: "Well, now, we'll have a little talk. Come here, Glory."

She clung closer to Ace, and Ace said in a low voice, almost a whisper: "Let her alone, Galt." His eyes was like fires burning under the ice.

Galt's muggs was grinning evilly and muttering to theirselves. Whithers was nervous and kept mopping perspiration. The air was tense. I was nervous and impatient; something was wrong, and I didn't know what. So when Galt started to say something, I took matters into my own hands.

"Bissett," I said, striding across the room and glaring down at him, "if they's a ounce of manhood in you, this here girl's devotion oughta touch even your snakish soul. Why don't you try to redeem yourself a little, anyway? Kick in with that paper! A man which is loved by a woman like Glory O'Dale loves you, oughta be above holdin' a forged confession over a innocent girl's head."

Bissett's mouth fell open. "What's he talking about?" he demanded from the world at large.

"I don't know," said Glory uneasily, snuggling closer to him. "He talked that way out in the other room. I think he's punch-drunk."

"Dorgan," said Bissett, "you don't belong in this crowd. Are you suffering from some sort of an hallucination?"

"Don't hand me no such guff, you snake!" I roared. "You know why I brung you here—to get the confession you gypped outa Whithers' sister, and blackmailed him with—just like you made him throw my fight tonight."

Bissett just looked dizzy, but Glory leaped up and faced me.

"You mean you think Ace made Whithers turn in that rotten decision?" she jerked out.

"I don't think," I answered sullenly. "I know. Whithers said so."

She jumped like she was galvanized.

"Why, you idiot!" she hollered, "they've made a fool of you! Jed Whithers hasn't any sister! He lied! Ace had nothing to do with it!

Whithers was hired to throw the fight to Leary! Look at him!" Her voice rose to a shriek of triumph, as she pointed a accusing finger at Jed Whithers. "Look at him! Look how pale he is! He's scared witless!"

"It's a lie!" gulped Whithers, sweating and tearing at his crumpled collar like it was choking him.

"It's not a lie!" Glory was nearly hysterical by this time. "He was paid to throw the fight! And there's the man who paid him!" And she dramatically pointed her finger at Diamond Joe Galt!

GALT WAS ON HIS feet, his small eyes glinting savagely, his jaws grinding his cigar to a pulp.

"What about it, Galt?" I demanded, all at sea and bewildered.

He dashed down his cigar with a oath. His face was dark and convulsed.

"What of it?" he snarled. "What you goin' to do about it? I've stood all the guff out of you I'm goin' to!"

His hand snaked inside his coat and out, and I was looking into the black muzzle of a wicked stumpy automatic.

"You can't slug this like you did Red, you dumb gorilla," he smirked viciously. "Sure, the dame's tellin' the truth. Whithers took you in like a sucklin' lamb.

"When you caught him in your dressin'-room, he told you the first lie that come to him, knowin' you

for a soft sap where women's concerned. Then when you fell for it, and offered to help him, he thought fast and roped you into this deal. We been tryin' to get hold of Bissett for a long time. He's got somethin' we want. But he was too smart and too tough for us. Now, thanks to you, we got him, *and* the girl. Now we're goin' to sweat what we want out of him, and you're goin' to keep your trap shut, see?"

"You mean they ain't no Constance Whithers, and no confession?" I said slowly, trying to get things straight. A raucous roar of mirth greeted the remark.

"No, sucker," taunted Galt; "you just been took in, you sap."

A wave of red swept across my line of vision. With a maddened roar, I plunged recklessly at Galt, gun and all. Everything happened at once. Galt closed his finger on the trigger just as Spike, standing beside him all this time, closed his jaws on Galt's leg. Galt screamed and leaped convulsively; the gun exploded in the air, missing me so close the powder singed my hair, and my right mauler crunched into Galt's face, flattening his nose, knocking out all his front teeth, and fracturing his jaw-bone. As he hit the floor Spike was right on top of him.

The next instant Galt's thugs was on top of me. We rolled across the room in a wild tangle of arms and legs, casually shattering tables and chairs on the way. Spike, finding Galt was out cold, abandoned him and charged to my aid. I heered Red Partland howl as Spike's iron fangs locked in his britches. But I had my hands full. Fists and hobnails was glancing off my carcass, and a thumb was feeling for my eye. I set my teeth in this thumb and was rewarded by a squeal of anguish, but the action didn't slow up any.

It was while strangling Limey Teak beneath me, whilst the other three was trying to stomp my ribs in and kick my head off, that I realized that another element had entered into the fray. There was the impact of a chair-leg on a human skull, and Jed Whithers give up the ghost with a whistling sigh. Glory O'Dale was taking a hand.

Dutch Steinmann next gave a ear-piercing howl, and Bill Reynolds abandoned me to settle her. Feeling Limey go limp beneath me, I riz, shaking Steinmann offa my shoulders, just in time to see Reynolds duck Glory's chair-leg and smack her down. Bissett give a most awful yell of rage, but he wasn't no madder than me. I left the floor in a flying tackle that carried Reynolds off his feet with a violence which nearly busted his skull against the floor. Too crazy-mad for reason, I set to work to hammer him to death, and though he was already senseless, I would probably of continued indefinite, had not Dutch Steinmann distracted my attention by smashing a chair over my head.

I riz through the splinters and caught him with a left hook that tore his ear nearly off and stood him on his neck in a corner. I then looked for Red Partland and seen him crawling out a winder which he'd tore the shutters off of. He was a rooin; his clothes was nearly all tore offa him, and he was bleeding like a stuck hawg and bawling like one, and Spike didn't show no intentions of abandoning the fray. His jaws was locked in what was left of Red's britches, and he had his feet braced against the wall below the sill. As I looked, Red gave a desperate wrench and tumbled through the winder, and I heered his lamentations fading into the night.

SHAKING THE BLOOD and sweat outa my eyes, I glared about at the battle-field, strewn with the dead and dying—at least with the unconscious, some of which was groaning loudly, whilst others slumbered in silence.

Glory was just getting up, dizzy and wobbly. Spike was smelling each of the victims in turn, and Ace was begging somebody to let him loose. Glory wobbled over to where he'd rolled offa the bench, and I followed her, kinda stiffly. At least one of my ribs had been broke by a boot-heel. My scalp was cut open, and blood was trickling down my side, where Limey Teak had made a ill-advised effort to knife me. I also thought one of them rats had hit me from behind with a club, till I discovered that sometime in the fray I'd fell on something hard in my hip pocket. This, I found, was Ace Bissett's pistol, which I'd clean forgot all about. I throwed it aside with disgust; them things is a trap and a snare.

I blinked at Ace with my one good eye, whilst Glory worked his cords offa him.

"I see I misjudged you," I said, lending her a hand. "I apolergize, and if you want satisfaction, right here and now is good enough for me."

"Good Lord, man," he said, with his arms full of Glory. "I don't want to fight you. I still don't know just what it was all about, but I'm beginning to understand."

I set down somewhat groggily on a bench which wasn't clean busted.

"What I want to know is," I said, "what that paper was they was talkin' about."

"Well," he said, "about a year ago I befriended a half-cracked Russian scientist, and he tried in his crazy way to repay me. He told me, in Galt's presence, that he was going to give me a formula that would make me the richest man on earth. He got blown up in an explosion in his laboratory shortly afterward, and an envelope was found in his room addressed to me, and containing a formula. Galt found out about it, and he's been hounding me ever since, trying to get it. He thought it was all the Russian claimed. In reality it was merely the disconnected scribblings of a disordered

mind—good Lord, it claimed to be a process for the manufacture of diamonds! Utter insanity—but Galt never would believe it."

"And he thought I was dumb," I cogitated. "But hey, Glory, how'd you know it was Galt hired Whithers to throw my fight to Leary?"

"I didn't," she admitted. "I just accused Galt of it to start you fellows fighting among yourselves."

"Well, I'll be derned," I said, and just then one of the victims which had evidently come to while we was talking, riz stealthily to his all fours and started crawling towards the winder. It was Jed Whithers. I strode after him and hauled him to his feet.

"How much did Galt pay you for throwin' the bout to Leary?" I demanded.

"A thousand dollars," he stuttered.

"Gimme it," I ordered, and with shaking hands he hauled out a fold of bills. I fluttered 'em and saw they was intact.

"Turn around and look out the winder at the stars," I commanded.

"I don't see no stars," he muttered.

"You will," I promised, as I swung my foot and histed him clean over the sill.

As his wails faded up the alley, I turned to Ace and Glory, and said: "Galt must of cleaned up plenty on this deal, payin' so high for his dirty work. This here dough, though, is goin' to be put to a good cause. The Old Man lost all his money account of Whithers' crooked decision. This thousand bucks will save his ship. Now let's go. I wanta get hold of the promoter of the Sweet Dreams, and get another match tomorrer night with Kid Leary—this time with a honest referee."

The SLUGGER'S GAME.

This short story was first published in the May 1934 issue of Jack Dempsey's Fight Magazine.

I WAS BROODING over my rotten luck in the Sweet Dreams bar on the Hong Kong waterfront, when in come that banana peel on the steps of progress, Smoky Jones. I ain't got no use for Smoky, and he likes me just about as much. But he is broad-minded, as he quickly showed.

"Quick!" quoth he. "Lemme have fifty bucks, Steve."

"Why shouldst I loan you fifty smackers?" I demanded.

"I got a sure-fire tip," he yipped, jumping up and down with impatience. "A hundred-to-one shot which can't lose! You'll get back your dough tomorrer. C'mon, kick in."

"If I had fifty bucks," I returned bitterly, "do you think I'd be wasting my time in a port which don't appreciate no fistic talent?"

"What?" hollered Smoky. "No fifty bucks? After all I've did for you?"

"Well, I can't help it if these

dopey promoters won't gimme a fight, can I?" I said fiercely. "Fifty bucks! Fifty bucks would get me to Singapore, where I can always talk myself into a scrap. I'm stuck here with my white bulldog, Mike, and can't even get a ship to sign on. If I don't scram away from here soon, I'll be on the beach, and you demands fifty bucks!"

A number of men at the bar was listening to our altercation with great interest, and one of 'em, a big, tough-looking guy, bust into a loud guffaw, and said: "Blimey! If the regular promoters turn you down, mate, why don't you try Li Yun?"

"What d'you mean?" I demanded suspiciously.

All the others was grinning like jassacks eating prickly pears.

"Well," he said, with a broad smirk, "Li Yun runs a small menagerie to cover his real business which is staging animal fights, like mongooses and cobras, and pit-terriers, and game-cocks. He's got a big gorilla he ought to sign you up with. I'd like to see the bloody brawl myself; with that pan of yours, it'd be like twin brothers fighting."

"Lissen here, you," I said, rising in righteous wrath—I never did like a limey much anyhow—"I may have a mug like a gorilla, but I figger your'n could be improved some— like this!"

And so saying, I rammed my right fist as far as it would go into his mouth. He reeled and come back bellowing like a typhoon. We traded some lusty swats and then clinched and went head-long into the bar, which splintered at our impact, and the swinging lamp fell down from the ceiling. It busted on the floor, and you should of heard them fellers holler when the burning ile splashed down their necks. Everything was dark in there, and some was scrambling out of winders and doors, and some was stomping out the fire, and somehow me and my opponent got tore loose from each other in the rush.

My eyes was full of smoke, but as I groped around I felt a table-leg glance off my head, so I made a grab and got hold of a human torso. So I throwed him and fell on him and begun to maul him. I musta softened him considerable already, I thought, because he felt a lot flabbier than he done before, and he was hollering a lot louder. Then somebody struck a light, and I found I was hammering the fat Dutch bartender. The limey was gone, and somebody hollered the cops was coming. So I riz and fled out the back way in disgust. That limey had had the last lick, and it's a p'int of honor with me to have the last lick myself. I hunted him for half a hour, aiming to learn him to hit a man with a table-leg and then run, but I didn't find him.

Well, my clothes was singed and tore, so I headed for my boarding-house, the Seamen's Delight, which was down on the waterfront and run by a fat half-caste. He was lying in the hall dead-drunk as usual, and I was glad because when he was sober he was all the time bellyaching about my board bill. Didn't seem to be nobody else in the house.

I went upstairs to my room and opened the door, calling Mike. But Mike didn't come, and I smelt a peculiar smell in the air. I smelt that same smell once when some crimps tried to shanghai me. And the room was empty. My bed was still warm where Mike had been curled up on it, sleeping, but he was gone. I started to go outside and call him, when I seen a note stuck to the wall. I read it and turned cold all over.

It said:

If you want to ever see yure dog agane leeve fiftey dolers in the tin can outside the alley dore of the Bristol Bar at the stroak of leven-thirty tonight. Put the money in the can and go back in the sloon and cloase the dore. Count a hunderd and then you will find yure dog in the ally.
—A Man What Means Bizziness.

I run downstairs and shook the landlord and hollered: "Who's been here since I been gone?"

But all he done was grunt and mutter: "Fill 'er up again, Joe!"

I give him a hearty kick in the pants and run out on the street, plumb distracted. Me and Mike has kicked around together for years; he's saved my worthless life a dozen times. Mike is about the only difference between me and a bum. I don't give a cuss what people think about me, but I always try to conduct myself so my dog won't be ashamed of me. And now some dirty mug had stole him and I hadn't no dough to buy him back.

I sot down on the curb and held my throbbing head and tried to think, but the more I thought, the more mixed up things got. When I'm up against something I can't maul with my fists, I'm plumb off my course and no chart to steer by. Finally I riz up and sot out at a run for the Quiet Hour Arena. They was a fight card on that night, and though I'd already tried to get signed up and been turned down by the promoter, in my desperation I thought I'd try again. I intended appealing to his better nature, if he had one.

From the noise which issued from the building as I approached, I knowed the fights had already started, and my heart sunk, but I didn't know nothing else to try. The back door was locked, but I give it a kind of tug and it come off the hinges and I went in.

They was nobody in sight in the narrer hallway running between the dressing-rooms, but as I run up the hall, a door opened and a big man come out in a bathrobe, follered by a feller with towels and buckets. The big man ripped out a oath and throwed out his arm to stop me. It was the limey I'd fit in the Sweet Dreams bar.

"So that table-leg didn't do the business, eh?" he inquired nastily.

"Looking for another dose of the same, are you?"

"I got no time to fight you now," I muttered, trying to crowd past him. "I'm lookin' for Bisly, the promoter."

"What you shaking about?" he sneered, and I seen he had his hands taped. "Why are you so pale and sweating? Scared of me, eh? Well, I'm due up in that ring right now, but first I'm going to polish you off, you Yankee swine!" And with that he give me a open-handed swipe across the face.

I dunno when anybody ever dared slap me. For a second everything floated in a crimson haze. I dunno what kind of a lick I handed that Limey ape. I don't even remember hitting him. But I must of, because when I could see again, there he was on the floor, with his jaw split open from the corner of his mouth to the rim of his chin, and his head gashed where it hit the door jamb.

The handler was trying to hide under a bench, and somebody else was hollering like he had a knife stuck in him. It was the promoter of the joint, and he was jumping up and down like a cat on a red-hot hatch.

"What 'ave you done?" he squalled. "Oh, blimey, what 'ave you done? A packed 'ouse 'owlin' for h'action, and one of the principals wyting in the bleedin' ring—and 'ere you've lyed out the other! Oh, my 'at! What a bloody go!"

"You mean this here scut was goin' to fight in the main event?" I

asked stupidly, because my head was still going around.

"What else?" he howled. "Ow, murder! What am I to do?"

"Well, you limeys certainly stick together," I said. And then a vast light dazzled me. I gasped with the force of the idea which had just hit me, so to speak. I laid hold on Bisly so forcibly he squealed, thinking I was attacking him.

"How much you payin' this rat?" I demanded, shaking him in my urgency.

"Fifty dollars, winner tyke all!" he moaned.

"Then I'm your man!" I roared, releasing him so vi'lently he sprawled his full length on the floor. "You been refusin' to let me fight in your lousy club account of your prejudice against Americans, but this time you ain't got no choice! That mob out there craves gore, and if they don't see some, they'll tear down your joint! Lissen at 'em!"

He done so, and shuddered at the ferocious yells with which the house was vibrating. The crowd was tired of waiting and was demanding action in the same tone them old Roman crowds used when they yelped for another batch of gladiators to be tossed to the lions.

"You want to go out there and tell 'em the main event's called off?" I demanded.

"No! No!" he said hastily, mopping his brow with a shaky hand. "Have you got togs and a handler?"

"I'll get 'em," I answered. "Hop

out there and tell them mugs that the main event will go on in a minute!"

So he went out like a man going to keep a date with the hangman, and I turned to the feller which was still trying to wedge hisself under the bench—a dumb cluck hired by the club to scrub floors and second fighters which didn't have none theirselves. I handed him a hearty kick in the rear, and sternly requested, "Come out here and help me with this stiff!"

He done so in fear and trembling, and we packed the limey battler into his dressing-room, and laid him on a table. He was beginning to show some faint signs of life. I took off his bathrobe and togs and clamb into 'em myself, whilst the handler watched me in a kind of pallid silence.

"Pick up them buckets and towels," I commanded. "I don't like your looks, but you'll have to do. Any handler is better'n none—and the best is none too good. Come on!"

Follered close by him, I hurried into the arener to be greeted by a ferocious uproar as I come swinging down the aisle. Bisly was addressing 'em, and I caught the tag-end of his remarks which went as follows: "— and so, if you gents will be pytient, Battler Pembroke will be ready for the go in a moment—in fact, 'ere 'e comes now!"

And so saying, Bisly skipped down out of the ring and disappeared. He hadn't had nerve enough to tell 'em that a substitution had been made. They glanced at me, and then they glared, with their mouths open, and then, just as I reached the ring, a big stoker jumped and roared: "You ain't Battler Pembroke! At him, mates—!"

I clouted him on the button and he done a nose-dive over the first row ringside. I then faced the snarling crowd, expanding my huge chest and glaring at 'em from under my battered brows, and I roared: "Anybody else thinks I ain't Battler Pembroke?"

They started surging towards me, growling low in their throats, but they glanced at my victim and halted suddenly, and crowded back from me. With a snort of contempt, I turned and clamb into the ring. My handler clumb after me and commenced to massage my legs kind of dumb-like. He was one of these here sap-heads, and things was happening too fast for him to keep up with 'em.

"What time is it?" I demanded, and he pulled out his watch, looked at it carefully, and said, "Five minutes after ten."

"I got well over a hour," I muttered, and glanced at my opponent in the oppersite corner. I knowed he must be popular, from the size of the purse; most performers at the Quiet Hour got only ten bucks apiece, win, lose or draw, and generally had to lick the promoter to get that. He was well built, but pallid all over, with about as much expression as a fish. They was something familiar about him, but I couldn't place him.

The crowd was muttering and growling, but the announcer was a stolid mutt which didn't have sense enough to be afraid of anybody, even the customers which frequents the Quiet Hour. To save time, he announced whilst the referee was giving the usual instructions, and said he: "In that corner, Sailor Costigan, weight—"

"Where's Pembroke?" bellered the crowd. "That ain't Pembroke! That's a bloody Yankee, the low-lifed son of a canine!"

"Nevertheless," said the announcer, without blinking, "he weighs one-ninety; and the other blighter is Slash Jackson, of Cardiff; weight, one-eighty-nine."

The maddened mob frothed and commenced throwing things, but then the gong clanged and they calmed down reluctantly to watch the show, like a fight crowd will. After all, what they want is a fight.

At the whang of the gong I tore out of my corner with the earnest ambition of finishing that fight with the first punch, if possible. It was my intention to lay my right on his jaw, and I made no secret of it. I scorns deception. If he'd ducked a split second slower, the scrap would of ended right there.

But I didn't pause to meditate. I sent my left after my right, and he grunted poignantly as it sunk under his heart. Then his right flicked up

at my jaw, and from the way it cut the air as it whistled past, I knowed it was loaded with dynamite. Giving him no time to get set, I slugged him back across the ring and into the ropes on the other side. The crowd screamed blue murder, but I wasn't hurting him as much as they thought, or as much as I wanted to. He was clever at rolling with a punch, and he was all elbows. Nor he wasn't too careful where he put 'em, neither. He put one in my stummick and t'other'n in my eye, which occasioned some bitter profanity on my part. He also stomped heartily on my insteps.

Little things like them is ignored in the Quiet Hour; the audience merely considers 'em the spice of the sport, and the referee is above noticing 'em.

But I was irritated, and in my eagerness to break Jackson's neck with a swinging overhand punch, I exposed myself to his right, which licked out again like the flipper of a seal. I just barely managed to duck it, and it ripped the skin off my chin as it grazed me. And as I stabbed him off balance with a straight left to the mouth, that peculiar lick of his set me to wondering again, because it reminded me of something, I couldn't remember what.

He now brung his left into play with flashy jabs and snappy hooks, but it didn't pack the power his right did, and all he done was to cut my lips a little. He kept his right cocked, but I was watching it, and when he shot it again I went inside it and battered away at his midriff with both hands. He was steel springs and whale-bone under his white skin, but he didn't like 'em down below. He was backing and breaking ground when the gong ended the round.

I sunk onto my stool in time to receive a swipe across the eyes with the towel my handler was trying to fan me with, and whilst I was shaking the stars out of my vision, he emptied a whole bucket of ice water over my head. This was wholly unnecessary, as I p'inted out to him with free and fervent language, but he had a one-track mind. He'd probably seen a fighter doused thusly, and thought it had to be did, whether the fighter needed it or not.

I was still remonstrating with him concerning his dumbness when the bell rung, and as a result, Jackson, who shot out of his corner like a catapult, caught me before I could get into the center of the ring, shooting his left and throwing his right after it. Zip! It come through the air like a hammer on a steel spring!

I side-stepped and ripped my left to his midriff. He gasped and staggered, and I set myself like a flash and throwed my right at his head with all my beef behind it. But I'd forgot I was standing where the canvas was soaked with the water my dumb handler had poured over me. My foot slipped on a sliver of ice just as I let go my swing, and before I could recover myself, that T.N.T. right licked out, and this time it didn't miss.

Jerusha! It wasn't like being hit by a human being. I felt like a fireworks factory hadst exploded in my skull. I seen comets and meteors and sky-rockets, and somebody was trying to count the stars as they flew past. Then things cleared a little bit, and I realized it was the referee which was counting, and he was counting over me.

I was on my belly in the resin, and bells seemed to be ringing all over the house. I could'st hardly hear the referee for 'em, but he said "Nine!" so I riz. That's a habit of mine. I make a specialty of getting up. I have got up off the floor of rings from Galveston to Shanghai.

My legs wasn't exactly right— one had a tendency to steer south by west, while the other'n wanted to go due east—and I had a dizzy idee that a typhoon was raging outside. I coulds't hear the waters rising and the winds roaring, but realized that it was my own ears ringing after that awful clout.

Jackson was on me like a hunting panther, just about as light and easy. He was too anxious to use his right again. He thought I was out on my feet and all he had to do was to hit me. Any old-timer could of told him that leading to me with his right, whether I was groggy or not, was violating a rule of safety which is already becoming a ring tradition.

He simply cocked his right and let it go, and I beat it with a left hook to the body. He turned kinda green in the face, like anybody is liable to which has just had a iron fist sunk several inches into their belly. And before he could strike again, I fell into him and hugged him like a grizzly.

I knowed him now! They wasn't but one man in the world with a right-hand clout like that—Torpedo Willoughby, the Cardiff Murderer. Whiskey and women kept him from being a champ, and kept him broke so much he often performed in dumps like the Quiet Hour under a assumed name, but he was a mankiller, the worst England ever produced.

I shook the blood and sweat outa my eyes, and took my time about coming out of that clinch, and when the referee finally broke us, I was ready. Willoughby come slugging in, and I crouched and covered up, weaving always to his left, and hooking my left to his ribs and belly. My left carried more dynamite than his left did, and I didn't leave no openings for that blasting right. I didn't tin-can; I dunno how and wouldn't if I could. But I retired into my shell whilst pounding his mid-section, and he got madder and madder, and flailed away with that right fiercer than ever. But it was glancing off my arms and the top of my head, and my left was digging into his guts deeper and deeper. It ain't a spectacular way of battling, but it gets results in the long run.

I was purty well satisfied at the end of that round. Fighting like I was didn't give Willoughby no chance to blast me, and eventually he was going to weaken under my body-battering. It might take five or six rounds, but the bout was sched-uled for fifteen frames, and I had plenty of time.

But that don't mean I was happy as I sot in my corner whilst my handler squirted lemon juice in my eye, trying to moisten my lips, and give me a long, refreshing drink of iodine in his brainless efforts to daub a cut on my chin. I was thinking of Mike, and a chill trickled down my spine as I wondered what them devils which stole him wouldst do to him if the money wasn't in the tin can at exactly eleven-thirty.

"What time is it?" I demanded, and my handler hauled out his watch and said, "Five minutes after ten."

"That's what you said before!" I howled in exasperation. "Gimme that can!"

I grabbed it and glared, and then I shook it. It wasn't running. It didn't even sound like they was any works inside of it. Stricken by a premoni-shun, I yelled to the referee, "What time is it?"

He glanced at his watch. "Seconds out!" he said, and then: "Fifteen minutes after eleven!"

Fifteen minutes to go! Cold sweat bust out all over me, and I jumped up offa my stool so suddenly my handler fell backwards through the ropes. Fifteen minutes! I couldn't take no five or six rounds to lick

Willoughby! I had to do it in this round if winning was going to do me any good.

I throwed all my plans to the winds. I was trembling in every limb and glaring across at Willoughby, and when he met the glare in my eyes he stiffened and his muscles tensed. He sensed the change in me, though he couldn't know why; he knowed the battle was to be to the death.

The gong whanged and I tore out of my corner like a typhoon, to kill or be killed. I'm always a fighter of the iron-man type. When I'm nerved up like I was then, the man ain't born which can stop me. There wasn't no plan or plot or science about that round—it was just raw, naked, primitive manhood, sweat and blood and fists flailing like mallets without a second's let-up.

I tore in, swinging like a madman, and in a second Willoughby was fighting for his life. The blood spattered and the crowd roared and things got dim and red, and all I seen was the white figger in front of me, and all I knowed was to hit and hit and keep hitting till the world ended.

I dunno how many times I was on the canvas.

Every time he landed solid with that awful right I went down like a butchered ox. But every time I come up again and tore into him more furious than ever. I was crazy with fear, like a man in a nightmare, thinking of Mike and the minutes that was slipping past.

His right was the concentrated essence of hell. Every time it found my jaw I felt like my skull was caved in and every vertebrae of my spine was dislocated. But I'm used to them sensations. They're part of the slugger's game. Let these here classy dancing-masters quit when their bones begins to melt like wax, and their brains feels like they was being jolted loose from their skull. A slugger lowers his head and wades in again. That's his game. His ribs may be splintered in on his vitals, and his guts may be mashed outa place, and his ears may be streaming blood from veins busted inside his skull, but them things don't matter; the important thing is winning.

No white man ever hit me harder'n Torpedo Willoughby hit me, but I was landing too, and every time I sunk a mauler under his heart or smashed one against his temple, I seen him wilt. If he could of took it like he handed it out, he'd been champeen. But at last I seen his pale face before me with his lips open wide as he gulped for air, and I knowed I had him, though I was hanging to the ropes and the crowd was yelling for the kill. They couldn't see the muscles in his calves quivering, nor his belly heaving, nor the glaze in his eyes. They couldn't understand that he'd hammered me till his shoulder muscles was dead and his gloves was like they was weighted with lead, and the heart was gone out of him. All they couldst see was me, battered and bloody, clinging to the ropes, and him cocking his right for the finisher.

It come over, slow and ponderous, and glanced from my shoulder as I lurched off the ropes. And my own right smashed like a caulking mallet against his jaw, and down he went, face-first in the resin.

When they fall like that, they don't get up. I didn't even wait to hear the referee count him out. I run across the ring, getting stronger at every step, tore off my gloves and held out my hand for my bathrobe. My gaping handler put the sponge in it.

I throwed it in his face with a roar of irritation, and he fell outa the ring headfirst into a water bucket, which put the crowd in such a rare good humor that they even cheered as I run down the aisle, and not over a dozen empty beer bottles was throwed at me.

Bisly was waiting in the corridor, and I grabbed the fifty bucks outa his hand as I went by on the run. He follered me into the dressing-room and offered to help me put on my clothes, but knowing he hoped to steal my wad whilst helping me, I throwed him out bodily, jerked on my street clothes, and sallied forth at top speed.

The Bristol Bar was a low-class dive down on the edge of the native quarters. It took me maybe five minutes to get there, and a clock behind the bar showed me that it lacked about a minute and a fraction of eleven-thirty.

"Tony," I panted to the bartender, who gaped at my bruised and bloody face, "I want the back room to myself. See that nobody disturbs me."

I run to the back door and throwed it open. It was dark in the alley, but I seen a empty tobacco tin setting close to the door. I quickly wadded the money into it, stepped into the room and shut the door. I reckon somebody was hiding in the alley watching, because as soon as I shut the door, I heard a stirring around out there. I didn't look. I wasn't taking no chances on them doing anything to Mike.

I heard the tin scrape against the stones, and they was silence whilst I hurriedly counted up to a hundred. Then I jerked open the door, and joyfully yelled: "Mike!" They was no reply. The tin can was gone, but Mike wasn't there.

Cold, clammy sweat bust out all over me, and my tongue stuck to the roof of my mouth. I rushed down the alley like a wild man, and just before I reached the street, where a dim street-lamp shone, I fell over something warm and yielding which groaned and said: "Oh, my head!"

I grabbed it and dragged it into the light, and it was Smoky Jones. He had a lump on his head and the tin can in his hand, but it was empty.

I must of went kinda crazy then. Next thing I knowed I had Smoky by the throat, shaking him till his eyes crossed, and I was mouthing, "What you done with Mike, you dirty gutter rat? Where is he?"

His hands were waving around, and I seen he couldn't talk. His face was purple and his eyes and tongue stuck out remarkable. So I eased up a bit, and he gurgled, "I dunno!"

"You do know!" I roared, digging my thumbs into his unwashed neck. "You was the one which stole him. You wanted that fifty bucks to bet on a horse. I see it all, now. It's so plain even a dumb mutt like me can figure it out. You got the money—where's Mike?"

"I'll tell you everything," he gasped. "Lemme up, Steve. You're chockin' me to death. Lissen—it was me which stole Mike. I snuck in and doped him and packed him off in a sack. But I didn't aim to hurt him. All I wanted was the fifty. I figgered you could raise it if you had to ... I'd taken Mike to Li Yun's house, to hide him. We put him in a cage before he come to—that there dog is worse'n a tiger ... I was to hide in the alley till you put out the dough, and meanwhile one of Li Yun's Chinees was to bring Mike in a auto, and wait at the mouth of the alley till I got the money. Then, if everything was OK, we was going to let the dog out into the alley and beat it in the car .... Well, whilst I hid in the alley I seen the Chinee drive up and park in the shadows like we'd agreed, so I signalled him and went on after the dough. But as I come up the alley with the money, wham! that double-crossin' heathen riz up out of the dark and whacked me with a blackjack. And now he's gone and the auto's gone and the fifty bucks is gone!"

"And where's Mike?" I demanded.

"I dunno," he said. "I doubt if that Chinee ever brung him here at all. Oh, my head!" he said, holding onto his skull.

"That ain't a scratch to what I'm goin' to do to you when you get recovered," I promised him. "Where at does Li Yun live at?"

"In that old warehouse down near the wharf the natives call the Dragon Pier," said Smoky. "He's fixed up some rooms for livin' quarters, and—"

That was all I wanted to know. The next second I was headed for the Dragon Pier. I run down alleys, crossed dark courts, turned off the narrer side street that runs to the wharf, ducked through a winding alley, and come to the back of the warehouse I was looking for. As I approached, I seen a back door hanging open; and a light shining through.

I didn't hesitate, but bust through with both fists cocked. Then I stopped short. They was nobody there. It was a great big room, electrically lighted, with a switch on the wall, and purty well fixed up generally. Leastways it had been. But now it was littered with busted tables and splintered chairs, and there was blood and pieces of silk on the floor. They had been some kind of a awful fight in there, and my heart was in my mouth when I seen a couple of empty cages. There was white dog hair scattered on the floor, and some thick darkish hair in big tufts that couldn't of come from nothing but a gorilla.

I looked at the cages. One was a bamboo cage, and some of the bars had been gnawed in two. The lock on the steel cage was busted from the inside. It didn't take no detective to figger out what had happened. Mike had gnawed his way out of the bamboo cage and the gorilla had busted out of his cage to get at him. But where was they now? Was the Chinees and their gorilla chasing poor old Mike down them dark alleys, or had they took his body off to dispose of it after the gorilla had finished him?

I felt weak and sick and helpless; Mike is about the only friend I got. Then things begun to swim red around me again. They was one table in that room yet unbusted. I attended to that. They was no human for me to lay hands on, and I had to wreck something.

Then a inner door opened and a fat white man with a cigar in his mouth stuck his head in and stared at me.

"What was that racket?" he said. "Hey, who are you? Where's Li Yun?"

"That's what I want to know," I snarled. "Who are you?"

"Name's Wells, if it's any of your business," he said, coming on into the room. His belly bulged out his checked vest, and his swagger put my teeth on edge.

"What a mess!" he said, flicking the ashes offa his cigar in a way which made me want to kill him. It's the little things in life which causes murder. "Where the devil is Li Yun? The crowd's gettin' impatient."

"Crowd?" I interrogated. As I spoke, it seemed like I did hear a hum up towards the front of the building.

"Why," he said, "the crowd which has come to watch the battle between Li Yun's gorilla and the fightin' bull-dog."

"Huh?" I gawped.

"Sure," he said. "Don't you know about it? It's time to start now. I'm Li Yun's partner. I finances these shows. I've been up at the front of the buildin', sellin' tickets. Thought I heard a awful racket back here awhile ago, but was too busy haulin' in the dough to come back and see. What's happened, anyhow? Where's the Chinees and the animals? Huh?"

I give a harsh, rasping laugh that made him jump. "I see now," I said betwixt my teeth. "Li Yun wanted Mike for his dirty fights. He seen a chance to make fifty bucks and stage a show too. So he double-crossed Smoky, and—"

"Go find Li Yun!" snapped Wells, biting off the end of another cigar. "That crowd out there is gettin' mad, and they're the scrapin's offa the docks. Hurry up, and I'll give you half a buck—"

I then went berserk. All the grief and fury which had been seething in me exploded and surged over like hot lava out of a volcano. I give one yell, and went into action.

"Halp!" hollered Wells. "He's gone crazy!" He grabbed for a gun, but before he could draw I caught him on the whiskers with a looping haymaker and he done a classy cartwheel head-on into the wall. The back of his skull hit the light-switch so hard it jolted it clean outa the brackets, and the whole building was instantly plunged in darkness. I felt around till my groping hands located a door, and I ripped it open and plunged recklessly down a narrer corridor till I hit another door with my head so hard I split the panels. I jerked it open and lunged through.

I couldn't see nothing, but I felt the presence of a lot of people. They was a confused noise going up, a babble of Chinese and Malay and Hindu, and some loud cussing in English and German. Somebody bawled, "Who turned out them lights? Turn on the lights! How can we see the scrap without no lights?"

Somebody else hollered, "They've turned the animals into the cage! I hear 'em!"

Everybody begun to cuss and yell for lights, and I groped forward until I was stopped by iron bars. Then I knowed where I was. That corridor I'd come through served as a kind of chute or runway into the big cage where the fights was fit. I reached through the bars, groped around and found a key sticking in the lock of the cage door. I give a yell of exultation which riz above the clamor, turned the key, throwed open the door and come plunging out. Them rats enjoyed a fight, hey? Well, I aimed they shouldn't be disappointed. Two men fighting for money, of their own free will, is one thing. Making a couple of inoffensive animals butcher each other just for the amusement of a gang of wharf rats is another'n.

I came out of that cage crazy-mad and flailing with both fists. Somebody grunted and dropped, and somebody else yelled, "Hey, who hit me?" and then the whole crowd began to mill and holler and strike out wild at random, not knowing what it was all about. It was a regular bedlam, with me swinging in the dark and dropping a man at each slam, and then a window got busted, and as I moved across a dim beam of light which come through, one guy give a frantic yell, "Run! Run! The griller's loose!"

At that, hell bust loose. Everybody stampeded, screaming and hollering and cussing and running over each other, and me in the middle of 'em, slugging right and left.

"You all wants a fight, does you?" I howled. "Well, here's some to tote home with you!"

They hit the door like a herd of steers and splintered it and went storming through, them which was able to storm. Some had been stomped in the rush, and plenty had stopped my iron fists in the dark. I come ravin' after 'em. Just because

them rats wanted to see gore spilt—
by somebody else—Mike, my only
friend in the Orient, had to be sacri-
ficed. I could of kilt 'em all.

Well, they streamed off down
the street in full cry, and as I emerged,
I fell over a innocent passerby which
had been knocked down by the
stampede. By the time I riz, they was
out of my reach, though the sounds
of their flight come back to me.

The fire of my rage died down
to ashes. I felt old and sick and worn
out. I wasn't young no more, and
Mike was gone. I stooped to pick up
the man I had fell over, idly noticing
that he was a English captain whose
ship was tied up at a nearby wharf,
discharging cargo.

"Say," he said, gasping to get his
breath back, "aren't you Steve
Costigan?"

"Yeah," I admitted, without
enthusiasm.

"Good!" he said. "I was looking
for you. They told me it was your
dog."

I sighed. "Yeah," I said. "A white
bulldog that answered to the name
of Mike. Where'd you find his body?"

"Body?" he said. "My word! The
bally brute has been pursuing four
Chinamen and a bloody gorilla up
and down the docks for half an hour,
and now he has them treed in the
rigging of my ship, and I want you
to come and call him off. Can't have
that, you know!"

"Good old Mike!" I whooped,
jumping straight into the air with
joy and exultation. "Still the

fightin'est dog in the Asiatics! Lead
on, matey! I craves words with his
victims. I got nothin' against the
griller, but them Chinees has got
fifty bucks belongin' to me and
Mike!"

GENERAL IRONFIST.

This short story was first published in the June 1934 issue of Jack Dempsey's Fight Magazine.

AS I CLUMB into the ring that night in the Pleasure Palace Fight Club, on the Hong Kong waterfront, I was low in my mind. I'd come to Hong Kong looking for a former shipmate of mine. I'd come on from Tainan as fast as I could, even leaving my bulldog Mike aboard the *Sea Girl*, which wasn't due to touch at Hong Kong for a couple of weeks yet.

But Soapy Jackson, the feller I was looking for, had just dropped plumb out of sight. Nobody'd saw him for weeks, or knowed what had become of him. Meanwhile my dough was all gone, so I accepted a bout with a big Chinese fighter they called the Yeller Typhoon.

He was a favorite with the sporting crowd and the Palace was jammed with both white men and Chineses that night, some very high class. I noticed one Chinee in particular, whilst setting in my corner waiting for the bell, because his European clothes was so swell, and because he seemed to take such a burning interest in the goings on. But I didn't pay much attention to the crowd; I was impatient to get the battle over with.

The Yeller Typhoon weighed three hundred pounds and he was a head taller'n me; but most of his weight was around his waist-line, and he didn't have the kind of arms and shoulders that makes a hitter. And it don't make no difference how big a Chinaman is, he can't take it.

I wasn't in no mood for classy boxing that night. I just walked into him, let him flail away with both hands till I seen a opening, and then let go my right. He shook the ring when he hit the boards, and the brawl was over.

Paying no heed to the howls of the dumbfounded multitude, I hastened to my dressing-room, donned my duds, and then hauled a letter from my britches pocket and studied it like I'd done a hundred times before.

It was addressed to Mr. Soapy Jackson, American Bar, Tainan, Taiwan, and was from a San Francisco law firm. After Soapy left the *Sea Girl*, he tended bar at the American, but he'd been gone a month when the *Sea Girl* docked at Tainan again, and the proprietor showed me that letter which had just come for him. He said Soapy had went to Hong Kong, but he didn't know his address,

so I took the letter and come on alone to find him, because I had a idea it was important. Maybe he'd been left a fortune.

But I'd found Hong Kong in turmoil, just like all the rest of China. Up in the hills a lot of bandits, which called themselves revolutionary armies, was raising hell, and all I couldst hear was talk about General Yun Chei, and General Whang Shan, and General Feng, which they said was really a white man. Folks said Yun and Feng had joined up against Whang, and some tall battling was expected, and the foreigners was all piling down out of the interior. It was easy for a white sailorman with no connections to drop out of sight and never be heard of again. I thought what if Soapy has got hisself scuppered by them bloody devils, just when maybe he was on the p'int of coming into big money.

Well, I stuck the letter in my pocket, and sallied forth into the lamp-lit street to look for Soapy some more, when somebody hove up alongside of me, and who should it be but that dapper Chinee in European clothes I'd noticed in the first row, ringside, at the fight.

"You are Sailor Costigan, are you not?" he said in perfect English.

"Yeah," I said, after due consideration.

"I saw you fight the Yellow Typhoon tonight," he said. "The blow you dealt him would have felled an ox. Can you always hit like that?"

"Why not?" I inquired. He

looked me over closely, and nodded his head like he was agreeing with hisself about something.

"Come in and have a drink," he said, so I follered him into a native joint where they wasn't nothing but Chineses. They looked at me with about as much expression as fishes, and went on guzzling tea and rice wine out of them little fool egg-shell cups. The mandarin, or whatever he was, led the way into a room which the door was covered with velvet curtains and the walls had silk hangings with dragons all over 'em, and we sot down at a ebony table and a Chinaboy brung in a porcelain jug and the glasses.

The mandarin poured out the licker, and, whilst he was pouring mine, such a infernal racket arose outside the door that I turned around and looked, but couldn't see nothing for the curtains, and the noise quieted down all of a sudden. Them Chineses is always squabbling amongst theirselves.

So the mandarin said, "Let us drink to your vivid victory!"

"Aw," I said, "that wasn't nothin'. All I had to do was hit him."

But I drank, and I said, "This is funny tastin' stuff. What is it?"

"Kaoliang," he said. "Have another glass." So he poured 'em, and nigh upsot my glass with his sleeve as he handed it to me.

So I drank it, and he said, "What's the matter with your ears?"

"You oughta know, bein' a fight fan," I said.

"This fight tonight was the first I have ever witnessed," he confessed.

"I'd never thought it from the interest you've taken in the brawl," I said. "Well, these ears is what is known in the vernacular of the game as cauliflowers. I got 'em, also this undulatin' nose, from stoppin' gloves with human knuckles inside of 'em. All old-timers is similarly decorated, unless they happen to be of the dancin'-school variety."

"You have fought in the ring many times?" he inquired.

"Oftener'n I can remember," I answered, and his black eyes gleamed with some secret pleasure. I took another snort of that there Chinese licker out of the jug, and I begun to feel oratorical and histrionic.

"From Savannah to Singapore," I said, "from the alleys of Bristol to the wharfs of Melbourne, I've soaked the resin dust with my blood and the gore of my enermies. I'm the bully of the *Sea Girl*, the toughest ship afloat, and when I set foot on the docks, strong men hunt cover! I—"

I suddenly noticed my tongue was getting thick and my head was swimming. The mandarin wasn't making no attempt to talk. He was setting staring at me kinda intense-like, and his eyes glittered through a mist which was beginning to float about me.

"What the heck!" I said stupidly. Then I heaved up with a roar, and the room reeled around me. "You yeller-bellied bilge-rat!" I roared drunkenly. "You done doped my grog! You—"

I grabbed him by the shirt with my left, and dragged him across the table top, drawing back my right, but before I could bash him with it, something exploded at the base of my skull, and the lights went out.

I MUST OF been out a long time. Once or twice I had a sensation of being tossed and jounced around, and thought I was in my bunk and a rough sea running, and then again I kinda vaguely realized that I was bumping over a rutty road in a automobile, and I had a feeling that I ought to get up and knock somebody's block off. But mostly I just laid there and didn't know nothing at all.

When I did finally come to myself, the first thing I discovered was that my hands and feet was tied with ropes. Then I seen I was laying on a camp cot in a tent, and a big Chinaman with a rifle was standing over me. I craned my neck, and seen another man setting on a pile of silk cushions, and he looked kinda familiar.

At first I didn't recognize him, because now he was dressed in embroidered silk robes, Chinese style, but then I seen it was the mandarin. I struggled up to a sitting position, in spite of my bonds, and addressed him with poignancy and fervor.

"Why," I concluded passionately, "did you dope my licker? Where am

I at? What've you done with me, you scum of a Macao gutter?"

"You are in the camp of General Yun Chei," he said. "I transported you hither in my automobile while you lay senseless."

"And who the devil are you?" I demanded.

He gave me a sardonic bow. "I am General Yun Chei, your humble servant," he said.

"The hell you are!" I commented with a touch of old-world culture. "You had a nerve, comin' right into Hong Kong."

"The Federalist fools are blind," he said. "Often I play my own spy."

"But what'd you kidnap me for?" I yelled with passion, jerking at my cords till the veins stood out on my temples. "I can't pay no cussed ransom."

"Have you ever heard of General Feng?" he asked.

"And what if I has?" I snarled, being in no mood for riddles.

"He is camped nearby," said he. "He is a white foreign-devil like yourself. You have heard his nickname—Ironfist?"

"Well?" I demanded.

"He is a man of great strength and violent passions," said General Yun. "He has acquired a following more because of his personal fighting ability than because of his intellect. Whomever he strikes with his fists falls senseless to the ground. So the soldiers call him .

"Now, he and I have temporarily allied our forces, because our mutual enemy, General Whang Shan, is somewhere in the vicinity. General Whang has a force greater than ours, and he likewise possesses an airplane, which he flies himself. We do not know exactly where he is, but, on the other hand, he does not know our position, either, and we are careful to guard against spies. No one leaves or enters our camp without special permission.

"Though Ironfist and myself are temporary allies, there is no love lost between us, and he constantly seeks to undermine my prestige with my men. To protect myself I must retaliate—not so as to precipitate trouble between our armies, but in such a way as to make him lose face.

"General Feng boasts that he can conquer any man in China with his naked fists, and he has frequently dared me to pit my hardiest captains against him for the sheer sport of it. He well knows that no man in my army could stand up against him, and his arrogance lowers my prestige. So I went secretly to Hong Kong to find a man who might have a fighting chance against him. I contemplated the Yellow Typhoon, but when you laid him low with a single stroke, I knew you were the man for whom I was looking. I have many friends in Hong Kong. Drugging you was easy. The first time a pre-arranged noise at the door distracted your attention. But that was not enough, so I contrived to dope your second drink under cover of my sleeve. By the holy dragon, you had enough drug in you to have overcome an elephant before you succumbed!

"But here you are. I shall present you to General Feng, before all the captains, and challenge him to make good his boast. He cannot with honor refuse; and if you beat him, he will lose face, and my prestige will rise accordingly, because you represent me."

"And what do I get out of it?" I demanded.

"If you win," he said, "I will send you back to Hong Kong with a thousand American dollars."

"And what if I lose?" I said.

"Ah," he smiled bleakly, "a man whose head has been removed by the executioner's sword has no need of money."

I burst into a cold sweat and sot in silent meditation.

"Do you agree?" he asked at last.

"I'd like to know what choice I got," I snarled. "Take these here cords offa me and gimme some grub. I won't fight for nobody on a empty belly."

He clapped his hands, and the soldier cut my cords with his bayonet, and another menial come in with a big dish of mutton stew and some bread and rice wine, so I fell to and lapped it all up in a hurry.

"As a token of appreciation," said General Yun, "I now make you a present of this unworthy trinket."

And he hauled out the finest watch I ever seen and give it to me.

"If the gift pleases you," he said, noting my gratification, "let it nerve your thews against Ironfist."

"Don't worry about that," I said, admiring the watch, which was gold with dragons carved on it. "I'll bust him so hard he'll be loopin' the loop for a week."

"Excellent!" beamed General Yun. "If you could contrive to deal him a fatal injury during the combat, it could simplify matters greatly. But come! I shall tangle General Feng in his own web!"

I FOLLERED HIM out of the tent, and seen a lot of other tents and ragged soldiers drilling amongst 'em, and off to one side another camp with more yeller-bellied gunmen in it. It was still kinda early in the morning, and I gathered it had tooken us all night to get there in Yun's auto. We was away up in the hills, and they was no sign of civilization anywheres.

General Yun headed straight for a big tent in the middle of the camp, and I follered him in. A lot of officers in all kinds of uniforms riz and bowed, except one big man who sot on a camp stool. He was a white man in faded khaki and boots and a sun helmet; his fists was as big as mauls, and his hairy arms was thick with muscles. His face and corded neck was burned brick-colored by the sun, and he wore a expression like he habitually hankered for somebody to give him a excuse to slug 'em.

"General Yun—" he begun in a harsh voice, then stopped and glared at me. "What the hell are you doing here?" he demanded.

"Joel Ballerin!" I said, staring at him. I might of knowed. Wherever they was war, you'd usually find Joel Ballerin right in the middle of it. He was from South Australia, and had a natural instinct for carnage. He was famed as a fighting man all over South Africa, Australia and the South Seas. Gunrunner, blackbirder, smuggler, pirate, pearler, or what have you, but always a scrapper from the word go, with a constant hankering to bounce his enormous fists offa somebody's conk. I'd never fit him, but I'd saw some of his handiwork. The ruin he could make of a human carcass was plumb appalling.

He glared at me with no love, because I got considerable reputation as a man-mauler myself, and fighting men is jealous of each other's fame. I couldst feel my own short hairs bristle as I glared at him.

"You have boasted much of your prowess with the clenched fist," said Yun Chei, softly. "You have repeatedly assured me that there was not a man in my army, including my unworthy self, whom you could not subdue with ease. I have here one of my followers whom I venture to back against you."

"That's Steve Costigan, an American sailor," snarled Ballerin. "He's no man of yours."

"On the contrary!" said General Yun. "Do you not see that he wears my dragon watch, entrusted only to my loyal henchmen?"

"Well," growled Ballerin, "there's something fishy about this. When you bring that cabbage-eared gorilla up here—"

"Hey!" I said indignantly. "You cease heavin' them insults around! If you ain't got the guts to fight, why, say so!"

"Why, you blasted fool!" he roared, jumping up off his stool like it was red hot. "I'll break your infernal head right here and now—"

General Yun got between us and smiled blandly and said, "Let us be dignified in all things. Let it be a public exhibition. I fear this tent would not prove a proper arena for two such gladiators. I shall have a ring constructed at once."

Ballerin turned away, grunting, "All right; fix it any way you want to." Then he wheeled back, his eyes flaming, and snarled at me, "As for you, you Yankee ape, you're going out of this camp feet-first!"

"Big talk don't bust no chins," I retorted. "I never did like you anyway, you nigger-stealin' pearl-thief!"

He looked like he was going to bust some blood-vessels, but he just give a ferocious snarl and plunged out of the tent. General Yun motioned me to foller him, and his officers tagged after us. The others follered General Feng. They didn't seem to be no love lost betwixt them two armies.

"Ironfist is caught in his own snare!" gurgled General Yun, hugging hisself with glee. "He lusts for battle, but is furious and suspicious because

I trapped him into it. All the men of both armies shall see his downfall. Call in the patrols from the hills! General Ironfist! Ha!"

GENERAL YUN DIDN'T take me back to his tent, but he put me in another'n and told me to holler if I wanted anything. He said I'd be guarded so's Ballerin couldn't have me bumped off, but I seen I was as good as a prisoner.

Well, I sot in there, and heard some men come marching up and surround the tent, and somebody give orders in broken Chinese, and cussed heartily in English, and I stuck my head out of the door and hollered, "Soapy!"

There he was, all right, commanding the guard, with a old British army coat three sizes too small for him, and a sword three sizes too big. He nigh dropped his sword when he seen me, and bellered, "Steve! What you doin' here?"

"I come up to lick Joel Ballerin for Yun Chei," I said. And he said, "So that's why they're buildin' that ring! Nobody but the highest officers knows what's goin' on."

"What you doin' here?" I demanded.

"Aw," he said, "I got tired tendin' bar and decided to become a soldier of fortune. So I skipped to Hong Kong and beat it up into the hills and joined Yun Chei. But Steve, the life ain't what it's cracked up to be. I don't mind the fightin' much, cause it's mostly yellin' and shootin' and little damage done, but marchin' through these hills is hell, and the food is lousy. We don't get paid regular, and no place to spend the dough when we do get it. For ten cents I'd desert."

"Well, lissen," I said, "I got a letter for you." I reached into my britches pocket, and then I give a yelp. "I been rolled!" I hollered. "It's gone!"

"What?" he said.

"Your letter," I said. "I was lookin' for you to give it to you. It come to the American Bar at Tainan. A letter from the Ormond and Ashley law firm, 'Frisco."

"What was in it?" he demanded.

"How should I know?" I returned irritably. "I didn't open it. I thought maybe somebody had left you a lot of dough, or somethin'.'"

"I've heard pa say he had wealthy relatives," said Soapy, doubtfully. "Look again, Steve."

"I've looked," I said. "It ain't here. I bet Yun Chei took it offa me whilst I was out. I'll go over and bust him on the jaw—"

"Wait!" hollered Soapy. "You'll get us both shot! You ain't supposed to leave this tent, and I got to guard you."

"Well," I said, "t'aint likely they was any money in the letter. Likely they was just tellin' you where to go to get the dough. I remember the address, and when I get back to Hong Kong, I'll write and tell 'em I got you located."

"That's a long time to wait," said Soapy, pessimistically.

"Not so long," I said. "As soon as I lick Ballerin, I'll start for Hong Kong—"

"No, you won't," said Soapy. "No ways soon, anyhow."

"What d'you mean?" I asked. "Yun said he'd send me back if I licked Ballerin."

"He didn't say when, did he?" inquired Soapy. "He ain't goin' to take no chance of you going back and talkin' and revealin' our position to Whang's spies. No, sir; he'll keep you prisoner till he's ready to change camp, and that may be six months."

"Me stay in this dump six months?" I exclaimed fiercely. "I won't do it!"

"Maybe you won't at that," he said cheeringly. "A lot of things can happen unexpected around a rebel Chinee camp. I see you're wearin' Yun Chei's dragon watch."

"Yeah," I said. "Ain't it a beaut? Yun Chei give it to me."

"Well" he said, "that watch has been give away before, but it has a way of comin' back to Yun Chei after the owner's demise, which is generally sudden and frequent. Four men that I know of has already been made a present of that watch, and none of 'em is now alive."

"The hell you say!" I said, beginning to perspire copiously. "This is a nice, friendly place I got into. Do you want to stay here?"

"No, I don't!" he replied bitterly. "I didn't want to before, and when I thinks they's maybe a million dollars waitin' somewhere for me to spend, I feels like throwin' down this fool sword and headin' for the coast."

"Well," I said, "I ain't goin' to spend no six months here. Yet I wants that thousand bucks. Let's us make a break tonight, after I collects."

"They'd run us down before we'd went far," he said despondently. "I got one of the few good horses in camp, but it couldn't carry us both at any kind of a clip. All the other nags are fastened up and guarded so nobody can desert and carry news of our whereabouts to General Whang, which would give a leg to know, so he could raid us. Yun Chei knows he can trust me not to, because Whang wants to cut off my head. I stole a batch of his eatin' chickens onst when we was fightin' him over near Kauchau."

"Well," I begun hotly, "I'll be derned if I'm goin' to—"

"Shhh!" he said. "We got to change guard now; here comes the other squad. I'm goin' off some-wheres and think."

Another gang of Chinamen come up with a native officer in charge, and Soapy and his men marched off, and I sot and wound my dragon watch, and tried to think of something, but didn't have no success, as usual.

TIME DRAGGED SLOW, but finally about the middle of the afternoon, a mob of captains or something come and led me out of the tent and escorted me to the ring which had been built about halfway between the camps. They was already a solid bank of soldiers around it, Yun Chei's on one side and General Feng's on the other, with their rifles. The ring was just four posts stuck in the ground, with ropes stretched between 'em, and a bare floor of boards elevated maybe a yard or more. General Yun was setting in a camp chair on one side, with his officers around him, and a big Chinee, which was naked to the waist, was standing right behind him. The other officers and the common soldiers of both armies sot on the ground or stood up.

I didn't see Soapy nowheres, and they wasn't no seconds nor handlers. The Chineses didn't know nothing about such things. I clumb into the ring and examined the ropes, which was too loose, for one thing, and the floor, which was solid enough but none too even, and no padding of any kind on it. They had had sense enough to put camp stools in the corners, so I shed my cap, coat and shirt, and sot down. General Yun then riz and come over to me and smiled gently and said, "Smite the dog as you smote the Yellow Typhoon. If you lose the fight, you will lose your head in this very ring."

"I ain't goin' to lose," I snarled, being fed up on that kind of talk, and he smiled benevolently and retired to his chair. Just then somebody yanked my pants leg, and I looked down and seen Soapy. He was shaking with excitement.

"Don't talk, Steve!" he whispered. "Just lissen! Yun Chei thinks I'm encouragin' you for the battle. But lissen: I've fixed it! I got wind of a Federal army camped in a valley to the south. They don't know nothin' about us, but I found a man who swore I could trust him, and I smuggled him off on my horse. He'll guide 'em back here, and they'll break up this den of thieves. When the shootin' starts, we'll duck and run for the Federal lines. I sent my man right after I talked to you this mornin', so they oughta get here in maybe an hour or so."

"Well," I said, "I hope they don't get here too soon; I want to collect my thousand bucks from Yun Chei before I run."

"I'm goin' to snoop amongst Feng's men," he hissed, and just then the crowd on the opposite side of the ring divided, and here come Feng hisself, alias Joel Ballerin.

He was stripped to the waist, and he wore his fighting scowl. His short blond hair bristled, and his men sent up a cheer. He was big, and well built for speed and power. He had broad, square shoulders, a big arching chest, and a heavy neck, and his muscles fairly bulged under his sun-reddened skin with every move he made. He stood square on his wide-braced legs, and they showed plenty of power and drive. He was a fraction of a inch taller'n me, and

weighed about 200 to my 190, all bone and muscle and hellfire.

Looking back on that fight, it was one of the strangest I ever mixed in. They wasn't no referee. They was a Chinaman who whanged a gong every now and then when he remembered to, but he wasn't no-ways consistent in his time-keeping. Some of the rounds lasted thirty seconds and some lasted nine or ten minutes. When one of us went down, they wasn't no counting. The idea was that we should just keep on battling till one of us wasn't able to get up at all. We hadn't no gloves. Bare knuckles don't jolt like the mitts, but they cut and bruise. It's hard to knock out a tough man in good condition with one lick or half a dozen licks of your bare maulers. You got to plumb butcher him.

They was few preliminaries. Ballerin vaulted into the ring, kicked his stool through the ropes, and yelled, "Hit that gong, Wu Shang!" Wu Shang hit it, and Ballerin come for me like a cross between a bucking bronco and a China typhoon.

We met in the center of the ring like a thunder-clap, and his first lick split my left cauliflower, and my first clout laid his jaw open to the bone. After that it was slaughter and massacre.

There wasn't nothing fancy about our battling. It was toe to toe, and breast to breast, bare knuckles crunching against muscle and bone. Before the first round was over we was slipping in smears of our own blood. In the second Ballerin nearly fractured my jaw with a blazing left hook that stretched me on the floor. But I was up and slugging like mad at the bell. We begun the third by rushing from our corners with such fury that we had a head-on collision which dumped us both to the boards nigh senseless. Ballerin's scalp was laid open, and my head had a bump on it as big as a egg. The Chineses screamed with amazement, seeing us both writhing on the floor, but we staggered up about the same time and begun swinging at each other when Wu Shang got rattled and hit the gong.

AT THE BEGINNING of the fourth I started bombarding Ballerin's mid-section whilst he pounded my head till my ears was ringing like all the ship bells in Frisco harbor, and the blood got in my eyes till I couldn't see and was hitting by instinct. I could hear him gasping and panting as my iron maulers sunk deeper and deeper into his suffering belly, and finally, with a maddened roar, he grappled me and throwed me, and, setting astraddle of me, begun pounding my head against the boards, to the great glee of his warriors.

As Wu Shang seemed inclined to let that round go on forever, I resorted to some longshoreman tactics myself, kicked lustily in the back of the head, arched my body and throwed him off of me, and

pasted him beautifully in the eye as he riz.

This reduced his available sight by half, and didn't improve his temper none, as he proved by giving vent to a screech like a steam whistle, and letting go a hurricane swing that caught me under the ear and wafted me across the ring into the ropes. Them being too loose, I continued my flight unchecked and lit headfirst in the laps of the soldiers outside.

I riz and started to climb back through the ropes, necessarily tromping on my victims as I done so, and one would've stabbed me with his bayonnet by way of reprisal if I hadn't thoughtfully kicked him in the jaw first. Then I seen Ballerin crouching at the ropes, grinning fiercely at me as he dripped blood and weighed his huge fists, and I seen his intention of socking me as I clumb through. I said, "Get back from them ropes and let me in, you scum of the bilge!"

"That's up to you, you wind-jamming baboon!" he laughed brutally. So I unexpectedly reached through the ropes and grabbed his ankle and dumped him on his neck, and before he could rise, I was back in the ring. He riz ravening, and just then Wu Shang decided to hit the gong.

At the beginning of the fifth we came together and slugged till we was blind and deaf and dizzy, and when we finally heard the gong, we dropped in our tracks and lay there side by side, gasping for breath, till the gong announced the opening of the sixth, and we riz up and started in where we'd left off.

We was exchanging lefts and rights like a hail storm when he brung one up from the floor so fast I never seen it coming. The first part of me that hit the boards was the back of my head, and it nigh caved in the floor. I riz and tore into him, slugging with frenzied abandon, and battered him back across the ring, but I was so blind I missed him as he side-stepped, and fell into the ropes, and he smashed me three times behind the ear, and then, as I wheeled groggily, he caught me square on the button with a most awful right swing. Wham! I don't remember falling, but I must of, because the next thing I knowed I was down on the boards and Ballerin was stomping in my ribs with his boots. Away off I could hear Wu Shang banging his gong, but Ballerin give no heed, and I felt myself slipping into dreamland.

Then my blood-misted gaze, wandering at random, rested on General Yun in his camp chair. He smiled at me grimly, and that half-naked Chinaman behind him drawed a great curved sword and run his thumb along the edge.

With a howl of desperation I steadied my tottering brain, and I fought my way to my feet in spite of all Ballerin could do, and I pasted him with a left that tore his ear nearly off his head, and he went reeling into the ropes. He come back with a roar and a tremendous clout

that missed me and splintered one of the ring posts, and I heaved my right under his heart with all my beef behind it. I heard a couple of his ribs crack under it, and I follered it with a hurricane of lefts and rights that drove him staggering before me like a ship in a typhoon. A thundering right to the head bent him back over the ropes, and then, just as I was setting myself for the finisher, I felt somebody jerking my pants leg and heard Soapy hollering to me amidst the roar of the mob, "Steve! Ballerin's got fifty rifles trained on you right now. If you drop him, you'll never leave that ring alive."

I SHOOK THE blood outa my eyes and cast a desperate glare over my shoulder. The front ranks of General Feng's warriors still leaned on their rifles, but behind 'em I caught a glimmer of black muzzles.

Ballerin pitched off the ropes, swinging a wild overhand right that missed by a yard, and he would of tumbled to the boards if I hadn't grabbed him and held him up.

"What'm I goin' to do?" I howled. "If I don't drop him, Yun Chei'll cut off my head, and if I do, his men'll shoot me!"

"Stall, Steve!" begged Soapy. "Keep it up as long as you can; somethin' might happen any minute now."

I cast a glance at the sun, and sweated with despair. But I held Ballerin up as long as I dared, and then I pushed him away from me and swung wide at him. He reeled and I tried to catch him, but he pitched face-first, and I ducked as I heard a click of rifle bolts. But he was trying to climb up again, and I never hoped to see a opponent rise like I hoped to see him rise. He grabbed the ropes and hauled hisself up, and stared around, one eye closed and t'other glassy.

He was out on his feet, but his fighting instinct kept him going. He come blundering out into the ring, swinging blind, and I swung wide, but he fell into it somehow, and I hit him in spite of myself. Soapy give a lamentable howl, and Ballerin pitched back into the ropes, and I was on him and locked him in a despairing grasp before he could fall. He was dead weight in my arms, out cold, his legs dragging, and I was so near out myself I wondered how long I couldst hold him up. Over his shoulder I see General Yun looking at me impatient; even a Chinese revolutionist could see that Ironfist was ready for the cleaners. But I held on; if I let go, I knowed Ballerin wouldn't get up again, and his men would start target practice on me.

Then above the noise of the crowd I heard a low roar. I looked out over their heads, and beyond the ridge of a distant hill something come soaring. It was a airplane, and nobody but me had seen it. I wrestled my limp victim to the ropes, and gasped the news to Soapy. He was too smart to look, but he hissed,

"Keep stallin'! Hold him up! The Federals have sent a plane to our rescue! Everything's jake!"

General Yun had got suspicious. He jumped up and shook his fist at me, and hollered, and his derned executioner grinned and drawed his sword again—and then, with a rush and zoom, the airplane swooped down on us like a hawk. Everybody looked up and yelled, and as it passed right over the ring, I seen something tumble from it and flash in the sun. And Soapy yelled, "Look out! There's a dragon painted on it! That ain't a Federal plane—that's Whang Shan!"

I throwed Ballerin bodily over the ropes as far as I could heave him, and div after him, and the next instant—blam!—the ring went up in smoke, and pieces flew every which way.

BOMBS WAS FALLING and crashing and tents going sky-high, and men yelling and shooting and running and falling over each other, and the roar of that cussed plane was in my ears as I headed for the tall timber. I was vaguely aware that Soapy was legging it alongside me, hollering, "That Chinaman of mine never went to the Federals, the dirty rat! I see it all now! He was one of Whang Shan's spies. No wonder he was so anxious to help! He wanted my horse—hey, Steve! This way!"

I seen Soapy do a running dive into General Yun's auto, which was setting in front of his tent, and I follered him. We went roaring away just as a bomb hit where the car had been a second before, and spattered us with dirt. I dunno where General Yun was, though I caught a glimpse of a silk-robed figure, which might of been him, scudding for the hills.

We went through that camp like a tornado, with all hell popping behind us. Whang was sure giving his enermies the works in that one plane of his'n. They was such punk shots they couldn't hit him with their rifles, and all he had to do was heave bombs into the thick of 'em.

I don't remember much about that ride. Soapy was hanging to the wheel and pushing the accelerator through the floor, and I was holding onto the seat and trying to stay with the derned craft which was bucking over that awful road like a skiff in a squall. Presently we hit a bump that throwed me clean over the seat into the back, and when I come up for air I had something clutched in my hand, at the sight of which I give a yell of joy—and bit my tongue savagely as we hit another bump.

I clumb back into the front seat like I was crawling along the cross-trees of the main-mast in a typhoon, and tried to tell Soapy what I'd found, but we was going so fast the wind blowed the words clean outa my mouth.

It wasn't till we had dropped down out of the higher hills along about sundown and was coasting along a comparatively better road amongst fields and mud huts that I

got a chance to catch my breath.

"I found your letter," I said. "It was in the bottom of the car. It must of slipped outa my pocket whilst I was tied up."

"Read it to me," he requested, and I said, "Wait till I see is my watch intact. I didn't get my thousand bucks for lickin' Ballerin, and I want to be sure I got somethin, for goin' through what I been through."

So I looked at the watch, which must of been worth five hundred dollars anyway, and it was unscratched, so I opened the letter and read: "Ormond and Ashley, attorneys at law, San Francisco, California, U. S. A. Dear Mister Jackson: This is to inform you that you are being sued by Mrs. J. A. Lynch for a nine months board bill, amounting to exactly—"

Soapy give a ear-splitting yell and wrenched the wheel over.

"What you doin', you idjit?" I howled, as the car r'ared and skidded and lurched around like a skiff in a tide-rip.

"I'm goin' back to Yun Chei!" he screeched. "My expectations is bust! I thought I was a heiress, but I'm still a bum! I ain't got the—"

Crash! We left the road, rammed a tree, and went into a perfect tailspin.

The evening shadders was falling as I crawled out from under the debris and untangled one of the wheels from around my neck. I looked about for Soapy's remains, and seen 'em setting on a busted headlight, brooding somberly.

"You might at least ask if I'm hurt," I said resentfully.

"What of it?" he asked bitterly. "We're ruined. I ain't got not fortune."

"I was ruined when I first met a hoodoo like you," I said fiercely. "Anyway, I still got Yun Chei's watch." And I reached into my pocket. And then I gave a poignant shriek. That watch must of absorbed the whole jolt of the smash. I had a handful of metal scraps and wheels and springs which nobody could tell was they meant for a watch or what.

Thereafter, a figure might have been seen flitting through the twilight, hotly pursued by another, bulkier figure, breathing threats of vengeance, in the general direction of the coast.

SLUGGERS *on the* BEACH.

This short story was first published in the August 1934 issue of Jack Dempsey's Fight Magazine.

THE MINUTE I SEEN the man which was going to referee my fight with Slip Harper in the Amusement Palace Fight Club, Shanghai, I takes a vi'lent dislike to him. His name was Hoolihan, a fighting sailor, same as me, and he was a big red-headed gorilla with hands like hairy hams, and he carried hisself with a swagger which put my teeth on edge. He looked like he thought he was king of the waterfront, and that there is a title I aspires to myself.

I detests these conceited jackasses. I'm glad that egotism ain't amongst my faults. Nobody'd ever know, from my conversation, that I was the bully of the toughest ship afloat, and the terror of bucko mates from Valparaiso to Singapore. I'm that modest I don't think I'm half as good as I really am.

But Red Hoolihan got under my hide with his struttings and giving instructions in that fog-horn beller of his'n. And when he discovered that Slip Harper was a old shipmate of his'n, his actions growed unbearable.

He made this discovery in the third round, whilst counting over Harper, who hadst stopped one of my man-killing left hooks with his chin.

"Seven! Eight! Nine!" said Hoolihan, and then he stopped counting and said: "By golly, ain't you the Johnny Harper that used to be bos'n aboard the old *Saigon*?"

"Yuh—yeah!" goggled Harper, groggily, getting his legs under him, whilst the crowd went hysterical.

"What's eatin' you, Hoolihan?" I roared indignantly. "G'wan countin'!"

He gives me a baleful glare.

"I'm refereein' this mill," he said. "You tend to your part of it. By golly, Johnny, I ain't seen you since I broke jail in Calcutta—"

But Johnny was up at last, and trying to keep me from taking him apart, which all that prevented me was the gong.

Hoolihan helped Harper to his corner, and they kept up an animated conversation till the next round started—or rather Hoolihan did. Harper wasn't in much condition to enjoy conversation, having left three molars embedded in my right glove.

Whilst we was whanging away at each other during the fourth, I was aware of Hoolihan's voice.

"Stand up to him, Johnny," he said. "I'll see that you get a square deal. G'wan, sink in your left. That right to the guts didn't hurt us none. Pay no attention to them body blows. He's bound to weaken soon."

Enraged beyond control, I turned on him and said, "Look here, you red-headed baboon, are you a referee or a second?"

I dunno what retort he was fixing to make, because just then Harper takes advantage of my abstraction to slam me behind the ear with all he had. Maddened by this perfidy, I turned and sunk my left to the hilt in his midriff, whereupon he turned a beautiful pea-green.

"Tie into him, Johnny," urged Hoolihan.

"Shut up, Red," gurgled Harper, trying to clinch. "You're makin' him mad, and he's takin' it out on me!"

"Well, we can take it," begun Hoolihan, but at that moment I tagged Harper on the ear with a meat-cleaver right, and he done a nose-dive, to Hoolihan's extreme disgust.

"One!" he hollered, waving his arm like a jib-boom. "Two! Three! Get up, Johnny. This baboon can't fight."

"Maybe he can't," said Johnny, dizzily, squinting up from the canvas, with his hair full of resin, "but if he hits me again like he just done, I'll be a candidate for a harp. And I hate music. You can count all night if you want to, Red, but as far as I'm concerned, the party's over!"

Hoolihan give a snort of disgust,

and grabbed my right arm and raised it and hollered: "Ladies and gents, it is with the deepest regret that I announce this bone-headed gorilla as the winner!"

With a beller of wrath, I jerked my arm away from him and hung a clout on his proboscis that knocked him headfirst through the ropes. Before I couldst dive out on top of him, as was my firm intention, I was seized from behind by ten special policemen—rough-houses is so common in the Amusement Palace that the promoter is always prepared. Whilst I was being interfered with by these misguided idjits, Hoolihan riz from amongst the ruins of the benches and customers, and tried to crawl back into the ring, bellering like a bull and spurting blood all over everything. But a large number of people fell on him with piercing yells and dragged him back and set on him.

Meanwhile forty or fifty friends of the promoter hadst come to the rescue of the ten cops, and eventually I found myself back in my dressing-room without having been able to glut my righteous wrath on Red Hoolihan's huge carcass. He'd been carried out through one door whilst several dozen men was hauling me through another. It's a good thing for them that I'd left my white bulldog Mike aboard the *Sea Girl*.

I was so blind mad I couldn't hardly get my clothes on, and by the time I hadst finished I was alone in the building. Gnashing my teeth

slightly, I prepared to sally forth and find Red Hoolihan. Shanghai was too small for both of us.

But as I started for the door that opened into the corridor, I heard a quick rush of feet in the alley outside, and the back door of the dressing-room bust open. I wheeled, with my fists cocked, thinking maybe it was Red—and then I stopped short and gawped in surprise. It wasn't Red. It was a girl.

She was purty as all get-out, but now she was panting and pale and scared-looking. She shut the door and leaned against it.

"Don't let them get me!" she gurgled.

"Who?" I asked.

"Those Chinese devils!" she gasped. "The terrible Whang Yi!"

"Who's them?" I inquired, considerably bewildered.

"A secret society of fiends and murderers!" she said. "They chased me into that alley! They'll torture me to death!"

"They won't, neither," I said. "I'll mop up the floor with 'em. Lemme look!"

I pushed her aside and opened the door and stuck my head out in the alley. "I don't see nobody," I said.

She leaned back against the wall, with one hand to her heart. I looked at her with pity. Beauty in distress always touches a warm spot in my great, big, manly bosom.

"They're hiding out there, somewhere," she whimpered.

"What they chasin' you for?" I

asked, forgetting all about my hurry to smear the docks with Red Hoolihan.

"I have something they want," she said. "My name is Laura Hopkins. I do a dance act at the European Grand Theater—did you ever hear of Li Yang?"

"The bandit chief which was raising Cain around here a couple of years ago?" I said. "Sure. He raided all up and down the coast. Why?"

"Last night I came upon a Chinaman dying in the alley behind the theater," she said. "He'd been stabbed. But he had a piece of paper in his mouth, which had been overlooked by the men who killed him. He had been one of Li Yang's soldiers. He gave me that paper, when he knew he was dying. It was a map showing where Li Yang had hidden his treasure."

"The heck you say!" I remarked, much interested.

"Yes. And the spot is less than a day's journey from here," she said. "But somehow the killers learned that I had this map. They call themselves the Whang Yi. They are the men who were the enemies of Li Yang in his lifetime. They want the treasure themselves. So they're after me. Oh, what shall I do?" she said, wringing her hands.

"Don't be afraid," I said. "I'll pertect you from them yeller-bellied rats."

"I want to get away," she whimpered. "I'm afraid to stay in Shanghai. They'll kill me. I dare not try to find the treasure. I'd give them the map if they'd only spare my life. But they'll kill me just for knowing about it. Oh, if I only had money enough to get away! I'd sell the map for fifty dollars."

"You would?" I ejaculated. "Why, that there treasure is likely to be a lot of gold and silver and jewerls and stuff. He was a awful thief."

"It won't do me any good dead," she answered. "Oh, what shall I do?"

"I'll tell you," I said, digging into my britches. "Sell it to me. I'll give you fifty bucks."

"Would you?" she cried, jumping up, her eyes shining. "No—oh, no; it wouldn't be fair to you. It's too dangerous. I'll tear the map up, and—"

"Wait a minute!" I hollered. "Don't do that, dern it! I'll take the risks. I ain't scared of no yeller bellies. Here, here's the fifty. Gimme the map."

"I'm afraid you'll regret it," she said. "But here it is."

Whilst she was counting the fifty, I looked at the map, feeling like I was holding a fortune in my hand. It seemed to represent a small island laying a short distance offa the mainland, with trees and things growing on it. One of these trees was taller'n the others and stood off to itself. A arrer run from it to a spot on the beach, which was marked with a "x." There was a lot of Chinese writing on the edge of the map, and a line of English.

"Fifty paces south of that tall

tree," said Miss Hopkins. "Five feet down in the loose sand. The island is only a few hours run from the port, if you take a motor launch. Full directions are written out there in English."

"I'll find it," I promised, handling the map with awe and reverence. "But before I start, I'll see you home so them Whang Yis won't try to grab you."

But she said, "No, I'll go out the front way and hail a cab. Tomorrow night I'll be safe on the high seas. I'll never forget what you've done for me."

"If you'll give me the address of where you're goin'," I said, "I'll see that you get a share of the treasure if I finds it."

"Don't worry about that," she said. "You've already done more for me than you realize. Goodbye! I hope you find all you deserve."

And she left in such a hurry I hardly realized she had went till she was gone.

Well, I wasted no time. I forgot all about Red Hoolihan—a man with millions on his mind ain't got no time for such hoodlums—and I headed for a certain native quarter of the waterfront as fast as I could leg it. I knowed a Chinese fisherman named Chin Yat who had a motor launch which he rented out, and being as I had given all my money to Miss Hopkins, I didn't have no dough, and he was the only one which I knowed would let me have his boat on credit.

It was late, because the fight card had been a unusually long one. It was away past midnight when I got to Chin Yat's, and I seen him and a big white man puttering around the boat, under the light of torches burning near the wharves. I bust into a run, because I was afraid he'd rent the boat before I could get there, though I couldn't figger what any white man would want with a boat that time of night.

As I hove up, I hollered, "Hey Chin, I wanta rent your boat—"

The big white man turned around, and the torchlight fell on his face. It was Red Hoolihan.

"What you doin' here?" he demanded, clenching his fists.

"I got no time to waste on you," I snarled. "I'll fix you later. Chin, I gotta have your motor-boat."

He shook his head and singsonged, "Velly solly. No can do."

"What you mean?" I hollered. "How come you can't?"

"'Cause it's already rented to me," said Hoolihan, "and I've done paid him his dough in advance."

"But this here's important," I bellered. "I got to have that boat! It means a lot of dough."

"What d'you know about a lot of dough?" snorted Hoolihan. "I need that boat because I'm goin' after more dough than you ever dreamed of, you bone-headed ape! You know why I ain't takin' the time to caulk the wharf-timbers with your gore? Well, I'll tell you, so you won't get no false ideas. I ain't got the time to waste on a baboon like you. I'm goin' after hidden treasure! When I come back, that boat'll be loaded to the gunnels with gold!"

And so saying, he waved a piece of paper in my face.

"Where'd you get that?" I yelped.

"None of your business," he said. "That's—hey, leggo that!"

I had made a grab for it, in my excitement, and he took a poke at me. I busted him in the snout in return, and he nearly went over the lip of the wharf. He managed to catch hisself—and then he let out a agonized beller. The paper had slipped outa his hand and vanished in the black water.

"Now look what you done!" he howled frantically. "You've lost me a fortune. Put up your mitts, you spawn of the devil's gutter! I'm goin' to knock—"

"Did your map look like this?" I asked, pulling out mine and showing it to him in the torchlight. The sight sobered him quick.

"By Judas!" he bawled. "The same identical map! Where'd you get it?"

"Never mind about that," I said. "The p'int is, we both knows what the other'n's after. We both wants the treasure Li Yang hid before the Federalists bumped him off. I got a map but no boat, you got a boat but no map. Let's go!"

"Before I'd share anything with you," he said bitterly, "I'd lose the whole shebang."

"Who said anything about sharin' anything?" I roared. "The best man takes the loot. I still got a score to settle with you. We finds the plunder, and then we settles our argument. Winner takes the treasure!"

"Okay with me," he agreed, blood-thirstily. "Come on!"

But as we sputtered outa the harbor in the starlight, a sudden thought hit me.

"Hold on!" I said. "Does this here island lie south or north of the port?"

"Cut off the engine and we'll look at the map," he said, holding up a lantern. I done so, and we peered at the line of English which was writ in a very small, femernine hand.

"That's a 'n'," said Red, pointing at it with his big, hairy finger. "It means the island lies north of the harbor."

"It looks like a 's' to me," I said. "I believe it means the island's south of the harbor."

"I say north!" exclaimed Hoolihan, angrily.

"South!" I snarled.

"We goes north!" bellered Hoolihan, brandishing his fists. He hadn't no control over his temper at all. "We goes north or nowheres!"

As I started to rise, my foot hit something in the bottom of the launch. It was a belaying pin. I ain't a man to be gypped out of a fortune account of the stubbornness of some misguided jackass. I laid that belaying pin over Red Hoolihan's ear with a full-arm swing.

"We goes south," I repeated

truculently, and they was no opposing voice.

Feeling your way along that coast at night in a motor-launch ain't no picnic. Hoolihan come to just about daylight, and he got up and rubbed the lump over his ear, and cussed free and fervent.

"I won't forget this," he said. "This here is another score to settle with you. Where at are we?"

"There's the island, dead ahead," I answered.

He scowled over the map, and said, "It don' t look like the one on the map."

"You expect a ignerant Chinese to draw a perfect map?" I retorted. "It's bound to be the one. Look for a tall tree standing kinda out alone. It oughta be on this end of the island."

But it wasn't; they wasn't nothing there but low, thick bushes rising outa marshy land. We tried the other end of the island, and I said: "This is it. The Chinee made another mistake. He put the tree on the wrong end of the island. There's a sandy beach and a tall palm standin' out from the rest of the growth."

Hoolihan had forgot all about his doubts. He was as impatient as me to get ashore. We run in and tied up in a narrow cove, and tramped through the deep sand to the trees, packing the picks and shovels we had brung along, and my heart beat faster as I realized that in a short time I wouldst be a millionaire.

That tall palm was a lot closer to the water than it looked like on the map. When we'd stepped off fifty paces to the south, we was waist-deep in water!

"I see where we meets with engineerin' problems in our excavations," I said, but Hoolihan scowled and flexed his enormous arms, and said, "That ain't worryin' me. I'm thinkin' about somethin' else. Here we are, there's the treasure, lyin' under five foot of sand and water. All we got to do is dig it up. But we ain't settled yet whose treasure it is."

"All right," I said, shedding my shirt, "we settles it now."

With a roar, Hoolihan ripped off his shirt and squared off, the morning sun gleaming on the red hair of his gigantic chest, and the muscles standing out in knots all over his arms and shoulders. He come plunging in like the wild bull of Bashen, and I met him breast to breast with both maulers flailing.

He'd never been licked in a ring or out, they said. He was two hundred pounds of bone and bulging muscle, and he was quick as a cat on his feet. Or he would of been, if'n he'd had a chance to be.

We was standing ankle-deep in sand. They wasn't no chance for footwork. It was like dragging our feet through hot mush. The sun riz higher and beat down on us like the pure essence of hell-fire, and it soaked vitality out of us like water out of a sponge. And that awful sand! It was worse'n having iron weights fastened to our ankles. There wasn't no foot-work, side-stepping—nothing but slug, slug, slug! Toe to toe, leaning head to head, with our four maulers working like sledge-hammers fastened on pistons.

I dunno how long we fought. It musta been hours, because the sun crawled up and up, and beat down on us like red hot lances. Everything was floating red before me; I couldn't hear nothing except Red's gusty panting, the scruff of our feet through that hellish sand, and the thud and crunch of our fists.

Talk about the heat Jeffries and Sharkey fought in at Coney Island, and the heat of the ring at Toledo! Them places was Eskimo igloos compared to that island, under that awful sun! I got so numb I could scarcely feel the jolt of Hoolihan's iron fists. I'd done quit any attempt at defense, and so had he. We was just driving in our punches wide open and with all we had behind 'em.

One of my eyes was closed, the brow split and the lid sagging down like a curtain. Half the hide was missing from my face, and one cauliflowered ear was pounded into a purple pulp. Blood was oozing from my lips, nose and ears. Sweat poured off my chest and run down my legs till I was standing in mud. We was both slimy with sweat and blood. I could hear the agonized pound of my own heart, and it felt like it was going to bust right through my ribs. My calf muscles and thigh muscles was quivering cords of fire, where

they wasn't numb and dead. Every time I dragged a foot through that clinging, burning sand it felt like the joints of my limbs was giving apart.

But Hoolihan was reeling like a stabbed ox, staggering and blowing. His breath was sobbing through his busted teeth, and blood streamed down his chin. His belly was heaving like a sail in the wind, and his ribs was raw beef from my body punching.

I was driving him before me, step by step. And the next thing I knowed, we was under the shade of that big palm tree, and the sun wasn't flaying my back no more. It was almost like a dash of cold water. It revived Hoolihan a little, too. I seen him stiffen and lift his head, but he was done. My body beating hadst took all the starch outa his spine. My legs were dead, and I couldn't rush him no more, but I fell into him and, as I fell, I crashed my right overhand to his jaw with my last ounce of strength.

It connected, and we went down together, him under me. I laid there for a second, and then I groped around and caught hold of the tree and hauled myself to my feet. Hanging on with one hand, I shook the blood and sweat outa my eyes, and begun counting. I was so dopey and groggy I got mixed up three or four times and had to start over, and finally I passed out on my feet, cause when I come to I was still counting up around thirty or forty. Hoolihan hadn't moved.

I tried to say, "By golly, the

dough's mine!" But all I could do was gulp like a dying fish. I took one staggering step towards the picks and shovels, and then my legs give way and I went headfirst into the sand. And there I laid, like a dead man.

It was the sound of a motor putt-putting above the wash of the surf which first roused me. Then, a few minutes later, I heard feet scruff through the sand, and men talking and laughing. Then somebody swore loud and freely.

I shook the red glare outa my eyes and blinked up. Four men was standing there, with picks and shovels in their hands, staring down at me, and I rekernized 'em: Smoky Harrigan, Bat Schimmerling, Joe Donovan and Tom Storley, as dirty a set of rats as ever infested a wharf.

"Well, by Jupiter!" said Smoky, with the sneer he always wore. "What do you know about this? Costigan and Hoolihan! How come these gorillas to land on this island?"

I tried to get up, but my legs wouldn't work, and I sunk back into the sand. Hoolihan groaned and cussed groggily somewhere near me. Harrigan stooped and picked up something which I seen was my map which had fell into the sand.

He showed it to the others and they laughed loud and jeeringly, which dully surprised me. My brain was still too numb from Hoolihan's punching and that awful sun to hardly know what it was all about.

"Put that map down before I rises and busts you in half," I mumbled through pulped lips.

"Oh, is it yours?" asked Smoky, sardonically.

"I bought it offa Miss Laura Hopkins," I said groggily. "It's mine, and so is the dough. Gimme it before I lays you like a carpet."

"Laura Hopkins!" he sneered. "That was Suez Kit, the slickest girl-crook that ever rolled a drunk for his wad. She worked the same gyp on that big ox Hoolihan. I saw her take him as he left the fight club."

"What d'you mean?" I demanded, struggling up to a sitting posture. I still couldn't get on my feet, and Hoolihan was in even worse shape. "She sold the same map to Hoolihan? Is that where he got his'n?"

"Why, you poor sucker!" sneered Harrigan. "Can't you understand nothing? Them maps was fakes. I dunno what you're doin' here, but if you'd followed 'em, you'd been miles away to the north of the harbor, instead of the south."

"And there ain't no treasure of Li Yang?" I moaned.

"Sure there is," he said. "What's more, it's hid right here on this island. And this is the right map." He waved a strip of parchment all covered with lines and Chinese writing. "There's treasure here. Li Yang didn't hide it here hisself, but it was left here for him by a smuggler. Li Yang got bumped off before he could come for it. An old Chinee fence named Yao Shan had the map.

Suez Kit bought it off him with the hundred bucks she gypped out of you and Hoolihan. He must have been crazy to sell it, but you can't never tell about them Chineses."

"But the Whang Yis?" I gasped wildly.

"Horseradish!" sneered Smoky. "A artistic touch to put the story over. But if it'll make you feel any better, I'll tell you that Suez Kit lost the map after all. I'd been follerin' her for days, knowin' she was up to something, though I didn't know just what. When she got the map from old Yao Shan, I tapped her on the head and took it. And here we are!"

"The treasure's as much our'n as it is your'n," I protested.

"Heh! heh! heh!" he replied. "Try and get it. Gwan, boys, get to work. These big chumps has fought each other to a frazzle, and we got nothin' to fear from 'em."

So I laid there and et my soul out whilst they set about stealing our loot right under our noses. Smoky paid no attention to the palm tree. Studying the map closely, he located a big rock jutting up amongst some bushes, and he stepped off ten paces to the west. "Dig here," he said.

They pitched in digging a lot harder'n I had any idee them rats could work, and the sand flew. Purty soon Bat Schimmerling's pick crunched on something solid, and they all yelled.

"Look here!" yelled Tom Storley. "A lacquered chest, bound with iron bands!"

They all yelled with joy, and Hoolihan groaned dismally. He'd come to in time to get what it was all about.

"Gypped!" he moaned. "Cheated! Swindled! Framed! And now them thieves is robbin' us right before us!"

I hauled myself painfully across the sands, and stared down into the hole, and my heart leaped as I seen the top of a iron-bound chest at the bottom. A wave of red swept all the weakness and soreness outa my frame.

Smoky turned and yelled at me, "See what you've missed, you dumb chump? See that chest? I dunno what's in it, but whatever it is, it's worth millions! 'More precious than gold,' old Yao Shan said. And it's our'n! While you and that other gorilla are workin' out your lives haulin' ropes and eatin' resin dust, we'll be rollin' in luxury!"

"You'll roll in somethin' else first!" I yelled, heaving up amongst 'em like a typhoon. Harrigan swung up a pick, but before he couldst bring it down on my head, I spread his nose all over his face with a left hook which likewise deprived him of all his front teeth and rendered him horse-de-combat. At this moment Bat Schimmerling broke a shovel over my head, and Tom Storley run in and grappled with me. This was about the least sensible thing he could of done, as he instantly realized, and just before he lapsed into unconsciousness he hollered for Donovan to get a gun.

Donovan took the hint and run for the launch, where he procured a shotgun and come back on the jump. He hesitated to fire at long range, because I was so mixed up with Storley and Schimmerling that he couldn't hit me without riddling them. But about that time I untangled myself from Storley's senseless carcass and caressed Schimmerling's chin with a right uppercut which stood him on his head in the hole on top of the chest.

Donovan then give a yelp of triumph and throwed the gun to his shoulder—but Hoolihan had crawled up behind him on all-fours, and as Joe pulled the trigger, Red swept his legs out from under him. The charge combed my hair, it missed me that close, and Donovan crashed down on top of Hoolihan, who stroked his whiskers with a right that nearly tore his useless head off.

Hoolihan then crawled to the edge of the hole and looked down.

"It's your'n," he gulped. "You licked me. But it busts my heart to think of the dough I've lost."

"Aw, shut up," I growled, grabbing Schimmerling by the hind laig and dragging him out of the hole. "Help me get this chest outa here. Whatever's in it, you get half."

Hoolihan gaped at me.

"You mean that?" he gasped.

"He may, but I don't!" broke in a hard, femernine voice, and we whirled to behold Miss Laura Hopkins standing before us. But they was considerable change in her appearance. She wore a man's shirt, for one thing, and khaki pants and boots, and her face was a lot harder'n I remembered it. Moreover, they was a bandage on her head under her sun-helmet, and she had a pistol in her hand, p'inting at us. She looked like Suez Kit now, all right.

She give a sneer at Smoky and his minions, which was beginning to show signs of life.

"That fool thought he'd finished me, eh? Pah! I don't kill that easy," she said. "Stole my map, the rat! How did you two gorillas get here? Those maps I sold you were for an island half a day from here."

"It was my mistake," I said, and I added, limping disconsolately towards her, "I believed you. I thought you was in distress."

"The more fool you," she sneered. "I had to have a hundred dollars to buy Yao Shan's map. That gyp I worked on you and Hoolihan was the best one I could think of, at the spur of the moment. Now get to work and hoist that chest out, and load it in my boat. You're a sap to trust anybody—ow!"

I'd slapped the gun out of her hand so quick she didn't have time to pull the trigger. It went spinning into the water and sunk.

"Just because you're smart, you think everybody else is a sap," I snorted. "C'mon, Red, le's get our chest out."

Suez Kit stood staring wildly at us. "But it's mine!" she hollered. "I gave Yao Shan a hundred dollars—"

"You give him our hundred," I snorted. "You make me sick."

Me and Red bent down and got hold of the chest and rassled it out of the hole. Suez Kit was doing a war-dance all over the beach.

"You dirty, double-crossing rats!" she wept. "I might have known I couldn't trust any man! Robbers! Bandits! Oh, this is too much!"

"Oh, shut up," I said wearily. "We'll give you some of the loot— gimme that rock, Red. The lock is plumb rotten."

I took the stone and hit the lock a few licks, and it come all to pieces. Smoky and his gang had come to, and they watched us wanly. Suez Kit fidgeted around behind us, and I heard her breath coming in pants. Red throwed open the lid. They was a second of painful silence, and then Suez Kit let out an awful scream and staggered back, her hands to her head. Hanigan and his mob lifted up their voices in lamentation.

That chest wasn't full of silver, nor platinum, nor jewels. It was full of machine-gun cartridges!

"Bullets!" said Hoolihan, kinda numbly. "No wonder Yao Shan was willing to sell the map. 'More precious than gold,' he said. Of course, this ammunition was more precious than gold to a bandit chief. Steve, I'm sick!"

So was Smoky and his gang. And Suez Kit wept like she'd sot on a hornet.

"Steve," said Red, as him and me

limped towards our boat whilst the sounds of weeping and wailing riz behind us, "was it because I kept Donovan from blowin' your head off that you decided to split the treasure with me?"

"Do I look like a cheapskate?" I snapped. "I knowed from the first that I was going to split with you."

"Then why in the name of thunderation," he bellered, turning purple in the face, "did you have to beat me up like you done, when you was intendin' to split anyway? What was we fightin' about, anyway?"

"You might of been fightin' for the loot," I roared, brandishing my fists in his face, "but I was merely convincin' you who was the best man."

"Well, I ain't convinced," he bellered, waving his fists. "It was the sand and the sun which licked me, not you. We'll settle this in the ring tonight, at the Amusement Palace."

"Let's go!" I yelled, leaping into the launch. "I'm itchin' to prove to the customers that you're as big a flop as a fighter as you were as a referee."

www.ingramcontent.com/pod-product-compliance
Lightning Source LLC
Chambersburg PA
CBHW050157030726
47505CB00005B/1415